DEATH AT THE END OF THE ROAD

by

John Morsell

Printed by Village Books in Bellingham, WA.

ISBN 9780692687086
LCCN 2016905863

Cover images: Top photo, northern lights over an old cabin. Shutterstock image, copyright Jens Ottoson. Bottom photo, seiner off the coast of the Kodiak Archipelago, Alaska, 2009. Nancy Heise, released to the public domain, sourced from Wikipedia.

Cast of Characters

Charlie Skyler – Boat-dwelling ecotour guide whose curiosity often leads to impromptu, if unhealthy, detective work

Kate Perkins – Swamp-dwelling Midwest transplant who gets sucked into Charlie's intrigues

Johann Sebastian Bachman (JB) – Enigmatic retired hippie academic with special skills and a mysterious background

Bob Stillwater (Super Trooper) – Enthusiastic Alaska State Trooper

Rodolfo – The body in the water; owner of a taco stand

Elena – Rodolfo's wife

Agent Phillips – Senior DEA agent from Los Angeles office

Agent Jankowski – Junior DEA agent from Los Angeles office with excessive macho tendencies

Aldo Fenstrom – Elderly commercial fisherman with a shady past and proclivity toward distribution of mind-altering substances

Darryl Swift – Amoral local drug dealer

Julie Fishbein – Darryl's girlfriend

Brett Fishbein – Dim-witted pothead and Julie's brother

Frank Halburg – Violent lieutenant in Aldo's operation

Jake Halburg – The body on the trail and Frank's brother

Stuart Halburg – Frank and Jake's father, southern gentleman, and associate of Aldo in the drug distribution business

Robert Fenstrom – Aldo's son and psychopathic syndicate enforcer

John Vander – Owner of the Rainbow Inn, partner in the drug distribution business

Izzy – Aldo's deckhand and brother-in-law

Astrid – Izzy's wife and Aldo's sister

Beverly Milford – Junior DEA agent with a bulldog mentality, love of Alaska, and infatuation with JB

Tom March – Another DEA agent, Beverly's immediate superior

Paul Larchmont (Frog) – Bush pilot and Aldo's emergency escape planner

Rob Smithers – Air traffic controller at the Wrangell airport

Ayers – Violent head of a rogue government black ops organization

The Mole –?

Prologue

Quang Ngai Province, South Vietnam
August, 1970

Sarge lay on his cot in the tiny tent wearing nothing but skivvies and dog tags. He was drenched in sweat and his bedding was brown from weeks without laundry facilities. He was holding a ragged old *Time* magazine but could not remember anything that he had read. His thoughts kept drifting to his home where the air was cool and crisp, and the snow-capped mountains rose from the water's edge. August was fishing season and his dad would be out on the bay, dropping the net, hoping to intercept a school of salmon. What kind of cruel god forced a young man to leave his northern homeland and travel to the jungle and rice paddies of Southeast Asia, only to be shot at by anonymous strangers?

Sarge and his squad were sequestered in a corner of the camp separated by a circle of razor wire and guarded by a couple of sleepy MPs. It was the third week of house arrest, and there had been no word from the brass. The untimely demise of Lieutenant Hellman was one of many potential fragging incidents that were being halfheartedly investigated by the powers-that-be. Sarge did not feel guilty that the M16 round had found its way into the Lieutenant's brain during yet another pointless engagement with the "enemy," whoever they were. However, he was concerned for the other four members of his squad (Christ, was that all that were left?). If the bullet had gone through and through, there would have been no question, but the medic who examined the Lieutenant found a bullet wedged between his skull and helmet and immediately identified it as a friendly fire round. The circumstances of the Lieutenant's death were then forwarded to authorities for an investigation. The source of the bullet was currently uncertain. After passing through the Lieutenant's helmet and his skull, the bullet had been severely deformed. It was unlikely that ballistic examination would be able to match it with a squad member's rifle. In any event, without eyewitness testimony, it would be impossible to determine whether the death was the result of accidental friendly fire or intentional execution.

The July 15 sortie had been another in a series of pointless attacks on poorly defined targets. It seemed like the platoon was always outnumbered and the targets carefully surrounded by booby traps. Ambushes were standard procedure for the Viet Cong, providing an atmosphere of continual terror. The Lieutenant had not been able to explain the rationale behind the attacks or put them into any kind of strategic perspective. Four of Sarge's squad members had been killed in the prior three months for no good reason that he could think of. The war had long ago ceased to make any sense. It was obvious to all the infantrymen that there was no enemy in the conventional sense. Most of the young men drafted for the war in Southeast Asia had naively visualized war as portrayed in the movies about WWII, as uniformed soldiers heroically battling each other with clear boundaries between the good guys and the bad guys. But here there was only jungle and booby traps and snipers. The Vietnamese themselves were inscrutable and fought for whatever side was in their momentary self-interest. The insanity had to stop.

During the previous year and a half, the squad had become almost intimate, as is often the case under the extreme circumstances of war. The time between engagements was especially oppressive. There was little to do and little to keep their minds off the danger that awaited the next troop movement. The interim periods were made bearable by marijuana and heroin. Several of Sarge's squad proved to be especially adept at scrounging and deal-making, normally a skill to be desired in combat zones. But under the conditions of low morale and pointlessness, drug acquisition and supply became the logical expression of their talents. While totally unintentional, circumstances were such that the squad evolved into a close-knit hierarchy devoted partly to keeping each other alive and partly to drug distribution. Sarge was the logical leader.

On July 15, they had been ordered to pacify a small village reported to be a haven for Viet Cong. Like most of their other combat missions, the day had begun with an endless hike along a muddy jungle path. Intermittent rain, hundred percent humidity, dripping vegetation, and mist rising from the jungle floor created an environment that was so moist they might as well have been swimming. Sarge had never gotten used to the ever-present leeches, but, like the rest of his squad members, he had trained himself to refrain from picking them off until the platoon stopped for a rest. As they approached their destination, they reached a small clearing that, prior to the war, had been a rice paddy, but now was being reclaimed by the jungle. Fanning out along the edge of the clearing, the platoon approached the village with Sarge's squad in the middle. Lieutenant Hellman was ahead and to the left, advancing much more quickly than Sarge thought was prudent. A scream from the right was followed by a frantically relayed message down the line that one of B Squad's men had been skewered by a bamboo spear launched from a booby trap along the trail. The Lieutenant signaled the spooked soldiers to move ahead, and when most of the platoon was in the middle of the field, they began to take heavy fire from three sides. Another fucking ambush. The platoon was forced back and took heavy casualties. The lieutenant fell as they started to retreat. Following procedure and tradition, platoon members, including members of Sarge's squad, dragged the body back to safety. But it soon became evident that safety for the Lieutenant was largely irrelevant. For whatever reason, the enemy did not pursue the ragtag platoon as it retreated through the jungle, eventually reaching their base camp in the early morning hours.

On the morning of July 16, Sarge and his four remaining squad members had a meeting. Although no one spoke of the possibility, all knew instinctively that the death of Lieutenant Hellman was likely not an accident. They had all been pushed to the brink, and any one of them could be responsible. But only the one who pulled the trigger knew for sure. A solemn pact was formed and all present swore to plead ignorance as far as the source of the deadly round.

PART I

Fall
Present Day

One

A cloud crept down the sides of the ridge, settling over the bog like a quilt. Ancient black spruce pierced the mist, the stunted, gnarly trees emerging at drunken angles from the spongy sphagnum soil. Pools of standing water between the mossy hummocks were frozen with a thin rime. The sweet smell of Labrador tea combined with the musky smell of fermenting highbush cranberries. Although it was only September, bone chilling cold seemed to rise from the muskeg and penetrate the body, ignoring any layers of clothing in the way. The night was totally still and crisp, as if it would shatter in the presence of a sudden noise. Fingers of fog reached for the front door of the remote cabin.

"Shit." The swamp lady tripped and landed face first in the blueberry bushes at the side of the trail. Having walked the trail hundreds of times, she had long since forsaken her flashlight. But she wished she had it now. The dim body-shaped lump in the trail could only mean bad things — at worst a dead friend and, at best, a serious complication in her life, a life which she had been attempting to simplify without much success. Picking herself up, she bent over the lump and, in the dim light, determined that it was indeed a body, most likely dead and most likely male. The clothing was typical coastal Alaskan — rubber boots, jeans, fleece jacket, and stocking cap. After debating whether to eat dinner before notifying the authorities (she was exceedingly hungry), the swamp lady decided in favor of civic duty--plus she was totally freaked out. Finding that her cell phone battery was dead as usual, she trekked back out to her rust-pocked Subaru parked at the trailhead and drove the five miles back into town to the State Trooper headquarters.

Kate Perkins had arrived in Homer two years before, on the run from her past life in New York City. After reaching a breaking point of sorts, she had moved out of her New York apartment, piled her belongings into her old car, and started driving. Kate had driven more or less randomly for days until she reached the end of the road, which happened to be a strange coastal town in south-central Alaska, of all places. Kate recognized that Homer, besides being scenically spectacular, was populated by assorted misfits and eccentrics with stories similar to her own. She immediately felt at home, even though the environment, both ecologically and culturally, was like no place she had ever been. And, after all, how bad could the weather be? Against the advice of newly-acquired local friends, Kate purchased 10 acres of scrubby spruce forest and bog with a small homebuilt log cabin, using the last of her inheritance from her grandmother. Although she possessed none of the skills needed for backwoods Alaska living, she managed to stumble through the essentials and turn the skuzzy cabin into a home. Following a series of seasonal jobs ranging from fish gutting to waitressing, she latched onto her current position as administrative manager for FlashFrozen Seafoods. Kate was still trying to figure out how her life had taken such a weird turn, from urban artiste to backwoods Alaskan.

†

Kate stared at the body. The harsh light from the trooper's flashlight revealed a face that probably had been handsome at one time, but now was pale, bloody, and distorted. The light also revealed a massive wound to the right side of the head – bone chips could be seen glistening through the bloody mess. On the back of the right hand was a blurry tattoo that seemed to depict a sort of Celtic dragon design. Both the tattoo and the dead man's face looked vaguely familiar, but she had no specific memory of ever having met him. Kate's stomach churned, both from the nauseating scene and a flood of involuntary unpleasant feelings that seemed to be associated with the man on the trail. Kate was suddenly frightened and asked Trooper Bob to accompany her to the cabin. The cabin was undisturbed, but seemed dark and creepy.

Returning to the body, Trooper Bob secured the area with crime scene tape and searched the man's pockets – all empty. Kate was finishing her second hamburger when Trooper Bob knocked on her door. As she opened the door for the young law enforcement officer, a wave of odd emotion went through her – Kate had a bad feeling that her life was about to undergo another major change.

Bob was a large man and loomed over Kate as she continued to eat her dinner. "Have you ever seen the victim before?"

"No," said Kate with obvious uncertainty.

"Since there was no blood at the scene, I think the man was killed somewhere else and brought here, but that seems like a lot of work. Can you think of any reason why someone would intentionally dump a body on your trail?"

"No, I really can't. My life has been pretty peaceful lately, with a minimum of drama." Bob was furiously writing on his notepad, which Kate found curious since her answers were very brief.

"Do you live here alone?" asked Bob.

"Unfortunately, yes."

"Have you always lived alone?"

"Thankfully not for my entire life, but during the two years that I've been in Homer I've been alone." Kate's mind involuntarily performed an inventory of her past boyfriends, resulting in the conclusion that alone was better. She was still trying to decide whether she had made poor choices or whether all men were jerks. The jury was still out.

"Can you estimate how many people know how to get to your cabin?"

"I have no idea what went on before I bought the place, but since I've lived here, I've probably invited maybe fifteen people to visit."

"I would appreciate it if you could make a list of all of those people and make a note if any of them might want to embarrass you for some reason."

"These people are all my friends and would not be involved in a murder." Kate wondered whether that was really true.

"I'm not accusing anybody at this stage, but I need to collect as much information as I can. I promise not to harass your friends other than asking a few questions. The fact that the body was on your trail suggests that whoever dumped it may have been familiar with the area. It's also possible that it is pure coincidence, but if someone wanted to simply get rid of a body, it seems to me that they would not place it in the middle of a well-used trail. Please don't leave town, Miss Perkins, without checking with me, and try not to mess up the area where the body was found." After a not-so-surreptitious look around the one-room cabin, Trooper Bob left.

Two

Gurgle, thump; gurgle, thump; gurgle, thump.

Charlie Skyler tentatively stuck his head out of his sleeping bag and listened to the uncharacteristic noise pattern. After ten years of boat living, he had become intimately familiar with every potential noise associated with the boat. This particular noise probably meant that something floating in the water was bumping against the outside of the hull. Since it was nearly time to get up and his curiosity was piqued, he slipped on his sweats and stuck his head out of the companionway, emerging into the early morning of the small boat harbor.

Charlie loved mornings in the harbor — the stillness, the silhouettes of the boats against the early morning light, the mewing of the gulls, and the pleasingly unpleasant organic smell of the tide flats. Wandering over to the port side, he looked down into the water and observed a lumpy brown object with a pale head sticking out of one end. Kelp fronds encircled the body and streamed in the current. The pasty yellow flesh left no doubt that the body had been in the water awhile. The head was face down and was bobbing up and down, hitting the boat side with every small wave.

"Shit." Charlie took a longline hook and a length of line and hooked onto the soggy brown Carhartt jacket attached to the head, then tied it to the side of the boat. He went into the pilot house and called the harbor master on the VHF radio, suggesting that she might want to get down to Charlie's boat slip as soon as possible. Although disturbed and intensely curious about the identity of the body, he decided to wait for the authorities before moving the soggy Carhartt man. He turned to the galley and started a pot of coffee.

Like many young people, Charlie had begun a quest for the perfect place to live after graduating from college. Ever since he could remember, he had been enthralled by the romance of the sea. He pictured himself like the logo on the frozen fish sticks box--an independent commercial fisherman fighting the elements to bring home the fish to a hungry nation. Because of this notion, he logically headed for Alaska, where it seemed most likely that this unrealistic dream might actually come true. He had just about reached the end of his resources when his ancient pickup truck limped into Homer in the late 1990s. Charlie immediately decided that this was the place.

The town of Homer is located in south-central Alaska on the Kenai Peninsula adjacent to the north side of Kachemak Bay, a long, narrow body of water that adjoins lower Cook Inlet. The city of Anchorage is about 75 miles north of Homer as the crow flies, but the highway connection between the two towns is 225 miles long because of inconveniently located mountains and fjords. Homer is, indeed, at the end of the road, and this characteristic has probably shaped its settlement demographics to a substantial degree. Many people living in Homer are there because of its location, having wanted to get away from the mainstream for a variety of reasons. Some are in search of beauty and tranquility; others are in search of a place to hide. Another factor driving Homer's existence is the extreme productivity of the marine environment. Because of a fortunate congruence of oceanographic factors, the area is rich in fish and shellfish, and thus has supported commercial fisheries since the early 20th century. Although some of these marine resources have become depleted, commercial fishing is still an important industry. The area surrounding Kachemak Bay, lying as it does within the transition zone between the Pacific Northwest rainforest and the boreal white spruce-birch forest that characterizes most of interior Alaska, is mostly heavily wooded with Sitka spruce and western Hemlock. Because of the maritime influence, the climate is somewhat milder than communities to the north. A narrow ridge of mountains along the south side of Kachemak

Bay provides a buffer from the stormy Gulf of Alaska, further creating a sort of special microclimate.

This new phase in Charlie's life had begun with a series of seasonal fishing jobs, working as a deckhand during the crazy halibut longline fishery and picking salmon out of gill nets during the salmon season. The other fishermen were impressed by his physical endurance and his knowledge of fish (aided by a barely-made-it biology degree). He eventually earned a position of respect in the fishing community. In 1998, he purchased an old 42-foot purse seine boat and invested all his money and sweat into refitting the boat. Unfortunately, due to a coincidence of poor salmon runs and lousy market conditions, the first three fishing seasons were pretty much a bust. Charlie was not making it in his dream profession.

He changed gears, refit his boat again with passengers in mind, and started an ecotour business that emphasized wildlife tours. The business was quite successful because of Charlie's friendly, offbeat personality and his broad knowledge of Alaskan ecology. Without really trying, Charlie had become an Alaskan "character," which he shamelessly exploited when marketing his business. He grew a bushy beard, donned a Greek fisherman's cap, and went to great pains to play the role. To reduce his cost of living, he lived aboard his boat year-round. During the long off-season, he earned money any way he could. He was currently unemployed but not worried about it.

"Jees, Charlie," said Eileen, the harbor mistress, when she glimpsed the body. "Why the heck didn't you just phone the police?"

"Sorry, Eileen, but I threw my cell phone into the harbor after my last fight with Jeanne. I didn't think it would be a good idea to broadcast the presence of a body floating in the harbor over the marine radio," replied Charlie.

"OK, I'll call them. Cripes, what's next?" Eileen dialed 911 on her cell phone.

Soon they heard the sound of a siren, which they could track for the entire six miles from town out to the end of the spit where the harbor was located. Bob, the Super Trooper, swaggered down the dock and approached Charlie's slip. Bob's appearance could best be described as large—not fat exactly, just really big. His large round head was topped by a crew cut and seemed to be attached directly to his shoulders without any intervening neck. In spite of his intimidating size, his facial expression was friendly and somewhat childlike.

"For cripes sake, Bob. The guy's dead. What did you need the siren for?" remarked Eileen.

Bob just shrugged and looked at the body. He called for a rescue vehicle and a body bag, then he and Charlie turned the body over with a boat hook.

"Oh, no! It's Rodolfo," Charlie said.

"Who the hell is Rodolfo?" Bob asked.

"He's the new owner of the taco stand across from the harbor."

"Uh-oh," Bob said.

The taco stand had achieved notoriety several months earlier when a herd of state and federal drug agents blew into town and closed it down. The gossip circulating around the harbor maintained that Buddy's Burritos was a front for a significant drug distribution network. Several arrests were made, but the general consensus was that the major players had been tipped off and had skipped town. The small stand had eventually been auctioned off, and Rodolfo had bought it for $800. He and his wife Elena had been selling excellent Mexican food for about three weeks to the harbor crowd.

Charlie, Bob, and the paramedics used the hydraulic boom on the boat to lift the body on deck. A wound at the right temple and eye suggested that blunt force trauma had, at least, contributed to Rodolfo's present condition. All of his pockets were empty. The body was placed in the bag, transferred to the dock, and hauled away on the first leg of its journey to Anchorage, where it would be autopsied at the state crime lab.

Three

Bob Stillwater, the Super Trooper, had earned his nickname when, as a new graduate from the academy, he had been assigned to the Homer area and had zealously closed down most of the small marijuana grow operations, thereby making a major dent in the local economy. Some of the residents were not happy with Bob, but his naïve friendliness and his dedication to law enforcement had eventually won him some degree of community acceptance. What Bob lacked in brain power, he made up for by sheer enthusiasm. The subsequent legalization of marijuana in the state had taken some of the wind out of Bob's sails, forcing him to concentrate on more serious crimes. Bob, Charlie, and Eileen were sitting at the galley table in Charlie's boat, mulling over possible motives for Rodolfo's death.

Bob asked, "Do you guys think that Rodolfo might have had connections to the original owners of the taco stand?"

"I really don't think so," Charlie said. "Rodolfo and Elena have lived here for several years and were just starting to make a go of it. It just seems unlikely."

Eileen said, "I agree."

"Maybe there was something left in the taco stand that the bad guys wanted. It's possible that Rodolfo found it," Charlie said.

"That seems like as good a theory as any at this stage. I guess I'm going to have to notify Rodolfo's wife and question her about the circumstances. What a crappy thing to have to do. I'm probably also going to have to deal with those jerks at the DEA. Things have suddenly gone to hell around here. You probably haven't heard, but another body was found last night west of town off Mission Road," said Bob.

"You're kidding! Who was it?" Eileen asked.

"We don't know. The body had no identification. It was a male, probably in his early thirties, dressed like a fisherman, good physical condition except for being dead. He was found by a woman named Kate Perkins as she was walking to her cabin."

"The Swamp Lady? Wow!" said Eileen.

"Do you know our Ms. Perkins?" Bob asked.

"Yeah. She works at FlashFrozen."

"What do you think of her?"

"I think she's a mixed up young woman who is trying to find her way. Why? Do you think she's involved?" Eileen asked.

"I have no real reason to think so, but I had a feeling that she was holding something back when I questioned her."

"What was the cause of death?" Charlie asked.

"We won't know for sure until we get the autopsy results, but he had head wounds similar to Rodolfo."

"Seems kind of coincidental," Charlie said.

"My thought exactly. You guys keep your eyes and ears open. I'll check with you later." Bob stepped from the boat to the dock.

"I've got to get back to work." Eileen followed him. "Let me know if you find any more dead bodies."

As Eileen was leaving, a disheveled head poked through the door of Charlie's boat. The bushy beard and long, graying wild hair reminded Charlie of various photos he had seen of Albert Einstein in his later years, or maybe commercials for products to prevent static cling. Unusual pale blue eyes and wiry build seemed incongruous with the bushy hair. "Hey, man. Was that what I thought it was?"

"Yeah, I'm afraid so," Charlie said. "Rodolfo from the taco stand is no longer with us. Come on in."

JB grabbed a coffee mug from the cabinet and poured himself a brew. "Wow. That was Rodolfo? What happened to him?"

"Looks like he was hit on the head. That's all we know at this point."

JB lived on an old boat, two stalls down from Charlie. His history was sketchy at best. The only thing Charlie knew for certain was that JB was one of the smartest, best educated people he had ever met. In the two years since JB had shown up in Homer, Charlie had tried to figure out what made JB tick. As best as he could patch things together, JB once had been a well-known professor of philosophy and political science at a California university. Something had happened to cause him to leave his job, and he subsequently underwent some sort of mental meltdown. A Google search indicated that JB (also known as Johann Sebastian Bachman) had written several books on topics relating to the history and origin of various political movements. There had been one Google reference to an editorial in a student newspaper that discussed whether it had been proper for the university authorities to dismiss JB simply because he had had an affair with a student in his class. It sounded like he had been a popular professor and the students were on his side.

JB did not like to talk about his past, and Charlie had the feeling that there was a lot more to JB than was immediately apparent. When asked how he spent his time, he claimed that he was writing a definitive treatise on American political polarization. But Charlie had never seen much evidence that that was actually the case. Since he had moved in next door, he and Charlie had become good friends. Charlie often asked JB for advice, and his answers, although they seemed to come out of left field, usually made surprising sense. Clearly, his mind worked differently from those of most people.

JB's boat, the Otterly Ridiculous, had once been a high-quality forty-foot sailboat, but age and lack of maintenance currently disqualified it from any pretentions. It definitely wasn't leaving the dock any time soon. The deck was piled high with junk, including crab pots, water jugs, ropes, buoys, ragged blue plastic tarps, and dead potted plants. Until recently, JB's pride and joy had been a six-foot tall marijuana plant displayed proudly on the foredeck during the summer growing season. Unfortunately, the patience of the authorities had finally worn thin, and he had been asked to remove it. JB had organized a going-away party for the plant (whose name was Fred). All the harbor rats had attended and toasted Fred's demise. Portions of Fred were very likely responsible for the degree of frivolity at the party. Charlie had only been inside the Otterly Ridiculous once – and that had been enough. It was so messy that he couldn't bear to see a boat treated so badly. Since then, any time that they spent together was on Charlie's boat.

One of JB's more interesting and confounding characteristics was his amazing ability to attract young women to his bed, something that Charlie could not even begin to imagine. Apparently, a liaison with a wild old hippie was exciting to select members of the Homer counterculture. What was even more amazing was that most of these young women remained friends with JB long after the affairs had ended. Charlie could only wish that his own relationships would end in the same way.

"What do you think happened to Rodolfo?" JB asked.

"I don't know. It doesn't make sense that he would have been involved in anything illegal. He seemed like an uncomplicated, good-hearted person. My guess is that he was an innocent victim of some kind. Maybe he inadvertently stumbled into something that put him at odds with some bad people."

"It seems pretty likely that the past history of the food wagon had something to do with it. That is too big a coincidence," replied JB.

Four

Charlie was lying on the bed in his boat cabin, reading the instructions for his new smart phone. The demise of the previous phone was a side effect of Charlie's miserable love life. His on-again-off-again, more or less girlfriend, Jeanne, had walked out when Charlie, once again, had been unwilling to commit to a long term relationship (or anything else). The phone had been pitched in the harbor when Jeanne had refused to answer his calls.

The "c" word gave Charlie major heebie jeebies but, at the same time, his affection for his numerous lovers had been sincere and honest. He could never quite understand their reaction when he shied away from promises of long-term fidelity. It was especially annoying since his slovenly neighbor JB seemed able to enjoy passionate short-term relationships and still be best of friends with all of his exes. It was as if the women considered a relationship with JB to be a mentoring experience or a rite of passage rather than potential commitment material.

Charlie was musing over the battle of the sexes for the umpteenth time when he heard footsteps on the boat and someone knocking on the main cabin door. As he emerged from the companionway of the aft cabin, he startled Elena, Rodolfo's wife.

"Oh, Señor Charlie, may I speak with you?"

"Of course. I'm very sorry about your husband. Please come into the galley. I've got some coffee ready." Charlie poured two cups. "What can I do for you? I can't even imagine what you and your children are going through."

"It has been very difficult. But right now I am most worried about the safety of my children and myself. I am afraid that the horrible people who killed Rodolfo may come for me."

"What makes you think that they may come after you?"

"The policeman asked me whether we had found anything in the food wagon that might be of value to the former owners. At the time I said no because I was not aware of anything. But last night I was going through some of Rodolfo's stuff and found this in a drawer."

Elena pulled a small, leather-bound portfolio from her purse and gave it to Charlie. The initials "GCTB" were embossed on the front side. The only thing inside the portfolio was an official-looking piece of paper with a twelve-character alphanumeric code written on it.

"I'm not sure what this is, but it looks like it could be valuable--maybe a code for a bank account. Have you told the police about this?"

"No," said Elena. "At first I was not sure whether it was important or not, but the more I thought about it, the more sure I was that the little book is not the kind of thing that Rodolfo would normally have in his drawer. I was worried that he might be involved with the bad guys somehow, and now I am worried that they may come after me."

"I don't know whether it's important either, but I think we need to get it to the police. The sooner it is out of your hands, the safer you and your family will be. Would you like me to go to the trooper headquarters with you?"

†

After Elena left Trooper Headquarters, Charlie and Bob were sitting in Bob's tiny office. After some persuasion, Elena had been convinced to leave town temporarily. She and her two children had been placed on a plane to Anchorage where they would be staying with friends.

"What do you make of the thing that Elena found?" Bob asked.

"I don't know," said Charlie. "It looks like some kind of code or password, maybe for a bank account. Such a thing could be worth killing for, depending on what the code accesses."

"I'm in the process of faxing photos of the portfolio to the DEA. I'm sure they'll have some ideas. I'll also check with the local banks to see if it might be one of theirs. I probably shouldn't be telling you this, but before the food wagon was auctioned off, someone broke into it in the middle of the night and totally tossed it, obviously looking for something. Judging from the extent of the damage, it appeared that they didn't find it. It looks like your instincts have been right so far. What we don't know is whether the person who broke in was a local resident or whether he specifically came to town to search the taco stand. Whoever it was, no one saw him."

"Did you ever find out the identity of the other dead body?"

"No. His prints are being run through various national databases, but no hits yet."

†

Charlie knew the signs. Over the years he had had a bad habit of getting involved in stuff that was basically none of his business, sometimes with unpleasant results. This mystery was sucking him in. Rodolfo and Elena were nice people, and he was pissed that a happy family had been destroyed just as they seemed to be getting ahead. Plus, he felt that he was somehow part of it, since he had found Rodolfo's body and Elena had come to him for help. He found his truck heading toward Mission Road in spite of himself. It was late afternoon and getting dark fast. Charlie figured that the swamp lady would be getting off work at 4:30 and would be home by about 5:00. The highway climbed to the top of the bluff as it headed west out of town, providing an unobstructed view of outer Kachemak Bay and lower Cook Inlet beyond. Augustine Volcano was silhouetted against the darkening horizon 75 miles away. In front of the volcano, the ocean shimmered like mercury behind a foreground of slate gray. The mountains across the bay were bathed in the pastel pink of alpenglow. Charlie never tired of Kachemak Bay sunsets.

He turned on Mission Road and began to look for the parking area at the head of the trail to Kate Perkins' cabin. He had a vague idea where it was located, but wasn't sure if he could find it in the dark. Charlie was starting to think that he had gone too far, when he saw a 1980s vintage Subaru station wagon parked on the right side of the road. For somewhat obscure reasons, old Subarus were the vehicle of choice for the Homer counterculture. Charlie hypothesized that most of the cars were originally owned by Anchorage yuppies but were discarded when they became too old to pass Anchorage's formerly strict emissions requirements. Homer had no such silly laws, so the cast-off cars eventually found their way south, like many of Homer's residents.

Charlie grabbed a flashlight, found the trail, and began what he hoped was a short hike. It was seriously dark in the forest, and he was glad he had the light. About 400 yards in, he saw the yellow crime scene tape that no doubt marked the body's former location. After another 200 yards, he saw the lights of the cabin. Off to the right was a large bog. It was noticeably colder in the lowlands compared to out on the road. Charlie shivered involuntarily, walked up to the cabin door, and knocked.

"Who the hell is it?" yelled a voice from inside.

"Charlie Skyler. I live at the boat harbor," replied Charlie through the closed door.

"What do you want?" said the voice.

"I'm wondering if I could talk to you about some of the stuff that has happened around here lately."

"Are you with the police?"

"No."

"Then why are you interested?"

"It's hard to explain. May I please come in?"

"How do I know you're not one of the bad guys?"

"Look, I live on the boat Shearwater and we've probably met somewhere around town. I've lived in Homer for fifteen years. I promise I'm totally harmless."

†

Kate instantly recalled an image of a handsome, bearded Viking standing on the deck of a fishing boat. She often walked around the harbor during her lunch break, and she was familiar with the boat and its bachelor owner. The Shearwater was a frequent topic of conversation among the horny women at FlashFrozen. Her desire to open the door suddenly increased.

"That's a cool boat," Kate said, and the door eased open. The man standing in front of her was about six-foot-two, with broad shoulders and a mostly slim waste that was just starting to expand into middle age proportions. He had longish, sun-bleached light brown hair and a full blond beard. His most striking feature was the pale blue eyes that shone brightly through the expanse of facial hair. The Viking analogy seemed especially appropriate. In spite of herself, her mind's eye began picturing him in fur clothing and wielding a battle ax.

†

Charlie was surprised to see an attractive young woman in her mid-twenties holding a short-barreled 12-gauge shotgun. The gun was pointed more or less at his private parts. The swamp lady was medium height, with auburn hair reaching the middle of her back. Her face was pretty in an unconventional way. Her eyes were remarkable – an intense green with specks of gold that seemed to glow like those of a cat in the dark. A lock of hair crossed her forehead and partially covered her right eye, somehow enhancing the feeling that the beautiful eyes were a window to what lay behind. She was wearing baggy sweat clothes, so Charlie's subconscious hindbrain was having trouble putting together all the pieces required for a complete assessment of her overall attractiveness. This was a frequent problem in Alaska, where people tended to wear bulky clothes.

"Well, come on in. What are you afraid of?" Kate asked.

"Do you think you could put the gun down?"

Thinking twice, Kate laid the gun on her bed. The log cabin was sparse but neat, emphasizing early fur trapper décor. A wood stove made from a 55-gallon oil drum dominated the center of the cabin. Light was provided by propane lanterns. A small hand-sawed spruce slab table occupied one side of the cabin, and a plywood bunk occupied the other. The mattress was incongruously covered by a plush down comforter, on top of which were several large stuffed animals. The shotgun barrel was resting on the lap of a purple hippo. The kitchen counter and cabinets at the far end appeared to be constructed primarily of old wood fruit cartons. A variety of shelves held books and an eclectic mixture of curios. Abstract mobiles hung from the log beams overhead.

An old chair constructed of willow branches creaked as Charlie settled into it. "Nice cabin," he said. Being appreciative of small living spaces, Charlie was actually sincere in his appraisal of the cabin, but Kate's scowl indicated that she thought he was being sarcastic.

"No, really," said Charlie, "I like it."

Kate sat on the edge of the bed, not too far from the shotgun. "OK, what is this all about?"

"You probably haven't heard yet, but Rodolfo Gonzalez's body was found in the harbor. Rodolfo and his wife owned the taco stand on the spit. I happened to be the one who found the body next to my boat. He was probably murdered. I think it will be announced in today's paper, so it's not a secret."

†

Kate was stunned. Rodolfo? The nice guy she bought a double-decker chicken taco from every Friday at noon? She'd never seen him without a smile on his face. Who would want to kill him? "Wow," she said. Then she thought of the dead man on her trail. This was getting creepy; not only was there a killer in town, but a *serial* killer? "Do you think there's a connection between Rodolfo and the guy on my trail?"

"I think there might be," said Charlie.

"So why are you running around asking questions? Shouldn't that be the job of the troopers?"

"Yeah, probably. But I found Rodolfo's body and then Elena came and asked me for help, so I sort of got sucked in. I have a pathological curiosity that sometimes gets me into trouble."

"Have they identified the body that I found yet?"

"Not that I know of. I'm not sure that the troopers would tell me if they had, which reminds me, I would appreciate it if you didn't tell the troopers that I was out here."

"Are you crazy?" Kate responded. "I think the Super Trooper is already suspicious of me. If I start having secret conversations with you, it will only add to the suspicion."

"OK, I'm not asking you to lie, just don't volunteer the information unless you have a good reason. Why do you think the troopers are suspicious?"

"I'm not really sure. After I found the body, I was sort of freaked out. There was something about the guy's face that gave me the creeps, but I couldn't put my finger on why. He also had a tattoo that I've seen someplace before. Sort of a weird déjà vu kind of thing. I think the trooper picked up on my feelings."

"Did you tell the troopers about your feeling?" Charlie asked.

"No. The whole thing is so vague that I didn't see how it would be very helpful. Plus, the trooper is already planning on questioning anybody who knows the location of my cabin. I didn't want to encourage him to look further into my personal life, although I don't know why I should care. My life has been really boring lately. However, a dead guy on my trail is way more excitement than I want."

"Well, I think you're going to get some excitement whether you want it or not. Are you involved in the murders?"

"Dammit, I didn't invite you in here to get accused of stuff. Why in God's name would I leave a dead body on the trail to my own cabin, then go and call the troopers? And, furthermore, I have no idea why anybody else would want to dump a body there." Kate's eyes sparked as her face became animated. In a reflexive, but somehow sexy, motion she pushed back the hair from in front of her eyes, giving Charlie a clear view of their intensity. He became more intrigued than ever with the swamp lady.

"OK, I'm sorry. I just wanted to see how you would react to the question."

"What is this? Are you trying to play good cop and bad cop at the same time?"

"Something like that," said Charlie.

"Well, you're not very good at it."

"That's for sure." He shrugged. "Look, I don't really think you're involved in the murders, but there may be some reason why the mystery man was left on your trail. If a connection exists, it could help solve the crimes. It could also mean that somebody doesn't like you. Your weird feelings about the guy just add credibility to the connection theory. Are you sure you have no idea why you reacted the way you did?"

"I've been wracking my brain trying to figure it out, but so far I haven't come up with anything."

"If something does come to mind, it would be a good idea to tell the troopers as soon as possible," said Charlie. "If you are feeling so inclined, you could also tell me. My cell phone number is on this card. Do you have a phone?"

"I have a cell phone, but since there's no power here, I have to charge it at work or in the car so most of the time the battery is dead."

"I think it would be a good idea to keep the phone charged and nearby until this situation is resolved. Would you be willing to give me your number?"

"Gosh, thanks for the advice. If I wanted to be close to my father, I wouldn't be living 4,000 miles away from him. And is there any other reason why you want my number?" Kate got up and headed for the door.

"Geesh, give me a break." Charlie took the hint that it was time to leave. "I was just trying to help. And there might be other reasons for wanting your number. Anyway, thanks for the frank conversation, and I really do like your cabin."

Kate handed him a scrap of paper with her phone number as he exited through the open doorway. She watched him walk away, her thoughts already reviewing her encounter with the tall man. As Charlie disappeared down the trail, Kate began to wonder why she had not invited him to stay longer, and she began to think about how lonely and vulnerable she was in her little cabin at the end of the trail. She locked the door and decided to actually load her shotgun for the first time. The symbolic act made her realize how frightened she was.

Five

Charlie was eating breakfast at the Mariners Café when Trooper Bob came in and sat down at the table. "What's up?" Charlie asked.

"We finally got an ID on the mystery man. He had no criminal record, so his prints weren't in the normal databases. But it seems he got printed when he obtained a Coast Guard Mariners License, so we got a hit on one of the non-criminal federal print files. His name was Jake Halburg, 36 years old, single, mostly employed as sort of a freelance captain in the charter fishing industry in southeast Alaska. He worked for a variety of upscale fishing lodges in recent years. According to his family, he had been living in Sitka during the off-season. I contacted one of his former employers and they said that he was reliable, good at catching fish, and that the clients liked him. Other than that, they said he was sort of a loner and nobody seemed to know much about him. There doesn't appear to be anything in his record that suggests involvement with drugs or other illegal activities. Nobody I talked to was aware that he was in the Homer area or that he had even left southeast. So I am not sure that we know much more than we did before."

"I agree," said Charlie. "That doesn't sound very helpful, at least on the surface. Why are you telling me all this?"

"Well, two reasons, I guess. When I first started this job I got a lot of people pissed off, and my bosses strongly suggested that I make more of an effort to involve local people in law enforcement. Plus, I was hoping that since you are part of the charter industry, you might have some ideas for getting more information on this guy."

"I don't know," said Charlie. "I don't talk much with the guys in southeast Alaska. What was the name of the lodge that he last worked at?"

"It was the Rainbow Inn, south of Ketchikan, one of those fly-in only, high roller kind of places. Caters to movie stars, CEOs, and other people that have way more money than they need. He worked there for two seasons."

"If he was hobnobbing with wealthy people, it might not be too much of a stretch for a guy like Halburg to get involved with illegal stuff. It would be a convenient way for a drug dealer to reach elite customers," said Charlie. "I know a guy in the charter fishing business in Ketchikan. I can check with him and see if he has ever run into Halburg or heard any rumors about the Rainbow Inn."

"That would be great. I'd appreciate it if your inquiries could be discreet. I talked to the drug enforcement guys last night and filled them in on what was going on. The Feds may be looking into the same angle, and it might be embarrassing if we messed them up somehow."

"OK. Is there any word on the stuff that Elena found?"

"Not yet. Actually, I'm not sure if the Feds would tell me anyway." Bob got up to go. "I'll see you later. I have to check up on some vandalism downtown. I've been so wrapped up in these murders that I've been neglecting my normal duties, which seem to mostly involve drunk teenagers."

Charlie went back to his boat and began working on a backlog of correspondence and email relating to his tour business. He hated having to deal with the marketing aspects of the business, but the Alaska tour season was so short that he needed to be solidly booked for most of the summer in order to make any money. It seemed since the harbor had installed wireless Internet capability, he was continually messing with email. What happened to actual letters?

But thoughts of Rodolfo's body floating next to his boat kept intruding on his concentration. He reached for his old address book, looked up Ralphy's number, and entered it into his phone. Ralphy was a college buddy who lived for fishing. He had started a sport fishing charter operation in Ketchikan and now spent his summers taking cruise ship passengers on half-day fishing trips. Ralphy answered on the second ring.

"Hey, Ralphy, it's Charlie from Homer."

"Charlie, what's happenin' man? I haven't heard from you in a long time."

"Yeah. How are things in beautiful Ketchikan?"

"Rainy, as usual. How are things with you?" Ralphy asked.

"Not much has changed. I'm still hanging out, doing my tour thing, going through girlfriends on a regular basis."

"I wish I had some of your problems," said Ralphy. "What can I do for you? Knowing you, I suspect there is a reason for this call."

"I'm working on something here, and I was hoping that you might be able to help shed some light on things. Have you ever heard of a charter boat operator named Jake Halburg? He apparently lives in Sitka, but has worked at the Rainbow Inn for the last two seasons."

"I can't say that I've ever heard of Halburg. But there is lots of scuttlebutt within the Ketchikan charter community about the Rainbow Inn."

"That was going to be my next question," Charlie said. "What have you heard?"

"Most of the stuff is just rumors of shady dealings. But on the slightly more specific side, one of the other charter operators here in town worked for Rainbow Inn a couple of years ago. He said that the clients were rich and the tips were good, but the place had a creepy feel to it. Some of the other captains were unfriendly and secretive. He always felt that there was something illegal going on in the background. He had no desire to become a part of it, so he left. He also said that there seemed to be an unusual number of attractive young women lurking in the wings who were obviously not interested in fishing. I think it was his assumption that these women had something to do with whatever was going on. Possibly an extra service included with the modified American plan."

"Wow, that's pretty interesting, Ralphy. I knew I could count on you."   "What are you getting yourself into now? I see you're still poking your nose into unsavory situations."

"Yeah, well, things keep happening to me. I can't help it – I'm just a magnet for weird stuff. Thanks a lot for your help. If you run across any other information on Halburg or the Rainbow Inn, I'd appreciate a call."

"OK, Charlie. Hang in there. Oh, one other thing. My friend said that some of the people working at the inn looked like they came straight out of a *Godfather* movie, so be careful."

Six

"How the fuck did two people end up dead? That wasn't supposed to happen." The tall, burly man with a bushy beard sat with another man and a woman around a table that occupied most of the second story of a strange three-story dwelling.

The tower-like structure was located in a primitive subdivision off of East End Road, a significant minor highway extending east from Homer some 30 miles through woodland and meadow along the bluff paralleling the north side of Kachemak Bay. An incredibly diverse array of residences were accessed from this single road, ranging from upscale homes with million dollar views to one-room shacks cobbled together with duct tape – from ranches with lush green pastures to mini-farms cluttered with car bodies and rotting boats. One of the attractions of the Homer area to young, independent-minded folks was the total lack of zoning and building codes. Here a person could still buy a couple acres of scraggly spruce forest, clear the land, and erect whatever kind of shelter his or her skills, imagination, and financial resources allowed. This resulted in whole subdivisions of homebuilt residences, each an individual creation. Some were amazing, some weird, and some downright crappy, but there were definitely no "little boxes" here. One interesting feature of these dwellings was that each builder seemed to run out of money and/or energy at about the same stage of construction, that is, prior to applying any kind of siding. Consequently, a disproportionate number of the buildings were encased only with white house-wrap material. It was rumored that unfinished houses were subject to lower property taxes, which may have provided another explanation for the number of chronically unfinished homes.

The single bare light bulb hanging from the ceiling shone dimly through a blue haze of marijuana smoke encircling the three residents of Tyvek Manor.

"I don't know. Things are spinning way out of control," said the second man. "These guys play for keeps. We're way out of our league."

"Let's calm down and think about this for a minute. We haven't killed anybody," the thin, long-haired woman pointed out.

"Yeah, but the cops might think we're part of a criminal conspiracy," the first man said.

"Maybe we should turn ourselves in and make the best deal we can. I liked Rodolfo – it was really shitty that he got killed for no good reason," the woman replied.

"You're forgetting that Aldo knows who we are. As long as he is loose, we don't stand a chance if we go to the police," the second man observed.

The first man agreed. "Even if he ends up in jail, he still has some very nasty friends.

Seven

Later that evening, Charlie was lying in his sleeping bag reading a book on celestial navigation. He was on another one of his brain improvement kicks. Periodically he would give up his normal fare of trashy detective novels and begin a brief, but intense, foray into some new area of intellectual pursuit. This month's topic had started out with a biography of Captain Cook, but he had become so fascinated with seventeenth century navigation that he had diverged a bit. It was amazing to Charlie that men set out on long voyages with only the vaguest notion of where they were at any given time. He was starting to doze off when the dramatic first movement of Beethoven's Fifth Symphony suddenly began emanating from the small shelf above his bed. He was caught in a brief surreal moment where classical music merged with visions of celestial patterns until he remembered that he had programmed Beethoven as the ring tone for his new phone.

"Yeah, this is Charlie," he said into the tiny phone.

"Hi, Charlie. It's Kate Perkins."

"I didn't expect to hear from you so soon. What's going on?" Charlie was suddenly wide awake.

"I thought of some stuff that I'd like to talk to you about," said Kate.

"Sure. When would be a good time?"

"How about now? I'm at the Rusty Harpoon."

"OK, I could come on over there. I just need to put some clothes on." The Rusty Harpoon was a harbor-side tavern just a few minutes' walk from Charlie's boat slip.

"Would it be OK if I came to your boat instead? It might be best to talk about this stuff privately."

"That's fine with me. Are you sure I'm trustworthy?"

"I guess I'll have to take that chance," said Kate. "I'll see you in a few minutes."

He put on some jeans, exited the aft cabin, crossed the deck to the main cabin, turned up the heat, and put some water on to boil. A few minutes later, he saw Kate walking down the dock. Her body was backlit from the harbor lights and her lithe profile was apparent in her tight work jeans. Charlie was gratified that Kate's body appeared to be every bit as attractive as her face, but at the same time he was ashamed of himself for his shallow, testosterone-driven view of human attributes. He came out on deck to meet her and invited her into the bowels of the Shearwater.

"Hi," said Charlie. "This is a pleasant surprise."

"Hi, yourself." Kate looked around the cabin. "This boat is a heck of lot cleaner and neater than any other fishing boat I've been on. Most male fisher persons are total slobs."

"Thanks, I think. I guess it's not really a fishing boat any more, but it was clean even when it was used for fishing." Make yourself at home. Would you like beer, coffee, or tea?"

Kate slumped down on the narrow settee adjacent to the miniscule dinette table. "I think I need another beer."

"So, what's this important stuff you want to talk about?" Charlie pulled two beers out of the refrigerator.

"It just sort of came to me last night as I was lying in bed." Kate paused.

"What came to you?"

"The dead guy had a tattoo that I've seen somewhere before, and his face looked vaguely familiar. What I realized last night was that his tattoo and facial features were similar to a man who caused me a bunch of trouble a while back. I guess what I'm saying is that the dead guy looked a lot like this other guy, but it wasn't the same guy."

"Why don't you start from the beginning?"

"OK. About a year ago, a guy came to work at FlashFrozen in the loading dock. He was sort of a tough guy with an attitude. He hit on almost all of the women at FlashFrozen, but for some reason became obsessed with me. I basically thought he was obnoxious and made a point of not encouraging his advances. This made for an awkward situation, but I tried to be polite and professional when he was around, without reducing myself to his level. I think this just ticked him off more than it would have if I had told him where to go. There were a couple of very ugly scenes where he called me a stuck-up bitch and threatened to make me pay. Anyway, as all this was going on, he was also making other folks angry by coming in late and being generally unreliable. One day he just wasn't there anymore. Management wouldn't tell anybody what had happened, but the rumor was that drugs were somehow involved. Several other men were fired at the same time, so maybe he was selling drugs to FlashFrozen employees."

"What was his name?" Charlie asked.

"Frank Halburg."

"I think that explains why you had strange feelings when you saw the body," Charlie said.

"What? Why?"

"The dead guy was probably Frank Halburg's brother."

"How the heck do you know that?"

"The troopers got an ID on the body. His name was Jake Halburg. My swift mind has put the evidence together and deduced that they were brothers – or possibly cousins."

"Damn! But that just makes it weirder. I can understand why Frank might want to dump a body on my trail to make trouble for me, but would he kill his own brother? And why?"

"I have no idea," Charlie said. "Would Frank have known where you live?"

"I never invited him there, but he could have found out easily enough. Or he could have followed me."

"Is there anything else you noticed about Frank Halburg that might help us to figure this out?" Charlie asked.

"Besides the fact that he was a total jerk? The only thing I can think of is that I sometimes saw him having a smoke with some of the fishermen that were unloading salmon at the FlashFrozen dock. It seemed like they were buddies."

"Do you know any of their names, or do you remember any boat names?"

"I didn't know any of the guys. They were just grubby fishermen dressed in yellow slickers. The one boat I remember was a white fiberglass boat with the net reel on the front – a bow picker. I don't think I saw the name."

"Can you think of anything else about the boat that might be distinctive?"

"The boat seemed like it was in pretty good shape, which might be distinctive compared to most of the other fishing boats around here, except yours, of course," Kate said.

"Thanks. Anything funny about the superstructure or how the boat was set up?"

"Yeah, now that you mention it. There was one of these hourglass-shaped things hanging from the rigging."

"That's called a day shape. It's an official signal to other boats to stay clear when the fishing boat is doing its fishing thing. Some boats just hoist them up and never take them down. Most fishing boats don't bother at all with day shapes, so that could help us to identify the boat. Bow pickers aren't all that common in Cook Inlet to start with, so a bow picker with a day shape might be pretty distinctive. I know most of the fishing boats in Homer, and that one doesn't ring a bell, but I'll keep my eyes open. Most likely that boat came from another port."

"What do we do now, Charlie?"

"You're probably not going to like this, but I think we should give all this information to the Troopers. If you want, I can tell Bob everything that we talked about. If he wants to question you further, he can get hold of you."

"Oh man! OK." Kate shook her head. "Why do these things happen to me? I really try to live a simple life, back to the land, organic food, sustainable living, and all that. But somehow the rest of the world keeps intruding in a major way."

"Unfortunately, I'm the wrong person to counsel you on simple living. I don't seem to be able to keep my nose out of other people's business. Want another beer?"

"I better go," Kate said. "Unlike some people, I have to work in the morning."

"Would you like to go out to dinner with me tomorrow night? It's Friday," Charlie blurted as Kate was going out the door.

Kate stopped in her tracks and paused for what seemed like a long time. "Is this like a date, or are you still playing detective?"

"I don't know what to call it, but I promise not to talk about dead guys unless, of course, you want to."

"How could I refuse such a romantic invitation? Let's meet at your boat at about 7:00."

"Boy. That was easy. I'll see you tomorrow night."

"Easy may not be the word that comes to mind after we get to know each other," Kate said.

Charlie could not shake the feeling that his impulsive invitation was the start of another complicated chapter in his mostly unsuccessful relations with the opposite sex.

†

As soon as Kate left, JB emerged from his floating cave and climbed aboard the Shearwater. "Who the hell was that?" he asked.

"Don't you have anything better to do than to spy on me?"

"Normally it's so dull around here that there is nothing to spy on. Would you deny me the pleasure of prying when there is finally something happening?"

"God forbid," said Charlie. "That was Kate. We have a date for tomorrow night."

"So how did you find her? And how did I miss her?"

Charlie related the circumstances of their acquaintance to JB.

"So you guys were brought together by dead bodies."

"Yep," said Charlie.

"I can't wait to see how this turns out," said JB.

Eight

"Have you heard anything from the Feds on any of this stuff?" Charlie asked.

Once again, Charlie was sitting in Trooper Bob's office. He had just finished briefing Bob on the information from his Ketchikan source as well as the saga of Kate Perkins and her mysterious feelings about the dead guy on her trail. He neglected to mention their upcoming dinner date.

"They haven't exactly been forthcoming. They did say that the portfolio that Elena found was most likely information needed to access a secret bank account at a bank in the Cayman Islands. If they know anything about the name of the account holder, they haven't told me. I'll email them a report of the information and ask them how they want to proceed on the investigation. Meanwhile, I still have two murders to investigate in my jurisdiction. It's not completely clear that the murders are drug-related, so I don't need their permission to ask questions. I guess I'll start with the FlashFrozen management and see what they have to say about Frank Halburg. There was no report to the troopers about any illegal drug activity at FlashFrozen, so, if drugs were a factor in the layoffs, they were keeping it from us."

"One problem I see," said Charlie, "is that word might leak out to the bad guys that someone at FlashFrozen is talking too much. I'm afraid that Kate Perkins could be in danger. She might already be on the killer's shit list."

"I don't know what to do about that," Bob said. "I have to follow the evidence where it leads."

"Maybe you could make up a story that would lead away from Kate. For example, you could say that you had received complaints about Frank Halburg last year, but you were unable to pursue the matter at the time because of lack of evidence. The death of Jake Halburg naturally leads you to follow up on a guy with the same last name," Charlie suggested.

"OK, I can do that," Bob said. "That would make me look better as well."

"Right," said Charlie.

†

Charlie and Kate entered Grandma's Fishhouse, a restaurant near the base of the Homer Spit. Picking a secluded table overlooking the bay, they settled in for Homer's version of an upscale meal. From their table they could see the six-mile long peninsula reaching well out into the middle of Kachemak Bay. Charlie often explained to his clients that the Homer Spit is one of the longest sand spits in the world – a geological feature created by centuries of storms that have moved sand and gravel adjacent to the shore. The direction and velocity of the currents, depth contours, and shape of the adjoining shorelines determine the patterns of deposition and ultimately the configuration of the spit. Under natural conditions, the spit probably changed its shape from year to year as the equilibrium between deposition and suspension changed with annual weather patterns. However, human intervention has assured that the long natural causeway remains in place. The presence of this unusual feature is another reason for Homer's existence. In earlier times it provided a natural lightering area for unloading ships, as well as providing sheltered anchorage on its east side. In more recent times, a road was constructed the length of the spit connecting downtown Homer to the boat harbor and marine industrial facilities near its outer end.

Charlie had dressed up by replacing his normal T-shirt with a buttoned denim shirt (jeans and rubber boots remained the same), whereas Kate was wearing a light blue turtleneck. Her long hair cascaded over her shoulders, and her incredible eyes seemed to glow in the candlelight. Charlie thought that Kate looked very nice – actually more than nice.

"I've been checking up on you, Charlie," Kate said as they sat down. "The word is that you haven't been very successful in maintaining relationships with members of the opposite sex."

"Let's not beat around the bush or anything," Charlie said. "I get the feeling that you haven't done all that well in that department yourself."

"I guess I can't argue with that, but I'm younger than you are. Have you ever been married?"

"No." Oh, crap, thought Charlie. Dinner conversation is not quite going according to plan.

"Why not?"

"Aren't we a little early in our relationship for these kinds of questions? Heck, we don't have a relationship – we just met, for crying out loud." Charlie hoped to deflect the conversation to another direction.

The waitress swooped in, and they ordered draft beer and fish and chips.

"I believe that a lot of time can be saved in human interactions by dispensing with the bullshit. According to the grapevine, you have had numerous girlfriends, but as soon as things get serious, you back out. Why is that?"

"OK, I'll try to come up with a serious answer. As it happens, I have been wondering the same thing myself lately. I have sincerely liked all of the women I've been involved with, and I didn't wish to hurt anybody. I was never conscious of leading them on, but obviously they felt that I was, judging from the fireworks as the relationships disintegrated. I have apparently been oblivious to things that should have been obvious. It's probably true that I'm scared of commitment – I'm sort of set in my ways, and my lifestyle doesn't exactly conform to the "Leave It to Beaver" model. But I think what it comes down to is that I haven't found the right person. I'm willing to make some compromises, but I don't think I should have to change my entire lifestyle in order to be a committed partner."

"Wow, Charlie. That was a pretty good answer. Way better than I was expecting."

"Thanks," said Charlie. "How about you? Can you tell me something about how you ended up in Homer and why you are living like a hermit?"

"I'm not living like a hermit. I have friends. But you answered my obnoxious question, so I guess I should answer yours. I'll give you the short version of my personal history. I grew up in a suburb outside Detroit. My mom and dad are very religious and conservative. In high school I was part of the popular clique, did all the right things. I went to college at the University of Michigan and sort of went nuts without my parents around. I got involved in theater and dancing and started running around with a pretty artsy, free-thinking group. One of my instructors said that I had potential as a professional dancer, so I left college in my junior year and went to New York to make my fortune as a dancer. I struggled for a couple of miserable years, working wherever I could, had a series of boyfriends, all of whom tried to exploit me in one way or another."

She blew out a breath. "I was just about at the end of my endurance when I had an opportunity to try out for a Broadway production. I was counting on that being my big break, but I was not selected for the show. At the same time, my boyfriend du jour had become possessive and abusive. I guess I had a mini-breakdown of some sort at that point. I threw all my stuff into my car and started driving. I didn't stop until I got here. I don't really even remember very much of the trip up here or how I made the decisions that got me to Alaska. One day I arrived in Homer, looked around, and decided that it was as good a spot as any. Anyway, my New York experience was so bad, I had more or less decided that the world was filled with assholes and that that was the normal condition. Maybe that helps explain some of my cynicism. Is that a pathetic story, or what? "

"That's a lot more dramatic than my personal history," Charlie said. "Has living in Homer helped to change your opinion of the human race?"

"Yeah, at least partly. I've met a lot of genuine people here. But people are still people. I think I've learned to have a more balanced view, and I'm starting to be more optimistic. But even within the Homer counterculture, there are a lot of desperate, unstable people."

"Like Frank Halburg?"

"Yeah."

The waitress delivered a pitcher of beer, two large platters of deep fried halibut, and a mountain of French fries. Kate dug in like she had not eaten in days.

"What about your family? Do you communicate with them?" Charlie asked.

"I've been writing to them pretty regularly in the last year or so," Kate said between bites. "They think I'm totally out of my mind and have no concept of life in Homer. The idea of their prom queen living in a log cabin in Alaska and splitting wood for heat is pretty foreign to them. But I also think they're glad that I'm not in New York anymore. I haven't seen them or my brothers in about four years, but I'm working up to a trip back to Michigan, maybe next spring. There are some hard feelings that will need to be overcome. With my newfound maturity I've realized that they're just trying to do the best they can, like everyone else." Somehow most of the food on Kate's plate had disappeared. "So, what's your story, Charlie?"

"I grew up in a fairly normal middle class family in Connecticut." Charlie stared at Kate's empty plate in amazement. "My father died a couple of years ago. He was an engineer, and my mother stayed at home. I have two sisters who are living the American dream – two kids, white picket fence, PTA, all that. I have always been pretty independent and adventurous and my father encouraged me in whatever I wanted to do. After finishing a biology degree, I took some time to travel and scope out various parts of the country. I always loved the small New England seaport towns – it seemed like they had a special mystique. I was interested in commercial fishing, but fishing on the East Coast has been pretty much shot for a long time. So it was a natural step to check out Alaska. Coastal Alaskan towns have much of the same feel with some of the wildness of the last frontier thrown in. I arrived in Homer in 1998 and thought it was the neatest place I'd ever been. So I'm still here. Commercial fishing hasn't worked out so well, but I like the ecotour thing that I do now better anyway. There is something fun and exciting about showing people cool stuff that they wouldn't normally see. Most of my clients are very appreciative."

†

As Charlie was talking, Kate took a good look at her dinner companion. She was fascinated by the expressiveness generated by his twinkling bright blue eyes, made more dramatic by crow's feet that seemed to move as he spoke. His sunburned face was framed by a full blond beard and shaggy light brown hair. She tried to picture what he would look like without a beard and decided that it would not matter. He would look great either way. He really did look like a character from a Viking movie set.

"Are you going to eat all of your French fries?" Kate asked.

"Help yourself. Do you always eat so much?"

"Yeah, pretty much," Kate said. "Are you really able to earn a living leading tours for only three months of the year?"

"Sort of," said Charlie. "I do other stuff during the off season. Some carpentry, some consulting for local environmental organizations. By living on my boat, I'm able to keep my cost of living down. Actually, it looks like the tour season is expanding. I'm taking a couple of people out next week to look at migratory seabirds and whatever else we can find."

"I take it you charge these people a lot." said Kate.

"You bet," said Charlie. "Fuel, boat maintenance, insurance, and the short season all contribute to my costs. Plus, they're paying for my amazing personality. In spite of that, I'm not exactly getting rich."

"I can understand why." Kate finished her third glass of beer. "Thanks for the dinner, Charlie. You're an interesting person."

"I'm not sure what that means, but you're pretty interesting yourself. I'm guessing that inviting you back to my boat to view my maritime art collection might not be in my best interest."

"You learn fast." Kate got up from the table. "Actually, I would like to see you again, but right now I'm really tired. I haven't been sleeping very well for obvious reasons."

Charlie walked her to her vehicle. "Be careful, Kate."

Nine

Trooper Bob was sitting at his desk filling out report forms about the interviews he had conducted at FlashFrozen. Basically, he had not discovered any new information. The facility manager had said that Frank Halburg was fired simply because he was a troublemaker and did not do his job. The other three men laid off at the same time had been friends of Halburg and had the same work ethic. When asked about drugs, the manager got somewhat defensive, but said that he had no knowledge of any special drug situation relating to Halburg and his friends. His exact words were: "This is Homer, for cripes sake. Most of the population drinks and smokes marijuana. My only concern is whether people do their jobs."

When asked if he thought that Halburg could be violent, he acknowledged that he appeared to be a pretty unstable individual. Apparently, Halburg had nearly lost it when told that he was being fired. The company had tried to find an address for Halburg after he left town so that they could send him his W2 forms, but he left no forwarding address, and Internet searches had been unsuccessful.

As Bob was finishing up the last sentence, his phone rang. Before he could get the phone to his ear, he heard, "What the hell do you guys think you are doing up there? You're jeopardizing the success of an ongoing investigation. I want you to stay out of it."

"Who is this, and what are you talking about?" said Bob.

"This is Agent Jankowski of the DEA, and I'm talking about your inquiries regarding the Rainbow Inn."

"Are you saying that you guys are already investigating the Rainbow Inn?"

"Yeah, you doofus, we've had an undercover operation in place for two years, and, thanks to you, it may be blown."

"Look," Bob said, while trying to regain his composure. "In the first place, our inquiries were through a third party who is totally unconnected to the Rainbow Inn, and it's very unlikely that word will ever get back to them. Secondly, I'm investigating two murders in my jurisdiction, which I am definitely empowered to do. I would be more than happy to work cooperatively with you guys if the murders are somehow connected to the Rainbow Inn operation or other drug activities, but you need to let me know what's going on. What role did Jake Halburg play in this whole drama?"

After a long pause, Agent Jankowski said, "Jake was our undercover agent."

"O…kay," said Bob. "I guess that would explain why people might want him dead. But why was he in Homer?"

"We don't exactly know why he was in Homer. We do know that some of the same players involved in last summer's drug distribution bust in Homer are also involved in the Rainbow Inn operation. We also suspect that one of the kingpins of the operation lives in or near Homer. We are speculating that Halburg was sent by the bad guys to take care of some unfinished business in Homer. Maybe the whole thing was a setup so they could dispose of him at a location that was not obviously connected to the Rainbow Inn."

"Believe it or not, we have some additional information that may be of help to you," Bob said. "A man named Frank Halburg was employed at the fish packing plant up here last year until he was fired. He is most likely Jake's brother or cousin, based on the resemblance and same last name. Frank evidently was not a very nice person. Has he been on your radar?"

"We knew that he had a brother, but the last we heard he was in the Army."

The Super Trooper continued to fill in Agent Jankowski on what little was known about Frank Halburg, making sure that Jankowski took note of Bob's alertness in picking up on the same last names. He promised not to make any more inquiries directed at the Rainbow Inn.

Ten

The following Tuesday, Charlie was up early, busy cleaning up his boat for his clients who were due to arrive on the 9:30 plane. It was a rare beautiful fall day with mirror-calm waters. Recent snowfall at the higher elevations had given the mountain peaks and glaciers across the bay a fresh coating of snow. The morning sun glistened on the mountain tops, highlighting a world of intense whiteness in contrast to the dark green forest and blue green waters below. His prayers had been answered; such incredible weather almost guaranteed that his clients would be pleased with their Kachemak Bay adventure, making his job of entertaining and educating much easier. Cold rain, rough seas, and seasickness usually did not enhance the overall experience.

Charlie had just finished talking on the phone to the Super Trooper and had been duly warned not to pursue inquiries that would piss off the DEA and thus shorten Bob's career. Charlie thought that the fact that Jake Halburg was a DEA informer was pretty interesting. He had suggested to Bob that he ask Agent Jankowski how Jake Halburg happened to be recruited as an informer. The fact that his brother might be somehow involved was too much of a coincidence. It seemed obvious that there must be more to the story.

John and Sarah Peters were die-hard birders from San Diego. As they got off the plane from Anchorage, Charlie immediately recognized his clients. Both were outfitted in clean, neatly creased Eddie Bauer khakis and Patagonia fleece jackets. Sarah even had binoculars around her neck. Charlie turned on the charm, helped them with their luggage, and ushered them to a reasonably clean SUV he had borrowed from a friend. On route to the harbor, he began his usual welcome to Homer speech. His approach was to assess his customers on the way to the boat, to determine how best to accommodate them. Charlie enjoyed teaching people about the natural resources of the area, but he had found that some clients did not enjoy being lectured or did not have the patience to listen. He was pleased that John and Sarah were friendly, not too pretentious, and genuinely interested in what he had to say.

The scenic drive to the boat harbor on a picture-perfect day was a great start to the adventure. Several bald eagles perched on the harbor light poles presented the first photo-ops. John and Sarah begged Charlie to stop the car and initiated a flurry of photography that was to continue for the next two days. The eagles, habituated to goofy human behavior, sat and stared with their inscrutable expressions.

After all the gear was loaded onto the Shearwater, Charlie started the big diesel engine and completed an orientation and safety briefing while the engine was warming up. Leaving the harbor, they first turned toward the shoreline of Mud Bay, adjacent to the spit, to observe birds feeding on the mudflats. They watched a flock of surf scoters diving for small clams in the shallow waters. Lines of these unusual diving birds took turns diving in rapid succession and then surfacing in the same rapid fashion, like some large comedic avian synchronized swimming team. They also watched large flocks of small sandpipers take flight as they wheeled in unison, alternately flashing the white undersides of their wings and the gray topsides. Charlie enjoyed explaining how the worms and clams inhabiting the mud in this rich area supported hundreds of thousands of migrating shorebirds in the spring and fall. Twenty-foot tides exposed large expanses of mud flat, making food available to both diving and wading birds.

After John and Sarah agreed that they had had enough of the mudflat scene, Charlie headed out into the bay toward Yukon Island on the far side, where he was reasonably sure they would be able to observe sea otters rafted up in the kelp beds. Few boats were on the water. The pleasure boating and sport fishing seasons were over, and most of the absentee boat owners had retreated to their snug homes in Anchorage.

Several commercial craft were approaching Homer from the outer bay, wisps of diesel smoke emanating from their stacks. One of the boats caught his eye and caused an involuntary shiver. He picked up his binoculars and confirmed his initial impression – the boat was a white bow picker with an hourglass-shaped object hanging from the rigging. Charlie tried to figure out how he could keep an eye on the boat without interrupting his tour and shortchanging his clients. He caught a glimpse of otters hanging out in the rocks near Cohen Island at the entrance to Eldred Passage. If they could spend enough time watching the otters, he would still have a clear view of the bay, and maybe he could determine where the mystery boat was going while simultaneously entertaining the Peters.

The Shearwater slowly approached the group of otters. Charlie's eyes were glued to the depth finder because of the close approach and presence of rocks just under the surface. About 20 animals were floating in a tight group between the rocks. Close observation indicated that some of them were hanging onto kelp fronds to keep from drifting away; others were hanging onto each other. Charlie explained that most of the otters were probably adult males or sexually immature animals that tend to gather together into groups during the non-breeding season. Females with pups were more solitary.

Occasionally, individual animals dove and soon after surfaced with an urchin or a crab. John and Sarah were totally occupied with their camera gear, trying to get memorable photos of the charismatic animals.

Periodically, Charlie looked back toward Homer and watched the progress of the mystery boat. He was only somewhat surprised when the boat went past the end of the Homer spit, bypassing the Homer harbor, and continued into the inner part of Kachemak Bay. After another 20 minutes, the Peters indicated that they were ready to move on. At this point, the white boat was nearly out of sight, but Charlie was pretty sure that the boat had passed most of the available sheltered anchorages and cove properties. Beyond where the boat had disappeared from view, stopover locations were very limited – Bear Cove and two shallow lagoons were the only possibilities. It would be easy to cruise along the shore and find the mystery boat, and in his mind, he had already modified his tour plans for the following day. He felt that John and Sarah would love to see the wild areas of inner Kachemak Bay.

The rest of the day went as planned. The Shearwater plied the calm waters, allowing the intrepid adventure couple to observe a variety of migratory and overwintering seabirds, more otters, and lots of beautiful scenery, topped off by a sighting of a minke whale. John and Sarah were happy and tired customers as Charlie dropped them off at the Fair Waters Bed and Breakfast, where most of his clients stayed. He arranged to pick them up at 8:30 the next morning.

After returning to the boat to fix himself some dinner, he checked his voice mail and found a message from Kate inquiring how his day had gone. "Oh, oh," Charlie thought as he envisioned a new, complicated relationship. "Here I go again."

†

Weather was not too bad on Wednesday morning when Charlie picked up the Peters. Winds were light, but the high cirrus clouds suggested a coming change in the weather. In fact, the marine forecast indicated that a storm was on the way, so Charlie warned John and Sarah that they might have to return to Homer by early afternoon to avoid nasty conditions. The Shearwater idled through the harbor entrance, then accelerated to cruising speed. They passed Gull Island, home to thousands of cliff-nesting seabirds during the breeding season, but now nearly deserted. A lone eagle perched on a scraggly stunted spruce at the top of the nearly naked island, as if wondering what had happened to his summer food supply. The eagle seemed somehow symbolic. The Shearwater, too, was alone – the only boat in sight in all of Kachemak Bay.

When describing the plan for the day, Charlie had intrigued John and Sarah by suggesting that they might be able to find a Kittletz's murrelet in the inner bay. The small diving bird was uncommon, and neither of the Peters had ever seen one, thus providing the potential for them to add another bird to their life lists, the birders' Holy Grail. Charlie knew that the feeding habitat of those birds was highly specific, consisting of the interface between fresh and salt waters where silty glacial streams enter saltwater. Consequently, they were usually found in the inner bay near the mouths of larger streams. In truth, Charlie was not really sure that the birds would be around in September, since he had never looked for them before in the fall. But it would provide an excuse to skirt the shoreline on the south side of the bay in search of the mystery boat.

As on the previous day, the wildlife continued to cooperate, providing enough interest through the morning that John and Sarah did not get bored. Sightings of harbor seals, sea lions, loons, and various other diving birds kept the cameras busy. Just after noon, they were approaching Bear Cove, the last deep water anchorage in the inner bay, when Charlie looked toward shore and saw the mast of a boat protruding from behind a low-lying island. He was able to see just enough of the rigging to recognize the mystery boat.

Looking at his chart, Charlie recognized the area as Fenstrom's Lagoon, a shallow tidal lagoon protected from the bay by a narrow barrier island. He remembered reading that a fox farm had been located there in the early 1900s. Raising foxes for their furs had been a significant industry during earlier times in southern Alaska. The farms were usually located on islands or other remote areas, and the farmers were noted for their hermit-like existence and antisocial tendencies. Fenstrom's Lagoon was only accessible to boats through a narrow channel during high tides. Charlie was surprised that a boat as large as the bow picker had been able to make it into the lagoon. In any event, the boat was nearly out of sight – if he had not been cruising near shore and looking for it, it would have remained hidden.

Charlie cruised on by, not wanting to arouse suspicion, and entered Bear Cove, where they anchored and ate lunch. As they left the cove, they spotted a lone Kittletz's murrelet bobbing on the water at the entrance. John scrambled for his camera and managed to get one shot before the little nondescript bird dove. The wind picked up as they began the 15-mile trip back to the Homer Harbor. By the time they approached the spit, the waves had built to six feet, and Sarah was looking green.

After happily accepting a check from John and Sarah, Charlie dropped them off at the airport for their return trip. They were more than pleased with the tour and Charlie was relieved that it had gone so well. He was also excited that he had acquired unexpected intelligence regarding the mystery boat.

After dropping off the badly-needed check at the bank, he returned to the Shearwater and fired up his computer. He navigated the Kenai Peninsula Borough's web site until he found a link to borough plat maps. After finally deciphering the complicated mapping system, he pinpointed the area on the south side of Kachemak Bay, where he had seen the mystery boat. Much of the land surrounding the bay was in public ownership with scattered private inholdings. He found that an 80-acre parcel surrounding Fenstrom's Lagoon was owned by an Aldo Fenstrom, presumably an heir to the original fox farmer. Charlie knew almost everybody living on the bay and was amazed that he had never heard of Fenstrom before. It was creepy that he had been able to maintain such a low profile. Charlie wondered what to do with the information. Fenstrom's possible connection to the murders was tenuous at best, based only on a hunch and Kate's observations. The police would obviously need some real evidence before they could take any action.

He felt the boat rock and then saw Kate's face in the cabin window. She was carrying a six-pack and a grocery bag.

The ensuing evening was long and pleasant with discussion ranging from politics to religion to music – everything except murder.

Charlie did not tell Kate about the mystery boat and its owner. He was not sure why. Kate cooked a spaghetti dinner in Charlie's galley and proceeded to eat most of it. Charlie was beginning to realize that if he and Kate should ever get together, he would have to allow extra money for an expanded food budget. They drank beer and talked until after 11:00 – way past Kate's bedtime as she informed him. It was somehow appropriate that the evening ended only with a kiss.

Eleven

The next morning, Charlie walked to the harbor boardwalk and bought an espresso, something that he did several times a week when the weather was nice. He sat on the wooden bench overlooking the harbor, as was his habit, and watched the harbor activity. In most small boat harbors in the lower 48, pleasure boats were segregated from the utilitarian and often scruffy work boats. The pleasure boat sections were dominated by streamlined craft in gleaming white fiberglass, each boat resembling an athletic shoe logo--what one marine architect has called "blob boats." In contrast, the Homer harbor was an eclectic and egalitarian mix of pleasure boats, commercial fishing boats, charter fishing boats, and other commercial craft, as well as some boats that defied description. Gleaming fiberglass was moored next to rusting hulk.

The charter fishing and tourist seasons were over, so the harbor was generally quiet, but there was some activity at the FlashFrozen dock, where a couple of small longline boats were unloading halibut and black cod. Charlie was mesmerized, watching as braillers full of large fish were hoisted from the holds of the boats up to the top of the pier and dumped onto sorting tables, beginning the fishes' journey through the processing plant. As he sipped his coffee and turned his gaze toward the harbor entrance, he did a double take. The mystery boat had pulled into the harbor and was heading to the fuel dock.

This was too much. Charlie ran down to his boat and retrieved his binoculars, ran back up to his perch on the bench overlooking the harbor, and focused on the mystery boat. The boat's name, Lucinda, did not seem very sinister. Like many fishing boats in lower Cook Inlet, the Lucinda was obviously used in several different fisheries. The large net drum used in the salmon gillnet fishery had been replaced by an aluminum chute for guiding the setting and retrieval of a heavy longline over the bow of the boat. Longlines were used for catching halibut and cod. Thinner lines with hooks at the end were attached to the main line at intervals of every ten feet or so. The strings of baited hooks were laid on the sea bottom, sometimes covering distances of thousands of feet with hundreds of hooks per line. Alongside the chute were barrels of precut herring chunks that were used to bait the hooks. The Lucinda was obviously headed out to go halibut fishing.

Two men were on board. One was a large man, 60 to 70 years old, with blond hair and blocky features; the other was younger and thinner, with dark hair. The former appeared to be in charge, and Charlie guessed that he might be Aldo Fenstrom, given his light complexion and Scandinavian name. The Lucinda completed fueling, then left the harbor and began steaming westward. Charlie bought another espresso and watched the mystery boat until it was nearly out of sight. Most of the longline boats fished in waters 50-70 miles away from Homer. They would not be back for at least two days.

This might be a perfect time to snoop around Fenstrom's Lagoon. Or was that idea totally nuts? Why would he risk an illegal activity like trespassing (and maybe breaking and entering) when there was no real evidence that Fenstrom was even involved in the murders? Plus he could not be sure that Fenstrom lived alone and that any cabins on the property would be empty. But, on the other hand, he might never get another opportunity.

Charlie's rational side debated with his incurably snoopy side for a little while, but he knew which side would win. "Why do I bother trying to be reasonable?" he asked himself.

He fired up the Shearwater's engine. He knew that he was assuming some risk. With the bay nearly empty of boats, people would notice that he was heading toward Bear Cove and would wonder what he was doing; Homer was a small town. He would need a convincing cover story. The only thing he could come up with was that he was testing out some alterations to his battery charging system and needed to run the boat for a couple of hours.

The Shearwater pulled into Bear Cove in early afternoon. Weather was cool and cloudy, with a light wind. Charlie anchored in the southwestern corner of the cove and launched the small kayak that he kept tied to the Shearwater's cabin top. The shoreline of Bear Cove was ringed by widely-spaced seasonal cabins. All of the structures visible from the Shearwater appeared to be empty. As he paddled out through the cove entrance and back along the south shore toward Fenstrom's Lagoon, he began to have second thoughts.

He was a very nonviolent person and felt strongly that there was little place for violence in the modern world except in situations of genuine self-defense, situations that appeared to be very rare. Having hung out in fisherman's bars, he had witnessed numerous fights between inebriated, testosterone-charged men (and a couple of women). These fights were supposedly to defend individual honor, but a look at the bloodied, embarrassed faces of the combatants after the fights were over suggested nothing other than stupidity. Honor was pretty much the last thing to come to mind. Although Charlie had not been in a serious physical confrontation since junior high, he always figured that he could probably defend himself if need be, by virtue of his size and strength and experience as a competition wrestler in high school and college. But he also suspected that people who participated in a violent lifestyle had an edge over normal people who did not lead their lives expecting violence and thus were unsure how to respond.

And so, as the kayak skimmed over the water's surface, he thought about the two murders. What kind of person could murder one and maybe two people? And why Rodolfo, who was one of the most genuinely nice people that Charlie had ever met? Charlie could not help but think that Rodolfo had to be a totally innocent bystander.

Hugging the shoreline to be as inconspicuous as possible, Charlie slowly approached the entrance to the lagoon and peeked around the corner. He was able to see a mooring buoy and a small, dilapidated dock. The usual fisherman's debris – old buoys, rusted crab pots, and coils of rope – littered the upper edge of the beach. No boats were present except a skiff that was tied to the buoy where the mystery boat had undoubtedly been moored earlier. The fact that there were no boats on shore was a good sign, probably indicating that no people were onshore, either. The corner of a cabin was visible through the thick alders growing above the beach. It was low tide, and there was just barely enough water for the kayak to make it through the entrance. While the entrance was shallow, the middle of the lagoon had to be quite deep to provide enough water to moor the mystery boat at all tide stages. A small stream entered the lagoon on the far side of the dock.

It was a very neat setup, and Charlie was envious of Aldo Fenstrom. He momentarily thought how nice it would have been if his grandfather had been a fox farmer in Kachemak Bay, allowing him to inherit such a cool spot. He paddled up to the beach near the dock, pulled the kayak well up on the shore to allow for the rising tide, and started up the path to the cabin. It occurred to him that sneaking around might be a good way to get shot, so he impulsively yelled to see if anyone was home. He had no idea what he would say if someone answered.

Receiving no answer, he walked up to the cabin. Although the siding was weathered to a uniform slate gray color, the structure appeared to be well built and reasonably well maintained. A small clearing with tall, unmowed grass surrounded the cabin. An open-sided storage shed was filled with lumber, tools, and more fishing equipment. Ruins of old buildings and cages at one corner of the clearing were in the process of being reclaimed by vegetation, presumably the remains of the original fox farm.

Charlie peered in through one of the front windows. The interior of the cabin seemed pretty normal – it looked like there were two rooms with a living and cooking area in front and another room toward the back. What had he hoped to find here? Crap, he would have to go inside to get any information at all. He tried the door and was surprised to find that it was open. Before opening the door all the way he carefully looked for booby traps or any kind of trip mechanism that would betray the fact that he had been there, but he saw nothing suspicious. Clearly he'd been watching too many James Bond movies.

He pushed open the door. There was nothing unusual in the front room, just the normal stuff of life. A large caliber bolt action rifle hung from pegs above the front doorway. In other places in the world this might be considered unusual, but in remote coastal Alaska bears were an ever-present concern, and a readily available firearm was standard equipment. Numerous magazines were scattered on a coffee table, including various commercial fishing trade publications and two recent magazines of the type read by wannabe soldiers of fortune and mercenaries. Charlie found these magazines, with their weapon ads and discussions of optimal techniques for disposing of other human beings, to be extraordinarily creepy. Their presence reinforced his notion that Aldo was a dangerous man.

The back room was a combination bedroom and office. At a small desk was a stationary phone that looked to Charlie like a satellite phone he had once seen on a friend's boat, but it was connected to a cable that went outside. There was also a cellular phone sitting in a docking station with another antenna cable. There was no computer or any sign of computer accessories. Aldo was not a high tech guy. Post-it notes with various notations were stuck haphazardly to the desk top and the wall behind it. He had thought to bring a small digital camera and used it to photograph the desk top, the phone, and notes on the wall. Looking at the tiny camera screen, he wasn't sure whether the images would be clear enough to read the scribbled notes, but he did not want to take the time to copy the many notes, most of which seemed to contain names accompanied by local phone numbers. Inside the single desk drawer were more miscellaneous papers. On top was a recent wireless phone bill. He photographed the phone bill and everything else that could be seen without rearranging the papers.

On the other side of the bed was a chest of drawers with several framed photographs on top. One was a photo of a large man and pretty woman in their twenties standing with their arms around each other on a beach in a warm part of the world. The woman was exceptionally beautiful and appeared to be of Asian descent, possibly Vietnamese or Cambodian. They were wearing shorts and T-shirts. Aldo Fenstrom in younger days? Another photo showed a man in his thirties wearing fisherman's clothes and standing on the deck of a 1940s style halibut schooner; by his side was a blond boy of about eight. Aldo and father? Another apparent father-son photo was just to the right. A thirty-something man and a dark-haired boy of about eight stood at the edge of Fenstrom's lagoon. Clothing was more modern, and Charlie assumed that the photo was Aldo and his son – but no wife.

The last photo was the most interesting. It showed five men in dirty, worn Vietnam-era uniforms standing in a jungle clearing. The posing was casual, almost intimate, suggesting the men had been together for a long time. Charlie thought he could pick out Aldo by his build and light complexion. He photographed all of the photos and left the cabin.

As he headed for his kayak, Charlie glanced at the side of the cabin where the phone cables came through and noticed that they went to antennas on the roof. Charlie recognized one of the antennas as being a directional type often used to extend the range of cellular phones. The cell phone towers at the end of the Homer spit would be well within range. Aldo probably had a combination of cellular and satellite service and, thus, would be reliably connected to the rest of the world.

The trip back to Homer was uneventful, except for the chaos that was ongoing in Charlie's brain. He wasn't really sure whether he had found anything useful, and his heart was still beating overtime from the stupid risks he had taken. Even if some of the information linked Fenstrom to the murders, he did not know what he could do with it, since he had committed a crime in the process of obtaining it. But he wanted to talk to somebody; the first person to come to mind was Kate.

Twelve

"Charlie, are you completely crazy? You commit a crime and risk your life all because I saw a white boat at the FlashFrozen dock over a year ago." Kate was perched in the pilot house of the Shearwater. The sun was setting and the harbor looked serene in the evening light.

"There's more to it than that." Charlie plugged his digital camera into his computer. "Fenstrom has maintained an unbelievably low profile in a community known for its gossip. That can't be an accident. Plus the DEA guys told Bob that they suspect that a local person is involved in drug dealing at a high level."

"Fenstrom may just be an antisocial hermit," said Kate.

"Maybe, but then why would he have expensive telecommunications equipment in his shack? Are you going to help me go through this stuff or not?"

"OK, OK. Let's see what the great detective found."

Charlie downloaded his photos into the computer and was impressed by the resolution. After manipulating the images with his photo program to optimize clarity, he printed them out and spread them on the galley table.

Kate was immediately drawn to the Vietnam-era photo. "I'm getting that weird feeling again. Why is it that everybody looks like Frank Halburg? This is getting creepy." Kate was looking closely at a tall man in the photo standing with his arm around the shoulders of the man presumed to be Aldo Fenstrom.

"Your feelings suggest the possibility that one of Fenstrom's war buddies might have been Frank and Jake's father. I wonder whether the other guys in the photo are in any way related to the events of the last few days?"

"That would be extremely farfetched. Plus, I don't see any way of finding out, short of getting names from military records, which is probably beyond our capability," Kate said.

"I'll bet the DEA could do it," Charlie suggested.

"That's great. All we have to do is show them your contraband and suggest that they look into it. They're already pissed off at the Super Trooper. They would probably be happy to throw you in jail."

"There might be a way to provide the information anonymously. Anyway, let's look at this other stuff while we're thinking about that." Charlie turned his attention to the photo of the wireless phone billing statement that had been in Fenstrom's desk drawer. "There seems to be one Homer number that Fenstrom called about once a day. Otherwise, I don't see any patterns."

"Here, give me that." Kate grabbed the bill and sat down at the computer. She accessed whitepages.com and typed in the repeated Homer number. The name Darryl Swift popped up on the screen, with an address on Olshanski Road.

Charlie was amazed. "Wow. I didn't even know you could do that."

"It's called a reverse look-up. A bunch of websites will do it for you."

"For an art major who lives in a cabin with no electricity, you're a pretty geeky person."

"What can I say? My family are all computer nuts. My older brother is a systems analyst and used to be a serious hacker. Come to think of it, he may be able to help us out with some of this stuff," she said. "Anyway, I'll go through all of the numbers on this statement and make notes on what I find."

"While you're doing that, I'll look at the pictures from the desk top."

A scruffy apparition wearing a Grateful Dead T-shirt suddenly materialized inside the cabin door. Kate jumped and stifled a scream.

Charlie frowned. "Cripes, JB. Could you please try knocking?"

JB ignored Charlie's comment, took a beer out of the refrigerator, and plopped himself down on the settee next to Kate.

"Kate, meet JB," said Charlie. "JB, meet Kate."

"What are you guys doing?" JB asked.

Against his better judgment, Charlie explained the whole sordid mess.

JB sat and thought for a while, then turned to Kate. "What do you think about getting involved in all this?"

"I think Charlie is slightly crazy."

"I'm glad to see that someone around here is a little bit rational," JB replied. Then he suddenly stood up and left. The Shearwater rocked as he stepped off the boat.

Kate raised an eyebrow. "What was that?"

"That was JB. He's weird as hell, but a good friend. He lives in that floating slum over there. He is probably just starting on his first joint of the day, so he is a little erratic."

"I'm surprised that you told him about everything that we are doing."

"JB is definitely eccentric, but he is smart and amazingly level-headed when the circumstances call for it. He is generally a good person to have around. We may need his help eventually."

✝

Darryl Swift was splitting wood in the backyard of his Olshanski Road "homestead." He was a big, strong man and enjoyed this task above all others required for his semi-subsistence, stoned mountain-man lifestyle. There was something about the rhythm of the act combined with the violence of the splitting maul tearing through the spruce bolts that he found soothing. He often did some of his best thinking while splitting wood. On this particular morning he had a lot to think about, and the thoughts bouncing about his brain were causing a major headache.

The previous morning he had received a call from Aldo ordering him to lie low until further notice and informing him that there would be no resupply for a while until things cooled off. The main problem with lying low was the total lack of income from his normal drug sales. Since drugs were his only source of livelihood and since his cupboards were currently devoid of food, he was concerned for his future welfare. He was actually contemplating the possibility of a real job – maybe selling firewood, since trees seemed to be the only resource he had at the moment. An additional problem was the fact that he knew his regular customers would soon be starting to come by for their normal purchases. They would not be happy and would become progressively more unstable as time went on.

But of perhaps more importance than his immediate business problems was the connection between him and the murders of two people. While Darryl had not killed anybody, and, in fact, only had the vaguest notion of why the killings had occurred, he did have knowledge of the murders. He could not see how the authorities could connect him or his associates with the killings, but if they did, he was totally screwed. It grated on Darryl that Aldo was out in the Gulf of Alaska chasing halibut around, keeping well clear of anything that might be going on in Homer. He could only hope that a storm would sink Aldo's boat.

To make matters even worse, his girlfriend Julie was coming over in a few hours and he would have to tell her that he was out of coke. He suspected that her infatuation with him was strongly related to his ability to supply her multiple needs. His prospects for finding another female companion were grim, given the limited availability of single females in Homer and his limited value as a human being. Julie and her brother Brett were the only other people in Homer who were familiar with his operation.

†

A short time later, back on the Shearwater, Charlie and Kate were still poring over Charlie's ill-gotten "evidence." In the process of examining the remaining numbers on the wireless phone bill, Kate found only two that seemed to be suspicious, or at least not obviously innocent. The first was an international call to an unlisted number in the Cayman Islands, and the second was to a San Diego number listed under the business name Offshore Enterprises, Ltd. Kate had googled Offshore Enterprises to see whether the company had a website, but the search resulted in no references to the company of any kind. The listing in the San Diego yellow pages was under the import/export category and consisted only of a small print name and number.

"That's kind of suspicious," Charlie said. "I wonder how we can get more information on the company. Calling them from Alaska might not be a good idea."

"We could have someone else call from another state, maybe from a pay phone," Kate suggested.

"Do you have anybody in mind?"

"I was thinking that maybe my brother in Michigan could help out. I might also be able to get his advice on computer spying techniques. Plus, I need an excuse to get back in touch with him – it's been too long."

"Sounds good to me."

"Did you find anything interesting in Aldo's desk debris?" Kate asked.

"Not much. Most of the notes seemed to be related to commercial fishing supplies. One of the notes said to call Darryl, and another note had the name, Brett Fishbein. Fishbein isn't listed in the Homer phone book."

Kate googled "Brett Fishbein," but found no references that seemed to apply to their situation, unless Fishbein happened to be a German psychiatrist who had published a treatise on male homosexual behavior.

"I've had enough detective work for the day," Charlie said. "How about a beer?"

"That would be great. Hey, Charlie, where do you sleep, anyway?"

Charlie realized that Kate had never seen his master stateroom, which happened to be the part of his boat of which he was the proudest and on which he had spent the most time and money. Grabbing two beers from the refrigerator he said, "Follow me."

Fishing boats set up for purse seining generally have the cabin located as far forward as possible, leaving a large back deck area used for storage and deployment of the large net, as well as storage of fish in holds under the deck. On Charlie's boat, the main fish hold had occupied much of the middle portion of the boat, beginning a few feet aft of the main cabin door. Charlie had raised the deck level above the hold by a couple of feet and had constructed an enclosed companionway that allowed easy access to the forward starboard corner of the hold area. He and Kate exited the main cabin and headed for the companionway door.

Kate asked, "You sleep down there with the fish?"

"Yup."

Charlie opened the door and let Kate enter first. When she was about halfway down the stairs into the dark void under the deck, he flipped a switch. Bright but subtle recessed lighting suddenly revealed a small but elegant master suite.

"Holy shit," said Kate. "This is incredible."

The walls were paneled with oiled teak. A queen bed occupied the aft center of the room, with cabinets built into the hull on both sides of the bed. Bookshelves covered the back wall above the bed. The curves of the boat hull were faithfully replicated in the superb woodwork. A porthole-type window was present on each hull side, and a clear hatch opened to the outside overhead. A small head and shower were located in the forward port corner, and a small desk on the other side. The room was amazingly warm and dry, considering the temperature was below freezing outside and they were in a cave, much of which was below water level.

Kate jumped onto the bed as Charlie turned on a sound system with bluegrass music that sounded amazingly good in the small space. "Have I just entered the master seduction suite?" asked Kate. "This looks like the maritime version of a playboy bachelor pad."

"I can honestly say that seduction wasn't on my mind when I designed and built this room. I built it completely for myself. I like wood crafts, and finish work on high quality boats is one of the few places where handcrafted woodwork is still valued. Most houses, even upscale ones, use cabinetry from a place like Home Depot that's mass produced in standard sizes. Boats, on the other hand, have curved surfaces, and much of the woodwork is crafted to fit the space."

"Is seduction completely out of the question?"

"Not necessarily," replied Charlie, his mind racing to figure out exactly what Kate's expectations were and what he should do next. He reasoned that Kate had so far been blunt and honest so he decided to take her at her word.

†

Later, when Kate awoke, the cabin lights were out and she could see stars through the overhead hatch. The bedside clock said midnight.

Charlie stirred next to her in the queen-sized down-filled sleeping bag that served as bedding on the Shearwater. "Hey," he said.

"Hey, yourself." Kate moved closer. "That was really nice."

"That it was," Charlie said. "More than nice, but it all happened pretty fast. I'm afraid of hurting yet another female companion."

"Let's take it as it comes, Charlie. I'm a voluntary participant and I promise not to be unreasonable."

"OK. You might as well spend the night rather than drive home on icy roads."

"I don't have any clothes for work tomorrow."

"I can't help you with that, but I do have a shower and an extra toothbrush."

"Okay," said Kate.

†

Kate shivered from the cold as she left the master suite and crossed the few feet of open deck to the main cabin of the Shearwater. It was still dark at 7:00, but a pink glow was starting to appear in the eastern sky. The frosty rigging of nearby boats starkly contrasted with the lightening sky, like spider webs covered with morning dew. As soon as she opened the cabin door, she smelled coffee and bacon and heard the NPR news on the local station. Charlie was cooking scrambled eggs on the old diesel stove and had set the galley table for two.

Kate poured herself a cup of coffee and sat down. "This is the coziest boat I have ever been on. How do you keep it so warm?"

"Most of the commercial fishing boats in Alaska have these terrific diesel stoves in the galley. They provide both heat and cooking and are usually left on continually so the boats stay warm and dry. Sort of like the wood cook stoves used in houses in simpler times," Charlie replied. "How do you feel this morning?"

"I feel great. I can't tell you how good it felt to spend the night in your bed."

Charlie set out two plates of bacon, eggs and toast, with a double helping for Kate.

Kate dug in and, after five minutes of non-stop eating, finally came up for air. "I can't help it," she said. "Lovemaking makes me hungry."

"As far as I can tell, everything makes you hungry," Charlie replied.

"So, what are we going to do with all the information you've dug up about Aldo?"

"I don't know. I've been giving it some thought, and I think we need to find some kind of more definite connection between Aldo and the murders before we go to the authorities. Unfortunately, I have no idea how to do that. Maybe we can get some more information on Darryl Swift. You must know some druggies you can ask about local suppliers."

"Why would you think I know some druggies?"

"Because I smelled weed when I visited your cabin," Charlie replied.

"The marijuana I use I grew last summer in my own personal secret plot. Believe it or not, that is the extent of my drug use. But my friend Sheila may have some ideas. I'll see her at work today and could ask if she has heard of Darryl."

"Are you good enough friends so that you can trust her not to tell anyone about your inquiries? Otherwise, it could be dangerous for you."

"Yes, I think so. Maybe to be safe I could ask about drug suppliers in general, as if I am in desperate need and see if Darryl's name comes up. If it doesn't, then I could ask about him specifically."

"Great idea," Charlie said. "Can you give me a call or stop by after work and let me know what you found out?"

"Yes, I can," She gave Charlie a passionate kiss before she went out the cabin door.

Charlie watched her walk down the dock toward FlashFrozen. He was thinking that last night was pretty terrific and that he was rapidly getting in pretty deep.

Thirteen

The Super Trooper was staring at the walls of his office, trying to drum up enough ambition to finish filling out his monthly office supply requisition forms, when the call came in. Agent Jankowski informed him that he and his assistant would be coming to Homer to spearhead the investigation of the murder of Jake Halburg. They would be arriving the following afternoon and would expect Bob to brief them on the case as soon as possible and accompany them as they questioned witnesses.

This did not make Bob happy. In the first place, he did not have much information to give them, and in the second place, he did not like the idea of the federal agents questioning people in his town. Especially folks like Kate Perkins, who was likely an accidental participant in the Feds' undercover drama. Although Bob took his law enforcement responsibilities very seriously, he was a rank amateur when compared to the intensity of the Drug Enforcement Agency. All the agents he had met appeared to be totally devoid of humor or any sort of perspective on life outside of their professional niche. It was his opinion that all those guys needed to lighten up – maybe take up yoga. It also made him uncomfortable that Charlie Skyler probably knew more than he did about the events surrounding the double murders. He was suddenly desperate to talk to Charlie, in hopes that Charlie could help him feel less stupid when dealing with Agent Jankowski.

†

Charlie had spent most of the day trying to figure out how to impart his illicit information to the proper authorities without

81

incriminating himself. He was toying with the idea of making an anonymous call to the Crime Stoppers hotline in Anchorage. But what would he tell them? There is this hermit who lives on Kachemak Bay who is probably a drug kingpin and murderer, but there is no real evidence against him? Charlie had just decided to put off any decision until hearing from Kate on the Darryl Swift situation, when he received the call from Trooper Bob. He agreed to meet Bob for breakfast in the morning.

While waiting for Kate to show up, Charlie began some overdue maintenance chores on his boat engine. The hatch for the engine compartment was located in the floor of the main cabin. Working on the engine involved climbing down into the very cramped space and contorting his body into various uncomfortable positions. The large engine occupied the center of the hole, with just enough room on each side for a very thin person to crawl through. Space on a fishing boat was at a premium, and space for comfortable engine maintenance had apparently not been a priority of the designer.

Charlie was immersed in oil, concentrating on the intricacies of valve timing, when Kate stuck her head in the engine compartment and said, "Hey."

Startled, Charlie whacked his head on the low ceiling – an action that was closely followed by a string of epithets. He looked up at Kate's grinning face and said, "Where the heck did you come from? I didn't even hear you get on the boat."

"I'm sneaky," said Kate. "I'm also turned on by the smell of motor oil, so my finely tuned pheromone receptors homed in on the engine compartment."

"Forget it. We're not even going near a bed until I get cleaned up. Give me about five minutes to finish this, and then I'll be right up. Help yourself to a beer while you're waiting."

Kate pulled a beer out of the neatly-stocked frig and sat at the galley table, concentrating for the first time on the contents of the boat cabin. Charlie had obviously redone this cabin as well as the master suite, but he had done so without altering the utilitarian feel of the original fishing boat. The L-shaped galley on the port side consisted of teak cabinets capped by a countertop made of light wood, probably birch. The original oil stove remained, with its salty brass grillwork. The dinette table was made of teak and birch with an inlaid radial design. Bookshelves and other fine woodwork complemented the rest of the cabin. In the front starboard corner was the inside pilot station with its large wood wheel, comfortable pilot seat, and array of instruments.

Charlie finally emerged, wiping his hands on a well-used oil rag. He grabbed a beer and sat across from Kate. "Well, what did you find out about our boy, Darryl?"

"Darryl is definitely a major supplier. I asked Sheila where a person could get weed around here and she mentioned several names, including Darryl's. Then, when I hinted that I might be interested in harder drugs, Darryl's name was the only one that came up. She said that Darryl was very careful about his contacts and that she would have nothing to do with any dealings with him. Now I think she is seriously worried about me, but I'm pretty sure she didn't pick up on the snooping aspect."

"Boy, you're really getting into this detective thing. Thanks for the information."

"I don't know," said Kate. "I felt pretty sleazy tricking a friend. I'm not sure I want to do that again. Besides which, everybody at work will think I'm a serious druggie as soon as word gets around."

"Things are probably going to come to a head pretty soon. I got a call from the Super Trooper this afternoon, and he wants to meet with me tomorrow morning. It seems that the DEA guys are coming to town tomorrow afternoon to launch a major investigation into Jake Halburg's death. Bob is worried that they will run over his authority, and he is anxious to look as good as possible. I guess he wants to see whether I've learned anything new about the case. If he only knew.

Now the problem is: how much do we tell him so he can relay the information to the Feds?"

"I don't see any reason why you can't tell him about Aldo Fenstrom, based just on my boat description and your research of borough property records. There isn't anything illegal in that. If he wants, he can take credit for the information and let the feds follow up on it," Kate suggested.

"I was pretty much coming to the same conclusion. But I still don't know what to do with the other information. What do you think about my calling the Crime Stoppers line in Anchorage and leaving an anonymous tip suggesting that Darryl and Aldo might have had something to do with Rodolfo's death?"

"I don't know. Don't they need something more to go on before they can take any action?"

"Maybe not," said Charlie. "The DEA guys may be able to check phone records and stuff like that to build up evidence for a search warrant or an arrest. It seems like it might be worth a try. By the way, did you talk to your brother about doing some phoning for us?"

"As a matter of fact, I did. He said he would do it after he got off work and while it was still working hours in California. Since it is later in Michigan, he may have already done it. I expect a call from him any time. It was good to talk to him. He sounded pleased that I called, in spite of the fact that I was exploiting him for nefarious purposes."

"Sounds great. It seems like having met me is already contributing to harmony in the Perkins family."

"Yeah, right. Hey, Charlie, would you like to come over to my place for dinner tonight? I need to check on the cabin, feed the cat, light the stove, and warm it up before stuff starts to freeze."

"Sure," replied Charlie. "Making out in a cold cabin is just what I had in mind. What cat?"

"Buster is my attack cat. He was probably out catching mice when you were there before. If you're interested in spending the night, we could just take my car, and I could bring you back tomorrow morning on my way to work."

"Good idea. I'm always willing to make some sacrifices for the sake of energy efficiency. As long as I'm back in time for my 9:00 am meeting with Bob. Give me about ten minutes. I need to take a shower after bathing in motor oil."

Fourteen

Kate's little station wagon was chugging up the hill heading out of town when her phone rang. Charlie, sitting in the front passenger seat, surmised that the call was from Alex, Kate's brother. He listened to one side of the conversation and tried not to wince too badly from Kate's erratic driving. When Kate was talking, the car veered to the right, and, when she was listening, the car veered to the left. By the time she was done with the long call, they were almost to Kate's trail and Charlie was a nervous wreck.

"What's the matter?" said Kate. "You look pale."

"Let's just say that multitasking may not be one of your strengths," answered Charlie.

Ignoring that remark, Kate picked up a bag of groceries and started down the trail. "C'mon, I'll fill you in on the call as we walk." It was nearly dark, and the cold from the bog could be felt as they entered the trees. "Alex called Offshore Enterprises posing as a representative of a specialty store wanting to import specific items from Southeast Asia. A woman answered and said that they weren't interested in his business. When he inquired what their main business was, she became rude and cut him off. Alex also did some advanced web browsing. He found one obscure reference to the company as the defendant in a civil lawsuit where they had been sued by an aircraft services company because they didn't pay their bill. The suit was settled out of court, so no other information is available. Apparently, Offshore Enterprises doesn't do anything in the open other than occupy office space."

"Well, I guess that's interesting, but it sure doesn't help us very much. Anything else? You were on the phone for twenty minutes."

"Mostly we talked about family stuff. I guess everybody is okay. The usual family dramas, but otherwise no major problems. Everybody is worried about their whacked-out Alaskan refugee. They all assume the worst, as if it's a given that I'm a drug-addicted prostitute on my way to an early grave. They can't comprehend that there are alternative lifestyles that don't involve mayhem and immorality."

"It sounds like you really need to go see them," suggested Charlie.

"Yeah, I know. But I'm afraid that we'll end up back at square one again."

"I think they will come around if you take a positive approach to what you are doing with your life and explain it to them. Love is a pretty strong force."

"I wonder if their tolerance will extend to my hanging around with an Alaskan wild man who lives on a boat?"

"It might be best to avoid that part," said Charlie as they approached the cabin.

The cabin door was locked with a giant hasp and padlock. Kate pulled out a large key.

"What happened to trust between neighbors on the last frontier?"

"My natural cynicism about the human race hasn't been totally overcome. Besides, somebody might steal my cat."

As if on cue, Buster met them at the door, meowing loudly. Kate went through her ritual of lighting the gas lamps and the stove. Within a few minutes, the small space was warm and cheerful.

†

On the other side of town, Brett scratched his beard. He had no running water at his hovel, and, consequently, the flora and fauna in his whisker ecosystem were flourishing. Plus, he was sweating with extreme anxiety. He had just hung up the phone with Frank, who scared the bejeesus out of him. He had heard nothing from Frank for months, and he was hoping that Frank had disappeared forever to a far-away location, but then suddenly, out of the blue, he received the call.

Frank's instructions were clear and horrifying. He had been ordered to take care of the meddling woman from FlashFrozen, Kate what's-her-name. The consequences of ignoring Frank's directive were unthinkable. But violence was not in his nature, and he was having difficulty thinking straight.

He violently swept the pizza boxes onto the floor from the top of his ancient chrome dinette table so that he had room to make notes. Eventually a desperate plan came to him. He gathered together the things that he would need, then lit a joint and sat down to wait until the time was right.

†

Kate served up cheeseburgers and hash browns. Since her only cooking implement was a propane cooktop, her repertoire was limited to fried or boiled food. Needless to say, fried usually won out. "The cheeseburgers are great," Charlie said. "But I have to wonder. You once made a reference to health food, and I have yet to see you eat anything that would normally be considered remotely healthy."

"What can I say? I'm a food hypocrite. Most of the Homeroids that I hang around with are health food nuts, so I've gotten kind of used to talking the talk even if I don't walk the walk."

Charlie grinned. "Conformity among the nonconformists?"

"Something like that. Pretty stupid, huh? I seem to need a lot of calories. If I ate nothing but broccoli, I would have to eat a bushel a day. Sort of like a moose – I've heard they have to eat a hundred pounds of twigs per day to stay alive. Cheeseburgers are much more efficient."

"I certainly can't argue with logic like that." Charlie laughed.

"What about you? You seem to be annoyingly devoid of hang-ups."

"I suspect that my ex-girlfriends would disagree. I guess the major personality trait that tends to get me into trouble is my insistence on independence. I have trouble taking orders from other people, which has sort of minimized my career options. It's not that I'm antisocial, but the hassle of dealing with the politics and infighting that occur in any hierarchical organization doesn't seem to be worth the potential reward. I would rather deal with people on a friendly social basis, rather than in a work atmosphere that is too often a setup for failure."

"I sympathize with that point of view, but I may be a little more flexible than you." Kate started clearing the dishes and put them in her "sink," which happened to be a giant fiberglass utility room basin that she had scrounged from the Homer landfill. "I enjoy the camaraderie of the women at FlashFrozen, even though it can get catty from time to time."

She removed a pot from the top of the wood stove and poured hot water into the basin, balancing it with cold water from a plastic jug hanging from the rafters above the sink. Charlie picked up a towel and dried as Kate washed. When the dishes were done, Kate pulled the plug at the bottom of the basin, and soapy water burbled out.

"Exactly where does the water go when it leaves the sink?" asked Charlie.

"You probably don't want to know. C'mon, let's find a more comfortable location." Kate grabbed Charlie's hand and led him to the bed, where they snuggled into the down comforter with their heads resting on the purple hippo. Buster curled up on Kate's stomach and immediately began purring.

"Boy, it doesn't get much better than this," Kate said. "In bed with a nice guy and a nice cat."

"You do have simple tastes."

✝

Minimal light from the new moon filtered through the scraggly spruce branches as Brett slogged through the bog. This was the worst place he had ever been, and things were not going well. It was dark and cold, the woody shrubs scratched his face, and the hummocky terrain made it almost impossible to walk. The soggy sphagnum had sucked off his left boot twice, causing him to lose his balance and topple sideways. Every time he took a step, the water in his boot made a squishing sound. His left foot was numb with cold. The gas can he was carrying in a backpack had leaked, and his back was saturated with petroleum products. He hated the smell of gas. And he was disoriented.

"I'm going to kill that fucking Frank," he thought. But he knew deep down that it was much more likely to be the other way around, which was why, after all, he was here. Brett tried to get his bearings from landmarks, but could not see more than five feet. He was very cold and starting to think that maybe his first priority should be the avoidance of hypothermia, when he saw the dark shadow of a cabin in front of him.

The cabin, built on a small rise overlooking the bog, was dark and quiet. Brett was relieved to finally get out of the disgusting swamp. As he walked by the front door, he noticed the large hasp and had an idea that might make his plan work even better. He quietly closed the hasp and inserted a stick through the lock loop. Brett circled around to the back of the structure and saw the small propane tank, right where he was hoping it would be. Removing the can from his gas-saturated backpack, he poured gas along the back edge of the cabin and on top of the propane tank with its copper pipe leading to the cabin. He then walked backward into the trees, pouring a stream of gas as he went. He lit a match, touched it to the stream of gas, and stood watching transfixed as the flame leaped toward the cabin.

†

Small footsteps on his back woke Charlie from a sound sleep. Buster was pacing and meowing frantically. In his semi-conscious state, Charlie smelled both gasoline and smoke. Abruptly sitting up, he saw flames flickering out the back window. He quickly awakened Kate and ran to the front door. "Kate, the door's locked from the outside. Is there an ax in here?"

"Shit, Charlie. The ax is outside."

Kate turned on a flashlight, and Charlie ran to the window on the side of the cabin opposite the fire. "Kate, there are fucking bars on the windows." The previous owner had installed a metal grate over the outside of the windows to prevent bears from getting into the cabin.

"How the hell are we going to get out of here?" Kate yelled, sounding panicked.

Time seemed to stand still and Charlie's senses focused with amazing clarity on the smell of the smoke, crackling of the fire, and flickering of the flames outside the window. "What kind of ammunition do you have in the shotgun?"

"Buckshot," Kate yelled as she turned the flashlight onto the gun.

"Outstanding. Shine the light on the door." Charlie grabbed the gun. He fired twice, aiming at the bolts that attached the hasp to the front of the door. The explosions were deafening in the small space, the smell of gunpowder overwhelming. A large hole appeared in the door, and it flew open, with Charlie and Kate close behind.

Charlie ran around to the back of the cabin and saw that the lower part of the back wall was on fire, flames licking at the propane tank. He ran back into the cabin and grabbed the large wool throw rug that covered most of the cabin floor, pulled it out the door in one pull, upending tables and chairs.

"Kate, grab an end of this, and we'll put it over the fire." They dragged the rug around to the back and draped it over the burning logs as well as the propane tank. Charlie then dipped a bucket into

Kate's water barrel and poured water over the top of the rug and the propane tank. The fire died down quickly, and Charlie was able to shut the valve on the tank.

"Whoever started this fire may still be out there. Where's the gun?" Charlie said.

"I've got it. For once, I'm way ahead of you." Kate brandished the shotgun toward the woods.

"Have you seen Buster? He probably saved our lives by waking me up. Another couple of minutes, and the fire would have been out of control."

As if on cue, meowing came from behind the woodpile, and Buster trotted out to greet them.

†

Brett watched with fascination as the flames licked at the side of the cabin. He had planned to run away as soon as the match was lit, but could not pull himself away from the eerie scene. He had the feeling that he was the director of his own private horror movie.

Two loud gunshots ended his reverie and brought him back to reality. He was further shocked by the sight of a large man running around the cabin. He had checked the parking area at the trailhead before beginning his mission, and there had been only one car present. Where the hell did this guy come from? He was even more surprised when the fire was efficiently extinguished. He began to back farther into the woods. Confronting the pair, given the fact that they had a gun and he did not, seemed out of the question. Thinking that they may have already called for help with a cell phone, he ruled out retreating along the trail and reluctantly re-entered the bog for the long slog back to his car.

"Shit, Shit, Shit." His plan had been a total failure and, what was worse, he had to retreat through the damn swamp.

†

"What do we do now?" Kate sat on the threshold in front of the demolished cabin door. "Should we call the Super Trooper?"

"I forgot my phone. Do you have yours?"

"No, my phone is in my car."

"You would think that between us we would have one complete brain, but apparently not. I guess we should wait here until it gets light in a couple of hours. I'm sure whoever lit the fire is long gone, but we probably shouldn't take a chance on the trail, since it would be a pretty easy place for an ambush. We can talk to Bob first thing in the morning. In the meantime, we should be pretty safe as long as we stay alert, keep the gun handy, and don't make easy targets of ourselves."

"I'm definitely not going to fall asleep any time soon," Kate went into the cabin and grabbed the down comforter. "Follow me."

Kate led Charlie through the darkness into the woods away from the cabin to a rock outcropping fronted by large boulders. Buster trotted behind them. Kate squeezed between two boulders and entered a perfect natural hideaway. She and Charlie lay on the mossy ground with the comforter over them and started to relax.

"You're a pretty handy person to have around in an emergency. I wouldn't have thought to use the gun to get out of the cabin or the rug to put out the fire."

"I'm just glad I was around to help. And don't forget about Buster."

Fifteen

"I gather you two have become friends. How am I going to explain to the Feds that each of you happened to independently find a dead body, then a few days later happened to be jointly occupying a tiny cabin in the woods that somebody happened to set on fire in the middle of the night? This whole thing gets weirder and weirder by the day," said the Super Trooper to Kate and Charlie.

The three of them were crammed into Bob's miniscule office at 7:30 am. Charlie and Kate had carefully made their escape from the swamp after sunrise without incident. Fortunately, the bad guys had not thought to disable Kate's car. Bob was already at trooper headquarters when they arrived at 7:00. They had described in detail the exciting events of the previous night.

"Whoever was at the cabin last night probably didn't know that I was there, since Kate's car was the only one at the trailhead," Charlie said. "So, for whatever reason, someone wants Kate dead. Presumably, the bad guys think that she knows too much. The connection has to be someone at FlashFrozen. I think the first priority is to protect Kate, and the second priority is to try to get a lead on who the killer is."

"My priorities may change after I meet with the DEA guys this afternoon, but I guess I agree for now. Let's take a trip to the cabin and see what we can find," said Bob.

"Wait a minute, guys. What about me? I'm supposed to be at work in a few minutes."

"What do you want to do, Kate? Are you up to going to work, knowing that someone there is passing on information?"

"I don't know. I guess I could call in sick. I'd like to get the cabin door fixed, anyway, after Charlie blew it to smithereens."

At Bob's suggestion, they all piled into the patrol car. As Bob passed Kate's Subaru, he noticed the shotgun lying on the back seat. "I hope that gun's not loaded. If that were the case, it would be a violation of state law."

Kate and Charlie just looked at each other.

†

Brett was stoned at 7:00 in the morning. In spite of his exhausted and altered state, he was unable to put the events of the previous night out of his mind. Images of the flaming cabin and the ensuing sequence of events kept running through his brain like an endless tape. On the one hand, he could not believe that he had actually tried to kill someone by burning them alive, and part of his muddled brain was relieved that they had survived. On the other hand, he had screwed up, and Frank was going to be pissed.

His trip back from the cabin had been hellish. He had become lost in the bog again, and it had taken two hours to reach his rusted-out Nissan pickup, which he had parked on an old logging road down from Kate's trail. His clothes were muddy and wet and saturated with gasoline – sort of a dead giveaway regarding his felonious activities. He was terrified that there would be a road block set up on Mission Road, so he waited until after dawn before leaving. By the time the sun came up, he was nearing hypothermia. Proceeding very cautiously, he somehow reached his cabin without incident and immediately burned his clothes in the burn barrel next to his woodpile. Standing naked and shivering uncontrollably by the outside wash basin, he scrubbed his body as hard as he could, but could not get rid of the gasoline smell.

He had no idea what to do now. Frank was due to call in two hours, and he did not know what he was going to say. At Frank's request, he had not consulted with Darryl or his sister after the initial call. He was wondering whether he should talk to them now. He knew that his sister would likely not speak to him again if she knew what he had tried to do. But he needed advice and felt very alone. He wanted to skip town and never come back. Ever since he had arrived in Homer, things had gone to hell. He would be more than happy never to set foot again in the "cosmic hamlet by the sea."

†

Charlie, Kate, and the Super Trooper surveyed the damage to the side of Kate's cabin. Aside from some superficial charring, the damage was not extensive. A charred and empty gas can was lying near the base of the cabin wall. Bob carefully bagged the can to preserve any evidence value. The copper pipe leading from the propane tank to the cabin wall had sagged somewhat from the heat, underscoring how close they had come to disaster.

Bob indicated that it was probably foolish to try and extinguish the fire given the presence of the propane tank. Charlie allowed that that was probably true. A trail of charred ground led back to the woods, and it became obvious where the perpetrator had stood prior to lighting the stream of gasoline. A concentration of dark bog mud was evident on the ground, along with one pretty good boot print, likely from a common pair of fisherman's boots. However, one of the tread impressions suggested that part of the left boot sole had been damaged in the right front corner, creating a V-shaped cut in the rubber. Bob photographed the print.

More muddy footprints approached the front cabin door and could be traced backwards to the bog edge, suggesting that the intruder had reached the cabin by crossing the bog rather than by using the dry trail.

Kate indicated that trying to track a path through the bog would be difficult. But she noted that there was only one logical place to park a car that would provide access to the other side of the bog. After Charlie made a list of materials that he would need to repair Kate's door, the intrepid group of sleuths piled into the patrol car once again and proceeded to the logging road east of the cabin. The ground was still wet from the morning dew, and fresh tire tracks could easily be seen on the dirt road. They followed the tracks about a half mile to their end. A fresh pool of motor oil and more muddy footprints reinforced the notion that the arsonist had recently parked at that spot. Bob took a sample of the motor oil and more photographs. "Okay, you've convinced me that a very nasty, and not too bright, person tried to kill you guys last night. The fact that he tried to lock you in suggests that his goal was elimination rather than simply scare tactics."

"Great," Kate said. "I've never had anybody try to kill me before. How did I get into this?"

"I'm afraid that my poking around has a lot to do with it. I'm really sorry," Charlie said.

"Yeah, well if you weren't so cute, I would probably be really pissed at you. But right now I'm just really scared for both of us," Kate replied.

"I hate to interrupt this tender moment, but I have a strong feeling that there is a bunch of stuff that you haven't told me," Bob interjected.

"Let's go back to your office, and we'll fill you in as much as we can,"
Charlie said.

Back at the office, Charlie summarized his suspicions regarding Aldo Fenstrom, based on Kate's observations of his boat at FlashFrozen and Charlie's detective work in tracking the boat to Fenstrom's Lagoon. Additionally, they dropped the name of Darryl Swift as being a possible drug source per Kate's inquiries of her FlashFrozen coworkers. They did not mention any information that resulted from Charlie's illicit breaking and entering expedition to Aldo's cabin. Bob indicated that he would relay the information to the DEA guys. He further indicated that it was likely that the DEA would want to interview both of them. Charlie asked if Bob could question the DEA agents regarding how Jake Halburg came to be their undercover agent.

"I'm really tired," Kate said as they drove toward town. "Can we go to the boat so I can take a nap? I'm hoping that things will look less bleak after some sleep."

"There is one thing that I would like to do first." Charlie asked Kate to take a back street to the pharmacy and park out of sight at the rear of the building. After suggesting that she keep watch to see if anybody may have followed them there, he went inside through the back door, where there was a row of pay phones. Because of the early hour, the store was mostly deserted.

He called the state Crime Stoppers hot line in Anchorage and spoke to a sweet-voiced dispatcher, anonymously relaying all of the information that he and Kate had uncovered regarding Aldo Fenstrom, Darryl Swift, Brett Fishbein, Offshore Enterprises, and the possible Vietnam connection with the Halburg family. He tried to impress on the dispatcher the importance of the information, emphasizing the possible connection to a double murder and suggesting that she talk to a detective right away. He also told her that DEA agents would be in Homer that afternoon, and it would be good if the information were passed on to them through the Homer trooper office. By this time, Charlie was pretty sure that the woman was humoring him, and he did not feel optimistic that the information would be relayed any time soon.

On reaching the harbor, they parked out of sight behind a marine electronics repair shop and crossed the docks to the Shearwater. Kate crawled into Charlie's bed and immediately fell asleep. Charlie was too keyed up to sleep. He sat in the pilothouse, the events of the past 24 hours running through his brain like a bad movie.

Sixteen

The ragged tops of the highest waves seemed to kiss the sky. Low overcast combined with dim fall light and endless sea painted a scene in shades of gray. The horizon had a slightly corrugated appearance, belying the heights of the waves. The shrieking wind blew the froth of the breakers horizontally so that sea spray was continuous, a telltale sign of Force 8 conditions. A large, soot-colored sea bird nonchalantly paddled in the waves, traveling up and down on a watery roller coaster. Try as he might, man would never become as comfortable on the sea as the bird.

Blue-green water repeatedly washed over the top of the pilothouse, overwhelming the windshield wipers each time the Lucinda bottomed out in a trough and stuck its bow into the next wave in a never-ending series. The pounding would likely continue all the way to Homer, still six hours away. Men of the sea the world over were familiar with the nauseating feeling that accompanied the realization that conditions were crappy, bordering on dangerous, and the only thing to do was to resign oneself to a long period of discomfort and pray that the boat's mechanical systems would hold out until the destination was reached.

Aldo was thinking that he was too old for this shit, and that maybe this would be his last trip. Lucinda's hold was about two-thirds filled with halibut, about two tons worth. At six dollars per pound, the fish would be worth $24,000 at the dock in Homer. Compared to the profits from Aldo's other enterprises, the money was relatively unimportant. But Aldo had been fishing since he was seven years old, and responding to the various fishing seasons had become a conditioned reflex. The tradition begun by his grandfather and continued by his father, and eventually Aldo himself, seemed like something that could not be lightly broken. Thoughts of the three generations of Fenstroms that had operated out of Fenstrom's lagoon brought back the deep sadness he felt because he had no son to carry on for him – but that was another story.

Through the windshield of the aft pilothouse, Aldo watched Izzy, his deckhand, work on the front deck to batten down the fishing gear for the long, rough ride home. Miles of line, hundreds of hooks, bait barrels, anchors, and marker buoys all had to be secured in their special places. Aldo was obsessive about keeping his boat shipshape. Although Izzy wore the usual rubber bib overalls and yellow slicker, he was drenched to the skin. Working on deck in rough conditions was like being in a rolling Jacuzzi filled with ice-cold water. More water seemed to go down his neck with each wave. But Izzy did not seem to mind, lending credence to Aldo's feeling that Izzy was not playing with a full deck. While Izzy was clearly not an intellectual giant, he was reliable and could be counted on to keep his mouth shut. Furthermore, he was Aldo's brother-in-law. Keeping business within the family, especially illicit business, was the best way to avoid betrayal.

In spite of himself, Aldo began to think about what might be awaiting him when he got back, and he was not thrilled. On the one hand, his drug customers would be getting very impatient. Darryl would, of course, take the brunt of their dissatisfaction, but unhappy addicts were unstable and could cause trouble. On the other hand, he had the murders to worry about. Frank had become a loose cannon and was in danger of unraveling 35 years of a carefully constructed network that had functioned very well until recently. He had no idea what he was going to do about Frank. The situation was delicate, involving decades of obligation and intricate alliances with the Halburg family.

And then there was the money. Aldo was not an expert in international banking, but he was pretty sure that it was going to be impossible to access the more than twenty million dollars sitting in a bank in the Cayman Islands without the account number and password, especially since no name was on the account. Jake Halburg had set up the account and had probably recorded the account number somewhere – but he was dead.

Killing Halburg was especially stupid. Aldo had a bad feeling that his long run might be coming to an end. He had long ago developed an exit plan for just such an occasion, but thought it would be a shame to destroy all those years of hard work.

Seventeen

After Charlie and Kate left, the Super Trooper sent the charred gas can off to the state crime lab by air courier, in hopes that there might be some usable fingerprints. The side of the can that had been lying on the ground was not badly burned, and he was somewhat optimistic about the print potential. He had a feeling that the bad guy was too dumb to wear gloves.

He also ran the names Aldo Fenstrom and Darryl Swift through the national criminal database. Aldo's file indicated that he had received a dishonorable discharge from the army in 1971, but the records did not indicate what the basis of the charges had been. The only other item was a misdemeanor drug possession charge in California in 1974. Apparently Aldo had escaped trouble with the law subsequent to 1974. Darryl Swift's record showed three drug charges during the last ten years, with the latest being a felony sale charge, for which he had spent six months in a California prison.

The fact that Aldo Fenstrom was a commercial fisherman in his sixties who had not been in trouble with the law for over thirty years did not lend much credence to Charlie's suspicions. Darryl, on the other hand, was clearly someone Bob didn't want in his town; he'd bear watching. Unfortunately, there was currently no evidence to link Darryl to either the murders or local drug sales, so there wasn't much Bob could do in the way of direct investigation. He hoped that the DEA agents might be able to make use of the information. They would be arriving in a couple of hours. He filled his coffee cup, took two antacid pills, and tried to figure out how he was going to present his (and Charlie's) findings to the Feds in a way that would make him look most favorable.

†

Bob had to laugh when the two federal agents got off the 2:00 plane. Both had short haircuts and wore black suits, dark ties, and aviator sunglasses. Anyone in Homer, or anyplace else in the world for that matter, would have recognized them as some sort of federal law enforcement personnel. The only other people that might dress similarly would be Mormon missionaries, but the men getting off the plane were too buff and their facial demeanor too cocky for that.

The DEA boys sauntered up to the Super Trooper who, unlike the Feds, wore an actual uniform and thus had no pretensions about being recognizable. Agent Jankowski introduced himself and his sidekick Agent Phillips. Bob drove them back to trooper headquarters, where he had instructed his part-time secretary to clear the boxes out of the spare office/storage room so that they would have some place to sit. As he passed his desk, he noticed a fax from state headquarters describing a Crime Stoppers report that had been received in Anchorage only a couple of hours earlier. Quickly glancing through it, his first thought was "Damn you, Charlie." Picking up the unexpected report, he carried it into his meeting with the Feds.

The meeting room overflowed with testosterone fumes as Agent Jankowski immediately sat at the head of the table and noisily removed files from his briefcase. Agent Phillips sat next to Agent Jankowski, forcing the Super Trooper to sit in a crowded corner stacked with file boxes. Bob wisely sat back and waited until the agent was through outlining the DEA role in the investigation, which basically relegated the Alaska State Troopers to the role of observer.

Bob then quietly indicated that he had quite a bit of information to share and an attempted homicide to investigate, and he was damn well not going to be relegated to a back seat. He calmly suggested that they share all their information and work together. As a first step, Bob recommended that the federal agents start from the beginning and describe their investigation to date. When Agent Jankowski complained, Bob described the attempted murder and arson of the previous evening and the almost certain connection to the deaths of Jake Halburg and Rodolfo. Agent Jankowski glanced at Agent Phillips, who gave a slight nod. Bob filed away this telltale behavior as an indication that Agent Jankowski was not as dominant as he would like people to think.

It seemed that a local police jurisdiction in an LA suburb had received a communication from a citizen who had recently returned from a vacation trip to a fishing lodge in Alaska. This man, who was of a socially conservative bent, had discovered the Rainbow Inn on the Internet, and the advertising materials had convinced him that it would be the ideal guy trip to promote some bonding between himself and his 15-year-old son. After a few days at the Inn, it had become apparent that the services offered at the Inn and the morals of the clientele were not in line with his own values. The final straw was reached when one of the ubiquitous young women patrolling the grounds of the Rainbow Inn had tried to seduce his son (who was very disappointed when the activity was vetoed by his father). Convinced that the Inn was a front for drugs and prostitution and who knows what else, the man reported the operation to a friend in the Los Angeles Police Department. The LA Police, having no jurisdiction in Alaska, reported the communication to the FBI.

The FBI, while skeptical, thought that there might be something to the report, especially since they had heard some vague scuttlebutt about illicit activities at upscale fishing resorts. At that point, the DEA was brought into the picture and asked if they had any information that would add credibility to the report. They indicated that they had heard reports of drug distribution through southeast Alaska. Additionally, one of the top agents in the LA office was a fanatic fisherman. Hoping to kill two birds with one stone, the agent quickly volunteered and was dispatched under cover to the Rainbow Inn.

During the first few days at the Inn, the agent had a great time, catching his limit of salmon and halibut each day. The other guests spent a lot of time carousing in the lodge in the evenings, but no obvious illegal behavior was noted by the agent. The fishing guide assigned to the intrepid undercover agent was a likeable young man named Jake Halburg. On the fifth day, Halburg showed up for the day's fishing noticeably upset. He loudly complained about his bosses and was threatening to quit.

Sensing an opportunity, as the agent was leaving the Rainbow Inn, he slipped his business card into the envelope containing the tip that is traditional for fishing guides. Written on the back of the card was the suggestion that the DEA would be very interested in any information that Halburg might have regarding illegal activities at the Rainbow Inn. The agent returned to LA with three freezer boxes filled with fish and bragged about the incredible fishing until no one could stand to listen to him anymore.

Nothing was heard from Halburg until the following November, well after the fishing season. Then he came in person to the district office in Los Angeles and asked to speak with the agent. He described a sophisticated operation at the Rainbow Inn that included drug distribution and prostitution, and admitted that he was part of it. He indicated that the illegal activities were carefully separated from the legitimate activities and that hard evidence would be difficult to come by. He also indicated that the DEA agent had been "made" as soon as he stepped off the plane, and Halburg had been ordered by his bosses to be the best fishing guide he could be. A deal was made whereby Halburg would go back to work at the Rainbow Inn the following summer and systematically collect evidence. In return, he would be granted immunity from any charges that might result from his past association. The LA agents agreed that Halburg was not totally forthcoming, but decided not to push him too hard, since his cooperation was vital.

As scheduled, Jake Halburg went back to work for the Rainbow Inn at the start of the fishing season in June. As far as the DEA knew, he was collecting information for them, but there had been no actual communication from him. In fact, he seemed to have dropped off the face of the earth until his body was found in Homer.

"That was pretty interesting. Thanks for sharing." Bob then related his suspicions about Aldo Fenstrom and his possible connection with Frank Halburg. He also mentioned Darryl Swift and his probable involvement in local drug distribution. The agents rolled their eyes, implying that the connections with their case were tenuous at best. Bob then pulled out the Crime Stoppers report and handed out copies to the agents. Except for the first paragraph, he had not had time to read the report himself, so he was flying blind as far as the content. The agents read through the report and continued to be skeptical of its value.

"What are we supposed to do with this?" asked Agent Jankowski. "It's all speculation. I want to know who put this information together."

Bob was reading through the report for the second time and was fascinated by the possible Vietnam connection between Aldo Fenstrom and the Halburg family. "With all due respect," Bob said, "I have a suggestion. Rather than worry about where the information came from, why don't we concentrate on whether the information is accurate? Do you guys have the resources to check military records and find out the names of the guys in Aldo Fenstrom's unit? If one of those guys was named Halburg, and if he was, indeed, the father of our murder victim Jake, then we have a very strong connection with current events."

Agent Jankowski started to speak, but agent Phillips broke in. "I think that is a reasonable suggestion. We'll make some calls and see what we can find out. We might also be able to get information on the circumstances of Fenstrom's dishonorable discharge."

"Meanwhile I'll look into this other guy mentioned in the report, Brett Fishbein," said the Super Trooper.

Eighteen

The call finally came in three hours late. Brett had become progressively more panic-stricken as the day wore on. His state of mind was not assisted by the fact that he was working on his third joint of primo Matanuska Thunderfuck, and he was having major difficulties putting thoughts together. During a mostly incoherent conversation, he managed to get across to Frank that his attempt to get rid of the FlashFrozen busybody had been unsuccessful.

Frank was not at all interested in the details of Brett's horrible night. After colorfully suggesting that Brett perform various anatomically impossible acts, he told Brett to make himself permanently scarce by leaving the state or possibly the country, implying that if either he or the authorities caught him he would likely not be long for this world. Frank's final words were something to the effect that if you want something done right, you have to do it yourself. Brett had not been able to tell whether Frank was calling locally or not; the connection had been poor, but that was pretty normal. Frank could be anywhere. He could be outside watching Brett's cabin for that matter. This last thought reverberated in Brett's dysfunctional brain.

Brett relit the doobie. To the extent that he was able, Brett mulled things over. His choices ranged from bad to really bad. Somehow he had to leave town without getting caught by the police or killed by Frank. Then he had to disappear without a trace, leaving his sister Julie behind. He and Julie had been together since they were kids, but he definitely could not get her involved in this mess. And then there was Darryl. He wasn't sure whether Darryl had been in contact with Frank as well. He suspected that Darryl was out of the loop, since he was Aldo's right hand man and Frank seemed to be operating independently of Aldo. For some reason, Frank was on a mission of his own and appeared to be out of control.

One of Brett's bigger problems was that he didn't have enough money for a plane ticket out of Alaska. Driving to the Lower 48 via the Alaska Highway was a poor alternative, since he would have to go through both Canadian and U.S. customs. He probably wouldn't even be able to get into Canada because of his felony record, much less back into the U.S. He knew that one of Julie's credit cards was not totally maxed out, but he wasn't sure how to convince her to help without having to explain the whole mess to her. But it seemed pretty certain that the only way to skip town quickly was to enlist Julie's help.

†

The Super Trooper had helped the DEA guys settle in to his secretary's work space where they had access to a phone and a computer. They began pounding the keys. Bob went to his office and entered Brett Fishbein's name into the national criminal database. In a few minutes, he had returns from the state of Arizona where Brett had been convicted twice of misdemeanor possession and once for felony possession, for which he had served six months in the state prison. While Brett was not exactly an arch criminal, he definitely had a problem with drugs. The report from Crime Stoppers had not indicated what information had caused Brett to become a person of interest, only that he was.

Bob didn't know where to go from there. So there were these two guys, Darryl and Brett, who were probably involved in the Homer drug trade, but there was no direct evidence connecting them to anything. Then there was the mysterious Aldo Fenstrom. He could only hope that the DEA guys could establish some definite connection between Fenstrom and the Halburgs so that the investigation could proceed on some kind of solid basis.

$\dagger$

Later that afternoon, Julie and Brett were sitting at the dinette table in Brett's shack. Since Brett had run out of weed several hours previously, his mind was uncomfortably clear, a situation that he regretted, given his predicament.

"Brett, why do you need to leave town?"

"I can't tell you."

"You want me to go $800 in debt, and you can't tell me why?"

"You have to trust me. It is better if you don't know."

"Look, little brother, I've been protecting you from your stupidity since you were nine years old. I'm not about to blindly contribute to the Brett fund without more information."

"All I can tell you is that I am in serious danger if I stick around here. You may also be in danger if we stay close to each other."

"Have you talked to Darryl about this?"

"I don't want Darryl to be involved. I don't trust him to keep quiet about my plans."

"So whatever has you totally spooked has to do with Darryl's operation."

"I guess you could sort of say that."

"Well that's just great, since Darryl is both my supplier and boyfriend. What am I supposed to do when he asks me where you have gone? He'll know if I am lying to him. He's not a very nice person when he's pissed."

"I know this puts you in a bad spot. But you can just tell Darryl the truth that I was scared and took off and didn't tell you why I was leaving or where I was going."

"If we use my credit card, I have to make the reservation. I think I can make the reservation in your name, but you will need to tell me where you're going."

"Okay. I guess once I have the ticket, I can change it. Does that mean you're going to help me?"

"What choice do I have? I don't want my little brother to get killed. How did we manage to get ourselves involved in this lifestyle where we have to deal with things like this? We have made so many bad choices, it's pathetic. When do you plan to leave?"

"As soon as possible. Let's make reservations now. I'll drive to Anchorage and leave from there."

After an interminable wait for the airline operator (during which a disembodied voice kept reminding her what a valuable customer she was), Julie managed to make a one-way reservation for her beloved brother to Las Vegas, via Seattle. Brett figured that once he was in Seattle, he could decide where to go from there. He had to be in Anchorage early the next morning, which meant leaving Homer late that night.

†

Aldo and Izzy turned into Kachemak Bay, exhausted and sore after fighting the waves for what seemed like forever. They unloaded their fish at the FlashFrozen dock. Izzy disembarked and went home to his wife. Aldo continued on to Fenstrom's Lagoon. For once, the tide was high enough for him to enter on the first try. He felt more tired than he had ever felt in his life. The combined effects of sleep deprivation, hard physical labor, rough water, advancing age, and a feeling of fatalism regarding events on shore had taken a major toll. He carefully removed a well-secured cooler from the Lucinda and stashed it in a hidden root cellar near his cabin. He opened a can of pork and beans, ate a hasty dinner, crawled into bed, and instantly fell asleep.

†

"Piece of shit car," Brett mumbled to himself as he kneeled in the slush trying to change his right rear tire.

Although he had left Homer at 2:00 am, he was only two-thirds of the way to Anchorage. His old car had a maximum speed of 50 mph under the best conditions. Unfortunately, it had started to snow, and he was forced to go even slower. Then his tire had gone flat. The bed of the pickup was filled with junk, under which he had hoped to find a jack and lug wrench. An archeological dig through the ancient layers of truck debris complicated by darkness had resulted in the discovery of a jack, but no lug wrench. He was in the process of trying to remove the lug nuts with a pair of pliers that he had happened upon during his search. His flight was scheduled to leave Anchorage at 11:00, but he was still a couple of hours away and it wasn't looking good. He was cold, hungry, tired, and disturbingly unstoned.

Nineteen

Kate was running from the wall of fire, but it was moving so fast…She wasn't going to make it. Her life flashed before her eyes and it wasn't a pretty picture. She sat up with a muted scream…and hit her head on the ceiling.

As she crumpled back into the softness of Charlie's bed, she realized where she was. Unfortunately, the memory of the last twenty-four hours also came back to her. It was still totally dark outside, although the bedside clock said 7:00. Charlie was snoring lightly beside her. She resented the fact that he was sleeping peacefully, when she had just had one of the most terrifying and realistic dreams of her entire life. The least he could do was share in her dream aftermath. But she figured if that was his only flaw, she could deal with it.

Rolling over, she began to cuddle with the adjacent warm body. Kate remembered that she had been sleeping since the previous afternoon. Apparently, being almost murdered was an exhausting activity. Charlie had joined her sometime in the night, but she was not sure just when. She was incredibly hungry, having slept through dinner the previous night.

Charlie stirred and reciprocated her cuddling.

"Mmmmm," said Kate. "Are there any bacon and eggs left?"

"I can see that romance doesn't have a very high priority," Charlie said.

"Normally romance has a very high priority, but there is a finely-tuned balance between stomach and other body parts. In this case, the stomach is winning."

"Got it," said Charlie.

†

As was his habit, the Super Trooper arrived at his office at 7:00. He started the coffee pot and turned on his computer. Just as he was about to settle down to mundane chores, his computer dinged the arrival of a new message.

"Bingo!" said Bob.

The state crime lab had found a good fingerprint on the gas can used in the attempt to burn down the Swamp Lady's cabin. Even more amazingly, the print had been identified as belonging to a Brett Fishbein. The e-mail included attachments providing Fishbein's arrest record and mug shot. It was too good to be true. The direct evidence would allow Bob to issue an arrest warrant for Fishbein and would corroborate the Crime Stoppers report. The DEA guys were due to arrive in ten minutes, and he could not wait to tell them about this latest development. Maybe they would take him a bit more seriously.

But the bad news was he had no idea where to look for Fishbein. Bob had checked phone, address, and vehicle records the previous day, but had been unable to find any listing for Brett Fishbein. Also, it seemed likely that his suspect might have taken off after the failed arson attempt. He completed the paperwork for an all-points bulletin and sent it out to all state authorities just as the DEA guys sauntered into his office. This morning each of the agents seemed to be slightly deformed because of the awkward underarm lump created by their holstered Glocks. Apparently, they were expecting action. Bob was a little concerned about what might happen if one of them was to actually remove his gun from his holster, but he hoped that he could accommodate their lust for justice.

Bob filled the agents in on the Fishbein situation, emphasizing that thanks to him, they were in pursuit of an actual suspect. They reluctantly acknowledged that Fishbein seemed to be a promising lead, but they were still not convinced that the arson had anything to do with the murder of Jake Halburg. But, all things considered, they seemed to be treating Bob with greater deference than they had the day before.

Agent Jankowski fired up his ever-present laptop computer and looked to see what his sources had found regarding Aldo Fenstrom, et al. Because of the likelihood that Fishbein would flee the area, the Super Trooper felt that time was of the essence in tracking him down. He left the DEA guys to their computer search and went downtown to where he hoped to find some contacts that would have a line on some of Homer's more nefarious citizens. Because of the dominant role that alcohol played in the routine crime of Homer, Bob was well acquainted with the bar owners and their daily schedules. Most of the bars did not open until 11:00 am, but he knew that the proprietor of Gertie's Bar would likely be cleaning up and preparing for the day's business. He knocked on the door and was greeted by Gertie herself.

Gertie's had the reputation of being the sleaziest bar in town and had been the source of far too many calls to Bob's office. Gertie herself was a bawdy woman in her fifties known for her enormous cleavage. As if the cleavage was not enough to attract attention by itself, she also had a tattoo of a large iguana that originated somewhere below her boobline and terminated on her neck, taking advantage of the contours of her plentiful body. Although Gertie's business operation had caused problems for local law enforcement, Gertie was a generally friendly person and tried to cooperate with the law within reason. She greeted Bob with a "what now" look on her face. Bob presented her with the mug shot of Brett Fishbein and asked if she knew him.

"Yeah, I know him. That's Brett. He comes in here a couple times a week with his sister Julie," said Gertie.

"What can you tell me about him? Does he hang out with anybody else?"

"I don't know much about him. He doesn't cause any trouble. He just has a few beers and sits there with a spaced-out look. I suspect he is a major pothead. I don't think he has much between the ears. As far as who he hangs out with, the only other person I've seen him with is a guy named Darryl who may also be Julie's boyfriend. Darryl is generally bad news."

"Why do you say that?"

"Some of the customers seem to be afraid of Darryl. He has a kind of power over them."

"Might drug distribution have something to do with Darryl's power?"

"You didn't hear this from me. But yeah, probably. I don't think transactions take place in here. I watch pretty carefully. I need to stay in business."

"I'm not accusing you of anything. But I need to find Brett very badly. Do you know where he or his sister lives? Anything about his habits? Kind of car that he drives?"

"He may live in one of the shacks off of Olshansky Road. I'm not sure where Julie lives – maybe with Darryl. Brett drives a beater white Nissan pickup with off-color paint patches. It's pretty distinctive – looks like a pinto horse. I think it has out of state plates. That's about all I can think of."

"Thanks, Gertie. You've been a big help. If he should happen to show up in your bar, I would appreciate it if you would call me. But be careful. He's wanted for attempted murder. I'm trusting you to keep our conversation quiet for a couple of days. I don't think he knows that we're looking for him, and I'd like to keep it that way."

"Wow," said Gertie.

The Super Trooper went out to his cruiser and radioed a statewide alert for an old compact pickup that looked like a pinto horse.

Twenty

"What do we do now, Charlie?" Kate shoveled in another forkful of scrambled eggs. After a light coat of snow, the sky had cleared and it was shaping up to be another beautiful fall day in Homer. Although it was almost ten o'clock, the horizon to the east was just starting to brighten and the mountains were taking on a pinkish tinge. The 360-degree view from the galley of the Shearwater was stunning with the sunrise to the east, the crisp silhouettes of boats to the north, high mountains to the south, and volcanic peaks protruding from Cook Inlet to the west. Several glaciers were visible, starting to reflect the early morning light.

"I don't know," Charlie said. "You probably shouldn't go to work until things have settled down. We know that at least one person at FlashFrozen has been relaying your inquisitiveness to the bad guys. Also, I suspect that the Super Trooper will want to see us. I am curious what the DEA guys have been contributing to the situation."

"I sort of need to work. There's a little matter of money. At the very least, I need to let my boss know that I haven't dropped off the face of the earth."

"How well do you know your boss? Can you tell him you need a couple of days off to sort out some personal stuff?"

"Fortunately it's slow at the plant right now, so I can probably charm him into giving me time off. Unless, of course, he is one of the bad guys."

"Do you think that's possible?"

"I don't know. I'd be really surprised. I guess I'll have to trust my instincts."

"Don't let him know where you are. He will probably assume you are at your house. I don't think anyone saw us come aboard yesterday. The harbor has been very quiet."

Kate called her boss, apologized for not showing up at work, and pleaded for time off to take care of important family affairs. Charlie called the Super Trooper at his office phone, but got the message machine.

†

Sergeant Wes Stark was on highway patrol duty on the Seward Highway about 20 miles from Anchorage. This stretch of highway had the reputation of being the most dangerous road in the state because of its many curves, icy conditions, and scenic beauty, which often caused drivers to gawk. He was parked at a scenic overlook gawking at the mountains, drinking an espresso, eating a giant cinnamon roll, and chuckling to himself about the alert that had just been broadcast regarding a truck that looked like a pinto horse. That was a new one.

Out of the corner of his eye, he caught a glimpse of an old white compact pickup with brown paint patches. Doing a double take while spilling his coffee in his lap, he realized that it was probably the pinto car. Ignoring the pain in his crotch from the hot coffee, he carefully secured his espresso and cinnamon roll in the console, called for backup, turned on his siren and lights, and took off after the subject vehicle. It appeared that it was not going to be a difficult apprehension. The old truck was laboring to make fifty.

The pickup pulled over, and Wes instructed the driver to remain in the vehicle. Another officer arrived on the scene from the north and they arrested the driver, Brett Fishbein, without incident. Brett cleverly noted that he was totally screwed.

†

When the Super Trooper arrived back at his office after talking to Bertie, he was met by the DEA guys, who were both excited and annoyed that he had not been immediately available. Agent Jankowski suggested that they all sit down in the conference room to discuss progress on the case. Bob informed the agents that he had, through his diligent investigation, uncovered a description of Fishbein's car which turned out to be quite distinctive, and that he had already issued a statewide alert on the vehicle. Agent Phillips actually smiled, which Bob took as a compliment. Agent Jankowski then described what he had found out about Aldo Fenstrom. Initial attempts by DEA headquarters staff to obtain Aldo's military records had met with resistance due to sealed files, but with persistence they had managed to get some basic information. Aldo had been an infantry sergeant in active combat in Vietnam. He, along with four other members of his squad, had been dishonorably discharged because of charges of drug use and general insubordination. The squad had also been implicated in the battlefield death of their lieutenant, but there had been no proof that the death was intentional, so the charges were dropped. There were many such fragging incidents in the latter years of the war, and the ability of the Army to investigate them all had been totally overwhelmed. After the U.S. pulled out of Vietnam, much of what went on in the battlefields was forgotten or swept under the rug.

Other squad members who survived the war included a man named Stuart Halburg, who later had two sons, Jake and Frank. Bob resisted the temptation to do a victory dance on the conference room table.

Trying not to gloat, Bob said, "That's great. That gives us a definite connection between Fenstrom and the Halburgs."

"Wait, there's more," said Jankowski. "Two of the other squad members were named John Vander and Carl Smithson. Vander is one of the owners of the Rainbow Inn, and Smithson is listed as CEO of Offshore Enterprises. We don't know exactly where Stuart Halburg fits into the organization. He is currently the CEO of a well-known construction company in Savannah, Georgia. Apparently, he is considered a pillar of the community and wields considerable political influence. For unknown reasons, his sons elected to pursue a life of crime rather than work in the legitimate construction business. It seems that the connections established in Vietnam resulted in a well-coordinated, multi-generational crime syndicate that has continued to operate for forty years."

"Obviously the information provided in the Crime Stoppers report is accurate and helpful. But, at this point, we have very little actual evidence to tie any of these people to the murders," said Agent Phillips.

The phone in Bob's office rang, and Mary, his part-time secretary, answered. Breaking into the meeting, she indicated that the call was important. Picking up the phone, Bob smiled. "Bingo."

Returning to the conference room, Bob announced that there may be a way of getting some hard evidence, after all. "Brett Fishbein was just picked up outside Anchorage. He is being held in the Anchorage jail on suspicion of arson and attempted murder."

"That's great, but where do we go from here?" Agent Jankowski asked. "We need an overall strategy for tying all this stuff together."

The three law enforcement officers discussed the options and decided that the first steps were to question Brett Fishbein and meet with Charlie Skyler and Kate Perkins, since they obviously had some inside information and were somehow tied into the events, albeit probably as victims. They decided it would be best to transport Fishbein to Homer for questioning rather than have all three of them go to Anchorage. They agreed that it would also be psychologically better to have Brett close to home so that he would be in reach of his colleagues. Fear of being silenced might encourage him to cooperate more quickly.

Bob called his boss in Anchorage and asked that Brett be secretly moved to Homer. He met with solid resistance, until Agent Jankowski got on the line and went into one of his rants. It was promised that

Brett would be in Homer early the next morning. Bob also called Charlie and asked to meet with him and Kate at their earliest convenience. A two o'clock meeting was arranged. Meanwhile, the officers began to collect background information on the other members of the Fenstrom syndicate.

†

Aldo awoke feeling groggy and out of sorts. His cabin was freezing, since he had not had the energy to light the stove before he went to bed. He needed to find out what was going on with his little empire. He had the same bad feeling that had stuck with him throughout the fishing trip. It was crucial that he make an assessment of his risk so that he could determine whether it was necessary to pull the plug and make his escape. Retirement was sounding better and better. Years of hard labor and working in cold, damp conditions had taken a toll on his body. Three days of baiting longline hooks in freezing conditions, combined with the forced necessity of a death grip on the wheel of the Lucinda during the long rough ride of the previous day, had caused his arthritic hands to swell and cramp into useless claws. Most people did not realize that commercial fishing was torture on the hands. Aldo could not imagine another season of baiting hooks or extracting salmon tangled in the coarse monofilament mesh of gill nets. As he fumbled to start the wood stove, he made up his mind that this was the last season. Tropical destinations beckoned.

After the cabin warmed up and he had had a substantial breakfast, Aldo sat at his desk and called Darryl on the cell phone. Darryl picked up on the second ring and, as expected, sounded frantic. He complained about customers who were about to kill him and asked when he could get some new supply. Aldo assured him that he had some fresh stuff and would deliver it to Darryl in Homer later that day. Darryl indicated that he had not heard of any law enforcement activities that might threaten the operation, but he did say that Brett

Fishbein had mysteriously disappeared. Brett's sister Julie had told him that Brett had seemed frightened the last time she talked to him, but she did not know where he had gone. He felt that Julie was holding back and had decided to question her further after receiving the new shipment. He thought that dangling a pharmaceutical carrot might make her more truthful, especially since she had become progressively more strung out in the past couple of days. Aldo asked Darryl to put out feelers regarding any increase in law enforcement activity and agreed to meet him at the Homer dock late that afternoon.

Aldo also pondered the Frank Halburg situation. As far as Aldo knew, Frank had been operating on his own for the last couple of months. Frank's discovery that his brother was collaborating with the DEA had pushed him over the edge. He had never been particularly stable, but now he was clearly irrational. Aldo needed to talk to Frank's father. One of the iron-clad rules of the organization was that Aldo and Stuart Halburg were to limit communication to emergencies only. Aldo left a coded message on one of Stuart's cell phones requesting a return call to Aldo's sat phone.

Twenty-one

Kate and Charlie were escorted into the trooper "conference room" followed by the federal agents and the Super Trooper. Bob had only four chairs, so he ended up standing. Agent Jankowski asked Charlie to review how they had gotten involved in this mess, and Charlie described how each of them had found dead bodies and that things had sort of progressed from there.

"Are you always so nosy?" asked Agent Jankowski.

"I don't know. Rodolfo's wife asked me for my help, so I tried to do what I could for her."

"So, if I understand you correctly, you and Ms. Perkins were brought together by dead bodies, and now you are intimate acquaintances."

"When you put it that way, it does sound kind of weird, but that's pretty much it. All couples have to meet somehow."

"I think we are getting off track here," said Agent Phillips. "The information you provided the trooper combined with the Crime Stoppers report seems to be very helpful. We would like to know if there is anything else you can tell us that would be helpful."

"I don't know anything about a Crime Stoppers report, but we will try to help in any way that we can," Charlie answered.

"Right," said Agent Phillips. "Look, we don't care where the information came from. We just want to find the guy who killed Jake Halburg and your friend Rodolfo. We may also be able to break up a major drug operation. So, do you have any suggestions on where we might go from here?"

"Well, based on Kate's inquiries at FlashFrozen, it seems like Darryl Swift is probably the primary local distributor, and it seems most logical that he gets his supply from Fenstrom. I suspect that any other local players are small-time drug users. Since someone tried to kill Kate, we're pretty sure that there is at least one person at FlashFrozen Seafoods who has been informing the bad guys, but we don't know who that person is. Kate could probably help narrow down the possibilities. The other wild card in the mix is Frank Halburg. He may well have killed his brother after learning that he had turned informant, and he may be behind the arson at Kate's cabin. He could be anywhere, and he may be very dangerous if, in fact, he is responsible for the murders. Meanwhile, is there any way to get warrants to search Darryl's house or Fenstrom's cabin?"

"Unfortunately, we don't have any hard evidence connecting these guys to actual crimes, so it is unlikely that a judge would issue a warrant," said Agent Jankowski.

"Should we tell them?" said the Super Trooper from his place at the back of the room.

"Tell us what?" Kate asked.

Agent Jankowski scowled at Bob. The two agents glanced at each other. Finally, Agent Phillips said, "Brett Fishbein's fingerprints were found on the gas can left at your cabin. He was apprehended yesterday near Anchorage."

"That's great," said Kate. "Maybe I can relax a little bit."

"Relaxation might be premature," Charlie said. "Frank Halburg is still on the loose. Has Fishbein provided any information?"

"Not yet. He's being brought here tomorrow morning for questioning," Bob said. "His arrest and transport are being kept secret, so please don't mention this to anyone. If word gets out, his life could be in danger. We are hoping that his fear might help him cooperate if we promise to move him from Homer to a secure facility someplace else. From what I have learned about him, he appears to be a loser with a drug habit, rather than a criminal mastermind. There is probably a good chance that he will open up, especially since he's facing major charges."

"So, if Brett implicates Darryl or Aldo, I assume that would provide enough evidence for a warrant," Charlie said.

"Probably," Agent Jankowski answered.

"By the way," Charlie added. "What happened to the stuff that Rodolfo's wife found? Did you guys get any information from it?"

"We've told you way too much about the investigation already. The only thing I will say is that the portfolio refers to a numbered bank account and a warrant is required to access it. We have been unsuccessful at obtaining one so far," Agent Phillips replied.

"I have one other suggestion," Charlie said. "I have a feeling that Aldo's organization includes the entire supply chain for his drug distribution business, starting with import of drugs from Asia, possibly from South Vietnam, and extending through distribution within the U.S. His points of distribution appear to be very selective – Rainbow Inn and Homer are the ones we know about so far. These are not the usual urban markets, which may explain why he has avoided detection for so long. All indications are that he is very smart, and I assume that he has planned an exit strategy for when things get too hot. We somehow need to proceed carefully, but quickly if we want to catch him."

Agent Jankowski bristled. "How the hell do you know all this? You need to stay out of our way."

"I have no intention of trying to apprehend anyone. That's your job, and you're welcome to it," Charlie answered.

"That's enough," Agent Phillips said. "The evidence so far suggests that Mr. Skyler may well be right, and we definitely need to be careful where we go from here. I appreciate the help that you guys have provided, but you do need to avoid stirring things up any more than they already are. There are some dangerous people out there. I suggest that you make yourselves scarce and stay away from Ms. Perkin's cabin for a while, until we have a better idea where Frank Halburg may be."

"I need to rescue my cat," Kate said.

"I'll go out there with you," Bob said.

"Charlie, do you mind if Buster stays on your boat?"

"I guess not, since Buster probably saved our lives the other night."

"Well, now that you guys have taken care of the important stuff, we have work to do," Agent Jankowski said.

Since it was nearly dark, Kate agreed to meet the Super Trooper the next afternoon, after the interrogation of Brett Fishbein, to go get Buster and check on her cabin. Kate and Charlie went back to the boat. Charlie suggested that Kate lie on the back seat of his car to avoid being seen and, once again, they parked in an out of the way location at the harbor. The problem was that it was impossible for Kate and Charlie to get to the boat without being seen walking on the dock. While it was dark, the bright harbor lights pretty much illuminated everything. But it was the best they could do. Charlie felt that the boat was pretty safe, especially in the master suite that had a heavy metal watertight door. Since boats conduct noises well, he was sure that he would hear anyone on or near the boat.

Kate sat on the edge of Charlie's bed and started sobbing. Charlie, totally surprised by the sudden change in Kate's demeanor, was at a loss as to what to do. It finally occurred to him that this might be a good time to provide comfort. He sat next to her and looked in her eyes.

"Sorry, Charlie. I'm totally freaked out, thanks to your warnings about Frank Halburg." Kate snuggled closer. "I can't go home, I can't go to work, I can't even go for a walk. How long is this going to last?"

"I don't know. I think the interrogation of Brett Fishbein is going to be the key to putting the bad guys in jail. But there is no way of knowing how things are going to play out. Hopefully, we should have a better idea of how much danger we're in after this afternoon. I'm not very good at this comforting stuff. What can I do to help?"

"Some beer and potato chips would help." Kate sniffed.

When Charlie returned from the galley, she was reclining on the bed and looked more perky in spite of red, puffy eyes. "Maybe we should take advantage of this time to get to know each other better," Charlie said as Kate crammed a handful of chips into her mouth.

"At this point most women would be pissed at you for thinking about sex when they are obviously in distress."

Charlie stared at Kate with a clueless expression.

"But, fortunately for you, I'm not most women," said Kate lustfully.

Twenty-two

Lonely clouds crossed the surface of the full moon, creating moving shadows in the forest. Fresh snow reflected the moonlight, causing the earth's surface to glow with a subdued white light. All sound was muted to silence. White birch bark with dark scars and snow-covered spruce boughs created a world of white and black patterns, blending foreground and background like the cryptic coloration of a zebra. The snowshoe hare munched on a willow twig, its big ears canting this way and that, listening, as always, for the approach of a lynx or the near-silent flight of a goshawk.

While cold, the softness of the snow presented a deceptive front of coziness. The log cabin stood out in contrast to the white surroundings. Isolated. Alone. A figure dressed in black wearing a dark-colored balaclava emerged from the spruce forest. It occurred to him that the black clothing was great as long as he was in the woods, but probably not optimal against the snowy background in the open. Oh, well. The lack of light in the cabin windows suggested that no one was home, a fact that was highly disappointing. He wanted this over with. The dark figure entered the cabin through the broken door and looked around. The shadow of a small animal streaked by him and disappeared behind the woodpile. The disarray inside the cabin and the charred wood on the outside confirmed Brett's account of the failed attempt. Where was she? No matter. He would find her eventually.

After talking to Frank the previous night, the Mole had made a similar reconnaissance of Fishbein's miserable cabin, finding it abandoned as well. Lucky for Brett. It appeared that he had left quickly, taking only the essentials. Hopefully, he was far away and would not be back to complicate things.

The Mole's nickname had originally started during his Army training, when he had gained a reputation for burrowing into the ground to avoid danger during live fire exercises. The Ninja look-alike oozed back into the forest, following the high ground around the bog back to his vehicle.

†

The paddy wagon containing Brett Fishbein arrived at trooper headquarters at ten o'clock. It was intended that Brett would spend the night in Homer's tiny jail downtown in the old federal building, but the interrogation was scheduled to occur in Bob's conference room, a room that had not seen this much use in years. The grumpy transport officials escorted him in his orange jumpsuit and shackles to his place at the table. After whining about the early hour and the long drive, they got back into the paddy wagon and left, leaving Brett at the mercy of the Homer trio. While the location was not very secure, it was assumed that the two DEA guys and the Super Trooper would be able to subdue him, if necessary.

Brett was miserable. He had slept very little at his temporary home in the crowded Anchorage municipal jail. Cellmates had included a strung-out junky and a very creepy biker type with huge biceps and a Porky Pig tattoo. Brett had been able to get some sleep on the drive from Anchorage, but was dirty and unshaven and felt terrible. He really wanted a joint. His fear of what would happen to him in the legal system was only surpassed by his fear of Frank, Darryl, and Aldo. There was no good outcome.

Agent Phillips began the conversation. "Good morning, Brett. I'm Agent Phillips with the DEA. On my right is Agent Jankowski and on my left is Trooper Stillwater. It appears that you're in a bunch of trouble. We have your fingerprints on a gas can left at the crime scene. We also have some footprint and motor oil evidence, which will likely finish pounding the nails into your coffin. You are being charged with attempted murder and arson, both very serious crimes leading to long jail time. The only chance you have of improving your situation is to cooperate with us. So, why don't you start at the beginning and tell us how you got yourself into this mess?"

"They'll kill me," said Brett. He squirmed in his chair, and his right eyelid began to twitch.

Agent Phillips leaned close to him. "Who will kill you?"

Brett leaned away from Phillips and focused his gaze on the tabletop. "I can't tell you or they will kill me."

Agent Jankowski crossed his arms. "Brett, any danger you might be in from your associates is going to be the same whether you talk to us or not. Your buddies have no way of knowing what you may or may not have told us, so it's not going to make any difference. We will protect you as best we can."

Brett looked up at Jankowski with a skeptical expression. "What about when I'm in jail? Can you protect me there?"

"There are ways that you can be protected in jail if we believe that there is enough danger," answered Jankowski. "It's up to you to make us believe that."

"If I cooperate, will you get me out of Homer and keep all of this secret?"

Jankowski gave Brett a cool stare. "If you tell us what we need to know, we will move you back to Anchorage as soon as possible. As long as the investigation is going on, we can try to keep things quiet. But eventually your name will be released. There are always some leaks in the legal system, so the sooner we get things wrapped up, the better."

Brett nervously cleared his throat. "I guess I don't have much choice. But the thing is, I really don't know very much. I'm just a pot head with no real agenda. The only reason I'm involved at all is because my sister is a serious coke addict and her boyfriend is a dealer."

"Can you provide names, please?" said Agent Phillips.

"My sister's name is Julie and her boyfriend is Darryl Swift."

"If, as you say, you are not deeply involved, then why would you set fire to Kate Perkins's cabin while she was in it?" Bob asked.

"Because he said he would kill me and my sister if I didn't find a way to get rid of her," Brett whined.

"Who would kill you?" Bob asked.

"Oh gees… Frank Halburg," Brett answered.

The three officers raised their eyebrows simultaneously. Charlie Skyler was right once again. "What role does Frank Halburg play in all of this?" Agent Jankowski asked.

"The funny thing is, I don't really know. He just showed up in Homer one day and started stirring things up. He worked at FlashFrozen for a while, then he left. Then he must have came back, 'cause now people are saying that he killed Jake."

"Why would he do that – kill his own brother?" Bob asked.

"I heard that Jake had become an informer for you guys. I didn't even know who Jake was until he was supposedly murdered in Homer."

"It sounds like Frank is a dangerous guy," Bob said.

"Frank is totally nuts. He scares the hell out of me."

"Do you know where Frank is?"

"I talked to him on the phone a couple of days ago, but there was no way of telling whether he was calling from Homer or from some other part of the world. Cell phone connections are always lousy, so it's hard to tell. I hope he's as far away as possible."

"What did you and Frank talk about?" Agent Jankowski asked.

"He called to find out whether I had succeeded in getting rid of Kate Perkins. When I told him that my plan didn't work, he told me to get out of town or he would kill me. The last thing he said was that if you want something done right, you have to do it yourself."

The agents looked at each other. "Okay," said Agent Jankowski. "What do you know about the drug distribution network that brings drugs to Homer?"

"C'mon, man, the whole town is going to be after me if I squeal." Brett became more and more agitated.

"If Frank Halburg is as dangerous as you say he is, it's probably not going to matter what the town thinks," Agent Jankowski answered. "So calm down and tell us about drugs in Homer."

"Aw, shit. As far as I know, Darryl is the main dealer for cocaine and heroin. Since weed has been legalized and half the population grows their own anyway, there is no profit in marijuana. I'm pretty sure that Darryl gets his stuff from a weird old hermit named Aldo who lives across the bay somewhere. Beyond that, I have no idea. I think the operation must be bigger than just Homer, but I never asked about it."

"What role does your sister play in all this?"

"Julie's not involved in drug sales at all, so leave her out of this." Brett suddenly became defensive. "She is a major coke addict and only hangs around Darryl because he gives it to her in exchange for being his girlfriend. Darryl is a major lowlife."

"One other thing," Bob said. "Is there a drug connection at FlashFrozen Seafoods?"

"I heard Darryl talking to a woman there. I think her name is Nancy."

The rest of the interrogation was dedicated to filling in details such as addresses and phone numbers for Darryl, Julie, and Brett. He had no further information on Aldo Fenstrom. Brett was secretly transported to the Homer jail and put under twenty-four hour guard. The DEA agents began the process of obtaining search warrants and subpoenas for phone records for Darryl Swift, Julie Fishbein, and Aldo Fenstrom as well as Brett Fishbein.

✝

Kate and the Super Trooper got into the police cruiser and headed for Kate's cabin. Kate tried to get Bob to talk about the interrogation of Brett Fishbein, but Bob said that he couldn't talk about it. He did, however, hint that most of Charlie's suspicions had turned out to be correct and that more arrests would be made in the near future.

The fresh snow on the trail to the cabin was untracked, but as soon as they reached the cabin they saw that someone had recently been there. Kate noticed that Bob unbuckled his holster and became more alert. Tracks led from the woods up to, and around, the cabin. Traces of snow inside the cabin indicated that whoever had been there had also gone inside.

As Kate approached, Buster emerged from behind the woodpile. He looked very cold. Buster jumped into Kate's arms and quickly snuggled inside her jacket. Bob photographed several clear boot prints in the snow on the cabin steps.

Kate looked around the cabin forlornly. "Now I'm really creeped out. I'm never going to feel safe in this place again," she said. "But as far as I can tell, there isn't anything missing."

Bob and Kate followed the tracks into the woods far enough to see that they skirted the bog heading toward the east. "Our bad guy probably parked on the same road that Brett used, except that he was smart enough to go around the swamp," Bob said. "Let's get out of here." They returned to the cruiser and headed back in the waning daylight. Buster stuck his head out of Kate's jacket, meowed forlornly, and then crawled back into the warm place.

"It was Frank Halburg, wasn't it?" Kate asked.

"I suspect so," said Bob.

The Super Trooper drove through Homer and out onto the spit, parking at one of the harbor entrance gates. He accompanied Kate to the Shearwater's slip. As she got out of the police cruiser and walked down the harbor ramp with Buster and the Super Trooper, she was painfully aware of the neighborhood gossipmongers staring at her from behind their curtains. So much for being inconspicuous. They found Charlie sitting at the galley table surrounded by a mountain of paper, furiously typing on his computer.

Charlie invited them in and served coffee. "What did you guys find?"

Kate filled him in on the tracks in the snow.

Bob summarized the interview with Brett that morning. "We're preparing arrest warrants for Aldo Fenstrom, Darryl Swift, and Frank Halburg right now. We'll search Aldo and Darryl's residences early tomorrow morning if we can get all the legal ducks in a row." He turned to Kate. "Do you know a woman named Nancy at FlashFrozen?"

She blinked at him, surprised. Nancy was the last person she'd suspect. "Yeah, Nancy Andropov works in accounting. Don't tell me she is involved with these guys."

"She might be," Bob said. "Where does she live?"

"Somewhere in the downtown area. I'm pretty sure that her address and phone number are listed in the phone book. She's a single mom with two little kids." Boy, if Nancy was a typical drug dealer in Homer, she needed to start looking more carefully at her colleagues.

"We're probably going to be questioning her tomorrow. Do you have any advice?"

Kate thought about it. Nancy was always quiet and seemed a little depressed. "If she is involved, it's probably out of desperation for money. She's had a bad time since her worthless husband left. On the other hand, if she really did tip off Frank about my snooping around at FlashFrozen, she must be a much different person than I thought I knew. But I still think that a low-key approach would work the best. Any kind of deal that would allow her to stay with her kids would likely be most persuasive."

Bob stood up to leave. "Be very careful. It looks like things are going to be happening around here, and you guys are not popular with certain individuals."

Charlie descended into the foc'sle of the Shearwater and, from the sound of it, was rummaging around in the storage cabinets. He returned with a funny-looking gun and a box of ammunition. Kate gave him a quizzical look.

He looked charmingly sheepish. "This is the only gun that I own. It's a compact .410 gauge shotgun designed for packing in survival kits. They're popular around here among halibut fishermen for dispatching halibut that are too big to bring on deck when they are alive."

Kate raised an eyebrow. "That's not exactly an assault rifle."

"The gun is loaded with slugs and will have plenty of stopping power at close range, but I doubt whether we will have to use it. I'm thinking that it might be a good idea for us to escape on the boat tomorrow if the weather is decent. We could go somewhere secluded and hide out," said Charlie.

"Sounds good to me," Kate said. "Also romantic."

"Right," Charlie said. "What do you want for dinner?"

"I don't care, as long as there is a lot of it. Being the target of a deranged drug dealer builds up an appetite."

Buster had spent the time since his introduction to the Shearwater exploring his new quarters with haughty suspicion, punctuated with an occasional pathetic whimper. After familiarizing himself with the boat cabin and foc'sle, he climbed onto the shelf above the pilot wheel, crouched between the radar screen and the fish finder, and stared at the people below.

Twenty-three

Aldo woke up in a funk long before sunrise. He had successfully delivered the cooler to Darryl the previous afternoon, thereby relieving himself of the possession of most illegal materials. But he was seriously worried about the disappearance of Brett Fishbein. Darryl had managed to intimidate the bar owner Gertie, into telling him that a trooper had been asking around about Brett. Apparently, she had given the trooper a description of Brett's car.

It seemed possible, maybe even likely, that Brett was in custody, especially given how clueless he was. He also had to assume that if Brett was in custody, then he was probably blabbing everything he knew. If that was the case, then things could bust wide open. Even though Brett did not know anything about the operation as a whole, he knew enough to get law enforcement heading in the right direction.

Aldo had also spoken to Stuart Halburg about Frank. The news was not good. Frank was ignoring attempts by his father to contact him. Frank's discovery that his brother had become an informant for the DEA had apparently caused him to come completely unglued and obsessed with thoughts of revenge. The relationship between the brothers had always been very tense. Sibling rivalry combined with obvious differences in intelligence and athletic ability had built up many years of resentment. The resentment had obviously boiled over big-time and was way beyond control. Aldo had to admit that the time had come to distance himself from all that he had built up over the years. He and Stuart had agreed to pull the plug on the operation. Aldo had a plan for escape that avoided all the normal routes of transportation, but unfortunately it would take some time to set things up. He wasn't sure how much time he had.

†

The Super Trooper and the two DEA agents left the trooper office at eight o'clock and headed for Olshanski Road in two vehicles, the police cruiser and a rented SUV (black, of course). They discussed the best approach and decided that they would simply drive up rapidly and hope to catch Darryl by surprise. As they pulled up to the odd-shaped cabin, they noticed that Darryl's truck was there, and so they expected that he would be home. All pulled their guns. One agent ran around the back, and the other two officers approached the front door. When they knocked on the door and announced their presence, the door was opened by a young woman with messy, long brown hair and a glazed look.

When asked where Darryl was, the woman said that she didn't know. A quick search of the cabin resulted in the conclusion that Darryl was not there. Further questioning did not result in any useful information. It became apparent that the woman was not totally connected to reality. The smell of marijuana in the house was strong, but the woman's behavior suggested that other substances were involved as well. When asked if her name was Julie Fishbein, she nodded her head yes and then began giggling and crying simultaneously. She curled up on the sofa in a fetal position and became unresponsive.

Agent Jankowski remained in the cabin while the Super Trooper and Agent Phillips looked around outside. There were no outbuildings or other obvious hiding places other than the surrounding forest. Many tracks in the snow and freshly split wood suggested that Darryl had recently been cutting the small spruce that surrounded his cabin and processing them into firewood. The tracks led in all directions, so it was difficult to tell which set, if any, would lead them to Darryl. Bob called in to headquarters to see if he could obtain any backup, but the nearest trooper was in Soldotna, more than an hour away. Since Bob was the only one wearing outdoor gear, he volunteered to make ever-widening circles around the cabin to try and pick up a trail leading away from the cabin. Agent Phillips insisted on accompanying him in spite of the fact that he was wearing black oxford shoes and dress pants.

After about 15 minutes, they reached the outer perimeter of Darryl's logging area where the snow was untracked. Continuing the concentric circles, they found a chainsaw lying in the snow and a single set of tracks leading to the west away from the subdivision. Agent Phillips asked Bob about the terrain and land use in the area. Bob indicated that ahead of them was about a mile of scrubby forest followed by a small ranch with cleared fields.

Agent Phillips revealed that his feet were wet and cold, possibly on the verge of frostbite. Bob knew that frostbite was unlikely since the temperature was above freezing; nevertheless, Agent Phillips was clearly not equipped for a cross-country pursuit, and it would probably be unwise for Bob to pursue the fugitive on his own. They turned back for the cabin, where they found that things were mostly unchanged. Julie opened her eyes when they entered, but then closed them again. Bob asked her if Darryl had a cell phone. Julie looked toward the kitchen counter and pointed. A phone was lying on the counter next to the toaster.

Agent Jankowski picked it up and scrolled through the recent calls, then placed the phone in his pocket. He looked at Agent Phillips and said, "Right now, Darryl has no way to contact anybody, so he either has to stay in the woods or go to somebody's house and call for help or maybe steal a car. Since he can be easily tracked in the snow, he will probably try to get some help as soon as possible. So, we have a little bit of time to try and head him off."

"I agree," Bob said. "I can call Mack Jefferson, whose place is in the immediate trajectory of Darryl's current path, and warn him that Darryl may be coming toward him. If Darryl is moving fast, he could get there in the next fifteen minutes or so."

"Good idea," Agent Phillips said. "Meanwhile, are there any helicopters in the area?"

"Yeah," Bob replied. "Kachemak Choppers is located near the airport."

Mack Jefferson happened to be home when Bob called, and his reaction to the possibility that Darryl was on his way was one of panic. Bob suggested that he vacate his home and head for town or some other friendly environment, a plan to which Mack readily agreed. Mack, while he had been an occasional customer of Darryl's operation, had no interest in getting involved in an aiding and abetting situation. He hopped into his pickup and took off for the nearest tavern. At Bob's suggestion, he had unplugged his only phone and taken it with him, thereby leaving Darryl with no transportation and no means of contacting anyone. Since it was too late to set a trap for Darryl at Mack's cabin, Bob drove his cruiser to the intersection of Mack's long driveway and East End Road to prevent Darryl from reaching nearby residences across the road. The DEA agents drove to Kachemak Choppers with the hope of chartering a helicopter.

Although Bob had warned Mack Jefferson to keep quiet about ongoing events, he knew that soon the whole town would be aware that Darryl was a fugitive on the run.

†

A lone figure crouched with binoculars behind a tree on a hillside overlooking Darryl's cabin. The figure was dressed in winter white camouflage and was nearly invisible in the dim autumn light. Leaning up against the tree was a bolt action rifle with a scope. He watched the agents load Julie Fishbein into the SUV. Unfortunately, he had reached his sniper position just before the law enforcement team had arrived, ruining any chance of getting a clear shot at Darryl. The police raid was totally unexpected and very bad news. He could only assume that Brett Fishbein had been apprehended and was blabbing to the authorities. He now knew that Darryl was on the run and decided that his only course was to follow Darryl in hopes of getting to him before the DEA. Darryl knew way too much.

†

Darryl had been just about to start his chainsaw and cut down yet another ten inch spruce when he heard vehicles in his driveway. Peering through the trees, he stood transfixed as the three officers rushed the cabin. He recognized the Trooper, but not the other guys. Reaching into his pocket, he felt for his cell phone, then realized that it was still in the cabin.

"What the fuck do I do now?" he said to the trees.

There appeared to be no other option but to try and get away somehow. He headed in a direction that he thought was west, toward Mack's place. Mack owed him big time and could probably be coerced to help him, but he had to hurry. He knew his tracks in the snow were visible to anyone who cared to look for them. If only he could levitate above the ground. He set off through the scrubby woods at a pace that was as fast as his pudgy body could go.

Darryl was starting to get cold as he broke out of the trees and approached Mack's pasture. Three horses were peacefully munching on a hay bale next to the fence. His clothes were sweat-soaked from anxiety and exertion, and his energy reserves were running down. He sprinted across the open field and up to Mack's doorway. No people or vehicles were in sight. "Damn."

The door was unlocked; he entered, tracking big clumps of snow into Mack's neat little cabin. He looked around for a phone and didn't see one. He knew Mack had a phone; where the hell was it? It finally dawned on him when he saw the empty phone jack – the phone had been removed. Mack must have been warned and told to get out of there. The authorities must be close behind. He may already have

145

walked into a trap. Peering out the front window, he saw no one approaching on the driveway.

Grabbing an Arctic parka from a hook in the entryway, he went back outside. A plowed service road for feeding the horses paralleled the fence line to the south. Since the road was hard-packed, Darryl figured that his tracks would not be visible, so he went to the south. He knew that eventually he would run into the steep, eroding bluff overlooking the bay. He wasn't sure what he would do then, but there should be plenty of hiding spots.

Terrain at the end of the fence line consisted of meadow and open forest. Wind off the bay had blown the snow into a hard crust so his tracks were almost invisible. Things were finally looking up. After about 20 minutes, he reached the bluff precipice, almost walking off the edge.

Darryl was familiar with the Kachemak Bay shoreline because he sometimes hunted for chunks of coal along the beach. The eroding sedimentary bluffs were another reason for Homer's existence. Early mariners had seen seams of coal exposed on the bluffs, and several small mining operations had sprung up to supply steam ships plying Cook Inlet. Continual erosion caused coal to slough off the bluff and fall to the beach below. Residents of Homer had scavenged coal off the beaches to heat their homes for 100 years. The smell of high-sulfur coal burning in space heaters was a distinctive characteristic of the Homer experience. These coal-scavenging forays had been enhanced in recent years by the ready availability of small all-terrain vehicles. Darryl wished he had an ATV now, as walking was getting tiresome.

Darryl skirted the cliff edge until he came to an erosion gulley that was not as steep as most of the cliff face. He carefully proceeded down the alder-choked gulley until reaching a well-hidden cave-like space in the face of the bluff at the edge of the gulley. He went in, sat down, covered himself with the parka, and tried to focus on his next course of action. But fear, fatigue, and cold made thought difficult.

Twenty-four

The crystal clarity of the sounds had a digital quality. While seeming to come from all directions, individual sounds were, nevertheless, clearly delineated, like the mental parsing of instruments within an orchestra that becomes possible under the influence of certain mind-altering substances. The old lady-like cackling of kittywakes; the whooshing breath of a sea lion surfacing after a dive; the eerie call of a loon in the distance; the lapping of tiny waves against the boat bottom; the distant fog horn at the harbor entrance. An otherworldly eeriness was created by the quiet fog. The boat seemed suspended in its own small universe bounded by the wispy limits of visibility.

"Well, this is just plain creepy," Kate said. "We wouldn't see any bad guys coming until they were ten feet away."

"Yeah, but they'd have to find us first," Charlie replied.

The Shearwater was anchored about a half mile offshore in Seldovia Bay. They had left Homer in the morning, cruised around for a while, and finally settled on Seldovia Bay as a hideout. Well, not exactly a hideout, since they were in clear sight of the community of Seldovia – or they would be if it were not for the foggy conditions. Charlie had originally considered hiding in one of the remote fjords that connect to the south side of Kachemak Bay, but he decided they could be too easily trapped, with no help available. So he had settled on anchoring near a town where they would be only a few minutes away from civilization, while at the same time providing a watery buffer from intruders. He had set the radar so that any boat approaching within a half mile of the Shearwater would set off the audible collision alarm. The dense fog had rolled in shortly after they arrived.

Charlie was lounging on the settee, nursing a beer and reading a commercial fishing trade magazine. Kate was propped up next to him, overseeing a wide array of snacks that covered the entire dinette table. With a mouth full of potato chips, she asked, "How can you be so relaxed? There are multiple killers on the loose, and somehow we became prime targets. How the hell did that happen? What did I do to deserve this?"

"I think we have done about all that we can. I'm trusting that the forces of good will prevail. Anyway, we should have a better idea of where we stand by this afternoon. I'll give Bob a call later on, after the dust settles. I'm assuming that people are actually getting arrested as we speak, at least I hope so. Meanwhile, there is not much point in worrying about things that we can't control."

"I hate it when people say that. That's supposed to make me feel better? I mean, isn't that when we need to worry? When bad things are happening and there is nothing we can do about it?"

"Sorry," said Charlie. "What am I supposed to say? That we're totally screwed and we might as well abandon all hope?"

"Well, no…I don't know. How do you think this is all going to end?"

"I assume that the Super Trooper and our intrepid DEA agents will clean up most of the Homer end of Aldo's operation. Aldo is smart, and I would be surprised if he hasn't already developed a plan to escape the clutches of the law. I don't think he is going to want to be directly involved in any violence. The biggest problem is still Frank Halburg. He is sort of a ghost. Nobody really knows where he is. His motivation is probably somewhat different than the rest of the motley crew. He may be marginally psychopathic."

"If that little speech was supposed to set my mind at ease, it sure didn't work," said Kate. "So we wait?"

"Yep."

†

After the law enforcement team left Darryl's house, the Mole moved very quickly. He made one circuit of Darryl's property, easily picked up his tracks in the snow, and followed them at nearly a run. In an earlier life, the Mole had been an Army Ranger, and he had always been obsessive about maintaining his physical conditioning. He was pretty sure that he was in much better shape than Darryl. After about 15 minutes, he reached the edge of the pasture and noted that Darryl's tracks proceeded across the field toward the house.

Just as he was about to follow, he caught a glimpse of a person in the distance heading across the meadow toward the bluff. It had to be Darryl. Outstanding. Taking his time, he skirted the pasture, heading west until he intercepted Darryl's faint tracks. Keeping well back, he continued to follow the tracks to the head of the gulley. He could see the beach. No sign of Darryl. He had to be hiding somewhere in the gulley. The Mole was not sure whether Darryl had a gun, but he doubted it, since the idiot had been clearly surprised by the sudden appearance of the cops. He carefully and quietly crept down the gulley with the rifle locked and loaded. About halfway down, Darryl's tracks went to the right, and he saw the corner of the cave. A few more steps and he came face to face with Darryl, who was hugging the back of the shallow cave.

"Yeeah! What the hell are you doing here?" yelled Darryl.

"I'm obviously following you," said the Mole.

"Why? The cops are probably right behind you."

"Probably, but I can't let them catch you."

"You're crazy," said Darryl. "You could be long gone. I would never rat on you and Aldo."

"Everybody talks sooner or later." He fired his rifle from the hip. The bullet entered the left side of Darryl's chest, exited from his back, and made a little crater in the back wall of the cave.

Switching from assassin mode to escape mode, the Mole devoted his thought processes to figuring out how to avoid detection from the ground and air. He assumed that helicopters would be deployed, as well as ground search teams. Hiding nearby for a while might be a better strategy than trying to run. Dogs would be a problem, but he didn't think that tracking dogs were readily available in Homer. He looked at the bluff face on both sides of the gulley. On the east side was a ledge created by a seam of harder rock. Because of the southern exposure, the snow had melted on the ledge. Testing the ledge, he found that the surface was hard enough that his boots made no impression. The ledge merged with another erosional gully about 300 feet away.

He started down the ledge toward the adjacent gulley. In some places the ledge was so narrow that he was afraid he would end up tumbling down the bluff to the beach below. But the hard sandstone held his weight, and he managed to make it to the ravine, then up to the top of the bluff. Traversing the top of the cliff face on bare ground, he found a small wooded area that provided a view back toward Darryl's hiding place, as well as a clear shot at anyone who might approach his position. The Mole created a nest-like blind using spruce boughs. The blind in combination with his white camo parka made him nearly invisible. He settled in for the duration, or at least until dark.

†

After leaving Darryl's cabin, Agents Phillips and Jankowski dropped Julie off at the hospital for observation. One of the hospital's security guards was assigned the job of preventing Julie from leaving her room, although such precaution seemed pretty unnecessary, since she was only semi-conscious. Following Bob's directions to the airport, they found that Kachemak Choppers was more than happy to fly them around. Business had been really slow, and Mike, chief partner and only pilot, was bored out of his skull.

He had learned to fly in the Army and had spent three years in Vietnam. Flying in Alaska was often challenging because of the rugged topography and changeable weather, but nothing compared to the adrenalin rush of being shot at while transporting critically injured soldiers. Consequently, Mike's demeanor in the cockpit was so calm as to be unsettling for most of his passengers. His idea of a good time was flying a helicopter through the mountains during a snowstorm. He was nearing retirement age and had spent so many hours in his chopper that all maneuvers were smooth and instinctive. Mike outfitted Agents Phillips and Jankowski with parkas and boots, and they took to the air, headed for the area of Darryl's cabin.

The Super Trooper was parked at the end of Mack's driveway. He was communicating with the agents by radio, and, when he heard that they were on their way, he began to drive toward Mack's house. Mike piloted the chopper around the perimeter of Darryl's property until picking up the tracks heading west. Like most helicopter pilots, Mike's vision and ability to pick out patterns on the ground was exceptional, and he was able to follow the trail in spite of the trees. Mike calmly relayed through the intercom that there were two sets of tracks. "Huh," said Agent Jankowski. "That's impossible."

"Nevertheless," Mike said, "it's true."

"Well, that sort of complicates things," Agent Phillips said.

They followed the tracks to Mack's field, and from the air they could see that one set went to the house and the other set traversed the pasture and headed toward the bluff. Mike relayed the information to the Super Trooper, who had pulled his cruiser up to Mack's house. Bob indicated that he would check out the house while the chopper reconnoitered the bluff area. From the helicopter, faint tracks were visible up to the edge of the bluff, then disappeared into a heavily vegetated gully where the tracks became obscured. The chopper circled the bluff area without seeing any sign of anyone on foot, then returned to Mack's pasture and landed so that the team could figure out what to do next.

After some discussion, they decided that Bob and Agent Jankowski would follow the tracks on foot while Mike and Agent Phillips would continue to search from the helicopter. They considered the possibility that Frank Halburg was responsible for the second set of tracks and agreed that he was likely armed and dangerous. Agent Jankowski was not happy about trekking through the Alaska wilderness, partly because he was from Newark and not comfortable in the out of doors, and partly because there was an armed wild man on the loose.

Bob and his reluctant companion hiked to the end of the pasture, where the two sets of tracks came back together. Following the tracks through the open forest, they soon came to the edge of the bluff. Tracking was getting more difficult on the wind-blown surface, but they were able to see the tracks up to the start of the gulley. They could hear the helicopter circling above them.

As they entered the dense alders within the gulley, they pulled their guns. Occasionally they picked up tracks in the snow under the alders and knew that they were still on the right track. Agent Jankowski swore at the poor footing. The common red alders that grow on Alaskan hillsides were a bane to anyone trying to get anywhere on foot. The trunks tended to grow horizontally before curving upward, making it necessary to step or climb over each trunk, only to be immediately tripped up by the next one. Progress was slow and exhausting. Agent Jankowski put his gun back in its holster so he could use both hands to negotiate the maze of three-inch alder trunks. He was muttering to himself that his partner had obviously chosen the easier job. Bob reminded him that, on the other hand, the helicopter was a big target and very vulnerable to gun fire. Agent Jankowski agreed that crashing and burning was not a good option either.

At a small clearing in the bushes, they could see two sets of tracks veering off to the right and observed what appeared to be mouth of a shallow cave. With guns at the ready, they peeked into the cave and observed a body face down on the cave floor. After confirming the lack of vitality of the man on the floor, they turned over the body and recognized Darryl from his various mug shots.

They radioed the helicopter and described the situation, emphasizing that the killer, likely Frank Halburg, was probably nearby and that they could all be in his sights. Since daylight was starting to fade, they agreed that they would retreat back to Mack's cabin and regroup, leaving retrieval of the body for later. Since it was almost dark and there was an armed fugitive on the loose, they decided to postpone any further pursuit until morning when they could assemble more personnel.

✝

When the Mole first saw the helicopter come over the bluff, he was tempted to see if he could shoot it down. It would be very cool to watch it smash into the ground and explode in a huge fireball. He also could have shot the trooper and the other guy at the cave. But, on second thought, while it would be fun, it might not be in his self-interest to trigger a major search and rescue operation. He still had other business to take care of, and he was getting cold. He needed to get back to Homer as soon as it was dark enough to avoid detection. The fact that the helicopter had flown directly overhead and not seen him proved he was generally smarter than everybody else.

Twenty-five

After the pursuit had been called off, Bob returned to his office to arrange for some help, and the DEA guys went to the hospital to see whether Julie had recovered sufficiently to provide any useful information. As they entered her room, she opened her eyes briefly, then closed them, pretending to be sleeping.

Agent Phillips said to Agent Jankowski, "I guess we need to start processing the paperwork so that Ms. Fishbein can be arraigned for attempted murder."

Julie's eyes popped open. "What? How do you figure that?"

"Your brother tried to burn up a couple of people. He is being charged with attempted murder. If I am not mistaken, you helped him in his escape plans, so you are an accessory," Agent Jankowski said.

"What? You guys are crazy. Brett is a totally nonviolent person. Where is my brother?"

"Your brother is in jail. He has confessed to arson and attempted murder."

"None of this makes sense. Brett said he was in danger and he was obviously very frightened, but he wouldn't tell me what was going on. All I did was help him buy a plane ticket, since he didn't have any credit cards. I guess he didn't get very far."

"What do you know about your boyfriend's drug operation?" Agent Phillips asked.

"Not very much," she said. "I've been addicted to cocaine since I was seventeen. I pretty much go where the drugs are, which in the last couple of years has been wherever Darryl happens to be. I try to stay out of the business of drug dealing. Brett is pretty much the same way. The only reason he was involved at all was because of my relationship with Darryl. Where is Darryl, by the way?"

Agent Jankowski looked at Agent Phillips, who nodded and told her, "Darryl is dead."

Julie's eyes opened to the size of saucers, and her face contorted. "You fuckers killed him? Damn it, damn it, damn it," she said as she buried her face in her pillow.

Agent Phillips gently replied, "We didn't kill him. Somebody else did. Do you have any idea who it might have been?"

Julie slowly lifted her head from the pillow. Tears streamed down her face.

Agent Phillips said, "Anything you can tell us will help us find Darryl's killer and will probably also help reduce the charges that you and your brother face. So let's start from the beginning. Where does Darryl get his drugs?"

"I don't know exactly. Every couple of weeks he would go out and come back with a cooler that he stashed in the root cellar under his cabin. Once I was in town and saw him driving toward home from the spit. That evening he had a new supply. He may have gotten the drugs from a boat or from somebody at the harbor."

"Exactly how is this root cellar accessed?"

"There's a trap door under the carpet in the lower entryway."

"Did you hear Darryl talk to anyone on the phone or in person who might have been possible suppliers?"

"He talked to lots of people on the phone, but there was one guy who must have been different from the average junkie, since Darryl talked to him like he was talking to a boss. Like he was intimidated. The guy's name was something like Waldo."

"Could the name have been Aldo?" Agent Jankowski asked.

"Yeah, that sounds right."

"What do you know about the deaths of two people in Homer in the last two weeks?" Agent Jankowski continued.

"Oh, jeez," said Julie. "All I know is that the deaths had something to do with the drug distribution business. I know that Darryl and Brett were not involved, but they were afraid of whoever was. I tried to get them to go to the authorities before we all got sucked into an investigation, but that obviously didn't work. It sounded like they were worried that Waldo or Aldo, or whatever his name is, would get them if they said anything."

"That brings us back to the question of who killed Darryl," Agent Jankowski said.

"I don't know. Look, I'm starting to feel really strung out. Can you ask the hospital people to give me something?"

"I'll see what we can do. Meanwhile, there will be a guard outside your door to keep you from leaving and to protect you. If someone out there is trying to eliminate witnesses, you may be on their list," Agent Phillips told her.

"Great. I thought my life couldn't get any worse, but I was wrong."

After leaving Julie, the agents went to Darryl's cabin to see if the drug stash was where Julie had said it would be. There was, of course, the possibility that the mysterious assassin would have gotten there first, but it was worth a try. It was also possible that the mystery man would be waiting in the woods to take out anyone entering the cabin.

It had become very dark while they were interviewing Julie Fishbein, and they approached carefully, using the SUV as a shield. They were able to locate the root cellar easily and inside they found a small white cooler labeled *salmon roe bait*. The cooler was carefully loaded into the back of the rented black SUV, returned to trooper headquarters, inventoried, and packaged up for secure shipment to the state crime lab.

Twenty-six

Kate gradually opened her eyes and peeked out from under the fluffy down sleeping bag. Charlie was snoring lightly beside her. The Shearwater rocked gently on small waves. Sunlight streamed in through the overhead hatch, providing a welcome contrast to the sinister atmosphere of the previous evening. Last night's fog and the knowledge that someone was likely trying to kill them had put a serious damper on Kate's normally sunny disposition.

She was determined that today would be a better day. Slipping on shoes and a sweatshirt, she went up on deck, followed by Buster, who was also feeling more perky. The scene that opened up before them was incredible. A brilliant sun was rising over the ridge to the east, illuminating lush green mountain slopes on three sides with bright strips of fresh snow at the tops. The town of Seldovia was nestled into the base of the mountains fronted by its picturesque harbor. Facing north toward the mouth of Seldovia Bay, Kate could see across Cook Inlet to the other side, where two volcanic peaks were visible, sunlight glinting off their snowy slopes. Artistic wisps of remnant fog completed the picture. A sea otter floated off the bow in casual nonchalance. A dozen gulls squabbled over a piece of food.

Kate knew from her reading that Seldovia was one of the oldest non-native communities in Alaska, having been established in the early 1800s by Russian fur traders. The community served as a gateway to the Cook Inlet region and a commercial fishing hub for many years. After the establishment of Anchorage in the early 1900s and the completion of a highway connection from Anchorage to Homer in the 1950s, Seldovia lost much of its early commercial importance. Until the middle of the Twentieth Century, most of the waterfront portion of the town was constructed on picturesque pile-supported platforms

159

built out over the tidelands. One of the stranger episodes in Seldovia's history was associated with the famous 1964 earthquake. Tsunamis accompanying the big quake damaged many seaside towns in south central Alaska and killed hundreds of people, but it initially appeared that Seldovia had been spared significant damage. The tsunami, when it hit, arrived at low tide, and thus flooding was primarily limited to areas that were within the normal intertidal zone. However, weeks later, during the first high spring tides after the quake, sea water rose above the ground level of many of the boardwalks and seaside structures. The people of Seldovia thought that the tides were unusually high, but the flooding continued to occur. It was eventually determined that the entire seashore had subsided during the earthquake by a couple of feet, causing many of the town's structures to be lower than the highest tides. A major portion of the waterfront was subjected to flooding several times each year. Using federal disaster assistance funds, the Seldovia oceanfront was totally reconstructed. Now Seldovia was a sleepy town of about 300 people, accessible only by boat or plane. The beautiful setting attracted a few tourists each year, and some residents still participated in commercial fishing. The sleepiness was occasionally interrupted by the contentious politics that seemed to plague all Alaskan small towns.

Kate rummaged around the galley, trying to find all the components to make coffee. The only coffee grinder was a little hand-operated thing, and the only coffeepot was a stovetop percolator. Hadn't those become extinct in 1960? Charlie's lifestyle was obviously more primitive than hers. At least she used pre-ground coffee and a French press. As the coffee was starting to perk, Charlie, looking wide awake and fresh, entered the galley.

Kate was still waiting for coffee so she could wake up. "Cripes, Charlie, it takes an hour to make coffee. I assume you have enough power on the boat so that you could have an electric coffee grinder if you wanted."

"It's sort of a Zen thing." Charlie looked amused. "Boy, what a beautiful morning."

"Now that we're here, what are we going to do for the rest of the day?"

"I don't know." He picked up his cell phone. "The Super Trooper should be in his office by now. Let's find out what's going on in Homer."

Bob answered on the second ring. "I've got good news and bad news."

"Shoot."

"We have Brett and Julie Fishbein in custody, and we're collecting lots of evidence. But Darryl is dead."

"What?" Charlie yelped.

"When we tried to pick him up, he escaped into the woods. Unfortunately, somebody else tracked him down and shot him before we were able to find him."

"Shit," said Charlie. "Is that somebody by any chance Frank Halburg?"

"Probably," Bob replied. "Mr. Halburg is proving to be a very dangerous, smart, and scary guy."

Bob filled in the details of the previous day's events. The fact that Darryl's killer had likely been watching the whole sorry episode unfold was particularly creepy. But at least the evidence suggested that the killer was probably in Homer and, therefore, a long ways from Seldovia. Bob also indicated that a team of search and rescue personnel was currently on its way to retrieve Darryl's body.

"What's the deal with Aldo Fenstrom? Are you going to try to pick him up?" Charlie asked.

"The DEA guys are putting together the evidence package for a search and arrest warrant as we speak. We're probably going to try and go over to Fenstrom's Lagoon this afternoon."

"Don't be surprised if Aldo is long gone," Charlie said.

He relayed the substance of his discussion to Kate, who had decidedly mixed feelings about the dramatic events. At least some of the bad guys were getting arrested, and maybe she would be able to get back to a normal life in the near future. On the other hand, a psychopath was likely gunning for her and Charlie. But the psychopath was likely at least 20 miles away from their current position.

Charlie said, "Let's go ashore and eat breakfast." Kate readily agreed.

†

The Mole woke up in his grimy motel room near the Homer airport. His whole body was sore from the combined effects of the previous day's exertion and the fact that he had spent six hours lying on the cold ground in his blind at the top of the Kachemak Bay bluff. He had watched the law enforcement team as they retreated from Darryl's hiding place. He had waited until he was sure that they were not coming back for the body. The night was dark and fog had moved in, making conditions perfect for his trek back to town. He had descended the bluff, followed the beach to the base of the spit, and remained in the shadows until reaching the old motel at about 1:00 am. The total distance was probably six or seven miles, and he had been very tired.

The previous morning, he had abandoned his car in the dense woods off a logging road not too far from Darryl's cabin. The car had been rented under an assumed name, of course, and he had never intended to go back for it. He expected that the authorities would eventually find his tracks and follow them back to the truck, but that would get them very little information. Fortunately, he had rented another car, under still another name, which was waiting for him at the motel.

He contemplated his future in Homer. Things were getting pretty hot and he needed to get out soon, but he still had things he wanted to do. Kate Perkins and Charlie Skyler were at the top of his list. He was dimly aware that, at this point, eliminating them was less about eliminating witnesses and more about his anger at their persistence. Nevertheless, in his mind, the two motives somehow merged, and he felt that his world would not be whole until the uppity pair was eliminated from his memory. He also thought about Aldo. He knew that Aldo was probably aware of what was going on – Aldo always knew what was going on. He figured Aldo was either gone or would soon be gone. He really didn't care.

He also thought about his screwed-up childhood and life on the Savannah estate of almighty Stuart Halburg. Stuart, the pillar of the community, might finally be brought down as the drug dealer that he was. The Mole's relationship with Stuart had always been severely strained, but the opportunities offered by the family business (the illegal one) were too good to pass up. So he had cooperated to the extent that he needed to assure himself a piece of the action. But now that the operation seemed to be crumbling, he was looking forward to the repercussions in Savannah when it was revealed that Stuart Halburg – esteemed businessman, Southern gentleman, and political hopeful – was one of the founding fathers of an international drug distribution network. He could hardly wait for the shoe to drop.

But he had more immediate matters to attend to. He needed to find out where Kate Perkins and her boyfriend were hanging out. He was pretty sure that she wasn't staying at her cabin, so he decided to first look at the harbor to see if Charlie Skyler's boat was there and maybe try to get a glimpse of the two of them. Planning a suitable means of lethality would proceed from his initial reconnaissance. His suitcase contained a variety of disguise items. He hadn't shaved in about a week, so he decided to stay the way he was and just add glasses and a Greek fisherman's cap. He checked his cell phone and saw that he had three calls from Aldo. He smiled and went out the door.

After arriving at the harbor overlook, he saw that Charlie's boat was gone. An old guy with a beard and long hair was working on a boat near where the Shearwater was usually moored. The Mole ambled down the dock and, putting on the friendliest face he could muster, asked the aging hippy if he knew where Charlie Skyler was.

†

JB looked at the stranger and said truthfully that Charlie's boat had been gone when he woke up, and he had no idea where it might be. "Why do you want to know?"

"It's a personal matter." The man in the fisherman's cap turned and abruptly left.

JB watched the man walk up the harbor ramp and get into a blue sedan. He immediately dialed Charlie's new cell phone number, but getting no answer, he left a voicemail message that a man had been looking for him. A man who had obviously been lying, and whom JB did not like.

†

Aldo was getting more and more frustrated. His informants in town had been keeping him posted on the various law enforcement activities that were going on. He knew that his name was either on, or would soon be on, a wanted list. But all his escape planning of the previous day had gone awry. He had initially arranged to meet the plane the prior evening, but fog in Cook Inlet had prevented the flight. Consequently, he was still at his cabin. Soon the tide would be too low to get the Lucinda out of the lagoon. He could still use the skiff, but it would be dangerous.

Aldo had packed a duffle bag that contained everything needed for an escape to a new identity, including money, false documents, and credit cards. Finally, he decided that it was time. He needed to get out of Kachemak Bay while he still could. He would continue to communicate with his pilot by satellite phone. He loaded his bags into the dinghy, rowed out to the Lucinda, and departed the lagoon. He barely made it on the falling tide. The Lucinda's prop was stirring up mud all the way out of the lagoon. Once in deeper water, he accelerated her to top speed, which was about 13 knots. He figured that he would reach his destination in about two and half hours.

Twenty-seven

Kate and Charlie were basking in the sun of a beautiful fall day. They had treated themselves to a good breakfast at a small harbor-side café, followed by a hike around the town. Now, as they reclined on the pebbles of a small beach at the north end of Seldovia, they had an incredible view of the entrance to Kachemak Bay and Cook Inlet. Sea otters frolicked in the kelp just offshore. Graceful lenticular clouds surrounded the tops of Mount Redoubt and Mount Iliamna, like twin Mount Fujis. The clouds were an indication of windy conditions aloft and probably portended a change in the weather.

"I could live in a place like this," Kate said.

"Me, too," Charlie said. "But economic opportunities are pretty limited, and the lack of road access makes living kind of inconvenient and expensive. I guess, since I live on my boat, I can pretty much live anywhere I want, as long as it's on the water. Maybe Seldovia isn't a bad idea."

"It seems odd to even be thinking about stuff like that when our immediate problems are sort of stressful. And don't tell me not to worry."

"Okay."

An eagle landed on the intertidal flat in front of them and started to consume some delectable long-dead sea creature. "Yum," said Kate.

A wisp of smoke from the stack of a boat became visible as a boat rounded the point heading out into the inlet. "Holy crap!" said Charlie. "That's Aldo's boat."

"Uh oh," Kate said. "I don't like this."

Charlie pulled his cell phone from his jacket pocket and dialed the Super Trooper's number. He got the answering machine and left a message. Then he dialed 911 and asked the dispatcher to contact

Trooper Bob and let him know that Aldo was leaving the bay by boat and that Charlie was going to follow him.

"Charlie, are you nuts?"

"Maybe," he said. "Are you coming or not?"

They sprinted for the dock, untied the Shearwater, and motored into Seldovia Bay. The Lucinda went out of sight as it rounded the corner out of Kachemak Bay and into the broad expanse of lower Cook Inlet. Buster lay in his newly appointed spot on a pillow in the galley. The look in his eyes was one of incredulity – what are these crazy people doing now?

Sea conditions were reasonably calm within the bay, but Charlie could see breaking waves ahead and knew that their journey would soon become unpleasant. As they rounded Dangerous Cape, the seas increased to about six feet. The Lucinda could be seen about two miles ahead. Charlie tried to adjust his speed so that he was just in sight of Aldo's boat but not too close. He knew that he would show up clearly on Aldo's radar screen, assuming it was turned on. Conditions were uncomfortable, but not a problem for a boat of the Shearwater's design. Kate and Buster, on the other hand, were not designed as well, and had a definite problem. Waves were coming from behind and slightly to the side of the boat so that the Shearwater rolled and pitched simultaneously with each passing wave. The slow compound motion was particularly nauseating.

Beethoven's Fifth Symphony incongruously broke the monotony of the droning engine and splashing water. They were approaching the edge of cell phone coverage, and Charlie could barely hear the Super Trooper. He managed to convey that they were following Aldo and were currently passing Flat Island, a well-known landmark. Bob was at a loss as to what to do.

Charlie yelled into the little phone, "How about enlisting the help of the Coast Guard? They could get a helicopter from Kodiak to our location in less than an hour. They're supposed to be involved in drug interdiction anyway."

"Okay, I'll talk to the DEA guys and see what we can do. How are we going to communicate when you are out of cell phone range?"

"I guess we'll have to use the marine radio. But, unfortunately, Aldo will be able to hear everything we say."

Charlie knew the U.S. Coast Guard Air Station Kodiak provided search and rescue operations over a huge area, including thousands of square miles of ocean stretching from the eastern Gulf of Alaska to the end of the Aleutian Islands. Their resources included long-range Hercules aircraft and Jayhawk helicopters. The latter machines had a range of 700 miles and could fly at 140 knots, providing great flexibility. The helicopter crews were known around the world for daring rescues at sea during extreme weather conditions.

"Can the Coast Guard really get here in time?" Kate asked.

"Yeah. We're only 90 miles from Kodiak and they can fly pretty fast. It probably depends on how fast they can mobilize."

Kate had reached a sort of gastrointestinal equilibrium. She no longer felt like she was going to barf, but she didn't feel good. Buster, on the other hand, looked very unhappy. Kate didn't think it was possible for a black cat to look green. He was tensely crouched on his cushion with claws dug in, trying to resist the constant rolling. His bug-eyed expression suggested panic.

Charlie did not tell Kate, but he was concerned about the weather. All indications were that it was going to get worse. He increased his speed so he could stay in sight of the Lucinda. It was becoming more and more difficult to see the small boat in the distance because of the lumpy sea and spray from breaking waves. Even the radar was having a hard time picking up the signal continuously because of the sea clutter and pitching of the Shearwater.

Aldo continued to skirt the west coast of the Kenai Peninsula. Charlie was puzzled: what was his destination? Under these weather conditions, it would be foolhardy to continue south into the Gulf of Alaska, but where else could he be headed? Charlie's phone rang again. He was barely able to hear the Super Trooper at the other end. It sounded like the Coast Guard was considering helping out, but they were waiting for assurance from Washington D.C. that it was alright. Also, the Coast Guard had suggested that they use VHF channel 83, which is normally for Coast Guard use only. Most marine radios were not set to scan that frequency, so it was unlikely that Aldo would be able to overhear their conversations. Charlie tuned his radio and established a dialogue with the radio operator at the Coast Guard station. He was relieved to find out that the operator had already been informed of the situation and would help relay messages to the troopers.

†

Shortly after leaving Fenstrom's Lagoon, Aldo tried to make contact with his escape pilot via the satellite phone. The fog of the last couple days had lifted, making airplane flight more viable, but now it was starting to look like a storm was on the way. The window of opportunity was probably going to be short. After several tries, he finally reached Frog, his designated escape pilot. Frog was a seasonal employee of the Rainbow Inn, flying fishermen around in the summer but living in Seward during the remainder of the year. Frog was a good pilot, but more important, he was seriously indebted to Aldo and John Vander, Aldo's former squad-mate and owner of the Rainbow Inn. Frog knew that one word from either of them would land him in jail for long time. Consequently, he was willing to risk his life to do whatever was necessary to keep his employers happy.

Aldo filled him in on his schedule, and Frog agreed to leave Seward in plenty of time to meet Aldo at the rendezvous location. He warned Aldo that aviation weather forecasts were calling for deteriorating weather conditions later in the day and that they were likely to have an exciting trip. As Aldo turned the corner into Cook Inlet, he was not happy with the choppy sea. Although the Lucinda was a sturdy and reliable craft, she had been designed for hauling in salmon nets in moderate coastal sea conditions rather than open ocean voyaging. But it couldn't be helped.

After about thirty minutes of plowing through the waves, he became aware of a radar blip about two miles behind him. Using binoculars, he tried to see what kind of boat it was, but conditions were too rough to see much. It appeared to be a fishing boat of some kind. Aldo was somewhat surprised that another relatively small craft would be out on such a nasty day, but Cook Inlet was a common travel route and most fishermen were slightly crazy. He was not overly concerned.

†

After another thirty minutes of nauseating motion, Kate was beginning to think that she might survive the ordeal. It reminded her of the Tilt-a-Whirl carnival ride that she had loved as a child in Michigan. She tried to imagine herself sitting beside her brother and laughing as he begged the infernal machine to stop. It had been several hours since breakfast, and she was actually starting to get hungry. As she reached for the potato chips, Charlie strongly suggested that snacking at this particular time was a bad idea. She was about to protest this infringement on her eating liberty when Buster jumped off the settee and threw up in the middle of the cabin floor.

"Guess who gets to clean up?"

"Yeah, yeah," Kate reached for the paper towels. Buster was just like her brother. Her stomach began to churn once more, and she put the chips back in the cabinet.

Charlie glanced at the radar and was mystified to find that the Lucinda had disappeared from the screen, in spite of having been there just seconds before. Then it became clear. Aldo had turned into Dogfish Bay, a long, narrow inlet abutting the Cook Inlet ship lane. Charlie had been in Dogfish Bay a couple of times during commercial fishing seasons. The sheltered anchorage was popular among the

171

fishermen during periods of bad weather. The relatively flat terrain at the head of Dogfish Bay had served as a staging area and camp for logging operations in years past. And then Charlie realized what Aldo was up to. Another remnant of the logging era was a small, primitive airstrip. Aldo was meeting a plane! Dogfish Bay was only five miles long, and Aldo would be at the head of the bay in half an hour. Allowing time to get to shore and transfer his belongings, he could be taking off in less than an hour, assuming that a plane was waiting.

Charlie radioed the Coast Guard and gave them the news of Aldo's location and probable plans. The radio operator told Charlie that the Coast Guard chopper was just taking off from Kodiak and could be at Dogfish Bay in about sixty minutes. They would be calling it pretty close. Rounding the headland at the mouth of the bay, Charlie entered calmer water and increased speed to Shearwater's maximum, which was none too fast. Aldo had also increased speed and was now more than two miles away.

It was probably just as well. Getting too close could be dangerous, especially if Aldo was carrying the rifle that Charlie had seen when he broke into his cabin. He had no clue what they would do if they were to catch up to Aldo. Handing the binoculars to Kate, Charlie pointed out the general location of the airstrip. There was no sign of an airplane. Aldo approached to within a couple hundred feet of the beach opposite the air strip and dropped his anchor. Charlie slowed and held back, still more than a mile away. With the engine idling, they continued to watch the Lucinda. A puff of smoke materialized from the rear of the Lucinda.

"Oh, shit," said Charlie and Kate simultaneously. A few seconds later, a gunshot reverberated off the mountainsides seeming to come from all directions. Charlie put the boat in gear and began to retreat.

"How far can a rifle shoot?" Kate asked.

"It probably has a maximum range of a couple miles, but the chances of hitting anything at this distance are pretty small."

"Small is good," Kate said. "But no chance would be better."

"Agreed. That's why we are retreating. I don't want any holes in my boat." As they motored away from the Lucinda, Charlie informed the Coast Guard radio operator that they were being shot at. The operator seemed incredulous and unresponsive. Charlie strongly suggested that he notify the helicopter of the situation as soon as possible so that they could be prepared.

The Shearwater turned and again faced the head of the bay. The wind was picking up and the clouds looked ominous, dark billows rapidly scudding over the ridge tops. Kate said, "I think I hear a plane." Charlie shut off the engine and they listened. All they could hear was the wind whistling through the rigging. Then they both heard it. A small plane cleared the top of the ridge and descended rapidly toward the small strip. Charlie again reached for the radio mike and called the Coast Guard. This time he talked directly to the chopper pilot.

"A plane is in the process of landing on the strip at the head of Dogfish Bay. Where are you guys?" asked Charlie.

"We're about 15 minutes away," answered the pilot. "The weather's getting really bad, but we're going as fast as we can. The plane picking up your bad guy is going to have visibility and turbulence problems very soon. I wouldn't want to be flying with him."

Kate yelled, "Aldo's moving!"

Charlie and Kate watched as Aldo drove the Lucinda up onto the beach, threw a couple of duffle bags off the bow onto the beach above the waterline, and then jumped off into ankle-deep water. Limping ashore, he picked up his bags and struggled over the dunes toward the airstrip. Through the binoculars, they could see a rifle slung over his shoulders. There was nothing they could do except move in a little closer and observe the drama.

✝

When Aldo turned into Dogfish Bay, he wondered whether the boat behind him would follow. All he could do was wait and see. In any event, he had a two-mile lead, which should give him enough time, assuming that the plane arrived according to schedule. Another call on the satellite phone alerted him that the plane would be there soon. Frog told him that the weather was bad and that their flight was going to be risky – the ceiling was dropping and the mountain passes were becoming socked in. All Aldo could say was to get there as soon as possible.

When the boat followed him into the bay and began to approach, he decided to warn them away with the rifle. He was relieved that the strategy worked, indicating that the people on board did not have equivalent weapons. But he assumed that they were in contact with somebody and was becoming very anxious. The arrival of the plane was a huge relief.

He debated whether to anchor the Lucinda and go to shore using the dinghy, then realized that was a stupid waste of time. Although he hated to leave the Lucinda to the mercy of waves and tide, running the boat up on shore was the only sensible solution. He had to come to grips with the fact that his life in Alaska was likely over, and it didn't really matter what happened to the Lucinda. However, as a last gesture to his faithful boat, he threw out the anchor after he had grounded it on the beach. That way it would likely stay on the beach, rather than drift on the high tide to points unknown and be smashed on the rocks.

As he jumped off the high bow of the Lucinda, he twisted his ankle. He strangely felt that it was somehow fitting that this day would continue to go to hell. As he hobbled up the beach, Frog ran out to meet him and grabbed his bags. Yelling over the sound of the wind, Frog urged Aldo to move as fast as possible. He had overheard radio conversations from a Coast Guard helicopter and knew that they were very close. They scrambled into the plane and Frog was taxiing before Aldo was in his seat. Whipping the plane around into the wind, Frog poured on the power, rising off the ground almost immediately because of the strong headwind. It seemed like they were standing still for a while, then gradually they began to climb. Out of the corner of his eye, Frog saw the orange and white Coast Guard chopper flying toward them. The Coast Guard pilot ordered him to land, but Frog ignored the call.

He looked at Aldo and said, "Here we go. This is where it gets exciting." Frog turned the plane toward the ridge top and flew into a massive cloud bank where he knew that the helicopter would not follow.

†

"Dammit," said Charlie. The Jayhawk circled back toward them and hovered.

"Sorry, Shearwater. There is nothing we can do now. Our procedures won't let us fly blind, even though we are probably better equipped to do it than the plane. We have his tail number and will alert all public aviation facilities to keep an eye out. He is going to be pretty limited where he can fly. If he makes it out of the clouds without hitting a mountain, he is eventually going to have to fly over the water in order to get below the clouds for a visual landing. There aren't that many landing possibilities. We'll research it and get the word out. Meanwhile, are you guys OK?"

"We're fine," Charlie said.

"The conditions on the inlet are nasty and getting worse as this storm passes over. We recommend that you stay put until the weather improves."

"I was thinking the same thing. Thanks for your help. I wish things had worked out better. I assume you will relay the status to the troopers in Homer."

"It is probably already being done. Good luck. Over and out."

"Well, that was interesting," Charlie said.

"Interesting!" We just wasted a day on a wild goose chase and now we're out in the middle of nowhere with a storm coming. My cat is sick. For all I know, we are out of food and will have to go ashore and trap rabbits or something to survive."

"Jeez, do you think you could be any more dramatic? We have lots of food, we're in a sheltered area, and the boat is warm and comfortable. But we do need to find a good place to anchor before it gets dark. Have some potato chips."

Charlie motored to the head of the bay, found the most protected site, and carefully set the anchor. He noted that the Lucinda was anchored and appeared to be all right for the night. The tide was going out and the boat would go dry in an hour or so, but, like most boats of its type, it was designed sit flat on its bottom and would not tip over. He was probably going to have to tow the Lucinda back to Homer. Or maybe Kate could drive it. Now that was a scary thought. He decided to wait and see what the sea conditions were like in the morning.

Theoretically, since the boat had been abandoned, it would be his property if he salvaged it. Maybe. Or, more likely, the DEA would confiscate it. He really didn't want to mess with another boat, but he didn't want to leave it there, either. The trip back to Homer would be long and slow; maybe he could leave the Lucinda in Seldovia instead of taking it all the way to Homer. He wasn't sure what kind of paperwork or legal actions needed to be taken to claim salvage rights, but he was pretty sure it would be way more complicated than necessary.

After shutting down the Shearwater's engine, he pulled two beers out of the frig and laid out cheese and crackers. Kate and Buster kicked back on the lounge and began to relax. After knocking back a beer, a half box of crackers, and a brick of cheese, Kate had to admit that she would probably survive. They agreed that it was pretty unlikely that any of the Fenstrom gang would be after them in their current location, and they tried not to think about having to return to town.

That night turned out to be unexpectedly special. After the discomforts of the day, Charlie's bed was unbelievably comfortable. The boat was rocking just enough to be sensual, and the pent-up stress of the last few days was released in a spectacular way.

Twenty-eight

The DEA duo was driving the Super Trooper crazy. Bob had received half a dozen calls relating to normal town stuff like domestic violence and drunken vandalism, but he had been unable to deal with any of them because the Drug Enforcement Agency felt that their business was more important than anybody else's. Bob did have to admit that having a psychotic killer loose in his town did have a pretty high priority. Like Jankowski and Phillips, he was disappointed that the opportunity to nab Aldo the previous evening had evaporated.

The agents were glued to their radios, phones, and e-mail in hopes that there would be some word about Aldo's plane. But they had heard nothing. There was no record of a small plane landing at any coastal strip within range of the plane's fuel supply. Either the plane had crashed, or it was hiding out at a private airstrip somewhere. Bob had the bad feeling that, if Aldo had lasted this long, he was probably still on the loose. He clearly didn't leave much to chance.

They had discovered that the plane was registered to a Paul Larchmont of Seward. Paul, alias Frog, had not been heard from since the previous morning, when several persons had seen him take off from his small backyard airstrip on the outskirts of town. He had not filed a flight plan. Big surprise.

Meanwhile, the DEA Los Angeles office was discreetly following up on the leads that Charlie had provided regarding the mysterious Offshore Enterprises. Unfortunately, Offshore Enterprises had closed its doors and appeared to be out of business. Attempts to determine exactly what that business had consisted of had resulted in very little information. There was no state business license, and no taxes had been filed. Neighboring business persons had seen a man and a woman come and go once in a while, but had not actually met anyone from Offshore Enterprises. Semi-trailer trucks were occasionally seen parked at the loading dock, but the trucks had no logos.

The Super Trooper was glad that Charlie and Kate were far from the action. At least he didn't have to worry about Frank Halburg getting to them until they got back to Homer. The nor'wester was slamming the whole peninsula, and he didn't see any way that Halburg could pursue them, even if he knew where they were. Bob had received a call from JB regarding the man looking for Charlie. The description that JB provided only roughly matched that of Frank Halburg.

Brett Fishbein had been returned to Anchorage and put into protective custody without incident. Hopefully, he would be safe there. Julie Fishbein was still being held in the hospital, but she would have to be released soon. She was asking to get into a rehab facility. Bob hoped that she would be successful since he had developed an inexplicable fondness for her.

†

Aldo's knees finally stopped shaking, and he felt like he could actually put something into his stomach. He and Frog were eating a quick breakfast of day-old doughnuts in a rundown cabin at the east end of Hinchinbrook Island in Prince William Sound.

After flying into the clouds at Dogfish Bay, they had remained totally blind for almost an hour. The little Cessna had been continually buffeted by the turbulent winds inside the storm clouds. Frog's plane was not equipped for instrument flying and, in any event, Frog did not have an instrument rating. But he was an experienced pilot and very familiar with the area. The GPS provided their general position, so he was pretty sure that there weren't any mountains in the way. When Frog had been certain that they were over open water, he had slowly descended.

180

Aldo had never been so scared in his life – he watched in terror as the altimeter wound down toward zero, and he was certain that they were going to plow into the water. They broke out of the clouds at just less than six hundred feet. Frog had then flown the plane within the narrow window of visibility between water and clouds all the way to Hinchinbrook. The sea a few hundred feet below them was a roiling maelstrom of waves and spray. It had become increasingly dark as the afternoon progressed. Fortunately the ceiling had remained at a constant altitude, and they were able to fly straight to their destination, arriving just before nightfall. When they landed on the bumpy abandoned airstrip, Aldo could barely walk.

Frog had scouted this location years ago as a possible link in an emergency escape route. Two weeks earlier, he had stashed several barrels of aviation fuel in a carefully hidden spot. The landing strip was on the south side of the island and so was not visible from the more heavily trafficked corridor inside the sound. Additionally, there was a convenient grove of cottonwoods at one end of the strip that provided partial cover for his airplane, making it difficult to see from above. But, regardless, they were not going to be there very long. The ceiling had lifted overnight, and it looked promising for them to keep going. Frog went to refuel the plane. Aldo tried to prepare himself for the next leg of their journey. He had always been afraid of heights.

†

The Mole was sick of the grubby motel room. The TV got only two channels, and he was going stir crazy. But there was nothing that he could do for the time being. Even if he knew where Kate Perkins and her boyfriend were, he had no boat, and the weather was too lousy to venture onto the water anyway. He did not know where Brett Fishbein was, but suspected that he was in jail. The sudden law enforcement activity strongly suggested that Brett was blabbing to everybody. He had discovered that Julie Fishbein was in protective custody at the hospital. He did not think that Julie had enough information to be worth worrying about, especially since Brett was already talking. Trying to get at Julie was probably too risky.

He was thinking that he probably should not have cut off communication with Aldo, since Aldo had contacts all over the place and could usually figure out what was going on. He had no idea where Aldo was either. His usual confidence was ebbing. His attempts to charm the single woman proprietor of the motel had been modestly successful, but he was still worried that she might put two and two together and figure out that he was the guy the cops were looking for. He needed to move to a less conspicuous place. He would try to hang on at the motel for one more day, then make some decisions about what to do next.

He had been checking the harbor every few hours to see if the Shearwater had returned. But no boats had been moving in the storm. However, the wind was subsiding and the clouds were lifting, suggesting that his quarry might be back within reach soon.

†

The Shearwater was rocking and gurgling. Residual swells from the passing storm were entering Dogfish Bay, enough to cause small waves to hit the boat broadside. Kate awoke and looked up toward the overhead hatch. The sun was coming up, and the broken clouds appeared to be moving back and forth. It took a few seconds before Kate realized that the boat was moving, rather than the clouds. There were even a few patches of blue sky. Charlie was still asleep, cuddling with his pillow like a small child. She wondered how guys could sometimes appear so innocent and peaceful and at other times be so totally obnoxious. Realizing that this sentiment was an artifact of her past experiences and not necessarily reflective of Charlie, she put the thought out of her mind. Thus far, Charlie had been a perfect gentleman. Maybe there was a chance of a relationship with a truly nice guy. But they had to survive the next few days.

Charlie stirred, opened his eyes, and kissed Kate passionately. "I hate to say this after the fireworks of last night, but we have got to get going."

"I suppose," Kate said. "Last night was pretty amazing."

They dressed and looked out at the world. The wind had diminished and there was a pink glow in the sky. The tide was high and the Lucinda was again floating. Charlie suggested that they tie onto the Lucinda and begin the long tow before eating breakfast.

The Shearwater eased up to the Lucinda, and Charlie was relieved that the water was deep enough to approach without grounding. He pulled in the Lucinda's anchor, rigged a tow rope, and they began the long, slow trip back. As they pulled out of Dogfish Bay, they were relieved to find that the waves were not too bad. They were able to maintain a speed of about six knots, which meant that they would be in Seldovia in about two hours. Charlie had decided to leave the Lucinda in Seldovia, where it would be less conspicuous. Nevertheless, it was likely that someone in Seldovia would recognize Aldo's boat and wonder what had happened. Charlie decided that he would tell curious onlookers that they had found the boat abandoned and that they had already alerted the authorities, which was basically true.

Cell phone signal strength reached an acceptable level as they approached Kachemak Bay, and Charlie made a series of calls. First he called JB, who he knew would be worried. JB had taken on a motherly role in his relationship with Charlie, which was often annoying, but at the same time comforting. After fending off JB's anger at being left in the dark, Charlie explained what he had been doing. JB filled him in on the mysterious stranger who had been looking for him. Furthermore, JB had been continuously watching the harbor overlook area since the stranger had approached him. He had twice seen the same blue sedan pull up to the harbor ramp, hang out for a few minutes, then leave. He was sure that the guy in the fisherman's cap was periodically monitoring the harbor to see if the Shearwater had returned. Charlie told him that they would be back in Homer by late afternoon, and they would discuss defensive strategy then. He smiled as he pictured JB sitting for hours peering out of his little boat cabin window, watching the parking lot through his binoculars.

He next called the Super Trooper and luckily reached him on his cell phone. Bob made several comments about Charlie having all the fun, chasing bad guys through Alaska's scenic waterways. Charlie filled him in on their status. They discussed the high probability that Frank Halburg was still intent on dispatching Kate. Charlie was somewhat surprised – and gratified – to learn that JB had been communicating with Bob. Frank's apparent single-minded determination to seek revenge suggested that setting a trap for him would have a reasonable probability of success. The obvious downside was that Kate and Charlie were the bait. The Super Trooper indicated that he would talk things over with the DEA agents. They arranged to talk by phone again when the Shearwater was about an hour out from Homer.

After entering the Seldovia harbor, they securely moored the Lucinda in an available spot and informed the harbormaster that the Lucinda was evidence in a crime, and that law enforcement officials would be in touch with him to discuss details of moorage and ultimate disposal. Charlie also suggested that the harbormaster keep quiet about the crime angle to avoid too much curiosity. But he knew that in a town like Seldovia, rumors would spread quickly and most likely wouldn't resemble reality anyway.

Before leaving Seldovia, Kate and Charlie searched the Lucinda for any information that might be useful in tracking down Aldo. All they found were a couple scribbled phone numbers on a scratch pad, which Kate stuffed in her pocket. As they were boarding the Shearwater for the passage to Homer, a grizzled fisherman with a hawk-like nose and cold blue eyes stopped them and inquired about the Lucinda. He knew that the boat belonged to Aldo Fenstrom and asked how Charlie had taken possession. Charlie indicated that the boat had been found abandoned and aground in Dogfish Bay, so they had brought it here. He said that the Coast Guard had been notified of the situation. When asked what he was doing in Dogfish Bay, Charlie indicated that they had been traveling from Kodiak to Homer and had sought refuge from the storm in the bay. The old fisherman looked dubious and quickly walked away.

"I don't think he believed you," Kate said.

"Me either, but I'm not sure it matters. He probably won't be able to contact Aldo, assuming that he is still alive. I suspect the last thing Aldo wants right now is someone calling him. Maybe there are other friends of Aldo in Homer that he could call. I guess we'll just wait and see."

Charlie and Kate departed for Homer, relieved that they were no longer responsible for the Lucinda. After about forty-five minutes, as promised, Charlie phoned the Super Trooper. Agents Phillips and Jankowski were in the same room, and they put Charlie on the speaker phone.

"So, Charlie, do you have any ideas?" Bob asked.

"Obviously, if we want to lure Halburg to the boat, we need to make things look as normal as possible from the time that we land. I'm thinking that Kate and I should just moor the boat and stay aboard, or at least pretend to stay aboard."

"What do you mean?" said Agent Jankowski.

"One possibility would be for Kate and me to sneak off the boat after dark. I think that we could exit the port pilothouse door, climb into a dinghy, row around the dock to JB's boat, and wait there. The way the docks are laid out, we should be able to accomplish that without ever being in the line of vision from anyone monitoring the harbor from shore side. We could leave a light on in the boat, with a timer set to turn it off at bedtime. You guys could figure out where you want to be. Frank is smart and will be watching for a trap. Everything needs to be set up before we get there."

"What's our strategy if Frank approaches the boat?" Bob asked.

"I guess we move in and arrest him," Agent Jankowski said.

"We should be prepared for an approach either on or in the water. Halburg's file indicates that he has had Special Forces training including diving, explosives, and water approach techniques," Agent Phillips said.

"Great," remarked Kate in the background.

"I would hate it if he blew up my boat," Charlie said.

"So, how do we defend against the diving possibility? He could swim in, plant a timed explosive, and leave without ever being seen," Agent Phillips said.

"I have a sensitive underwater hydrophone that I use on tours so people can listen to whale sounds. We could deploy that from JB's boat. The sounds of a diver's bubbles are very distinctive," Charlie said.

"If we do hear him, what do we do?" Bob asked. "He could be pretty hard to catch under the water."

"Shine lights, shoot into the water," Agent Jankowski said.

"If he is cool, he would still be able to escape. Pistol bullets only penetrate a few feet into water. He could swim deep under the docks, and it would be difficult to track him in the dark," Charlie said. "One possibility that just occurred to me would be to surround the boat with a gill net. A diver swimming in the dark would not see it and would likely get tangled up."

"That's a great idea, but how would you place the net without being seen?"

"I don't know – I might have to swim it around the boat. I also don't know where I would get a short piece of netting."

"I'll find some netting for you," Bob said. "I'll have one of the dock workers put it into the storage box at your boat slip."

"Okay, that sounds good. How about communications?"

"Let's use mobile marine radios set on the Coast Guard frequency at low power," Bob said. "Where are you guys going to be hanging out?"

"We'll figure something out," Agent Jankowski said.

"Okay, we'll be there in about twenty minutes and I guess we'll just stay on the boat until dark, then we'll sneak over to JB's boat."

"Good luck, everybody," Agent Phillips said.

Charlie called JB, informed him of the plan, asked him not to greet them when they landed, and indicated that they would be coming on board the Otterly Ridiculous after dark.

Twenty-nine

A sliver of new moon peeked out from behind fast-moving clouds. Pale moon shadows came and went. Eerie silhouettes from the rigging of the commercial fishing boats came in and out of focus. The harbor lights were partly obscured by misty halos that glowed like large rainbow-tinged lollipops. Individual piers protruded into the water from the main walkways like the fingers of a deformed hand. The ends of the fingers, away from the lights, were bathed in darkness. The cold clamminess was oppressive. Breath from all warm-blooded living things was visible as a dense cloud.

A cloud of vapor arose from the sea as one of those living things emerged from the water. Charlie removed his snorkel and climbed up the ladder on the dark side of the Otterly Ridiculous.

"How was it?" Kate asked.

"Fucking cold."

"Sorry. Stupid question."

Inside the cave-like cabin of JB's boat, Charlie removed his dry suit. His face was bright red where it had been exposed to the forty-degree water, and welts from the dive mask made him look somewhat like a raccoon. Kate, however, was observing lower on Charlie's body, where the tight long underwear exaggerated other features.

"For Pete's sake, Kate. Could you be any more obvious? This is a G-rated boat," JB said.

"That's not what I heard," Kate replied.

After dark, Charlie and Kate had carefully moved from the Shearwater to the Otterly Ridiculous by climbing over the adjacent boats and generally staying in the shadows. They had left a light burning in the Shearwater that would turn off automatically at 10:30. JB had even cleaned up his boat somewhat in expectation of company, although it was still marginally disgusting. While waiting for darkness, he had also continued his vigil of the harbor overlook. Just before dark, the blue sedan had again appeared and quickly departed. This information had been relayed to the Super Trooper, and anxiety was running high within the law enforcement trio.

Charlie set up the hydrophone and hung it off the side of the boat. Occasional propeller sounds from within the harbor indicated that it was functioning correctly. They began the long wait. JB rummaged around in a small closet and pulled out an M-16 assault rifle.

Charlie and Kate stared. "Do you actually know how to shoot that thing?"

"As it happens, I am an excellent shot," JB said. "There is a lot you don't know about me."

"Well, yeah. Maybe the fact that you never talk about your past has something to do with my ignorance. Please be careful with that thing," Charlie said as JB expertly fitted the magazine and checked the action. For some reason, Charlie was not totally surprised by this turn of events. JB's athleticism and physical confidence had always seemed somehow uncharacteristic of what would be expected for someone who had spent a lifetime as an academic.

"So, how is it that everyone calls you JB?" Kate asked.

"An excellent question. My full name is Johann Sebastian Bachman. Yeah, really. I don't know whether my parents were trying to be funny or whether my name is a sincere tribute to the composer. Regardless, when I was in seventh grade I began to tire of having to deal with Johann or J. S. Bachman, so I decided that I would rename myself JB. And there you have it. Not too interesting."

"Did you ever ask your parents about your name?"

"They both died when I was ten, so I didn't get the chance."

"I'm sorry," Kate said.

Kate had known JB for ten minutes, and already she had extracted more information from him than Charlie had in two years. How did women do that?

"Who did you live with after your parents died?"

"I lived with my aunt and uncle until I was seventeen then went out on my own."

The little radio came to life, and the Super Trooper asked if the team was ready for a long night. He assured them that the dynamic trio was in place and ready to go if any bad guys showed up.

†

The Mole had been trying to figure out the best strategy for dispatching Kate and Charlie. He didn't have time to wait for them to conveniently drive to a secluded location, and he had to assume that they knew someone was after them so they would be watching. Walking up to the boat and shooting them would be simple, but, if anything went wrong, he would be trapped. He could easily be cornered at the end of a dock or apprehended as he tried to leave the harbor on one of the three approach ramps.

The more he thought about it, the more he felt that he needed to approach from underwater at night. But it would be cold and dark, and the idea did not appeal to him at all. Of all the miserable exercises in which he had participated during his military training, night diving was his least favorite. And then there were the diving equipment requirements. Nevertheless, it was the only almost foolproof scheme he could come up with.

He had paid a visit to Izzy, Aldo's brother-in-law, the previous afternoon. Izzy worked off and on as a commercial diver and was well equipped with diving gear as well as underwater explosives. The Mole had convinced him to loan his gear without any guarantee of ever getting it back. Izzy was terrified of him and would have done anything to get rid of him. The Mole had also asked Izzy where Aldo was, and Izzy had truthfully replied that he didn't have any idea.

Now that the Shearwater had returned, he knew that he had to act as soon as possible. His plan was to wait until after midnight, slip into the water in the darkest, most remote corner of the harbor, proceed underwater across the boat channel to the Shearwater's location, attach an explosive charge to the bottom of the boat at the location of the fuel tank, activate the fuse, and swim far enough away from the boat so that he could get his head out of the water before the explosive shock wave hit. The instantaneous fireball generated from several hundred gallons of fuel would solve his problems. Confusion after the blast would assure his escape.

As he entered the cold water, the Mole's usual self-confidence was beginning to wane. He checked the compass heading from his location across the harbor to the end of the pier where the Shearwater was parked, and quietly submerged. It was incredibly dark, like being suspended in ink. The feelings of claustrophobia that he had felt during his training came back to him in full force. Swimming a few inches off the bottom at a depth of about twenty feet, he periodically pushed the back-light button on his compass to get his bearings. He discovered that he tended to veer to the right between compass readings. Consequently, his course was a zigzag. Use of his dive light was out of the question, since it would make him highly visible from the surface.

One positive aspect of the darkness was that he was not able to see what he was swimming through. Harbors are not generally considered desirable diving locations. Every once in a while he felt some sort of sea creature brush against him. Twenty minutes of blind creepiness passed, and he began to get concerned. His tank held about an hour's worth of air, less than that for a diver under stress, which he certainly was. Just as he was starting to panic, he ran head first into a piling. Swearing through his regulator, he willed himself to calm down. He needed to make sure that he was at the right pier, since his course had been anything but straight. The previous day he had memorized the configuration of the boats parked at the end of the pier where Charlie's boat was kept. Starting at the outer end there were two sailboats, a fast sport-fishing boat, a small commercial fishing boat, and then the larger Shearwater.

There was just enough illumination from the harbor lights so that the Mole, looking up through the water column, could vaguely make out the silhouettes of the running gear. The first two boats were definitely deep-keeled sailboats, the next was a smaller planing hull with a stern drive system, and the fourth boat had a traditional hull with a shallow keel and inboard engine. This was the right place.

He briefly stopped under the dock next to Charlie's boat and removed the explosives package with its timed detonator from the pocket of his buoyancy compensator jacket. Waiting a few seconds to get his bearings, he swam under the boat next to the Shearwater, then turned to approach his target under where he knew the fuel tanks would be located. As he crossed the space between the boats, he felt an odd resistance to his forward motion, which at first he did not understand. Reaching out with his gloved hand he felt the monofilament netting and realized that he was in trouble.

He tried to turn sharply away from the net, but by that time he was more or less engulfed. The valves behind his head at the top of the air tank caught in the netting and, as he turned, the net wrapped around him. During his dive training, he had spent many hours practicing various exercises designed to guard against panic. The sadistic trainers had intentionally subjected the trainees to various kinds of harassment while they were fifty feet underwater, which they were expected to overcome by slow, deliberate thought and action.

He reached for the knife strapped to his leg and began to cut away the netting, but the more he moved the more tangled he became. Unfortunately, his inherent claustrophobia combined with stress and lack of recent practice caused him to panic past any ability at self-control. He began to thrash violently.

†

Kate, Charlie, and JB were comfortably cocooned in the small cabin of JB's boat with the lights out. The hydrophone receiver was on, and they had been listening to the sounds of occasional boats going in and out of the harbor. Every twenty minutes the intrepid cop trio checked in on the radio. Charlie had been educating them on the types of boats that he was able to distinguish by their distinctive underwater sounds.

"Well, that is just truly fascinating." Kate yawned.

"I dunno," JB said. "I think it is kind of interesting."

They were just beginning to think that the whole apprehension plan was a fool's errand, when a faint new sound began to emanate from the speaker every couple of seconds. "That's it," Charlie said. "He's coming."

Charlie called the Super Trooper and told him that the suspect was approaching underwater. Bob indicated that he and the DEA agents would begin to approach the boat and warned Charlie to let law enforcement deal with the bad guy. The noise got louder. Amazingly, the sound of bubbles underwater sounded pretty much like, well, the sound of bubbles. Charlie and JB got up to go on deck. "Stay here, Kate," Charlie murmured.

Kate frowned. "Not on your life."

Jeez, the woman was not in the least obedient. Charlie shrugged, and they all quietly ascended the narrow companionway and watched to see what would happen at the Shearwater, two boats away.

Please don't let him blow up my boat, Charlie chanted inside his head.

As the Super Trooper and the agents approached the Shearwater, the space between the boat and the dock looked like a Jacuzzi with frothy bubbles rising almost continuously. Charlie approached and showed where the ends of the net were secured. Bob untied one end and began to pull toward the main pier, while Charlie pulled the other end.

A wriggling black mass totally wrapped in netting appeared as they reeled the net in. It reminded Kate of a large fly caught in a spider web. When the head of the diver could be seen, Agent Jankowski pulled his gun and ordered the black figure to stop struggling. The diver spit out the regulator, took a couple of deep breaths, and calmed down somewhat. The six people present at the bizarre scene all pulled on the net and managed to drag the dead weight onto the dock like a net full of herring. JB was the first to see the explosive package still in the diver's hand. Moving very fast, he stepped on the man's wrist, pulled a knife to cut away a piece of the net, and carefully removed the sinister object, all in one fluid movement. JB handed the small, square package to Agent Phillips and informed him that it was a device used by commercial divers with a built-in fuse activated by pulling a pin, like a hand grenade.

"It's totally safe as long as the pin's in place." JB told Phillips, pointing at the device.

Once again, Charlie was surprised to see his professorial friend be the one to react most quickly in response to a dangerous situation. And what was with the explosives expertise?

Bob and Agent Jankowski worked to free the diver from the net while, at the same time, trying to restrain him. Agent Jankowski pinned him down while Bob cut away the netting and unbuckled the Scuba gear. After the diver was free of his gear, Agent Jankowski reached for his handcuffs.

The diver kicked rapidly, hitting the agent in the hip and catapulting him into the water. The neoprene man stood up rapidly, still hanging on to the dive knife, and began running down the dock toward JB.

Charlie thought, "Uh oh."

JB stood nonchalantly in the middle of the dock as the black figure ran toward him with knife arm extended. At the last minute, JB deftly parried the knife arm, brought his knee into the man's stomach, and chopped him on the back of the neck. The diver collapsed onto the dock, a pile of wet neoprene.

Charlie walked up and quietly said to JB, "You've got some explaining to do."

Agent Jankowski pulled himself out of the water with Kate's help and angrily walked over to the diver, who had already been handcuffed by Bob. He reached down, pulled back the neoprene hood, and said, "We finally got you, Halburg, you son of a bitch."

Kate approached the handcuffed man and returned his direct gaze. He was average height with a compact, muscular build. His hair and complexion were dark, and his eyes revealed a hint of Asian in their ancestry. Kate said, "That's not Frank Halburg."

Thirty

Agents Jankowski and Phillips were severely frustrated. After capturing the midnight marauder, they had interrogated him for two hours, during which time he had said exactly nothing. He just sat there half asleep, apparently totally immune to police interrogation techniques. The agents yelled, cajoled, threatened, and nearly resorted to physical violence, but the Mole's expression never changed. In spite of themselves, they were impressed by the Mole's ability to resist all of the psychological tricks they could muster without even breaking a sweat. Ultimately, they gave up. They collected his fingerprints and a DNA sample and locked him up in the Homer jail.

No reply had arrived regarding the mystery man's prints as of Saturday morning. So far they didn't even know who the guy was. They discovered that he had apparently rented two cars under two names using two different IDs, neither of which was actually his. They found a duffle bag containing some clothes and personal items in the sedan that he had left at the harbor before his underwater adventure, but nothing in it gave any clue to his real identity. His forged driver's licenses were very well done and may have been provided by a professional document forger.

They had arrested Nancy, the FlashFrozen connection, at her home that morning. She had been quite a busy lady as far as recruiting customers for Darryl, but her overall knowledge of the drug distribution business in the Homer area was pretty much limited to local end-users. They determined that she probably did not know very much beyond her limited sphere. She had been acquainted with Frank Halburg when he worked at FlashFrozen and knew that he was somehow connected to drugs, but she had not seen him since he was fired. She claimed that the only person with whom she had discussed

Kate's inquiries was Darryl; no one else at FlashFrozen had been involved. She knew she was going to be fired and was very concerned about the welfare of her daughter. She was placed in jail while she made arrangements for bail. The agents decided to let the Super Trooper question her further regarding members of his town who had been purchasing illegal substances. They were only interested in the big picture.

†

Izzy reclined in his favorite chair with a light beer in one hand and the TV remote in the other. A football game had just ended, and he was searching for a new sporting event to fill his Saturday morning. He clicked to the outdoor channel, which was featuring trophy bass fishing in Alabama; that seemed like a good mindless choice. He had no desire to do anything else for the entire day.

The fishing trip with Aldo, in combination with the stressful visit from the Mole, had wiped him out. On the one hand, he was ticked that he had not heard from the Mole, since he was now without $2,000 worth of his favorite diving gear, but on the other hand he would be happy never to see the Mole again. He just wanted to vegetate for the rest of the day, actually for the rest of his life.

His wife Astrid had spent half the morning ranting about his laziness, but she had finally left to visit friends, thank goodness. Astrid was a strong-willed woman and ruled the household with an iron fist. While Izzy was short and wiry, Astrid was tall and big-boned like her brother, with blond hair and a square, plain face. Izzy knew that Astrid could probably beat the heck out of him if she ever wanted to, but fortunately she was a basically gentle person and their conflicts were all verbal.

The phone rang, and when Izzy picked up, he was surprised to hear that it was Erik Johnson, an old friend of Aldo's from Seldovia. He told Izzy that Aldo's boat had been towed to Seldovia from somewhere out in Cook Inlet and was now moored in the Seldovia harbor. The rumor going around town was that the boat had been confiscated by the authorities. Izzy had no idea what was going on, but told Erik that he would look into it and retrieve the boat if necessary. He had some knowledge of Aldo's various enterprises and was not totally surprised about the law enforcement angle, but he was puzzled as to why the boat had been out in the inlet, especially since they had just returned from a long, harrowing fishing trip.

In the back of his mind, Izzy had always coveted Aldo's boat, and now it sounded like Aldo might have abandoned it. He and Astrid would be the logical people to assume ownership. The thought of calling the authorities and asking about it did not appeal to him. He had always treasured his anonymity, and not many people knew of the relationship between Astrid and Aldo. But, on the other hand, how else was he going to find out anything? The Lucinda was a great boat and, he wanted it badly.

He picked up the phone and hesitantly dialed Trooper headquarters. The answering machine picked up, and he left a brief message asking about the status of the Lucinda. He grabbed another beer out of the refrigerator and went back to his recliner. Just as the manly TV fishing guide was repeating for the tenth time, "That sure is a beautiful fish you have there, Stan…what a dandy," a black SUV pulled into his driveway, spitting gravel onto the side of his house as it came to a rapid stop. Izzy peeked out the window. Shit, he'd managed to screw things up again.

Agent Jankowski knocked hard on the door to the cabin and announced that he was a drug enforcement agent. Izzy meekly opened the door and was more or less pushed aside by the agents. He wisely cooperated and did his best to answer questions. Everything he told them was mostly the truth. He was married to Aldo's sister and he sometimes worked as a deckhand for Aldo during salmon and halibut fishing seasons. He had no idea where Aldo was and had no clue how his boat ended up in Seldovia. He considered the boat a valuable family asset and simply wanted to retrieve it. The agents informed him that, for now, the boat was evidence in a federal drug investigation, and they did not know when it might be released, if ever.

When asked about Aldo's involvement with drug distribution, he indicated that he didn't know anything about it. In truth, all he knew was that Aldo had rendezvoused with another boat in the Gulf of Alaska on two occasions when he was on board, and a cooler labeled "salmon roe bait" had been transferred between the boats. He was pretty sure that the cooler contained something other than bait. He felt it would be best not to mention the secret rendezvous.

The agents did not ask and he did not mention his visit from the Mole. He indicated that Astrid would be returning in late afternoon and the agents said that they would be back then to question her. Izzy allowed that that was okay. Astrid and Aldo had become estranged long ago. She knew even less about Aldo's life than he did.

†

Frog placed the stencil over the tail section of his beloved Cessna and sprayed black enamel, superimposing a new registration number over the old number, which had been hidden by white paint the previous evening. He was standing inside a small run-down hangar on a remote island south of Ketchikan. The Rainbow Inn was about two miles away on the other side of the island. The short, grassy runway was little used and the hangar doors were about to fall off, but the plane was hidden from view. A trail through the forest led to a small cabin on the water a few hundred yards from the airstrip.

Frog returned to the cabin for lunch. Aldo was sitting at a ratty dinette table staring out the window at the ocean, a full glass of scotch in front of him. At one time, the cabin had been used by married employees of the Rainbow Inn, who had commuted to the Inn via a trail over the top of the island using ATVs. Now the trail was overgrown and barely visible, but still marginally usable. Aldo was dreaming of a steak dinner prepared by the Inn's chef, but he knew that they needed to stay out of sight. It was just a matter of time before the authorities started snooping at the Rainbow Inn. For now, their hideout was ideal; few people even knew about the airstrip and the hangar looked abandoned. The primary problem was that the kitchen cabinets contained only canned beans and packages of pilot bread. Food was evidently not a high priority for the previous occupants. It was going to be a long couple of days.

Aldo gazed out at the seals and water birds playing in the calm waters of the Inside Passage. He had always been a man of the northern seas and was wondering how he was going to adapt to the warm waters and white sand that awaited him at the end of his escape route. He had weighed various options for getting to his final destination, but had opted for the simplest solution. Reservations had already been made on commercial airline flights starting from Ketchikan and continuing on through. His new identification documents were foolproof, and he was well on his way to growing a full beard. The plan was for one of the float planes owned by Rainbow Inn to drop him off in Ketchikan the following day. By that time, things should have cooled down somewhat.

A quiet knock on the door was followed by the entrance of a tall man carrying a large backpack. He was slender and appeared very fit for a man in his sixties. His longish white hair and boyish features belied his age. He and Aldo embraced. Aldo had not seen John Vander in person in over twenty-five years, although they had spoken occasionally on the phone. Vander had been Aldo's corporal during those awful times of long ago. He and Aldo had been close friends and had traveled around together in the years after the war. Eventually they went their separate ways – Aldo inevitably wandering back to the family homestead on Kachemak Bay and John starting various businesses in the Pacific Northwest. But they had always been connected by the drug distribution network that had somehow survived the Vietnam War and continued to the present day. Even though both were self-supporting in legitimate ways, the profits from the drug business were too high to give up.

And so here they were, the drug empire finally crumbling after nearly forty years of successful operation. Now they both had to take refuge. Vander had secretly sold the Rainbow Inn several weeks earlier to a buyer who had no knowledge of the illicit activities that had gone on there. All the employees had been laid off. The new buyer was scheduled to take over the operation in a week's time. It was the start of the off-season, and the Inn would be inactive until the following spring. John and Aldo were going to follow similar, but different, escape paths and maybe meet up at some time in the future.

The plan was for Frog to fly Vander to the small town of Wrangell, where he would catch a commercial flight on route to a southern destination. Like Aldo's, his new documentation included an identity that provided him with a long-term visa to a convenient foreign destination where substantial funds would be waiting for him. Frog had reasonably asked John and Aldo what he was supposed to do after dropping Vander off. The answer had basically been that he could do whatever he wanted, but they didn't want to know what his plans were. As a reward for Frog's dedicated service, they had provided him with new identity papers, as well as forged documentation for his airplane that matched the new registration numbers. They told him that he should be able to start a new life somewhere without too much problem. He was not so sure.

Frog and John Vander took off from the small strip. Both of them were beginning a new chapter in their lives. Aldo was left to sit and wait for his floatplane pick up the following afternoon. He tipped the bottle of whiskey and refilled his glass.

Thirty-one

Buster prowled the perimeter of the small master's cabin of the Shearwater, impatient for his people to wake up. He wasn't used to the confined space of a boat and badly needed to get some exercise. Plus, there was no litter box in the sleeping cabin, and he really needed to pee. In frustration, he jumped up on the bed and pounced onto Kate's chest, immediately burrowing into the down comforter. In spite of himself, he began purring.

Kate opened one eye and scowled at Buster. Turning her head, she looked at the alarm clock and was surprised to see that it was almost noon. The events of the previous night began to come back to her, and she wasn't sure what to think. She had hoped that the capture of the guy who was running around shooting people would solve all their problems, but there were still major loose ends. Who was the mystery man? Where the hell was Frank Halburg? Was he even in Alaska? And which one of them had actually killed Rodolfo and Jake Halburg? Were she and Charlie still in danger? Could she ever go back to work again? Aghhh!

Kate slipped on some sweat clothes and quietly went out on deck, followed by a relieved Buster, who immediately ran to his litter box and squatted. The frantic look on Buster's face was immediately replaced by a look of rapture and contentment. If only human beings could achieve inner peace so easily. The quiet beauty of the morning was such an extreme contrast to the previous night that she was having trouble getting her mind around the drama and violence that had occurred just a few hours earlier. A man nobody knew had tried to blow up the Shearwater in hopes of permanently eliminating both her and Charlie. It was the second attempt on their life, but the attempts

203

had involved two different people. It seemed confusing and highly improbable that someone could want them dead that badly.

Entering the pilothouse, Kate started the coffee and thought about breakfast. Attempted murder was no reason to stop eating. In fact, it was probably all the more reason to eat like crazy. She scarfed a stale donut left over from last night's vigil to tide her over until she could come up with something more substantial.

The boat rocked, and JB swung his gangly frame on board by hanging on the rigging and dropping to the deck. "It's about time you guys got up." He poured himself a cup of coffee.

"Come aboard and have some coffee," Kate said. "How are you feeling this morning? Did you get hurt last night?"

"No, I'm fine."

"I won't even ask how you acquired the skills you exhibited last night. I'll wait for Charlie to do that. But I would like to thank you for your help."

"You're welcome. It appeared that the local authorities weren't quite up to the task."

"You are a very enigmatic person."

"I do my best." JB grinned.

Kate began to get some feel for the depth of the very strange person sitting next to her. "Charlie said you were writing a scholarly book. What is it about?"

"Back when I was a genuine academic, I did a bunch of research on political polarization in America. It has always fascinated me how seemingly reasonable people can end up with such divergent opinions, given that the reality of the universe is the same for everyone. But, more important, it is even more puzzling why divergent groups become so obsessive about their points of view that they lose all sense of perspective and basically sabotage any real hope for reasoned solutions to real problems. Various events in my life have caused me to become pretty cynical about human nature, which might not be a totally healthy thing. Therefore, I concluded that writing a book about this stuff might serve as a form of therapy. So that is what I am doing."

"That sounds pretty noble. How much have you written?"

"I was afraid you were going to ask that. I have completed an outline and the first couple of chapters. Progress has been slow, and my ability to focus hasn't been optimal. I keep getting diverted by sex and underwater marauders."

"I know the feeling. Let me know if you need any help. I'm a pretty good editor."

"Thanks. I'll consider your kind offer."

Kate cracked eggs into a frying pan as Charlie entered the cabin looking fresh and wide awake.

"You look like you got a good night's sleep," Kate said.

"Yeah, I guess sleep deprivation was able to overcome last night's adrenalin rush. I feel ready to tackle the world's problems."

"How about if we start with our problems?"

"Speaking of which, has anybody heard from the Super Trooper this morning?"

"Not yet. Let's eat." Kate dished out eggs and toast.

"OK, Mr. Martial Arts, time for an explanation," Charlie announced as they sat at the dinette.

"All right, I guess I can give you a partial explanation. For various reasons, I can't go into detail. In your attempts to get information on my life from Google, you may have noticed that my illustrious academic career did not start until I was twenty-six. So that leaves a gap of nine years between the time when I left home at age seventeen and when I started college. During those years, I had the opportunity to learn and practice a range of physical and mental skills that prepared me for survival in a wide variety of circumstances. The training was similar but more extensive than that received by special military units. I also received training in selected worldwide languages, history, and culture."

"But there is no record of your having been in the military."

"You have been busy. That is correct."

"That's it. That's all you're going to say?"

"Yep."

"So you were sort of a spy? An off-the-books government agent?" Kate asked.

JB shrugged his shoulders and looked inscrutable. Charlie looked frustrated, but Kate chimed in. "Well, I'm satisfied. Sort of. Maybe we should move on."

JB smiled, nodded his head, and took a final bite of eggs. The Shearwater shuddered as the Super Trooper came on board and joined them at the table. "How are the three musketeers this morning?"

"We're better than we were last night," Kate answered. "I hope you have some encouraging news for us this morning."

"Not so much. The mystery man refused to answer any questions, and we have not received any hits on his prints, so we still have no idea who the hell he is. The DEA guys interrogated him for a couple of hours. He just sat there with a blank look on his face. Jankowski came close to clobbering him, but his expression never changed. We've been following up on other leads. It turns out that Aldo's sister and brother-in-law live in Homer. The brother-in-law got wind of the fact that Aldo's boat was abandoned and called my office to inquire about it. The agents immediately swooped down and questioned him, but didn't find out much. They'll question the sister this afternoon. On another front, the Feds have plans to raid the Rainbow Inn sometime today. I think they are also going to try to question Jake Halburg's father. Still no word on Aldo's whereabouts. So the bottom line is, we are still trying to piece things together."

"Thanks for the update. So what now?" Charlie asked.

"I guess we wait for the Feds to do their thing. I'm not sure what we can do around here to help things."

JB looked at Bob. "I think it is kind of odd that there are no records of the midnight marauder's prints. Given his set of skills, it seems likely that he had military training somewhere along the line. His prints have to be on record some place unless they have been intentionally classified."

Charlie looked at JB and could not help thinking that maybe JB was in a special position to understand these things.

"The Feds also took a DNA sample, but it will be a while before the results are in. It seems kind of unlikely that there would be DNA records if there aren't any fingerprint records. I don't know how we find out who the guy is if he isn't willing to divulge any information," Bob said. "I have to go take care of some town business, so I'll check back with you later. Meanwhile, keep your eyes open. We still have no idea whether Frank Halburg is in the area or what his connection is to the mystery man."

"Hey, Bob," Kate yelled as the Super Trooper stepped onto the dock. "Tell the agents to ask Aldo's sister whether Aldo had a son."

†

Rob Smithers was sitting at his station in the small control tower at the Wrangell Airport. He generally worked alone, alternating shifts with another part-time controller. Just as he took a large bite of his bologna sandwich, his radio came alive with the disembodied voice of a pilot requesting permission to land. The pilot identified the plane as a Cessna 180 and recited his tail number.

Prominently displayed on the wall above Rob's desk was a notice from the FAA and DEA requesting that all controllers be on the alert for a white Cessna 180 with a designated tail number. The number reported by the approaching pilot did not match the number in the notice. Choking down a big chunk of sandwich, Rob proceeded to instruct the pilot. As the plane approached, he noticed that it was, indeed, white, but, since white Cessna 180s were one of the most common planes in Alaska, he did not think much about it. At least ten white 180s had passed through the airport since the notice came out.

But as the plane taxied in front of the tower on its way to the tie-down area, Rob noticed that the paint at the tail end of the fuselage was a slightly different shade than the rest of the plane. Grabbing his binoculars, he looked at the registration numbers; the black paint was glossy as if freshly applied, and faint dark shadows were visible under the surrounding white paint. Old numbers had been recently painted over and replaced with new.

The plane continued to the public area at the end of the taxiway, and two persons disembarked. One of the persons, apparently the passenger, walked toward the commercial terminal, carrying a large backpack. Rob picked up the phone and dialed the Wrangell Police Department. Getting no answer, he dialed 911 and asked the dispatcher, with whom he played poker on Thursday nights, to contact the police chief and have him call the tower. A few minutes later the chief called and Rob filled him in on his suspicions. The chief, who was also a member of the Thursday night poker group, indicated that he would look at the plane and maybe check the registration papers and pilot ID. The alert that had also come to his office contained the wanted pilot's name, Paul Larchmont, but no photo or description had been supplied, so visual recognition was not possible.

The chief pulled his black and white SUV alongside the white Cessna and hailed the pilot, who was attaching tie-down ropes to the ground anchors. The chief indicated that he was investigating an airplane theft and asked if he could see the registration papers and pilot's license. Frog produced all the paperwork, including his pilot's license and driver's license with his new identification. Everything appeared to be in order. Fortunately for Frog, the chief just looked at the papers and did not ask him for his name, because he had forgotten to look at the new documents to see what it was. The chief walked around the plane and surreptitiously looked at the new registration numbers. The painted-over numbers were too obscured to read, but it was obvious that the number had recently been changed or at least repainted.

The chief went back to the station. Since all of the plane's papers were in order and the pilot's name did not match the one that was given in the wanted notice, there was no basis for arrest. But changing plane numbers is a big deal, and he was not comfortable with the situation. He called the Los Angeles number provided on the wanted notice and was connected to a drug enforcement agent who recorded the information and promised to forward it to the agents working the case. The chief felt that he had done all that he could under the circumstances. He closed the office and went home for lunch.

Agent Jankowski's cell phone rang as he was finishing his lunch with Agent Phillips at the Mariner's Café. The home office agent briefed him on the call that he had received from Wrangell. Agent Jankowski asked the agent from LA to check the manifest for any commercial flight that was due to leave Wrangell that afternoon to see if the name Aldo Fenstrom appeared on it. He then called the Wrangell police chief and, with some intimidation, enlisted his help in investigating further. He asked the chief to question the air traffic controller further in hopes of obtaining a physical description of the man who had walked from the Cessna to the commercial terminal. He also asked him to take another look at the tail numbers to see if he could make out any of the old numbers.

The chief did as he was requested. The passenger from the mystery plane was described as a tall and lanky man in his sixties with longish white hair. He had been carrying a large hiker's backpack. When the chief returned to the Cessna, the pilot was nowhere to be seen. Consequently, he was able to take a long, careful look at the newly-painted area of the fuselage. Tilting his head just right to achieve the maximum angle of sunlight, he was able to see shadows of some of the old numbers and letters, allowing a partial reconstruction of the original tail number. He immediately reported back to Agent Jankowski, who was disappointed and confused that the passenger did not match Aldo Fenstrom's description. However, the partial tail number did match the number of the wanted plane.

The DEA agent informed the chief that there was an arrest warrant for Paul Larchmont and asked the chief to arrest the Cessna's pilot. The chief complained that the pilot had identification and plane registration papers that gave a different name. How was he to be sure that this was the right guy? Agent Jankowski indicated that he would fax Larchmont's Alaska driver's license photo for confirmation, but he stressed that Larchmont should be picked up right away, before he had a chance to take off again.

The chief regretted that he had called the DEA in the first place. He was used to the quiet tempo of Wrangell life, and having to do things quickly went against his nature. Nevertheless, after confirming that the pilot was indeed the guy that the DEA was after, he went to the only place where he figured that Larchmont, or whatever his name was, would be – the only restaurant within walking distance of the airport. Before he entered Kathy's Deli, he could see the pilot sitting at a table in the back. He contemplated calling his only deputy, who was currently off duty, for backup, but decided to go ahead and make the arrest on his own. Frog was not too surprised to see the chief again. Since leaving Seward, he had assumed that his life was pretty much out of his control, and he had begun to take a fatalistic view of his sorry existence. Much to the chief's relief, he went quietly.

Thirty-two

The Mole was hungry. He was sitting on the edge of his rock-hard bunk in the Anchorage jail. Fortunately, he had been given special status as a federal fugitive and was in a cell by himself. He was not afraid of other inmates, but he was in no mood to deal with the drama that cellmates always seemed to cause. How had things gotten so screwed up? He was used to being one step ahead of his opponents, but somehow this time they had been one step ahead of him. He was pretty sure that the law enforcement officers had not figured things out on their own. He blamed Charlie Skyler and his nosy girlfriend for his present situation.

The jail officials had informed him that he would be transferred to a federal facility in the lower forty-eight within a couple of days. He knew that his chances of communicating with the outside world would diminish once he was actually in federal prison; consequently, he hoped to maximize his opportunities while in the moderately leaky Anchorage facility.

He heard the guard coming down the corridor with the afternoon meal and eagerly anticipated his arrival, not only because he was hungry. As the tray with its plateful of generic meat, potatoes, and gravy was passed through the food slot, the guard made momentary eye contact. The Mole carried the food back to his bunk and began to eat hungrily. The food was terrible, but his training had prepared him and he was able to blank out the taste, knowing that it was important to get enough to eat. He imagined that it was filet mignon. Reaching for his fork, he slipped his finger under the plate and felt the presence of a folded piece of paper. Pretending to drop his bread, he turned his body to block the surveillance cameras and slipped the paper under his pillow. He sat back down and finished the disgusting meal, eating every morsel.

The Mole had learned that there was a time period after lights out when there was still enough dim light from the small window high overhead to read, but probably not enough light for the surveillance cameras to get a clear picture. He carefully placed the note inside a Penthouse magazine and lay back on his bunk. The note was handwritten in small script:

How the hell did you get caught? A. is on his way south. The operation is toast. Will try to get info on your transfer. Keep eyes open.
F.

The Mole smiled. He knew he could count on him. But after a few moments reflection, the Mole's mood changed back again. The easy life that he had known for the last twenty years was coming to an end. Although he was good at it, he was tired of being the enforcer. It was exciting at times, but also involved a lot of careful planning, which was boring. The thought of a legitimate career also seemed to be out of the question. Talk about boring. Maybe he could be a beach bum. But that idea involved a couple of difficult assumptions: first, he would need to escape from jail and successfully change his identity; and, second, he would need money. He was not sure how the money situation would play out, especially since a lot of the money appeared to be in an offshore bank account to which nobody currently had access – except possibly himself.

†

The DEA agents managed to make their way back to Izzy's house in late afternoon. Astrid had agreed to talk to them, although she was clear that she did not know much about Aldo's affairs and could not care less about his alleged illegal activities. In spite of her tough front, Astrid was a naturally friendly and talkative person, and once she got started, she enthusiastically described what it was like growing up at Fenstrom's Lagoon. Her grandfather had originally settled in Fenstrom's Lagoon in 1915, purchasing the eighty acres for next to nothing. He developed a fox farming operation in the 1920s at a time when the market for blue fox pelts was at its peak. Commercial fishing had always served as a second occupation as well as a means of acquiring food for the foxes. But the market for farm-raised foxes gradually diminished during the Depression and disappeared completely during WWII. After the mid-1940s, the primary family occupation was commercial fishing. Her grandparents had only one child, Astrid's and Aldo's father. Both of Astrid's grandparents died when she was a little girl. The next ten years were relatively happy with all family members contributing to their difficult lifestyle. But then, when she was twelve years old, her mother died of cancer. Since she was female and three years older than Aldo, she ended up taking over most of the household management. Their father was a stern, unemotional man who became even more detached after his wife died. He lived for fishing and mostly moped around the cabin during the rest of the year. To his credit, he did take a couple of hours every morning to homeschool Astrid and Aldo. He felt that education was important and did a reasonably good job providing basic skills.

Astrid had fond memories of the times the three of them spent on their fishing boat. Her father seemed to come alive, and the fishing trips almost seemed fun. But then they would come home, and her father would resume his position on the sofa with his ever-present glass of whiskey. He was never physically abusive, but when he was drunk, he would withdraw as if he was not there. When Astrid turned fifteen, she rebelled and arranged on her own to move into Homer with her aunt so that she could have a normal life and a normal high school education. Aldo remained at Fenstrom's Lagoon with his father. Aldo never forgave Astrid for leaving the lagoon.

When Aldo was seventeen, his father made him take the test for high school equivalency, which he easily passed. A few months later, he was drafted into the Army. He spent two years stateside and then was shipped to Vietnam. Astrid was vaguely aware that things did not go well in Vietnam, but she had no idea of any of the details. When Aldo returned, he was a different person. He was totally obsessed with arranging the immigration of a Vietnamese woman whom he had met during his tour and with whom he was apparently in love. After about a year and a half, she finally arrived in Homer, and they went to live at Fenstrom's Lagoon.

Astrid had met Aldo's common-law wife only a couple of times, but she could tell that she was not happy. About a year after they began to live together, they had a son. Rumor was that she wanted to take the child and return to Vietnam, but Aldo would not let her. She lived at Fenstrom's Lagoon for a couple more years, until she finally could not take it anymore. Vietnamese friends living in Homer helped her escape and paid her way back to Vietnam. The boy, whose name was Robert, stayed with Aldo for a while longer. Then the strangest thing happened – the boy just disappeared. When asked what had happened, Aldo just said that the child was living with the family of one of his Army buddies in the lower forty-eight. He claimed that this family would be able to take much better care of Robert than he could. And that was the last that Astrid had heard of the boy. Aldo continued to live a solitary life across the bay.

By the time Astrid finished her monologue on the Fenstrom family, Agent Jankowski was yawning and bored. He could not care less about her family drama – he just wanted to go catch bad guys and could not see that talking to this dowdy woman and her mousy husband was helping to accomplish that objective. But Agent Phillips was not so sure that Aldo's history was irrelevant. He was beginning to get vague feelings that it was all interconnected. In particular, he wondered about Kate Perkins' suggestion that they ask Astrid whether Aldo had a son. Clearly, Kate had some insight that they did not have.

As much as he hated to admit it, Charlie Skyler and Kate Perkins were pretty much responsible for most of the progress that they had made on this weird case. He decided that they deserved more respect and that another discussion was in order. All he had to do was rein in his overenthusiastic and not very perceptive partner.

†

Agent Tom March and his young partner, Beverly Milford, had been dispatched from the Los Angeles DEA headquarters to investigate a remote fishing lodge in Alaska suspected of being involved with drug trafficking. They had a warrant for the arrest of the owner, one John Vander. The partners had left early in the morning and had finally reached their destination in the afternoon.

The Rainbow Inn was harder to get to than some third world villages. The flights from LA to Seattle to Ketchikan were bad enough. Approaching the Ketchikan airport between the mountains in low overcast conditions was scary, but then, since the airport was on an island, they had had to take a ferry from the airport to the mainland. This was followed by a taxi ride to the float plane terminal. Their chartered plane was a six-passenger de Havilland Beaver with a humongous radial engine. Agent March thought that radial engines had gone out with WWII. It had to be the loudest plane he had ever encountered. Appropriately, the passengers were all issued earplugs.

On takeoff, the plane plowed through the whitecaps, threading its way between various small boats and alongside a monstrous cruise ship before lifting off and leaving the busy Ketchikan waterfront. Because of the low ceiling, the plane flew at an altitude of about four hundred feet, following the complex straits and passages between the islands of the Inland Passage. Beverly thought that they might as well be in a boat. After an hour, they banked left, touched down next to an island, and taxied up to a well-maintained dock. Before they even reached the dock, Agent March knew that they were too late. The place looked deserted.

The Rainbow Inn compound consisted of a large, well-groomed grassy area between the waterfront and the beautiful three-story lodge building constructed of large diameter logs. About twelve individual log cabins were arranged in a semicircle around the lodge. All was immaculate. Scattered old-growth Douglas fir completed the rustic, yet luxurious atmosphere. The partners approached the lodge and found that it was locked. Hearing a noise behind the lodge, they approached what looked like a maintenance garage and found a scruffy, bearded man wearing Carhartt pants with suspenders over a wool shirt. He was working on an industrial-size lawn mower, and, judging from the number of parts scattered around, he was not having much luck. They identified themselves as Federal agents and the man immediately said, "Holy shit. What have I done now?"

"As far as we know, you haven't done anything," replied Beverly. "We're looking for the owner – Mr. Vander."

"I don't know anything about a Mr. Vander, and, as far as I know, the owner lives in San Diego."

"Who are you, and what are you doing here?" asked Agent March.

"My name is Don Livingston, and I was just hired yesterday to be caretaker of this incredible place through the winter. From what I understand, the resort was just sold and the old occupants cleared out last week. I answered an ad in the Ketchikan newspaper for a caretaker and was hired sight unseen yesterday. I never met the owner. All the arrangements were made over the phone. So, here I am. This is my new home for the next seven months. I wasn't expecting visitors so quickly."

Agent Milford smiled at the likable Mr. Livingston and took in the beauty of the surroundings. She was thoroughly enjoying the adventure and was relieved to get out of the office. Unfortunately, Agent March did not share her appreciation of the situation. They had just wasted a lot of time on a wild goose chase, and his butt was sore from sitting on hard airplane seats.

"Do you mind if we look around?" Beverly asked.

"Actually, we have a search warrant, so it doesn't matter whether you mind or not," Agent March interjected.

"Help yourselves. You can spend the whole winter here if you want," Don said as he handed Beverly a ring of keys and winked lasciviously.

The two agents headed for the lodge. It was even more beautiful inside than outside. Although there were the token dead animal heads hanging on the wall, the interior furnishings had obviously been selected by a professional designer. Even the expression on the moose head appeared upbeat, as if he had felt it was a privilege to be killed and put on display in this cool spot. All the furniture and furnishings were still in place.

There were two computers behind the registration desk. Beverly turned one of them on and found all the latest office and hotel management software installed and ready to go, but there were absolutely no non-program files, as if the computer were brand new. She checked the hard drive status and found that it was almost empty. Opening the computer, she noted that the hard drive had no dust, suggesting that it had been recently replaced. Donning latex gloves, she removed the hard drive and put it in an evidence bag. She repeated the exercise with the other computer. Beverly informed her boss that they would get no information from the hard drives, except possibly the fingerprints of whoever had installed them. A computer-savvy person had obviously gone over everything to remove past records. All drawers and filing cabinets were empty.

A storage room for office supplies still contained some miscellaneous office items such as paper and equipment manuals. In the far back corner of the closet-like space was a pile of empty cardboard boxes and other discarded items. Beverly pulled out some of the boxes and uncovered an old dust-covered computer that had been thrown away years before. The people who had sanitized the inn had missed this item. She removed the hard drive and added it to her evidence stash, thinking that maybe something useful could be found in the old piece of equipment.

Beverly emerged from the closet, brushing dust off her clothes, and found Agent March sitting on the cushy leather sofa facing the large picture windows that looked out on the mist-shrouded islands in the distance. He was scowling and muttering to himself, when his phone rang. The home office had outfitted them with a fancy combination satellite and cell phone so that they would be reachable regardless of their location in the Alaska wilderness. Beverly inferred from his attitude that he was talking to someone who was his superior. His final words were, "Okay, we're on our way."

Agent March explained to his partner that he had been speaking to Agent Phillips, and they had been ordered to immediately take the float plane to Wrangell, wherever the hell that was, and take over the custody and questioning of a small plane pilot who was suspected in the escape of Aldo Fenstrom. He had dropped off a passenger, but the passenger did not fit Aldo's description. The description did, however, fit Vander's description so it was also possible that John Vander was in Wrangell and about to take off for parts unknown. Agent March proceeded to complain about having to spend more time in this godforsaken primitive territory. Beverly thought it was way cool.

Thirty-three

Kate and Charlie were determined to have a normal evening, so they spent a couple of hours with JB drinking beer at the Rusty Harpoon. Kate was introduced to some of the harbor regulars, all of whom were interesting in their own ways, but at the same time exhibiting most of the normal annoying characteristics that men in bars seem to assume when there is an attractive woman around. Kate had long since stopped being impressed by macho games, and it quickly grew tiresome. Charlie suggested that they go out for dinner, and JB, sensing that they wanted to be alone, elected to go back to his boat and "work on his book."

They went across the road to a small restaurant that sold wood-fired pizza and settled in at a table on the balcony overlooking the bay. After their pizza had arrived and they had gazed out at the water for a while, Kate said, "Have you had enough of this normalcy so we can go back to talking about drug dealing and mysterious killers?"

"I thought you would never ask. Why did you want to know whether Aldo had a son?"

"I don't know if you have been thinking the same thing that I've been thinking, but the midnight marauder had some Asian features, suggesting some kind of Eurasian heritage. The boy in the father and son picture that you found in Aldo's cabin also had Asian features, and the woman pictured with Aldo as a young man looked like she could be from Southeast Asia. It all sort of fits together. Aldo's organization seems to be anchored by the friendships he made in Vietnam, including with Stuart Halburg and his two sons. It seems logical that Aldo's son might be involved also."

"I have been thinking the same thing, but we still don't know why the mystery man is so mysterious. If he is Aldo's son, why has his existence been erased from the earth?"

"If his specialty is eliminating people, then there would be a definite advantage to being anonymous and untraceable."

"It's not that easy to remove records of your existence. He probably would have required professional help. Nevertheless, I like your theory," Charlie replied.

"So I guess a crucial question is whether Frank Halburg and the mystery man were working together. Brett Fishbein claimed that he got his orders to torch my cabin from Frank. And then the mystery man shows up and takes over the business of eliminating witnesses and other assorted annoying persons. It seems like they must have been working together. If that's the case, then who is giving orders to whom?"

Charlie took a bite of pizza. "I agree with everything you say. Maybe the Halburg brothers and Aldo's son were basically equal in the eyes of the organization. Aldo probably called the shots. Maybe he is still calling the shots from wherever he is. I don't think the DEA guys ever went back to Aldo's cabin to get information on his communication equipment. It seems like it would be worth a shot."

"Sounds good to me. Let's suggest it to the three stooges. It might be a good excuse for a boat trip."

"I thought you've had enough of boats for a while."

"I don't know. I was starting to enjoy myself until it got too calm."

"Right."

Charlie called the trooper office and left a message suggesting that they might want to visit Aldo's cabin to see what they could learn.

†

For reasons known only to God or the forces of evolution, depending on your personal viewpoint, the Super Trooper was back in Julie Fishbein's hospital room. He had unaccountably become very fond of the troubled young woman. The forces of lust and compassion had become combined in Bob's brain, and he was trying to figure out ways to help her. He had convinced the DEA guys to allow her to remain in the hospital, ostensibly for her own protection, but in reality so that she could be given drugs to help her deal with cocaine withdrawal. He did not want her to be in a lonely jail cell. The doctors had prescribed a combination of narcotic drugs on a gradually reducing schedule, which seemed to have taken the edge off the withdrawal process. Julie understood that Bob was acting on her behalf and was very grateful. Since Bob had last visited, she had cleaned herself up and looked quite attractive. The chemistry between the unlikely couple appeared to be mutual.

"So, what's going to happen to me?" Julie asked.

"I don't know what charges the DEA guys might bring against you, but I'll ask them to be lenient. You were an innocent bystander to all of the bad stuff that was going on around you, plus you've been totally cooperative. The fact that you have already suffered because of the death of Darryl and the incarceration of your brother will likely also play into how they view your case. If it were up to me, I would only charge you with misdemeanor possession. With your clean record, there would be no jail time involved."

"I guess we wait to see what happens."

"Yeah. You may be able to increase your bargaining power by voluntarily agreeing to enroll in a drug treatment facility."

"I've looked into treatment before. Public treatment options are almost nonexistent in Alaska, and private programs are too expensive."

"I'll see what I can find out," Bob said. "There may be some other alternatives."

Julie reached out and took Bob's hand. Bob leaned over and kissed her on the forehead. As he did so, he was thinking how unprofessional his behavior was and wondering how many trooper regulations he was breaking. But, for once in his life, he didn't care.

†

Agents March and Milford observed a Boeing 737 lift off from the Wrangell Airport just as their float plane was approaching the Wrangell harbor. "Looks like half of our job here just left for parts unknown," said Agent March.

Beverly looked at her notes on the Wrangell flight schedules and nodded her head in agreement; it was the last flight south of the day, and the mystery passenger was most likely on it. But they still had to question the Cessna pilot and escort him back to the Los Angeles holding facility. She was looking forward to testing her interrogation skills and hoping that they could contribute something useful to the overall investigation.

After a twenty-minute wait, a dirty purple taxi pulled up to the harbormaster's office. The driver wore a cut-off Grateful Dead T-shirt and dirty jeans. His hair was in a single long braid. Colorful tropical birds frolicked on both of his arms. He threw their bags in the cluttered trunk and closed it using bungee cords. As they got underway, the cabby started chatting about Alaska's recent efforts to legalize marijuana. He explained that this latest effort was the third time that marijuana had been semi-legalized in Alaska. The marijuana laws vacillated depending on which political party happened to be in power. Seeing that her boss was about to explode, Beverly preempted his reply by agreeing that this was, indeed, an interesting situation.

Exiting the cab in front of the tiny police station, Agent March asked, "How can you be so nice to people like that? I'm beginning to think that most Alaskans are only half human."

"Well, for one thing, he may be the only cab driver in town, and we will probably be calling on him later. It's probably not a good strategy to get him pissed at us. Plus, the initiative process is perfectly legal. It's better to have people go through legal channels than to ignore the law altogether."

Agent March rolled his eyes and grumbled something unintelligible.

Inside the station they encountered the chief, who was briefing his deputy on the day's events. They introduced themselves and got as much information from the chief as they could. The deputy, Phil, showed them the way to the single holding cell where Frog was lying on his bunk staring at the ceiling. Frog was led to a small interrogation room and handcuffed to the chair.

Beverly began the questioning. "We know that your name is Paul Larchmont and, as of a few days ago, you lived in Seward, Alaska. We have a copy of your driver's license right here, and it matches your birth records and other documentation from your life up to this point. We also have your fingerprints, which match a misdemeanor arrest record from California. So you might as well forget about pretending to be someone else. OK?"

"OK." Since being thrown in jail, Frog had been in an intense debate with himself regarding what would be the best strategy, given his impossible situation. If he cooperated with the authorities, he would likely be eliminated by one of Aldo's men – unless everyone else was also put away. But what were the chances of that? On the other hand, he really didn't know all that much. Aldo had been very careful not to divulge any of his plans or his new identification. He had decided that he really didn't have that much to lose by cooperating. If Aldo was going to kill him, he would probably do it anyway.

"So, Paul, do you know a man named Aldo Fenstrom?"

"First of all, please call me Frog – everyone else does. Second, you already know that I know Aldo Fenstrom. My major problem is that Aldo and the people who work with him are very dangerous people. If he finds out that I am cooperating with you guys, he will kill me one way or another if he can find me. So I need some assurance that you can protect me."

"We understand that Fenstrom is dangerous. There have already been three murders in Homer. We'll do what we can to protect you."

"Three murders! Shit. I didn't have anything to do with them. Hell, I don't know anything about them. What about the witness protection program?"

"If information you provide us leads to the capture and conviction of any of the main players, then I will talk to my bosses about witness protection. Meanwhile, we'll keep you under guard and isolated. OK?"

"OK."

"My first question is, who was the passenger you dropped off here in Wrangell and what were his plans?"

"The man's name is John Vander. He had a new passport, but I don't know what name was on it, and I don't know what his final destination was."

"So Vander was the owner of the Rainbow Inn and was an associate of Aldo Fenstrom?"

"That's right."

"Was Vander on the flight that left here about an hour ago?"

"I assume so."

Agent March left the room to call the home office and report the presence of a fugitive on the Wrangell-Seattle flight that was currently still in the air.

Beverly continued, "It seems like they were closing down the entire operation. Did it seem like that to you?"

"They didn't tell me what was going on, but part of my job was to plan and execute Aldo's emergency escape plan. He wouldn't leave the family property unless there was a good reason. Also, the Rainbow Inn was sold, and Vander flew the coop. That seems pretty drastic."

"Speaking of Aldo, when you were last seen up north, he was with you. What happened to him?"

"We flew down here, I left Aldo and picked up Vander, and here we are."

"Exactly where did you leave Aldo? And what were his plans?"

"I don't know what Aldo's plans are. They only told me what I needed to know. As far as his location, that is the first piece of information that might be really useful to you. I'm feeling a little uncomfortable about revealing it without better assurances of my safety."

At that point, Agent Morse came unglued. He grabbed Frog by the shirt and told him that his safety was in danger if he didn't answer. Agent Milford intervened and asked if she could continue the questioning. Frog wasn't sure whether they were playing good cop-bad cop or whether Agent March was just naturally obnoxious.

Beverly wasn't sure either. "Frog, after we leave here, we are both going to escort you to a Federal holding facility in Los Angeles. When you are there, you will be placed in isolation and guarded day and night. There is no reason why Aldo would even know that you have been captured, much less where you will be located."

"It's a mistake to underestimate Aldo. He knew that I was going to Wrangell. He has informers everywhere. He probably already knows that I am in jail."

"We have a chartered float plane, and we hope to leave as soon as we can. We can go wherever we want, and nobody will know where we're going. You have my word that Aldo is not going to know your location."

"Alright, but if I get killed, I'm going to be really pissed. I honestly don't know when Aldo was planning on leaving, but the last I saw him he was in a cabin on the other side of the island from the Rainbow Inn."

"Oh, shit," said Agent March. "We just came from there." He was going to be spending a lot more time in the torture chamber known as a Beaver. Beverly called the float plane pilot, who was hanging out at the docks with the other pilots. She asked whether it would be possible to fly back down to the Rainbow Inn. He said that the combination of darkness and approaching bad weather would make it impossible to fly back until the next day.

†

The Alaska Airlines flight from Wrangell to Seattle landed on time and taxied to the gate. Vander looked out the window and saw two black SUVs waiting at the jet way. He picked up his cell phone and dialed. When Aldo picked up, he said, "They're waiting for me at the gate. You need to change your plans and get out of there now." Vander hung up.

Aldo knew that Frog must have been intercepted in Wrangell, if they had already tracked down John Vander. He had to assume that Frog would blab his location, and that he could be next. He and Vander had discussed an alternative plan. One of the Rainbow Inn's outboard powered fishing skiffs was parked at the small dock below his cabin. It had plenty of gas. Although Aldo was not familiar with the area, he had spent his whole life on the water and had a portable GPS with marine charts installed. Vander had recommended an abandoned cabin in a hidden cove not too far away for an initial hideaway.

Aldo needed to figure out where he was going after that. Achieving his goal of a tropical getaway had just become much more difficult. He quickly packed some food, his belongings, and a couple bottles of whiskey down to the boat. The channel was deserted, and nobody saw him take off to make his way to the south.

Thirty-four

Mottled black and white pillowy clouds oozed over the narrow ridge of mountains separating Kachemak Bay from the expanse of northern ocean that extended unchecked to Hawaii and beyond. Descending whiteness engulfed rugged peaks and glaciers as gusty southeast winds pushed the waves up into a closely spaced chop with continuous whitecaps. The panorama was slate gray with a meringue topping. The salt air smelled of seaweed, decaying marine life, and storms.

The Shearwater slammed into the steep waves, one after another, wind-blown salt spray wetting the windshield with each dip of the bow. The windshield wipers were clacking like a crazed metronome. Charlie and Kate were comfortably settled into the pilot seat, Agents Phillips and Jankowski seated at the dinette table. Agent Jankowski had that peculiar look on his face that accompanies the early stages of seasickness. Kate was feeling especially smug, since she felt great in contrast to the obvious discomfort of the macho DEA guys. The harrowing experience while chasing Aldo into the inlet had given her a feeling of being an accomplished mariner.

While the wind was strong, the waves were not excessively large because of the short fetch in the sheltered bay. Charlie steered the Shearwater directly into the waves until they reached the windward side of the bay where conditions were more comfortable, then turned to the east toward Fenstrom's Lagoon. Once again he anchored in Bear Cove, only this time Charlie launched an inflatable dinghy with a small outboard to ferry everyone into the lagoon. Rain mixed with snow started to spit from the darkening clouds above. Agent Jankowski grumbled about Alaska's perpetually miserable weather.

Aldo's cabin appeared mostly unchanged since Charlie's last visit. The door was still unlocked, and most of Aldo's possessions were still there. The rifle that had hung from the rack above the door was conspicuously absent. The sink was filled with dirty dishes, clothing scattered on the floor and furniture. The photographs that had been on Aldo's dresser were untouched and were quickly thrown into an evidence bag, as were the contents of Aldo's desk drawers. His communication gear was gone, leaving only the wires dangling from the antennas. Agent Jankowski confirmed Charlie's suspicions that Aldo had used both satellite and cellular phone technology that would give him the ability to communicate to anywhere in the world.

"You guys had better look at this," yelled Kate, who had been rummaging around outside the cabin. One of the storage sheds was built into the side of a hill, and at the back of the shed was a hinged doorway apparently leading to a sort of root cellar excavated into the hillside. It appeared that lumber and plywood had been recently moved aside to expose the doorway and allow clear access. Agent Jankowski opened the heavy door and shone a flashlight into the dank space. At one side was a casket-shaped wooden box and, at the other, was an old cooler. Bob and Agent Jankowski carried the box into the open air and pried it open. Inside, packed in heavy plastic, were about two dozen AK-47 assault rifles and several hundred rounds of ammunition. "Wow," said Kate.

Agent Phillips brought out the small cooler. Inside was a brick-sized plastic-wrapped package containing a white powder. Oriental characters crudely scrawled in red ink were visible on the dirty plastic wrapping.

"This is Southeast Asian heroin," said Phillips, who had seen many such packages. "It probably originated in Myanmar and ended up in the U.S. via China. The question is why is only this one package left here? We know that Aldo delivered drugs to Darryl a couple of days ago."

"I think I know the answer to that." Charlie handed a waste basket to Agent Phillips. Inside the wastebasket were three used syringes. "Aldo was an addict himself. That would help explain why he continued to be involved with drug trafficking, even though his chosen life style did not seem to center around large quantities of money. He probably became addicted in Vietnam along with the rest of his squad."

"But would a heroin addict be able to lead a normal life for forty years without anyone noticing?" Agent Jankowski asked.

"Some people with heroin dependency have enough self-discipline to regulate dosage and remain reasonably productive. But it could be argued that Aldo's life wasn't exactly normal," Agent Phillips replied.

It took three trips in Charlie's dinghy to transport people, bags of evidence, and a casket full of guns to the Shearwater. By the time they got back to Homer in late afternoon, the temperature had fallen to near freezing, and big fluffy snowflakes were falling from the sky. In a word, everything was soggy – a typical fall day in Homer.

†

Aldo hit the disconnect button on his secure satellite phone and directed a few epithets in the direction of his whiskey glass. After months of silence and unauthorized rogue operations that contributed to the total disintegration of Aldo's life work, Frank had decided to finally call and ask for Aldo's help. His ability to help anyone, least of all himself, was severely limited by the fact that he was a fugitive stranded in the middle of the Alaska wilderness. Somehow Robert had managed to get thrown in jail, and now he wanted out, naturally assuming that Aldo and Frank would help spring him from the clutches of the law. Frank claimed that he had a plan to free Robert as he was being transferred from the Anchorage jail to the Federal transport aircraft, which was supposed to deliver him to prison in

California. All Frank wanted from Aldo was new identification documents for Robert, and money.

Should be no problem, considering that he was currently sitting on a ratty, mouse-eaten chair in a partially-collapsed log cabin on an island whose name he did not even know. Nevertheless, Aldo called a contact in California and arranged to have ID papers prepared with Robert's photo and sent to a P.O. Box in Anchorage. Also included in the package would be five thousand dollars in twenty-dollar bills. Now all Aldo had to do was figure out how he was going to get himself to a more favorable location without generating any suspicion.

He injected himself with the minimum maintenance dose of heroin that he could tolerate. Long experience had taught him that the low dose, in combination with alcohol, would get him through without much discomfort and still allow him to be reasonably alert. The imported Scotch whiskey from the bar at the Rainbow Inn was a bonus, one that was sorely needed, given his squalid living quarters.

Aldo reviewed his options. He still had his false identification papers, and his appearance was substantially different than it had been prior to his escape from Fenstrom's Lagoon. He thought the chances were pretty good that he could take the boat to Prince Rupert in northern British Columbia and catch a plane from there to a U.S. hub. Reporting his arrival by sea to Canadian customs was obviously not a good idea, but he figured it would be pretty easy to simply tie up the boat at a dock and walk into town. The other option would be to take the small, outboard-powered boat all the way down the Inland Waterway to the U.S., a trip of about 900 miles. Refueling would be a problem and, in some ways, he would be more conspicuous. Some of the sea crossings would be stretching the capability of the small skiff. He finally went to sleep in spite of the rustling of small creatures sharing his cabin.

†

Agents Morse and Milford were once again locked in the noisy confines of the float plane, as seemingly endless tracts of spruce and fir flew by beneath them. Beverly was looking out the dirty Plexiglas window and wondering at the beauty of the spider web-like waterways, mist-shrouded mountains, and dark green forest. Agent Morse sat rigidly with his jaw clenched and eyes scrunched shut. Clearly they were having different experiences. They had instructed the pilot to search the east side of the island on which the Rainbow Inn was located and look for an abandoned airstrip and small cabin as described by Frog, preferably without tipping the occupant that they were looking for him.

A stomach-churning loss of altitude caused Agent Morse to awaken and groan with discomfort. Beverly saw Aldo's hideout from the window and suggested that they fly past and land around the end of the island, well out of sight and earshot of the cabin. The flying torture chamber landed smoothly on the calm water and taxied up to shore. Low tide provided a convenient margin of dry land between the water and the trees, and, hopefully, a relatively easy means of access to their quarry. The agents, decked out in hip boots by the air charter company, exited the plane, jumped off the pontoon into the water, and waded to shore. The pilot was asked to remain there until hearing from them by radio, at which time he was to taxi around the island to the small dock at the cabin and pick them up.

The agents began their trek on the rocky intertidal beach. In some places their rubber-soled boots slipped on slimy, rockweed-covered boulders. In other places ball bearing-shaped cobbles rolled underneath their feet. Occasional fallen trees extended across the beach out into the water, requiring that they clamber over huge, mossy trunks. At no place were they able to walk in any kind of a relaxed manner. It was exhausting.

Beverly lost herself in wildlife observations. Two river otters slid off a rock into the water and chattered curiously at the intruders; a bald eagle took flight, temporarily abandoning a delectable dead goody; black oystercatchers, odd birds with oversized beaks and bright orange feet, cavorted on the rocks, looking strangely like avian clowns. Meanwhile, Agent Morse grumbled. He fell twice on the slippery rocks and succeeded in cutting his hand on the abundant barnacles. He mumbled that if they ever caught this guy, he was going to shoot him. Beverly rolled her eyes.

It had taken the float plane only thirty seconds to get from the cabin to their drop-off point; how could it take so long to walk back? After about forty-five minutes, they rounded a small bend in the shoreline and suddenly came upon the rickety dock structure that presumably led to the cabin where Aldo was holed up. Suddenly realizing that he was the man in charge, Agent Morse shifted to his macho law-enforcement-guy persona. He and Beverly drew their guns and crept up the overgrown path to the cabin. All was quiet as the cabin came into sight. Beverly went around to the back of the cabin, and Agent Morse knocked on the door, announcing with great flourish that he was a DEA agent.

Nothing but silence. He opened the unlocked door and burst into the cabin, assuming a cinematic crouch with gun raised, but all he saw was two empty whiskey bottles and an empty glass on an old dinette table. Given the "all clear," Beverly entered the cabin and looked around. In a state of exhaustion, Agent Morse flopped down on the ratty couch and put his head in his hands.

"Someone was here recently, probably as late as last night. The glass is still wet on the bottom, and the dirty pans in the sink still have moist crust on them. I think Aldo is one step ahead of us again. Maybe Frog was right. Somehow he got a tip that we were coming," Beverly said.

"Great," replied Agent Morse.

"I don't think there is much more we can do in Alaska. We have no idea where Aldo went or even what means of conveyance he may be using. I guess we should probably go home."

"I couldn't agree more." Agent Morse contacted the pilot on his portable radio. Unfortunately, they still had to return to Wrangell, pick up Frog from the city jail, then fly to Ketchikan, where they would get a commercial flight back to civilization. He did not want to think about another couple of hours in the plane from hell, followed by four or five hours in a commercial aircraft, all the while escorting Frog to his new home in Federal custody.

Beverly observed that her boss was scratching his arms and appeared to be in pain. She looked at the small red welts and said, "Nettles."

"What?"

"There were nettles on the path coming up here. You must have walked through them."

"Why the hell didn't you warn me?"

"You told me to be quiet."

"Yeah, yeah."

"The pain will go away in an hour or so."

"Thanks for the encouraging information."

†

John Vander was in an interrogation room at a Federal facility in Seattle. From the time of his capture, he had played dumb, minimized his conversations, and insisted on calling his lawyer, who conveniently lived in Seattle. He was currently waiting for his lawyer's arrival. The DEA agents had tried to intimidate him into self-incrimination, but he was much too smart to fall into their boring traps. He was simply a businessman who had sold his Alaska lodge business and was returning home to his primary residence in a Seattle suburb.

He was not all that concerned. He did not think there was much evidence that would directly link him to illegal activities. Any incriminating records had been destroyed or wiped from his computers. They had been very careful over the years to cover their tracks. All conversations with other members of the syndicate had been on secure phones or by encrypted e-mail. He fully expected that he would either be released or bailed out in a few hours.

Thirty-five

Three inches of light snow from the previous afternoon covered the docks, and sun was beginning to peek through holes in the clouds. Melting snow on the rigging of the Shearwater dripped onto the cabin top, causing an annoying drumming. JB and Charlie sat at the settee and drank coffee. Charlie had just finished relating to JB the results of the search of Aldo's place, and JB thought it was very interesting that Aldo was a heroin addict.

"Where is the beautiful Kate this morning?" JB asked.

"She went to work. She figured she had to go back to FlashFrozen some time, so thought she would get it over with."

"Does she think there are going to be hard feelings from her coworkers?"

"She's not sure. She hopes her boss will help out."

"On another topic, is there some way you could get me a copy of the mystery man's fingerprints and maybe his photo?" JB asked.

"What? Why would you want that?"

"I may be able to shed some light on his history."

"I gather that this is one of those things that I shouldn't ask about, but how the hell would you be able to do that?"

"You're right. You shouldn't ask."

"Okay. I'll ask Bob, but it is probably illegal for him to give us that kind of information. Since he owes us, thanks to your heroics, he might cooperate."

"Thanks, but don't sell yourself short." JB got up to leave. "It was your idea to plan for an underwater attack and to use the net, the results of which were most excellent. Anyway, I guess I'll get on with my busy day. I've got important things to do."

"Right."

Charlie drove into town. Most of the snow on the roads had melted, creating a wet but reasonably unslippery driving experience. Winter conditions were just beginning, and Charlie was not looking forward to another six months of freezing, thawing, ice, and snow. Homer had some of the worst driving conditions in the world. Farther north, when things froze up, they generally stayed that way so that conditions, while snowy, were at least predictable. But in Homer, relatively warm, wet storm fronts from the Aleutian Islands alternated with cold Arctic air that swooped down from the north, providing constantly changing conditions that were hard to prepare for. Temperatures could go from minus twenty degrees to plus forty degrees in a matter of hours.

Stopping at trooper headquarters, he found the Super Trooper grumbling to himself and poring over paperwork.

"What's the matter? State bureaucracy getting you down?" Charlie said.

"You could say that. Cooperating with Federal agencies involves a whole new layer of paperwork. What's on your mind?"

"I wonder if I could coerce you into providing me with a scan of the mystery man's fingerprints."

"I'm sure you know that I'm not supposed to go around handing out evidence in a murder case to any old interested citizen. I'm afraid to ask why you would want such a thing."

"I'm not old, but I'm certainly interested. I think our track record in helping with this case should entitle us to some privileges."

Cracking a smile, Bob said, "In the last few days I've been violating regulations right and left. I guess there isn't any good reason to stop now. Hang on." Bob went out to the office reception area, opened a file cabinet, pulled out a single page, copied it, put it into a plain manila envelope, and handed it to Charlie.

Nodding his thanks, Charlie said, "I heard a rumor that you've been spending a lot of time in Julie Fishbein's hospital room."

"Boy, nothing is secret in this town. Yeah, for some reason I like her and would like to see her get a break. The hospital has to release her tomorrow. The Feds aren't interested in prosecuting her, and I'm just going to push for a misdemeanor possession charge. She wants to get into a treatment program, so I've been researching options. My behavior could be considered unprofessional, but I don't care."

"For whatever it's worth, I think that's very nice," Charlie said. "Good luck with the treatment thing."

Charlie returned to the harbor and went aboard the Otterly Ridiculous. He found JB hunched over his laptop computer at the tiny navigation desk in the dark, mahogany-paneled cabin. JB quickly closed the computer as Charlie approached and accepted the plain brown envelope.

"Outstanding," said JB. "I'll get right on this."

"I know when I'm not wanted. Besides, my coffee is much better than yours. Let me know if you find something." Charlie gladly departed from the claustrophobic sailboat cabin.

†

JB opened a cabinet under the desk, pulled out a sophisticated scanner, and scanned the fingerprint image into his computer. He then went to a bookshelf and pulled out a dusty copy of Shakespeare's sonnets. Inserted on page 111 was a small slip of paper with a series of alphanumeric codes. Returning to his computer, he typed in the first code, which pulled up a web site containing only a Celtic design. Entering the next series of codes brought up more content and allowed him to transfer the fingerprint file. He typed a query, pushed Enter, and sat back to wait for the results. A couple of minutes later he was staring at a photo of the mystery man – Robert Fenstrom, aka Niles Gerber, aka "the Mole." His personal history was about what JB had expected. Trained in military special operations and undercover intelligence, Robert had apparently gone AWOL and off the radar screen about ten years earlier. The implication was that he possessed information sufficiently embarrassing for certain people that his disappearance had been considered classified, and, thus, he was not listed in normal law enforcement databases. Whatever Robert had done, or whatever incriminating information he had, was not revealed in the file.

Since JB was already viewing highly-classified information, Robert's transgressions were obviously sealed at a very high level. He had, in effect, become a non-person, except to those high-level officials who were probably still looking for him. "The plot thickens," thought JB. Not only was Robert Fenstrom an anonymous enforcer for a secretive drug syndicate, but his past was evidently of great interest to selected high-level government officials in the intelligence community.

Thoughts of the amoral, possibly psychopathic, Robert Fenstrom brought back unpleasant memories of some of his associates in JB's past life. While some of the acquaintances that he made in those years were motivated by patriotism and strong ideals, others attracted to the shadowy life of a paramilitary undercover operative were simply adrenaline junkies who cared little about other human beings and enjoyed the feeling of power combined with the lack of accountability that accompanied black operations. These people were one of the primary reasons that JB had chosen to alter his life course.

†

Kate and Charlie were lounging over beers in the galley of the Shearwater when JB entered in his usual dramatic way, eyes wild, long hair flying. "Kate was right," he said. "The midnight marauder is Aldo Fenstrom's son, Robert. His identity is being protected by the government, probably a few individuals in one of the intelligence branches. It looks like he went missing from his official duties about ten years ago, but government officials don't want him to come into the public eye, presumably because he has information that is embarrassing. He may be trading his freedom for his silence."

Charlie was impressed. "Wow. How the hell do you know all that?"

"I could tell you, but then I'd have to kill you," replied JB.

Kate rolled her eyes. These macho games would be humorous if they were not so dangerous when played by people in power around the world. "So what the heck do we do with this information?" she asked.

"For now, we probably don't do anything," said JB. "We could be in even more danger if the wrong people found out that we knew this stuff. The DEA guys already suspect that the mystery man is Aldo's son, because of their interview with Aldo's sister. Let's see what happens. If they confirm his ID and word reaches whoever is protecting him, then all hell could break loose."

"Great. I thought all hell had already broken loose, but I guess there is more to come," Kate said.

"By the way, Kate, how was your first day back at work?" JB asked.

"It was okay. Some of Nancy's friends were very cool, but fortunately my boss got everyone together and sort of explained what was going on. I think it will be all right."

"That's a relief," said Charlie. "I feel badly enough that your life has been totally screwed up since you met me."

"Oh well, I'm pretty much used to a screwed-up state of affairs. If things are going to be chaotic and dangerous, I might as well share it with somebody."

"This is all very touching," said JB, "but I've got to go. I'm meeting a new female friend for coffee in a few minutes." JB leaped off the boat, landing with amazing grace in spite of his gangly frame.

"Shall we make bets on how long it takes JB to get his new friend into bed?"

"You are way too cynical," Kate replied.

"Maybe," said Charlie.

Thirty-six

Beverly Milford was sitting at her cubicle at DEA headquarters in Los Angeles. Sitting next to her was their resident geek. He had spent most of the previous day analyzing the hard drives from the Rainbow Inn's computers. As Beverly suspected, the drives from the main computers were brand new and contained no information; however, the drive that she had taken from the old computer in the storage closet was full of stuff from hotel activities that had occurred before the computer had been replaced by newer models. Many of the files had been created by programs that were currently obsolete, but retrieving them and converting to modern formats was child's play for the IT specialist.

Beverly had met with Agent Morse first thing in the morning, and he had informed her that they would likely have to release John Vander unless she could come up with some substantive evidence pointing to drug dealing. It just so happened that Beverly's undergraduate major had been accounting. One of the reasons that she had switched to law enforcement was because she had come to the realization that a career in accounting would be like watching paint dry for the rest of her life. Ironically, however, by virtue of her education, she had become the de facto expert in forensic accounting in the Los Angeles DEA office. Since the advent of the wars on drugs and terrorism, the detection of money laundering had become a field in itself, and, in the last few years, Beverly had become quite good at it. She was looking forward to taking a crack at the Rainbow Inn files.

Plugging in a flash drive containing all the reformatted information, Beverly sorted through the array of directories and files. Dates of the files stored in the drive ranged from ten to fifteen years earlier. Right away she began to see a pattern of duplication of

241

accounting – basically two sets of books. But she knew that proving wrongdoing from the accounting records was going to be a difficult, tedious task, especially since the records were so old. Any trail that involved following the money through various financial institutions would be obscured by the passage of time.

Earlier, Beverly had talked to agents who were involved in the search of the Offshore Enterprises office. She hoped there would be some link between the Rainbow Inn and Offshore Enterprises. But, unfortunately, nothing incriminating was found, and, in fact, the offices had been totally emptied. No business license was recorded, no bank accounts were found, and no credit cards were issued in the company's name. The business phone line had been recently cancelled and call records were extremely boring, suggesting absolutely nothing suspicious. Public documents indicated that Offshore Enterprises was incorporated in the State of California and listed Carl Smithson as CEO. Corporate income tax returns had been filed for the last three years, showing a small profit, but, again there was nothing overtly suspicious. In short, other than a few legally-required public records, there was hardly any evidence that a business had ever existed.

Beverly went to the break room and got a giant cup of coffee. It was going to be a long day.

†

Agents Phillips and Jankowski as well as the Super Trooper were having a high-level conference in the tiny storage room at Homer trooper headquarters. The only decoration in the room was a three-year-old calendar that had originated from a Swedish chainsaw manufacturer. Each month displayed a beautiful blonde in a bikini in a provocative pose, usually cuddling a chainsaw. The calendar had been left over from the construction company that had previously rented the office. The Super Trooper found himself looking at the calendar and wondering why he had never removed it; it was obviously inappropriate for a trooper office. At the same time, the calendar made him think about Julie. While she was not quite as voluptuous as the Swedish models, she was still pretty darned cute. Focus, he told himself.

The law enforcement team had been briefed earlier in the day by the Los Angeles agents regarding their adventures in Southeast Alaska. Meanwhile, Agent Phillips had been trying to confirm the identity of the midnight marauder –whether he was, in fact, Aldo's son, Robert Fenstrom. DEA staff had searched various records and discovered that Robert Fenstrom had strangely disappeared from the face of the earth about ten years previously. But some old passport photos matched the face of the mystery man, and there appeared to be little doubt that the two were one and the same. The whole situation surrounding Aldo's operation was becoming ridiculously complicated.

Agent Phillips wondered what the heck was going on. He was starting to long for the good old days when he had first started in the law enforcement business. As a cop in south central LA, he and his partner concentrated on busting street corner gang-bangers. The bad guys were easy to identify and usually not too bright. Things had been much simpler then.

"So, where the hell are we at?" Bob asked.

"Well," Agent Phillips said, "I guess the good news is that we have three bad guys in jail, one guy sort of in jail, and one bad guy dead. As far as Homer is concerned, I suspect that drug traffic will be substantially reduced. Aldo is smart and may escape, but I think he is going to try and get as far away from here as possible. His business is in the tank and he is likely on the way to permanent retirement. Unfortunately, as far as the murders of Rodolfo and Jake Halburg are concerned, we're not exactly sure who killed whom. While Robert is obviously a potential candidate for the murders, we know that Frank Halburg ordered the torching of Ms. Perkins' cabin, and the fact that Jake Halburg was found on the trail to her cabin also implicates him in Jake's murder. With Frank Halburg on the loose, we may still be facing a whacko killer bent on creating havoc. We don't have a clue where he is – whether he is in Homer or even has any interest in anything going on here."

"He may be just crazy enough to still want to get revenge on Kate Perkins and Charlie Skyler. I have a feeling that we haven't heard the last from him," Bob replied. "And what about the rest of Aldo's syndicate? Is anyone looking into the role of Stuart Halburg?"

"Agents in our Savannah office have been looking into Stuart Halburg for several days. Because of his political standing in the community, he is completely untouchable until we get some real evidence. There has even been talk of his running for governor."

"A crooked politician. I'm shocked," Agent Jankowski said.

"Yeah, well, a review of his finances showed nothing suspicious. These guys are experts at money laundering."

"Okay," said the Super Trooper. "My problem right now is protecting Kate and Charlie and solving three murders that occurred in my jurisdiction."

"It seems to me that those guys are pretty good at taking care of themselves, plus they got themselves into this mess. And don't forget they have the protection of the Kung Fu hippie," Agent Jankowski said.

"Or, looking at it another way, they have been a big help with this investigation and have helped to make the DEA look good," Bob replied.

"All right, gentlemen. Enough bickering," Agent Phillips said. "Let's figure out where to go from here. There may not be much need for us to be in Homer any more. A concentrated effort from LA may be more useful in trying to put together a case to derail the whole operation. I think we'll plan to leave in the morning. We need to escort the midnight marauder to a secure federal facility as soon as possible. Meanwhile, Bob, maybe you can question some local folks and pick up some additional insight into Aldo's operation or into the psychology of Robert Fenstrom."

†

The Mole was jogging in place in the middle of his cell, trying to get his heart rate up to a point of satisfactory stress. He was just starting to work up a sweat when he heard several sets of footsteps echoing in the corridor between the cells. Were they coming for him?

Ivan, one of the daytime corrections officers, approached his cell, accompanied by two large men in navy blue suits. "Well, Mr. No Name, it looks like you're going to be accompanying these two nice men to a government-operated resort in the lower forty-eight."

The Mole just glared. He was placed in arm and leg shackles and led directly out of the Anchorage municipal building to a waiting black SUV with tinted windows. After about five minutes, the older of the two men said to the Mole, "We don't know who you are and we don't care. Our orders are to escort you to Seattle and hand you over to authorities there. Meanwhile, you are our prisoner. Please don't talk to anybody or try to escape. We would like this to be a relaxing trip."

The Mole nodded his assent.

The flight from Anchorage to Seattle was uneventful except for the ten-year-old boy across the aisle, who entertained himself by playing a game of staring at the prisoner. The Mole occupied himself by imagining the various ways in which he could make the boy's life miserable. If the kid only knew what the Mole had done and what he was capable of doing.

At Sea-Tac Airport, the Mole was escorted into a small, secured room adjoining the concourse. The door was locked behind them, and the Mole was ordered to sit in an immovable metal chair, where he was further secured by a pair of handcuffs attached to the frame of the sturdy chair. After about ten minutes, two other men entered the room through a doorway on the opposite side from which they had entered. Both men were tall, but one was heavy with red hair, a round, bloated face, beady eyes, and pale skin; the other man was thin to the point of being gaunt, and mostly bald. The Mole recognized the man with red hair, but did not change his expression. The heavy man nodded to the agents who had escorted the Mole from Anchorage and they both immediately left the room through the back door without saying a word.

"Well, Robert, it seems you've been up to your old tricks, except this time you were dumb enough to get caught."

"Fuck you, Ayers." These were the first words the Mole had uttered since being laid out on the Homer dock.

"Okay, this is how it's going to go. To keep up the charade, we're going to escort you out of here in shackles and drive to a safe house, making sure that we are not followed. There you will be given a new identity, a process with which you are intimately familiar, along with a small financial stake. We will then drop you off in Pioneer Square, where you can mingle with the other nameless, homeless folks of our fair city. Where you go from there is up to you, except that a return trip to Alaska is strongly discouraged. I'm sure you are pissed off at some of the citizens of the last frontier, but do not pick this moment to get revenge. That would be colossally stupid and an unnecessary risk both to you and to us. This is your last chance. If we find ourselves in this position again, we will kill you without a second thought. Is all of that clearly understood?"

"Sounds like a plan," said Robert.

†

"What!" exclaimed Agent Phillips. "You're shitting me. How could he be gone?"

The warden of the Anchorage municipal jail related his tale of the two FBI agents who had come that afternoon to escort the no-name prisoner to federal lockup in the Lower Forty-eight. The warden assured them that he had followed normal verification procedures, and all had been proper. He provided the names that the FBI guys had given, along with the verification phone numbers and codes.

Agent Phillips reluctantly walked to the Super Trooper's office and informed him of the situation. He and Agent Jankowski then checked with the FBI regarding the men who had been sent to Anchorage to pick up the prisoner. No agents with those names existed in the FBI roster, but more disturbingly, all the verification procedures had been exactly right. Since verification codes were changed regularly, the persons who took the prisoner had to have been insiders. A quick check of airline manifests indicated that a shackled prisoner had been transported on a commercial airline flight from Anchorage to Seattle – a flight that had landed two hours previously. Their man was gone.

A furious Agent Phillips reported the events to his boss, who claimed to have no knowledge of any special handling of the prisoner. "There is obviously stuff going on here that we don't know about. We are being intentionally kept out of the loop. But I do know that Robert Fenstrom, or whatever his name is, is a dangerous man and should not be on the loose. Damn it!"

Thirty-seven

Kate awoke to the sound of rain drumming on the overhead hatch. It was totally dark in the love nest of the Shearwater. Extending her leg over to Charlie's side of the bed resulted in the disappointing realization that Charlie was no longer present. The red glow of the digital clock indicated that it was past 7:00 — she needed to be at work in less than an hour.

She dressed in the tiny head, following an abbreviated morning routine. The space over the sink was so small that her elbow kept hitting the wall as she was brushing her teeth. A blast of cold, wet wind hit her as she opened the companionway door and stepped onto the deck. The mountains in the east were starting to glow with a feeble light, but for all practical purposes, it was still dark, and the dismal weather suggested that it was going to stay that way throughout the day. Stepping into the brightly lit galley, she was met by warm air smelling of bacon and coffee. Charlie kissed her and poured a cup of coffee, causing an immediate improvement in her state of mind.

Just as Kate was beginning to think that she might survive the day, the boat lurched and the Super Trooper bounded aboard with the agility of a water buffalo.

"Oh great," said Kate. "There is no peace around here."

Charlie was pouring Bob a cup of coffee when JB's wild visage appeared in the doorway. "I guess you guys forgot to tell me there was a meeting this morning."

Kate groaned. "Jeez, if I'd known that we were having company this morning, I would have ordered a catered breakfast. So why are you out so bright and early this morning, Bob? Good news, I hope."

"Not exactly," Bob replied. He told them about the fake FBI agents making off with the midnight marauder. "Agent Phillips is sure that our mystery man is Aldo's son, Robert, and that he apparently has friends in very high places."

Charlie and Kate looked at JB, who smiled smugly.

"Why do I get the feeling that you guys knew all this stuff already? Anyway, I guess the good thing is that he was not in Alaska as of yesterday afternoon."

"Great," said Kate. "Both Frank Halburg and Robert Fenstrom are on the loose, and both seem to want us out of the way. The key question is whether their desire for revenge is strong enough to lure them to Homer with the intent of killing us, when such a course of action would clearly put them at risk of being caught."

JB chimed in, "I don't know much about Frank Halburg, but, as far as Robert Fenstrom is concerned, I looked into his eyes as he was running toward me on the dock. They were not the eyes of a rational man. I suspect that I have now been added to his list of revengees. The only thing helping us out is that Alaska is a hard place for a fugitive to access, because he would have to run the gauntlet of border checks and Homeland Security checks. On the other hand, whoever is protecting Fenstrom will probably give him new identity papers, which might allow him to fly to Alaska pretty easily, especially combined with altered appearance."

Kate glared at him. "Thanks, JB, for those encouraging thoughts."

"JB is just being realistic," Charlie said. "So what can we do to keep Fenstrom from getting to Alaska, and, if he does get here, what can we do to protect ourselves?"

"The DEA guys are pretty pissed. I suspect they will do everything they can to make sure that airport security folks are looking for this guy. His appearance is pretty distinctive, so that may help. I don't know what to say about what you can do if he gets to Homer. I can increase my harbor patrols, but I obviously have other things to do," the Super Trooper replied.

"One thing we can do is alert the harbor rats to look for suspicious activity. Between the live-aboards, harbor staff, maintenance people, and businesses that overlook the harbor, there are a lot of eyes. At this time of the year there are not many strangers in town. Plus, most of the town folks are naturally nosey. We can distribute photos of Frank and Robert to all the harbor people in an afternoon," Charlie said.

"Great idea," said JB. "As one of the nosey people, I resent the implication, but I can testify that we don't miss much."

"Meanwhile, if you guys have any more information that would be useful to us, this would be a good time to cough it up," Bob said.

Kate and Charlie looked at JB.

"The only thing I can say is that Agent Phillips is right about his assumptions -- the mystery man is, indeed, Robert Fenstrom, and he is being protected by high officials in the national law enforcement or intelligence community. I honestly don't know any more than that," he said.

"Okay," said Bob. "While I'm tempted, I won't ask how you know this stuff. I'll make a bunch of copies of the bad guy photos so you can pass them out. But I think it would be best if you are selective and ask the harbor crowd to keep quiet about their surveillance and not post the photos in any public places. If either of our bad guys gets wind of the fact that their faces are known, they may take precautions to avoid being seen."

†

Beverly was back in her cubicle first thing in the morning after a late night. Her eyes were bloodshot, and she was on her third latte. But, in spite of her weariness, she was feeling invigorated. While lying in bed at 6:00 a.m., it had come to her. Figures from the Rainbow Inn's account sheets were dancing in her head when she remembered from their visit that the Inn only had twelve cabins. But some of the weekly records indicated that guests had paid for up to twenty sets of accommodations. The Inn was receiving income from accommodations that didn't exist. That fact suggested that the guests registered for those accommodations probably also did not exist. She compiled a list of guest names from two of the busiest weeks in 1998 and parceled them out to the DEA staff of researchers. The age of the data would create some difficulty but should not be insurmountable. Meanwhile, looking only at the last year for which she had records, she added up the total income that likely came from the ghost accommodations. The annual total came to about $600,000. Of course, all of this income had been reported and taxes paid as required. All in all, it seemed like a very slick system of laundering. All she had to do was somehow prove that the phantom guests (and their credit card accounts) were bogus.

At 11:30, a young staffer excitedly burst into Beverly's office. It seemed that, of the six names given to her by Beverly, three were identities that had been manufactured from dead people. Additionally, credit card accounts to which Inn expenses had been charged had only been open for a period of a few months. The evidence was clear – and it was probably only the tip of the iceberg.

Beverly called her boss, who immediately contacted the Seattle office where John Vander was still in custody. In fact, Vander was in the process of being released as the call came in, thanks to extreme pressure from his politically connected lawyer. Over the protests of his attorney, he was returned to custody while formal charges were prepared. Beverly thought that finally they had some leverage to uncover the inner workings of the syndicate. She knew that Agents Phillips and Jankowski were returning to the office that afternoon. She looked forward to helping develop a strategy for putting these sleaze balls away.

†

The Mole awoke abruptly to the sound of dumpsters being emptied into giant garbage trucks in the alley below his cheap hotel room. In his life he had stayed in many hotels from five-star to no-star, and the one annoying common thread had been early morning disturbance caused by dumpster dumping, accompanied by the beeping of insane backup alarms, one of mankind's stupidest inventions. He briefly pondered the mystery of why such activity would be allowed in the early morning hours adjacent to a place where hundreds of people were sleeping.

Putting aside such trivial thoughts, he began to think about a strategy for the future. His specialty was survival and adaptation, so he was not the least bit worried, but reestablishing himself as a different person might take a little time. Ayers and his crony had given him only $500, so obviously a first priority was getting more money. He had cash stashed at various locations, but unfortunately Seattle was not one of them. He needed to get to Los Angeles, where he had a storage unit with a combination lock that he could access anonymously. In the storage unit was $200,000, a motorcycle, satellite phone, several handguns, passports and driver's licenses in several different names, clothing, and personal items. Given his shortage of cash, his only option for the immediate future was to catch a Greyhound bus to California. He would first stop at a theatrical supply store and pick out some simple disguise items, probably just a mustache and hair piece to complement his grubby clothes.

After reaching LA, he would spend a couple of days at a nice hotel to pamper himself and remove the stink of jail. He also needed to establish a bank account and credit card under his new name of George Miamoto. But in any future movements he would use one of his alternative identities. He knew that Ayers and his crew would be monitoring the purchases and whereabouts of Mr. Miamoto. He also knew that he should call his father and get a status report on what was happening to the business. Aldo was the only person who frightened the Mole, and he wasn't looking forward to the conversation. He knew that Aldo would order him to stay away from Alaska. But he had no intention of staying away. After he had time to relax, he would consider a return trip to Homer and his unfinished business.

The Mole had one ace in the hole that he knew would buy him cooperation if he needed it — he was the only one left who could gain access to the bank account in the Cayman Islands.

Thirty-eight

A greenish-brown gecko stood on the rock wall rhythmically inflating and deflating its vivid scarlet throat pouch, at the same time assuming the rigid posture indicative of lizard lust. A smaller lizard stalked insects in the red dirt of the pathway, periodically lunging with head and tongue to suck up a hapless ant. Palm fronds rustled in the wind, while a yellow and black bird flitted from branch to branch. Sounds of the surf harmonized with the trade wind. A frigate bird wheeled with motionless wings on the updrafts above the sloping shoreline. Smells of the tropical sea combined with jasmine, bougainvillea, and marijuana to create the distinctive aroma of the Caribbean. Rugged mountains cut by valleys and ravines rose from the ocean, the dark green hillsides punctuated with occasional bursts of fluorescent orange where tall flowering tulip trees stood above the dense jungle foliage. It was extraordinarily beautiful.

Aldo lay in a hammock stretched between two palm trees in front of his cabana. He cradled a glass of rum with ice on his bare stomach, the condensation dripping into his navel. His escape to the remote island of Dominica had been ridiculously easy. He had simply driven the skiff to Prince Rupert, British Columbia, and tied up his boat at a public dock. The twenty-five-mile crossing of Dixon Entrance had exposed the skiff to large ocean swells, but nothing that Aldo couldn't handle. From the Prince Rupert dock he had grabbed a taxi to the airport and purchased a ticket to Los Angeles. From there, he had flown to San Juan, Puerto Rico. In San Juan, he had switched identification once again, purchasing a ticket to Dominica under a new name in the unlikely event that someone had managed to track him to Puerto Rico. Border crossings had proved to be no problem, his new passports and credit cards serving him well. His simple, but comfortable, accommodations in Dominica were courtesy of a former acquaintance who owed him allegiance because of past favors. He currently had enough cash to last a year or two, but not forever. He would eventually have to do something about that. His biggest problem for the moment was the scarcity of Scotch whiskey on the island, but rum was cheap and a reasonable substitute. Obtaining heroin was somewhat more problematic. While drugs of all kinds were readily available on the island, he had to be careful to avoid bringing attention to himself. An ambitious local official or informer would not think twice about turning him in if there were a monetary benefit. Meanwhile, his friend had provided a temporary supply and had promised the cooperation of the local authorities. In other words, they had been paid off.

Finally feeling relaxed after a week of extreme stress, Aldo retrieved his satellite phone and dialed Stuart Halburg, using the agreed-upon emergency number. He left a coded message that he was safely ensconced in his tropical refuge. The second call was to Robert, again leaving a coded message to call him back. He could only hope that Robert was using the satellite phone that Aldo had given him a year earlier. He hesitated before making the third call – to Frank Halburg. Damn Frank, anyway; he'd always been a jerk, and now he was responsible for the collapse of their little empire. But he badly wanted to know what the hell was happening in Alaska, and Frank would be the best source of information, especially since he and Robert kept in close contact.

Frank and Robert had been as close as brothers ever since Aldo had shipped Robert off to the Halburgs as a child. The two boys had an alliance that often did not include Frank's real brother, Jake. Consequently, Jake had felt alienated and had resented Robert's presence. Throughout their childhood, Frank and Robert had been inseparable, wandering the pine forests and swamps of Georgia. They had been in the same class at school and had fought over the same girlfriends. When they were both eighteen, they had joined the army.

Military service did not allow them to stay together, so they had drifted apart. After his discharge, Frank had tried to find Robert, but it seemed that he was involved in some sort of clandestine operation and was not reachable. Then, three years later on Christmas day, Robert just showed up at the family home in Savannah.

Much to Aldo's surprise now, Frank answered his phone. Aldo held his tongue and encouraged Frank to fill him in on events in Homer. As Frank related the tale of Robert's exploits, Aldo became more and more angry. He was somewhat relieved when he heard that Robert had been mysteriously transferred from the Anchorage jail to an unknown location. Aldo was aware that his son was being protected by some high-ranking individuals within the national intelligence community, but he had little knowledge of exactly what Robert had done to justify his treatment. In light of Robert's skills and proclivities, Aldo was pretty sure that he was better off remaining ignorant of whatever unsavory black ops the kid had participated in. For now, he hoped that Robert's protectors had taken over, and that he was out of official custody. But that also meant that he would be free to do more stupid things. On the one hand, he hoped that Robert would call him back, but, on the other hand, maybe he didn't want to have anything more to do with events happening beyond his small world on Dominica. When it came down to it, he knew that his affection for and obligation to his son would not let him simply walk away.

†

The Super Trooper pulled his beat-up jeep in front of the Homer Hospital. He was dressed in civilian clothes and had taken a well-deserved day off. Julie came through the hospital door, and Bob held the car door open for her in a gentlemanly fashion. She looked good in jeans and a clean white blouse and carried most of her worldly possessions in a small duffel bag. They quickly headed up the highway out of town, trying to be inconspicuous. Word would get around eventually, but he wanted to avoid as much gossip as possible. He knew it was improper for a trooper to be fraternizing with someone who was involved in a major drug investigation, but as a human being and a man, this was something that he had to do. Bob had found a place for Julie in a chemical dependency treatment center near Anchorage, and she was scheduled to check in the following morning. He had enough savings to cover the cost and hoped that he could get some donations from town people to help out. Gertie had already volunteered to collect money at her drinking establishment.

Bob and Julie had reservations at one of the best hotels in Anchorage so that they could spend one night together before she entered treatment. Aside from his obvious sexual desire, Bob hoped that spending a night together and cementing their relationship would give Julie something to look forward to and help her through the ordeal she was about to undergo.

"How are you feeling?" he asked.

"A little strung out," Julie replied. "The Doc gave me a few pills to carry me over until I get to the center, so hopefully I won't become a raging maniac during our time together."

"I can't imagine that you would ever become a raging maniac."

"You're a glutton for punishment. But I really appreciate your help and I'll try to keep things together."

"That's all I ask," said the Super Trooper. The old jeep pushed on down the highway, propelling Julie toward a potential new life.

†

Very large men with no necks and colorful helmets raced across the wide-screen TV and smashed into each other. Crazed fans wearing cheddar cheese wedges on their heads were jumping up and down. Izzy was glued to his recliner, nursing his third beer of the day, and it was not even noon. Once again, Astrid had abandoned him and gone to visit with her cousins. Izzy's mind was wandering, and he had completely lost track of what was going on in the game, not that he cared anyway.

He had received another worrisome call from Frank. Somehow he had become Frank's eyes and ears in Homer, and now the man was nagging him to report on local events, this time at the hospital. He made some calls and discovered that Julie Fishbein had been released that morning, but no one knew where she had gone. He also found out that the State Trooper had spent a lot of time in Julie's room.

Following procedures ordered by Frank, he relayed the information to a particular message machine. Besides the harassment from Frank, he was still miffed that his best diving gear was gone. And to top it all off, Aldo's boat was still sitting in Seldovia mired in bureaucratic red tape. Izzy had pretty much given up the idea of ever getting hold of the boat, even though, in his mind, he should be the one to take over ownership. It seemed that the boat was currently considered DEA property because it was involved in drug smuggling. And, if the DEA should elect to give up the boat, Charlie Skyler apparently had salvage rights because he retrieved it from where it had been grounded. None of this made any sense. With all Izzy had done for Aldo and the other whackos who worked with him, the boat should rightly belong to him.

†

Frank Halburg was tired of the tiny apartment in south Anchorage where he had spent most of the last two months. In spite of a steady stream of expensive young ladies, he was extremely bored. Utilizing feedback from various sources in Homer, he had orchestrated much of the disastrous activity that had occurred on behalf of Aldo's drug business. From his point of view, all of the problems they had encountered were the result of the meddling by Kate Perkins and Charlie Skyler, compounded by the stupidity of the local yokels they had enlisted to help with distribution. In addition to his conversation with Aldo earlier in the day, he had received two other recent messages of significance: the first was from his father in Savannah, who had just heard from John Vander's lawyer that Vander was in serious trouble with the Feds and likely would not be able to beat the rap; the second was from Robert, who was now free and clear. So, on the positive side, he and Robert were free of the authorities, Aldo was out of danger, and his father Stuart Halburg had not been implicated. On the negative side, the Homer and Rainbow Inn operations were out of business, one of the founding fathers – John Vander – was in jail, and a large sum of drug money was locked in a bank in the Cayman Islands that they could not get to.

He despised the Homer do-gooders and would have liked to teach them a lesson, but a return to Homer was a bad idea for the time being. Robert also wanted revenge and was capable of acting very impulsively. His first priority was to find Robert and convince him to proceed carefully; otherwise he could put the whole family in jeopardy. He and Robert had worked through difficult times before, and he was usually able to control Robert, in spite of the fact that the guy was certifiably crazy.

PART II

*Spring
Present Day*

Thirty-nine

Dark blue skies contrasted with blindingly white mountains. Water dripped everywhere from melting snow, building into rivulets, melting frozen ground. Western sandpipers, interrupting their journey from San Francisco Bay to the Arctic tundra, wheeled in a synchronous aerial dance, like a thousand Blue Angels. Effortlessly they alighted on the huge expanse of mud flat exposed by the vernal tides, probing the mud for worms and small crustaceans to refuel for the next leg of their journey. Surf birds frantically followed the leading edge of small waves – in and out, in and out. A crisp wind, cooled by ice-cold sea water, competed with the warm sun that built momentum in the lengthening May days. The transition from winter to summer was as if the gods had thrown a switch, electing to skip spring altogether, except for the brief period when the unpleasantness of muddy roads, accompanied by the emergence of detritus from under seven months of snow cover, converged with the pleasant singing of recently arrived birds and the warmth of long, sunny days.

It was almost hot in the pilothouse of the Shearwater, a welcome relief from days past. Charlie, Kate, and JB were celebrating Saturday morning with coffee and cinnamon rolls. Buster was chowing down on a liver snack.

"I talked to the Super Trooper yesterday and got the latest update on the Fenstrom situation," Charlie said. "There isn't much in the way of new information. They have pretty much lost track of all the fugitives. Meanwhile, Stuart Halburg is still carrying on his business in Savannah and has become politically more popular than ever. I'm losing hope that they will ever be able to tie the pieces together."

"Having to constantly worry whether someone out there is trying to permanently dispose of us is too friggin' stressful and frustrating. Is there anything we can do to help the authorities?" Kate asked. "JB, do your super powers allow you to get any more classified information that might expedite things?"

"I've already tried almost everything I can think of. There is one more line of inquiry that I might try, but it involves calling in a favor from someone who is not going to be happy to hear from me. Let me think about it."

"Kate, would your brother be willing to do some hacking into Stuart Halburg's life?" Charlie asked.

"I don't know. I don't want to put him in danger. Plus, I assume the DEA has already done their thing without success, so I'm not sure there will be anything to find. But I'll ask him. He probably knows some tricks that will make it difficult for anyone to trace the inquiries. When I'm in Michigan for that long overdue visit with my family, I should have plenty of time to explain the whole ridiculous situation to my brother."

"Another more promising idea might be to put pressure on Aldo's brother-in-law Izzy," Charlie suggested. "I'm pretty sure he knows more than he's told the authorities. It would be impossible for him to be Aldo's deckhand without learning something. I'll ask Bob about the possibility of questioning him more thoroughly. Looking at his phone records might also be a good idea."

The long winter had been uneventful. Kate continued to work at FlashFrozen, and Charlie worked at marketing his ecotour business. JB claimed that he was working on his book. Initially, they had been extra vigilant, sure that an attack from Robert Fenstrom or Frank Halburg was imminent. They even deployed motion-detecting alarms around the perimeters of Charlie's and JB's boats. But monitoring the alarms had gotten old and eventually had gone by the wayside. Kate was homesick for her cabin in the swamp, especially with spring arriving. She had agreed to stay with Charlie through the winter, not that it was a terrible hardship. The Shearwater was warm and cozy, and Charlie's bed cozier still. She did not miss the daily chore of splitting firewood and feeding her ravenous wood stove. Their relationship was stronger than ever, and she was feeling good about it, but a boat is a small space, and she missed the peacefulness and wildness of the spruce woods. Buster missed the multitude of small animals on the forest floor, especially the slow and dim-witted red-backed voles that had become his predatory specialty; he was getting fat and lazy.

They had assumed that the infinite resources of the Drug Enforcement Agency would bring an end to their concerns, but it had not happened.

†

Coincidentally, Beverly Milford was also thinking about the Fenstrom affair. She had long since moved on to other projects, but was profoundly unsatisfied with the outcome of her investigation of the Alaska drug operation. Her diligent forensic accounting combined with testimony from Jake Halburg before his untimely death had provided strong evidence against John Vander and, as a result, Vander was going to jail for a long time. But Vander had totally refused to cooperate with authorities, and, thus, the investigation had become stymied. She was now more familiar with the case than any of the other agents. It was obvious that Aldo's squad in Vietnam was the origin of the criminal enterprise, and it was also obvious that the founders were not going to give each other up. Trying to get Vander to talk was pointless. During her investigation of the records from the Rainbow Inn, she looked hard for any hint of connection to Stuart Halburg or to Carl Smithson at Offshore Enterprises. She had been unable to find anything and Smithson had disappeared. It was especially frustrating that Stuart Halburg was hailed as a pillar of the community in Savannah, when she knew darn well that he was part of a nasty criminal enterprise. She wondered what he thought of the death of his son Jake, probably at the hand of either his brother or Robert Fenstrom, who had also been part of the family. No father can forget the death of a son. How would a man deal with one son killing the other?

Beverly decided to spend more time on the case, whether her bosses liked it or not. In her conversations with Agents Phillips and Jankowski, she had learned of the involvement of Kate Perkins and Charlie Skyler, as well as the exploits of Johann Sebastian Bachman. She was intensely curious about the three of them from both personal and professional standpoints. She wondered if they could help provide new angles of inquiry.

She found Charlie's cell phone number in Agent Phillips' extensive notes and dialed. Charlie was sitting at his little desk working on modifications to his website when he received the call. At first, Charlie was defensive, but eventually he came around and opened up and told her they were also in essence "reopening the case" and had some ideas. Beverly conceded that formal law enforcement agencies were hampered by annoying legalities and that perhaps Charlie and the gang could do some things that she could not do and vice versa. They agreed that teamwork was essential.

Beverly also revealed the love for Alaska that she had discovered during her odyssey in southeast Alaska. Charlie offered her a free wildlife tour and fishing trip. Beverly made a spur of the moment decision to travel to Homer on her vacation in early June. Charlie marked it on his calendar.

†

Robert Fenstrom sat on the lanai of his beachside cottage in Malibu, watching the surf scene with special attention to the multitude of bikini-clad young women. He fantasized seducing each one while simultaneously beating up their buff young companions. But his brain was sufficiently intact to prevent him from acting on his impulses. He had business to attend to and did not want to attract attention to himself. He was renting the cottage in the name of George Miamoto so his handlers would at least be under the illusion that they were keeping track of him. The stash of money he had acquired from his emergency supplies was still providing his living expenses, but, considering the atrociously high rent in Malibu, it was not going to last much longer. He had fulfilled his promise to Frank that he would lie low at least until spring, and it was now time to make some decisions regarding his future plans.

Before returning to Alaska, he needed to set the stage for the future, which included a trip to the Cayman Islands to retrieve funds from the syndicate account, establishment of yet another new identity, complete with bank accounts and credit cards, and development of a foolproof plan that would allow him to disappear, thus avoiding both law enforcement authorities and the shadowy people from his past. He hated the fact that Ayers and his goons were watching him.

While he was essentially devoid of conscience, he was, nevertheless, conflicted over the Cayman funds. The other members of the Fenstrom operation did not know that he had the information to access the account, and he could probably get away with taking all of it. But he felt some loyalty to Frank and Aldo. On the other hand, he despised his de facto stepfather. Stuart Halburg had treated him like an indentured servant all his life, and his "holier than thou" image was such a load of crap that Robert was seriously looking forward to the day when his true nature was exposed to the uptight citizens of Savannah.

To further complicate things, he knew that Aldo had ways of finding things out, and he could not discount the possibility that Aldo might discover all the funds had been withdrawn. He was pretty sure that Aldo felt some affection toward him as his biological offspring, but he also knew that Aldo put very high priority on loyalty. He did not want to find out how Aldo would react to the loss of many years of business proceeds. Considering all these factors, Robert decided that he would withdraw only a couple million dollars and leave the rest in place. At some point, he would provide the access information to Aldo and let him deal with the remainder.

Using his secure satellite phone and one of his alternative identifications, Robert made airline reservations to Grand Cayman Island for the following morning. While he did not think that he was under constant surveillance by Ayers, he nevertheless left the cottage by the back door in the early morning hours, walking along the beach to the nearest taxi stand. His appearance had been substantially altered through the use of a prosthetic nose and selected facial hair. He was not able to do much about his Asian eyes other than divert attention to other facial features.

†

After breakfast on the Shearwater, JB retreated to his boat and dug out his hammock, which had been put away for the winter. He rigged the hammock between the mast and forestay, brought out his favorite pillow, and celebrated the coming of spring by basking in the sun. He did his best thinking while reclined in his hammock, which had become threadbare with use. He thought long and hard about whether he should call his old boss, Karl.

He had left government service at a time that was very inconvenient for his boss, although it had probably been essential for retaining his own sanity. Karl owed him big time for various reasons, but JB was not sure whether he would be honest enough with himself to admit his debt. JB did not know how cooperative he would be, and there was some danger that the call could backfire. But, in the end, JB decided that Karl was an honorable man and would likely be willing to help out.

JB dialed the number he had not called in over ten years, and entered the codes he had memorized long ago. The following silence seemed deafening and lasted for about thirty seconds; JB was about to hang up when the familiar voice answered, "Johann, I'm surprised to hear from you. How are things in beautiful Alaska? I suspect you wouldn't have called me unless you needed a favor. What can I do for you?"

JB was surprised and a little suspicious that Karl was so cooperative. The reference to Alaska was Karl's way of reminding him that they were still keeping track of his whereabouts. Nevertheless, he explained the situation regarding the mysterious Robert Fenstrom and asked Karl to see if he could find out any information that would help track Robert down. JB emphasized Fenstrom's psychotic nature and the very real danger to himself and his friends. Amazingly, Karl agreed to look into the situation and reply via e-mail.

An hour later, as JB was eating lunch, the bell on his laptop signaled incoming mail. The terse message from an anonymous sender said only, "George Miamoto, California."

Walking the twenty feet back to Charlie's boat, he found Kate and Charlie lounging, each with a book. JB informed them of his new piece of information. Charlie reported that Beverly Milford from DEA was coming to see them in a couple of weeks. Since Kate was going to be in Michigan the following week, they decided to hold onto the information until Kate returned. That way they could combine any information that Kate might obtain from her brother's hacking with JB's intelligence and, hopefully, assist the DEA.

"I have a good feeling about Agent Milford's involvement," Charlie remarked. "She sounded less uptight and more flexible than her macho colleagues."

Forty

Six people sat at the big mahogany dining table. An enormous crystal chandelier illuminated the perfectly set table. On Kate's right sat her brother, Ned; at the ends of the table sat her mother Rose and her father Phil; and across sat Reverend and Mrs. Foster, who had been the Perkins' family spiritual advisors for twenty-five years. It was Kate's second night home, and things were pretty tense. Kate noticed that her mother had brought out her grandmother's good china and the sterling silver place settings. The mashed potatoes and bean casserole were each in silver bowls. A large hunk of prime rib sat in front of her father on a silver tray.

She had spent most of the day before recovering from jet lag and calling a few old friends. Her mom had been affectionate as usual, and her Dad had been friendly, but cold. It was obvious that tonight's dinner was going to involve some heavy and annoying conversation. Kate was not sure that she was up for it, but her intent was to be honest and sincere in a mature and confident manner without being childishly defiant. Remembering past dinner table conversations that did not go well, she was not sure she could pull it off.

After Reverend Foster said grace, Mrs. Foster began the interrogation. "So, Kate, I understand you live in Alaska. What is it like being way up there in a foreign country?"

Ned rolled his eyes. Kate spent the next ten minutes explaining politely that Alaska was a state just like Michigan and had been since 1959. She went on to describe the weather conditions and demographics with the intent of debunking most of the myths about the state that were common among easterners.

"Have you been able to find a job up there?" asked Reverend Foster.

"Yes, I work as an administrative manager for a seafood processing company."

"Would it be possible to find a job more appropriate for your skills and education?" Kate's father asked.

"Actually, my current job is pretty appropriate, but I don't plan to work at FlashFrozen forever. I'm still trying to figure out what I want to do in the long term."

Kate went on to calmly describe living conditions at her cabin and overall lifestyle. Although the persons seated at the table were somewhat appalled, they seemed genuinely interested.

But Kate's father could not help himself. "With all the advantages that you have here at home, why would you want to live in such a place?"

"Homer is an unusual place. It provides the opportunity for people to be themselves without having to conform to any preconceived notions of what they should be like. I realize that you have provided a secure life for me, but what I need right now is the freedom to work out what I want my life to be like."

"I still don't get it," Phil said.

"Well, I think that was a very eloquent explanation," Rose said as she gave Phil the evil eye. "On another topic, are there any men in your life?"

"Yeah, I've been hanging out with a great guy for about seven months."

"Does this guy have a job?" asked Phil.

"Yep, he operates an ecotourism business."

"What the heck is that?"

"He takes tourists on wildlife tours on his boat. He used to be a commercial fisherman, but the fishing business is not too good right now."

"Does he make any money?"

"He makes enough. He owns and lives on his boat, so his expenses are very low."

"He lives on a boat? Is he some kind of hippie?"

"Look, Dad. Charlie is a great guy. He is definitely more respectful of me that any of my other boyfriends. He has a college education, he makes a good living, and he is respected in the community. He was even the one who suggested that I come down here and attempt to restore communication with you guys. So don't jump to conclusions."

Phil frowned and started to open his mouth, but Rose gave him another look and he thought better of it. Reverend and Mrs. Foster wisely decided to stay out of it.

The rest of the dinner conversation was mostly small talk. Kate, of course, did not mention the presence of drug-dealing conspiracies and psychopathic killers on the loose in peaceful Homer, Alaska. After dinner, she and Ned went for a walk. It was the start of summer in southern Michigan. Fruit trees were blooming, and the air felt balmy compared to Homer, where the bite of the ocean was always present.

"Well, I thought that went pretty well," Ned said.

"Yeah, I guess."

"Mom is on your side, and Dad will come around. He can see that you are growing confident with your own place in the universe. So, what is happening with the drama in the North?"

Kate brought Ned up to date on the Fenstrom situation and explained that she and her friends were hoping to get some more information that would help the authorities. She asked Ned if he had any interest in trying to ferret out some information on Stuart Halburg using his superior hacking abilities. Kate warned him that the Halburgs were dangerous people and that he might be putting himself at risk. Ned thought it would be fun. His mainstream IT job was extremely boring, and he missed the rush of illicit hacking. Besides, he had written software that made it almost impossible for anyone to trace the source of unsolicited queries. He was so excited that he planned to start on the project that night.

†

Frank was at a total loss. Since the drug business had come to a screeching halt, he had little to do and even less money. He had managed to seduce a relatively attractive woman whom he had met in a bar and had been living in her run-down house in Seattle for the last six months. Unfortunately, the relationship was becoming frayed. He was starting to think that he might have to get a real job. His father had ordered him to stay away from Savannah, effectively cutting him off from any benefit that might be derived from his father's legitimate or illegitimate businesses. Robert had given him some of the money from his stash, but it was almost gone. He had been communicating with Robert fairly regularly, but then Robert had told him that he was going away for a while. The good news was that Robert had implied that he might be coming back with some money. Meanwhile, Frank was stuck.

Forty-one

The Shearwater bobbed gently on the waves of Cook Inlet, creating a hypnotic gurgling sound. It was a beautiful early summer day with little wind and blue sky. Kate, Charlie, and Beverly stood in the cockpit, each with a heavy fishing rod extended over the side. It was the optimum time of the year for halibut fishing, and Charlie had guaranteed that they would catch fish. Hooks baited with chunks of herring and weighted with heavy lead balls bounced off the sea bottom fifteen fathoms below the boat. According to Charlie, the halibut were supposed to smell the bait and come from far and wide for the privilege of getting caught. They had been drifting for an hour, and the only catch was a very weird otherworldly anemone-like creature that had become snagged on Kate's hook.

"Boy this is fun," she said. "Where are all the monster fish that you promised us?"

"Be patient. The fishing will pick up when the tide turns to slack in a little while."

"Yeah, well it certainly can't get any worse. I think this is the Alaska version of a snipe hunt."

Beverly just smiled and took in the beauty of the day. She was enjoying the interchange between her new friends and soaking up new experiences. Meanwhile, JB was lounging against the cabin bulkhead on a pile of pillows, content to relax and ogle Beverly with undisguised lust. He claimed that his personal beliefs forbade him from being cruel to fish and so he did not want to participate. Charlie, knowing that JB's freezer was full of fish sticks, suspected that laziness was a more likely explanation.

The tip of Beverly's rod suddenly bent nearly to the water, and line started streaming out from her reel, making a screeching sound as the creature on the end of the line pulled against the reel's drag.

"Yikes, what do I do now?"

"Hang on and keep the tip up. When he stops running, start reeling. Keep all slack out of the line."

"Okay."

Beverly fought the fish for about twenty minutes, gradually reeling it closer to the surface. She was in very good physical condition and needed no help. Finally, they were able to see the large halibut about ten feet down in the water. It looked huge.

"Looks like about a hundred and twenty pounds. Do you want to keep it or let it go? Your option," Charlie said.

"I think I'd like to let it go. Such a magnificent fish."

"Okay, bring her up a little farther and I'll let her loose."

As the fish neared the surface, it seemed to look up at them, both eyes swiveling bizarrely on the top of its flat head. It lay there calmly as if hypnotized. Charlie took advantage of the fish's stillness to quickly remove the hook from its lip with a long pliers-like tool. The large halibut lay there for another second, then realizing it was free, slapped its tail and dove with amazing speed, splashing the three fisherpersons.

"Wow, that was something!" Beverly said. "I noticed you called it a 'her.' How do you know it was female?"

"Most of the big fish are females. It was a good decision to let her go. She will lay lots of eggs – the bigger the fish, the more eggs."

They continued to fish for a while longer, catching two small halibut, which Charlie kept for food. On the way back they saw minke whales, porpoises, and sea otters. Beverly was overwhelmed by the scenery as they motored through the back islands on the south side of the bay.

Beverly Milford had arrived the evening before. Charlie had picked her up at the airport and was somewhat surprised by her appearance, probably due to unfair stereotypes of female law enforcement officers. She was average height with short blond hair, a pretty face, dark blue eyes, and a well-toned body. What was surprising was her very expressive face that exuded warmth and congeniality. It was a major contrast to the stoic agents they had dealt with in the fall. In short, she was cute and friendly. He had a feeling from his earlier phone conversations that she was also a bulldog when on a mission. He drove her to the boat and introduced her to Kate. JB, knowing of her arrival, had been on the lookout. As soon as they arrived, he quickly showed up at the cabin door.

Taking a few seconds to adjust to JB's wild appearance, Beverly had said, "And this must be the infamous Johann Sebastian Bachman."

JB's face had lit up like a child getting his first birthday cake. "Please call me JB."

Beverly had requested, since she was supposedly on vacation, that they not talk about the Fenstrom affair until she had had a chance to have some fun. They all went out to dinner at Mama's Fish House, drank a lot of beer, and told stories. JB's infatuation with Beverly had become more and more obvious as the evening progressed and Charlie was getting a little worried.

†

After returning to the dock from their leisurely adventure on the water, they agreed it was time. They gathered around the dinette table, and Charlie broke out the beer and snacks.

"Thanks for a great day, you guys," said Beverly. "But now I guess we should talk about criminal conspiracies. Have you come up with any new and useful information?"

Charlie looked at JB, who winked and said, "Well, I managed to stumble on some stuff. It is likely that the midnight marauder, alias Robert Fenstrom, is currently going by the name George Miamoto and probably lives in California."

"Where in the hell did you come up with that?" asked Beverly.

JB just shrugged and said, "You will have to trust me."

"Fine, is there more stuff that seems to have eluded the professional law enforcement community?"

"I just got some information from my brother that might also help," Kate said. "He's been looking into Stuart Halburg's affairs."

"And of course these investigative activities are all legal?"

"Of course."

"Okay. What did he find?"

"On the surface, Halburg's construction business is clean. Everything is done by the book. And his public image is very carefully maintained by a team of public relations experts who make sure he does the right stuff, such as attending fund raisers and other community benefits. His PR people also effectively deflect any questions about his past personal life, which has not been so clean. For example, his first wife, Jake and Frank's mother, left him about fifteen years ago. There were rumors of abuse, but apparently they were cut short by a confidential divorce settlement that involved a lot of money. An independent weekly newspaper ran some stories after the separation, implying that Stuart was not a nice person, suggesting that he was involved with drugs, and that he bullied his ex-wife into giving up child custody. Amazingly, the stories ended after a few days, and nothing has been in the media since. After the divorce, he even managed to gain the reputation as Savannah's most eligible bachelor, and he eventually married a local beauty queen about five years ago. After three years, he again divorced, citing irreconcilable differences. His latest wife has disappeared from the scene. In fact she seems to have disappeared from the planet. So, as a first line of inquiry, I suggest trying to get at his ex-wives. Presumably, his first wife has heard that her son was murdered. I'm guessing that she might be more willing to cooperate if she suspects that Jake's death was related to Stuart's illicit business enterprises."

Kate took a deep breath. "On another front, Ned spent some time trying to track the money. There is definitely some funny stuff going on there, but it is very convoluted, involving shadow corporations and offshore accounts. You guys at DEA are probably better able to figure out the details. But apparently Ned was able to find enough discrepancies in Stuart's accounts to determine that more money is passing through than can be accounted for by his reported business income. One other thing--Stuart is an unlisted customer of a satellite phone service. He pays for a special encryption service to assure anonymity."

"Your brother has been busy," Beverly said. "Some of this stuff I already knew from my own investigations, but there is enough new information here to give us some better direction. One of my specialties is forensic accounting, so I might be able to pursue some of these leads and determine if there is enough information for warrants. Maybe you can get your brother to send me the details of his findings."

"Already done." Kate pulled out a manila envelope from one of the galley drawers and handed it to Beverly. "So, how are things going from your end of things? Obviously, our biggest concern is that there are still people out there who may want us dead."

"As I told Charlie on the phone, we're pretty much at a dead end. But I really want to keep going on this, and I appreciate working with you guys. I will do my best to keep you out of trouble in spite of your nefarious methods. I've been trying to figure out how best to handle JB's information. Assuming we can find an address for Mr. Miamoto, we can probably set up a surveillance based on an anonymous tip. If we can establish that Miamoto and Robert Fenstrom are one and the same, then we can arrest him, since there is an outstanding warrant."

"I suggest you ask your agents to watch for disguises and multiple identities. Fenstrom has probably had training in changing his appearance," JB said. "Also, he may already be alert to surveillance, since whoever is protecting him may well be watching him. You will need to discuss with your superiors how you are going to handle it if you do arrest him. The people who freed him from the Anchorage jail will either try to take over the arrest or kill him. If you arrest him, he may be considered such a hot commodity that continuing to keep him alive is too big a liability."

Beverly was beginning to get some feeling for JB's weirdly contradictory and complex persona. She was fascinated. "I know I shouldn't ask how you come by all this insight, but I can't help it. How the hell do you know this stuff, and why should I believe it?"

"If Miamoto and Fenstrom turn out to be the same person, it would provide pretty good proof that the information is accurate. All I can say is that I suspect that Robert Fenstrom and I have been through some of the same life experiences. I, however, am probably not a psychopath – eccentric perhaps, but hopefully not completely nuts."

"Well, that's encouraging." Beverly flashed JB a cute smile. Kate and Charlie rolled their eyes, amazed by the chemistry that seemed to be emerging.

"What about the State Trooper involved with the case? What kind of guy is he?" Beverly asked.

"He's a good, solid law enforcement officer. He handled himself well when your colleagues were in town – helped to keep them out of trouble in spite of the fact that they were pretty obnoxious. He's not a genius, but he does alright," Charlie said. "He can help out by keeping his eyes and ears open. If you want, we can introduce you."

"It may be better if my visit here remains off the record. Our collaboration is a little unusual, and my bosses might not like it too much."

The newly united investigative team finished off the last of the two six-packs and went out to dinner once more. The two women tried to pry more information from JB, but were unsuccessful in spite of the amount of alcohol that all had consumed. Walking back to the docks, it was no surprise when Beverly and JB veered off and elected to go for a walk on the beach in the extended daylight of a June night in Alaska.

"I think we may have set up the weirdest couple known to man," Kate said.

"Yeah, I can't even begin to imagine those two in an intimate relationship. I hope it ends up okay."

"It is a pretty nice night. Want to go for a walk?"

"Let's go the other way."

The two couples walked off into the midnight sun holding hands. A rosy glow extended from the water to the tops of the mountains, and the last of the sun disappeared behind the Alaska Range, the silvery glimmering sea gradually changing to slate gray. Observant persons would have noticed small waves coming from both the Shearwater and the Otterly Ridiculous just after midnight.

Forty-two

The Mole was hot, tired and grumpy. His face itched constantly at the point where his fake nose was attached. Scratching was pretty much out of the question given the circumstances. The trip to Grand Cayman Island had been long and unpleasant, with the normal airline frustrations – late planes, crowded seats, and chatty passengers. Fortunately, clearance through Cayman Island customs was no problem, since he was just another tourist. After collecting his luggage, he had gone into the restroom, entered a toilet stall, and removed his disguise. He could not stand the itching any longer.

Now he was on a crowded bus with a dozen other tourists heading from the airport to hotels along the famed Seven Mile Beach. It had to be at least ninety-five degrees, and his shirt was soaked with sweat. His fellow passengers were a ridiculously uniform group of upper middle class Americans, all wearing print shirts and khaki shorts. They were starting their vacations and were jovial to the point of nausea. After checking in at his small upscale hotel, he removed gin and tonic water from the mini-bar, fixed himself a strong drink, and sat on his seaside balcony.

Once again, he found himself watching the people on the beach. The average age of the sunbathers was substantially higher than in Malibu. Most of the bikini-clad women were trophy wives in their thirties and forties, some of whom looked very nice, usually much nicer than their companions, who were often in their fifties and sixties with a paunch and graying hair. Looking beyond the tourists, he noted that the islanders of all professions were of various mixed races, and he surmised that racial equality had reached a more advanced stage on Grand Cayman than in most other places in the world. As an Asian American, the Mole was sensitive to perceptions of racial difference.

But nothing is perfect, and he knew that money and power were still concentrated in the hands of old white men.

All the bare skin on the beach focused his thoughts on how long it had been since he had enjoyed female company. Grand Cayman Island had a reputation for some of the most beautiful call girls on the planet. A discreet call to the concierge finalized arrangements for a mixed race beauty to arrive at his suite later that evening. It was a risk to see a prostitute, since it guaranteed that at least one person would have a strong memory of his presence on the island, but it would be worth it.

Grand Cayman Island was one of the most prosperous of the Caribbean islands. Tourists were part of the reason, drawn by the beautiful beaches, upscale accommodations, and superb diving, but the thing that made the Caymans different from other destinations was the international banking industry. Account privacy and favorable taxes drew money from all over the globe, allowing wealthy clients to play all kinds of legal and illegal games with their money. There was usually a reason why people parked their money in Cayman banks. The combination of big money and recreational opportunities had resulted in a jet-set atmosphere.

†

The next day, Robert wandered the streets of the George Town financial district where all the large banks were located. He was trying to get a feel for the area and calm himself before entering the bank holding the Fenstrom account. He was not entirely sure what the procedure was for withdrawing money and knew that he would have to be on his toes. The long alpha-numeric account number and accompanying access code had been tattooed on the bottom of his foot long ago. During one of the few times that he, Frank, and Jake were in the same room, he had managed to secretly photograph the bank documentation. The foot tattoo idea was something that he had picked up during one of his prison stays. He was not sure whether there were signature requirements or not. He knew that Jake Halburg had originally set up the money drop, but obviously, Aldo and the other principals would need access as well.

The Mole assumed that he would need only the number and access code, but he was not positive. As a back-up plan, he had practiced his father's signature, since he was sure that Aldo would be listed as an account signatory. He was dressed in tropical white pants and open collared shirt with a navy blue sport-coat, matching the type of apparel worn by most of the prosperous customers he had observed entering the banks.

He started to panic as he climbed the marble steps of the bank, but willed his heart to slow down. Stopping in the lobby, he filled out a withdrawal slip for four million dollars. Stepping up to a teller, he asked for two cashier's checks, one made out to a Malibu bank for twenty thousand dollars and the other to a different Cayman bank for the remainder. The teller typed information into her computer and then left, saying she would be right back.

Robert did not like having her out of his sight. She returned all smiles, carrying two checks. She handed them to him, thanking him for his business. Before leaving, he inquired about the procedures for electronic banking, and the friendly teller gave him a brochure that explained it all. The withdrawal receipt gave the remaining account balance as twenty-seven million dollars.

Finally relaxing, Robert then walked two doors down the street into another bank and set up an account with the larger of the two checks under the name he was currently using. The smaller check would be deposited in his Malibu bank under the name of George Miamoto to supply his immediate needs.

Back at his hotel, he again sat on the balcony gazing out to sea and fantasizing in gruesome detail how he might be able to settle the score with the annoying Alaska trio.

Forty-three

Storm clouds built over the Caribbean, changing the color of the water from blue to gray. A lightning bolt extended from the clouds to the sea surface, and heavy rain started to fall at the exact same time as the jarring thunderclap. Aldo clumsily got out of his hammock and stumbled to the shelter of his cabana. He tripped on the front steps and fell to the side, hitting his shoulder on the porch railing. As he struggled back to his feet, the pain in his shoulder created a moment of clarity, and it occurred to him that this shit had to end.

Since moving to Dominica, he had been drinking and shooting up regularly. There was nothing else to do on the island. Pulling himself together, he sat on the porch bench, watched the storm, and tried to focus his foggy brain. He had always prided himself on the fact that he was a functioning addict and had looked down on his customers who often ended up in a downward spiral of uselessness. But now he was just like them. He told himself that the next day he would go back to his old schedule of minimal mind alteration.

Aldo awoke the next morning determined to remain clear-headed at least until happy hour. He had not checked on the status of his various co-conspirators in a couple of months. It was time, and besides, it would take his mind off his cravings. Calls on the secure satellite phone to Stuart, Robert, Frank, and Carl Smithson all went unanswered. In a message to each, he asked that they reply with a brief status report. In his restlessness, he started to think about Alaska and his long life there. He wondered what was going on with his property. He was tempted to call Izzy, even though he knew that it would be a crazy idea. Even though there was no love lost between Aldo and Astrid, it would be logical for his sister and Izzy to take over the family bay property, rather than let it fall into a state of decay. Instead of risking a call to Izzy's land line and providing some clue to his whereabouts, he decided to call Frank back and have him call Izzy.

He missed commercial fishing and needed to find something more or less constructive to do. The choices were limited. Maybe he could get involved in a poker game with the drunken ex-patriots who hung out at the old colonial hotel in downtown Roseau. If he could keep his mind less fuzzy than the other players, he might actually make some money, which would be a good thing, since his money supply was dwindling. The alcoholic colonial holdovers that frequented the hotel were a pretty useless bunch.

Aldo took a long walk along the shore and through the town to clear his head. He watched the Creole children playing and envied their carefree, innocent lives. Life on Dominica was simple. While most of the people were poor, they would never have to deal with the complexity and endless choices required to survive in the large country to the north. Unfortunately, satellite TV had exposed the populace to the seductive luxuries and lifestyles of the U.S. and Europe, causing young people to become dissatisfied and restless.

"Oh well," Aldo thought. "Not my problem." On returning to his cabana, he found that he had messages from Stuart and Frank. Stuart indicated that all was quiet in Savannah; Frank's message was more complicated. The word from Izzy was that the situation in Homer was unchanged; he had not been questioned any further by the authorities. Izzy had tried to lay claim to Aldo's boat, but that seemed like a dead end. The DEA had confiscated it and would probably auction it off eventually. Izzy was definitely interested in trying to occupy Aldo's property across the bay, but he was pretty sure that Astrid would not want to live there full time. Of greatest concern to Aldo was the fact that Robert seemed to have disappeared from his known California address and was not answering phone calls.

†

Two days after returning from Alaska, Beverly found herself sitting at a beachside restaurant in Malibu. The view from her table overlooked George Miamoto's apartment from the side, allowing her to see the lanai and its sliding glass door, which provided the back entrance to the apartment. She also had a view of the entrance to the underground parking garage and a partial view of the approach to the front of the building. This was her second day, and to avoid being too obtrusive, she had been alternating between several viewpoints, trying to look like a tourist with a few days off to soak up the sun and the beach ambience. A DEA team had made an initial approach to the apartment and determined that no one was home. Discreet discussions with neighbors indicated that the tenant had not been seen for several days. After being shown photos, one of the building residents was sure that the renter was Robert Fenstrom, but another resident indicated that it did not look much like him. Beverly and her superiors had decided that with two conflicting versions of photo recognition, they did not have enough evidence for a search warrant. Furthermore, a search warrant would create too much attention and might prevent them from catching Fenstrom.

So here she was. Stakeouts were unbelievably boring, and Beverly was on her own since the LA office was short staffed. She had had to fight to even get permission to conduct the surveillance. Sipping her fourth latte of the morning and nibbling a chocolate biscotti, she was daydreaming about Homer and JB.

The two nights that she had spent with JB were totally out of character. In fact, it was the only time in her life that she had jumped into bed with somebody without a prolonged courtship and deliberative thought. The several men in her past had been nice guys, but the relationships had all expired after a time. No drama, just loss of interest. But the situation with JB was somehow different. She did not feel the least bit guilty and was thinking that she might have finally found someone who was complex and interesting enough to fuel a long-term fire. But JB was an enigma, and she had no idea whether he thought of her as a temporary dalliance or something more. Plus, he lived on an incredibly messy sailboat, for cripe's sake. On the positive side, he was probably the smartest person she had ever met, and he was great in bed. She had also become very fond of Kate and Charlie and liked everything about Homer. Of course, she had not spent a winter there, which might affect her opinion. Like most people who are smitten with life-changing events, she had no clue what to do with all these feelings, but they had suddenly put a wedge into her previous vision of how her life would proceed.

Since Beverly was on stakeout alone, she obviously could not keep watch twenty-four hours a day — she had to get at least some sleep. She had rented a tourist apartment across the beach frontage road from Miamoto's apartment. At one o'clock in the morning on the third night of her vigil, she left her surveillance post to brush her teeth and get ready for bed. On her way to bed, she glanced out the window, just in time to see a figure dressed in black exit from the parking garage on a sleek motorcycle. The figure accelerated very fast and was immediately out of sight.

Although there was no way of knowing for sure, Beverly felt certain that the biker had been Robert Fenstrom. There was no point in following — it would take too long to get to her vehicle. She called the DEA dispatcher and asked him to get the word out to local law enforcement, but she did not have much hope that he would be found. He was way too smart.

The next day on a hunch, Beverly questioned the neighbor again — the one who had originally told them that George Miamoto's face did not match the photo of Fenstrom. This time she was able to tell that he was lying. On further questioning and threats of arrest, the neighbor admitted that Miamoto had given him a thousand dollars to watch carefully to see if anyone asked about him or appeared to be watching the apartment, with an additional bonus if his information allowed him to avoid detection. Fenstrom had called him late the previous afternoon and inquired what was going on. The neighbor told him that some official-looking people had asked about him and also told him that he thought a woman was watching his apartment.

Beverly was annoyed that she had been so easily discovered and wondered who this guy was who had time to keep track of everything that was going on in his neighborhood. But it did not matter – Robert Fenstrom had escaped once again. He had apparently been able to sneak into the apartment without being seen, to gather his belongings and motorcycle. At least now with two confirmations of identity, they had enough evidence for a search warrant.

Forty-four

Storm clouds were beginning to gather when the Shearwater pulled into her slip at about five o'clock. Charlie had spent the last two days entertaining a high school science class from Idaho with adventures in marine biology in Kachemak Bay. It had been a good day, and the rowdy Idaho contingent thanked Charlie, gave him a large check, and departed for their overnight quarters at a local motel. Kate and JB converged on Charlie as he was hosing slime off the aft deck. JB had a six-pack of beer and Kate had a huge bag of chips and a giant bowl of guacamole. It was an uncharacteristically warm evening, so they set up lounge chairs on the back deck. JB and Kate lit a joint but did not bother to pass it to Charlie, knowing that he would not partake – some silly rule about Coast Guard licensees not using semi-illegal substances.

They laid back and watched the approaching storm while toking, swigging, dipping, and crunching.

"What do you hear from the enchanting Beverly?" Charlie asked.

"I spoke to her last night," JB replied. "She has been busy." He filled them in on Beverly's activities over the past few days.

"So you were right about George Miamoto being Robert Fenstrom," Kate said.

JB gave her a quizzical look. "Of course I was right."

Charlie whistled. "That Beverly is one tough lady! Are you sure you want to get involved with such a pit bull?"

"I'll risk it."

"Well, I think she is very nice and you should go for it," Kate said.

"Gee, thanks for all the advice, guys. But I think I can figure this one out on my own."

Kate noticed the far-off look in JB's eyes. The man was in love.

The conversation turned to more mundane matters. Kate and JB started telling stupid jokes and giggling. The chips and guacamole disappeared, mostly into the bottomless void of Kate's digestive tract. Charlie just sat there, drank beer and smiled at his stoned companions, wishing he could join them. Large raindrops and gusty wind caused the partiers to retreat to their respective floating caves.

†

The Super Trooper threw his pencil at the wall. It was late afternoon, he was tired, and he was filling out more endless paperwork related to the activities of some troubled teens that had consumed much of his time in the last few days. The reports of vandalism had necessitated his getting out of bed in the early morning when normal people should be sleeping. He was recovering from his minor meltdown when Izzy walked in the front door. Crap. He knew that Izzy was here to check once again on the status of Aldo's boat. On the other hand, it was an opportunity to question the man further about his involvement with the murder suspects. He'd found a number of suspicious calls on Izzy's phone records. So Bob pulled himself together and invited Izzy to sit in the most comfortable chair in the office.

"I don't have any new information on the boat, but I might be able to move things along if you help us out," he said.

Izzy pretended to pick a piece of lint from his sleeve. "I don't know how I could help you."

"You worked for Aldo as a deckhand for several years, plus your wife is Aldo's sister. I think you know more about what Aldo was into than you told the DEA guys. Why don't you give us something so we can work together?"

"I really don't know very much. Besides, Aldo would kill me if he knew that I snitched."

He was tired of that old song. "Aldo is long gone and probably isn't coming back. So I don't buy that excuse."

"The only other thing I can tell you about the drug business is that twice we met another fishing boat in the middle of the Gulf of Alaska during halibut season. A cooler full of something was transferred to our boat and then they left."

"What was the name of the boat?"

Izzy's gaze darted to the far wall. "I didn't notice."

Bob frowned. "I find that hard to believe. Two boats out in the middle of nowhere, and you don't remember the name? You can do better than that."

Izzy squirmed. "Okay. Maybe it was something like the Esmeralda."

Now they were getting somewhere. "Do you know where they came from?"

"I don't know exactly, but I remember watching the radar screen, and they approached from a long way to the east. I think they must have come from southeast, maybe Sitka."

"Alright, that sounds good. On another topic, we know that you have received several calls from some kind of mobile satellite phone in the last month or so. Can you tell me who made those calls?"

Izzy's mouth dropped open. "Shit! If I tell you who made those calls, then I really will be in danger."

"There is a good chance that whoever made those calls is responsible for the murders of three people. If you cover for him, then you become an accessory to murder. Plus, you are probably already in danger, since you could be a link to some very dangerous people who don't like to leave loose ends behind."

"I don't know anything about any murders. I've heard the local gossip, but that's all. The calls I have been getting were from Frank Halburg. He told me to snoop around and keep him up to date on anything that is going on that he should know about. He calls me and I give him a status report. But so far I haven't really had anything to tell him, because everyone who was involved with Aldo is gone."

"Have you had any contacts with Robert Fenstrom?" asked Bob.

"I don't know who Robert Fenstrom is. I mean, I know that Aldo had a son, but I've never met him."

"There is another man who may have worked for Aldo that you might have run into. He is about six feet tall, muscular, dark complexion, and has Asian features. Does this person sound familiar?"

Izzy's face showed a moment of panic, and it was clear that he knew who Bob was talking about.

"Look, I know that this guy is very scary, and I don't blame you for being frightened," Bob said. "But right now your best chance is to help us catch him so he can't hurt anybody. When was the last time you saw him?"

"He came by the house last fall and forced me to give him my diving equipment. I haven't seen him since and I hope I never see him again, even though he owes me a couple thousand dollars."

"What name did he go by?" asked Bob.

"He just calls himself The Mole."

"As it turns out, The Mole and Robert Fenstrom are the same person," Bob said.

"What! That's crazy." Izzy looked severely stressed. "Can I go now?"

"Thanks for the help, but don't leave town," said the Super Trooper. He took a few minutes to summarize the information from Izzy and e-mailed it to the DEA in Los Angeles.

Forty-five

The search of the Mole's apartment had yielded no clues to his whereabouts, but fingerprints from the apartment confirmed without a doubt that George Miamoto was, in fact, Robert Fenstrom. Beverly was relieved that JB's information had been correct, and his shady past was not just something he made up to appear mysterious.

Armed with renewed credibility, Beverly used all of her persuasive power to convince her boss that she needed to go to Georgia to pursue some of the leads related to Stuart Halburg's potential misdeeds. DEA agents and analysts in Georgia had been assigned the task of finding Stuart Halburg's first wife, Mitsy. It was not known whether she was using her maiden name, Garner, or her ex-husband's name, or possibly another name entirely. The search soon turned up a Mitsy Garner living in a small town near where she had grown up, about a hundred miles from Atlanta.

Beverly was on her way there in her rented compact sedan. Country rock music was playing on the radio, and Beverly tapped her foot as she cruised along rural highways through piney woods and small crossroads communities. Red clay dirt swirled up from the highway, finding its way into the car and covering all the surfaces with a thin red dust layer. Her face felt dirty, and she could feel grit between her teeth. Still, it was good to be back in the field and following promising leads – taking positive action rather than sitting in her office cubicle back home.

She had received several semi-romantic e-mails from JB. His professorial writing style was amusing and somehow touching. She had replied in kind and looked forward to her next trip to Homer. She hoped that any future travel to Alaska would be voluntary and not associated with an attack on her friends by Robert Fenstrom. JB had warned her to be careful of the people who were protecting Robert. Consequently, she had taken actions on route to determine whether she was being followed. She was confident that she was alone.

Arriving in the community of Black Water Crossing, Beverly tried to follow the directions to Mitsy Garner's address that she had obtained from an Internet map site. She did not want to ask directions and risk warning Mitsy that she was coming. As usual, the mapped instructions were not quite right and she had to navigate a couple of dead-end streets before finding a viable route to the correct block. She stopped in front of a small, freshly painted house with a neatly-kept yard. The front door opened when she was half way up the front walk, and Beverly was greeted by an attractive woman in her early fifties. Beverly summoned up her friendliest manner and tried very hard not to intimidate Mitsy with her DEA credentials. She was defensive at first, but after Beverly provided condolences on the loss of her son, Mitsy's defenses broke down and she invited Beverly into the house. The interior was charming and comfortable, and Mitsy offered lemonade and cookies with graceful Southern hospitality.

Initial conversation centered around compliments on the house and the excellent cookies. Then Beverly got to the point. "We know that your ex-husband was involved with drug dealing and is not a very nice man, and we understand that you are frightened of him, but we're hoping that you might reconsider your past silence and help us put him in jail. Jake was probably killed as a direct result of Stuart's illegal business concerns."

Mitsy sat very still, tears streaming from her eyes. Beverly waited patiently for her to regain control. "Jake was the only good one," said Mitsy. "Frank and our stepson Robert were bad from the start. I really don't know how it happened – whether it was genetics or the influence of their fathers, but those two grew up with no sense of morality. I tried my best, but it was not good enough. It's not right that the only good one would die."

Mitsy began crying again. Beverly knew then that she was going to cooperate, and waited for the other woman to pull herself together.

Finally, Mitsy said, "I'll help out any way I can, but you probably already know that Stuart has some very influential friends, including state judges and high-level Savannah law enforcement personnel. It will be an uphill battle, and my life will be in danger. He may even know that you are here."

"I don't think anybody knows that I am here – I was careful to avoid being followed. But I agree that you have reason to be concerned, and I have permission to offer you protection. One critical question is whether you have any information that would definitely lead to his arrest. We will probably need more than your testimony to overcome the odds."

"I think you'll be happy with what I have to give you," Mitsy said. "About six months after Stuart and I got married, I started to realize what kind of person he really was and how dangerous he could be. So I began to collect incriminating evidence that I could use as a lever to protect myself. Hidden in the house is a box full of copied correspondence, account sheets, bank records, and notes that I made during that time period. Another full set of copies is filed with a lawyer who has instructions to release it if any harm comes to me. I wasn't exactly sure how Stuart was going to react when I asked for a divorce, and I intended to use the evidence as insurance against possible violence. As it turned out, I didn't need to use the insurance, so Stuart doesn't know that it exists. I guess he was just as happy to get rid of me as I was of him. He is so arrogant that it probably never occurred to him that I was anything but an ignorant bimbo. So where do we go from here? If I turn my box of goodies over to you, I'm going to need a safe place to go immediately."

"How do you feel about picking up and leaving with no notice?" asked Beverly.

"There's really nothing keeping me here. I can be ready to go in fifteen minutes. I have some bags already packed."

"Wow, that's amazing."

"I've actually been expecting that this day would come. If you hadn't shown up, I think I would have gone to the authorities myself."

On the road again, the little sedan pushed toward Atlanta at seventy miles per hour. No one spoke for the first hour, then Mitsy said, "Where are we going?"

"We're going to Los Angeles. That's where I live, and the DEA has some safe apartments for witnesses. They are actually pretty nice. We'll work out the details of where you might go after that later. Everything may be cool if Stuart gets put away."

"Yeah, maybe," Mitsy said. "Do you guys know where Frank is?"

"No, but we're looking for him."

"What did he do?"

"Do you really want to talk about this?" Beverly asked. "You've had a lot to deal with for one day."

"It's OK. I've known for a long time that Frank had a one-way ticket to jail."

"He's wanted for questioning in two murders and one attempted murder."

"Oh, God," said Mitsy. "My life has been a fucking disaster."

Beverly was at a loss for words. She felt sorry for Mitsy. From the standpoint of her investigation, things could not have turned out better, but the human toll associated with the Fenstrom drug operation seemed to be growing.

The remainder of the trip to Los Angeles was uneventful. After dropping Mitsy at the DEA apartment complex and completing the associated paperwork, Beverly went home to her own small apartment, which seemed especially lonely and creepy. She called JB and told him as much as she could without violating department policy too badly.

Back in her cubicle in Los Angeles the following morning, Beverly finally had the opportunity to see what was in the box from Mitsy. It turned out to be a treasure chest of incriminating evidence. In addition to documents, records, and notes, there were cassette tapes. It took Beverly a while to find an old cassette recorder. The first tape she listened to was one side of a phone conversation between Stuart and Aldo discussing delivery of product. She began the long process of cataloging the contents and determining which items were the most useful. Because of Stuart's political standing, Beverly knew that any evidence had to be foolproof. She was painfully aware that the federal prosecutors would require an ironclad case before even thinking about indicting someone of Stuart Halburg's stature. She was looking forward to putting such a case together.

Forty-six

Ayers was pissed. George Miamoto had dropped off the radar screen once again. He knew from intermittent surveillance that Miamoto had been hanging around Malibu for most of the last six months, but then a few days earlier he had disappeared. A routine check of his bank account in Malibu showed that a $20,000 deposit had been made in person on the sixth day after his absence, indicating that he had returned to the area, but, strangely, his apartment still seemed to be empty. Finally, Ayers's agents had questioned the neighbors and discovered, first, that the DEA had been looking for him and had staked out the place, and, second, that he had been warned of the surveillance and had taken off. Both of these facts were bad news. Ayers was at a loss regarding how the DEA had tracked him down. Nobody knew his George Miamoto identity except for a few people under his direct command. But a leak in his group was unthinkable. To further confuse things, the money in the Malibu bank had all been withdrawn from another branch in Sacramento the next day. So The Mole was now on the move with plenty of money. Where was he going, and where did the money come from?

It was evident to Ayers that Robert Fenstrom had become too big a liability. He needed to be permanently removed from the earth. Ayers did not like to think about the possibility of dispatching a former member of his operation – they were all like family – but he did not have any choice. Robert had been warned. He was pretty sure that Robert was going back to Alaska to take care of old business, if not immediately, then soon. The only good news was that, in order to do so, he would need to go through various checkpoints, either at airport terminals or at Canadian border checks. Either way, it provided an opportunity to track him down.

Ayers's first call was to a top official in Homeland Security. Fenstrom, as a wanted criminal, was already on their alert list, but Ayers provided additional information that would assist in his identification and insisted that he be notified, rather than other law enforcement agencies, if Fenstrom were spotted. His second call was to the U.S. Border Patrol, where he provided identical information and instructions.

His third call was to the Deputy Director of the Drug Enforcement Agency. The Deputy Director was well aware that Ayers was a powerful, dangerous, and scary guy, since he and Ayers had worked together on several covert Latin American drug enforcement efforts. Ayers asked him for the names of the agents that were pursuing the Fenstrom investigation and strongly suggested that he alert them that Ayers would be calling to set up a meeting in Los Angeles. Ten minutes later an email arrived, indicating that the principal agent was Beverly Milstrom and her boss was Agent Phillips. Ayers waited fifteen minutes then called Agent Phillips and set up a meeting for 10:00 am the next morning. It was a positive that the lead agent was female, since he might be able to avoid the usual testosterone-fueled territoriality that was so common among law enforcement personnel. He wanted to find out what the DEA knew and, at the same time, pre-empt their investigation and pursuit of Robert Fenstrom. The worst outcome would be for Fenstrom to be apprehended and go to trial, causing his background in black ops to come out into the open.

†

Beverly was apprehensive when she was called into Agent Phillips's office. There had been something about the tone of his voice that had alerted her to the probability that she was not going to like what he had to say. Agent Phillips related his conversation with the

Deputy Director along with the explicit orders to cooperate with this guy, Ayers, to the fullest extent.

"What the hell is going on? I don't even know who this guy works for, and he's trying to take over the investigation," Agent Phillips said.

"I was afraid something like this would happen. We already know that some shadowy group in the intelligence community is protecting Fenstrom, since they sprang him from the Anchorage jail. They obviously know that we had Robert's apartment under surveillance, which means that they were also watching him. They knew where he was, so they weren't trying to apprehend him, they were simply trying to keep track of him. He apparently possesses information that poses a serious threat to them. If they catch him before we do, they may permanently eliminate him."

"That's crazy. What makes you think that they would try to kill him?"

"The stakes must be very high for them to do what they're doing. Eliminating him seems like the next step, especially if there is a chance that Robert Fenstrom is going to go back to Alaska to seek revenge and make himself vulnerable to capture," Beverly replied.

"I have a feeling that you've been infected by those crazy folks in Homer. Do you have any ideas on where we go from here?"

"I'm worried that the first thing they are going to ask is the source of the information that led us to Malibu in the first place. They probably supplied Robert with the new identity, and they're going to want to know where we got the name."

"You said it was an anonymous tip. It was, wasn't it?"

"Yep," said Beverly.

"Well, we had better damn well stick to that story, even if they believe it about as much as I do. And you had better come up with an explanation regarding how the name was transmitted to us without leaving any record that would allow us to prove how we actually got the information."

"Okay, I'll work on that. What are we going to do about our pursuit of Robert Fenstrom?"

"It appears that our mystery agency is dead set on eliminating him one way or another. Maybe we should just let them do their thing. There are still other avenues to investigate as far as the overall Fenstrom operation. How about if you concentrate on building the case against Stuart Halburg for the time being?"

"That's alright with me," said Beverly. "Hopefully, the evidence against him won't depend on anything to do with Robert. It's probably going to be difficult to link him to murder in any event, since he's been so carefully cloistered in his good citizen cocoon."

"So our strategy tomorrow is to agree to back off our pursuit of Robert Fenstrom and let Ayers handle it the way he wants, but, if he suggests we back off the drug syndicate as a whole, we dig in our heels and simply tell him that we are doing the job that our agency was created to do."

"Sounds good to me," Beverly said.

Driving home from work, she felt bad about not being totally truthful with her boss. Phillips was a good guy, and she had a lot of respect for him. On the way she stopped at a Radio Shack and purchased a throw-away cell phone and a bunch of minutes. She had a bad feeling that her phones might be tapped. After eating a quick microwave dinner, she went out the back door and walked to a local park, where she sat on a bench and called JB. She told him about the contact with Ayers and the upcoming morning meeting. JB agreed with their general strategy, but he sounded very concerned and cautioned Beverly to be careful. He was definitely not his usual goofy self. Beverly was pretty sure that JB had recognized Ayers's name.

†

After an affectionate goodbye, JB grabbed a beer and settled into his hammock. He was not happy. He had never met Ayers, but knew

306

of him and knew that he was not a person to mess with. Ayers represented the worst of the people who let a sense of misguided patriotism dictate their lives and justify actions that by any other standard were unjustifiable. These people lived by the concept that the ends justify the means – one of mankind's most dangerous and pervasive principles. JB was not sure whether Ayers was aware of his existence or his past connections, but if he was, then Ayers would know where the name George Miamoto came from.

JB's old boss, Karl, was one of the few people who could intimidate Ayers, but still Karl would not be overjoyed at the prospect of confronting Ayers. It could be a big mess, and he wondered whether he should warn Karl of the potential confrontation. He decided to wait until he heard back from Beverly about the meeting with Ayers. She might be able to glean some insights from Ayers regarding whether he suspected the information came from the Homer contingent. JB lay there for a long time thinking about the fact that his past just wouldn't let go.

Forty-seven

The ethereal flute song of the Swainson's thrush came first from the right, then the left, then from all angles within the surrounding forest – singing without pause all day and all through the endless twilight of Alaskan summer. The varied thrush whistled its monotonal call, waited, then repeated at a higher pitch. Another thrush answered from far away with yet another note. The indescribable melodic warbling and chicka-dee-dee of small birds mixed with the rattle of aspen leaves in the breeze while red squirrels chattered their general annoyance at all intruders. The buzzing of bees in the heather and constant drone of mosquitoes provided a white noise background that seemed to accentuate the bird songs. Sunlight penetrated the canopy, creating dappled patches of brightness and harsh shadows that confused the eyes. The cloying smell of sweet gale and heather mixed with the smell of moss and spruce needles and mold and decaying leaves, like entering a restaurant with a hundred meals in preparation.

Kate and Charlie sat on the small porch at the front of the old log cabin overlooking the bog. It was warm and they were drinking lemonade, taking a break from their cleaning chores. A cloud of mosquitoes hovered around them, kept from bare skin by a force field of DEET. When Kate had first moved to the cabin, the insects had caused a major problem for her. After a few minutes of mosquitoes swarming around her head, she just wanted to scream and run back into the relative sanctuary of the cabin. But eventually she realized that the whole insect thing was just another psychological hang-up, and she became determined to beat it. She trained herself to ignore the bugs – at least most of the time.

Finally they were nearly done restoring the cabin to livability. Considering that the cabin had been abandoned for an entire winter, it was not in bad shape. The original builder had done a good job, making the structure rodent-proof, which was half the battle. Dampness and freezing had taken its toll, and most of the food had to be thrown out, but otherwise things were cool. Mattress and bedding were airing in the sunshine and all inside surfaces were now spic and span.

When they had first arrived, Kate had released Buster at the trailhead, and he had immediately run full tilt down the trail to the cabin and disappeared. As Kate and Charlie reclined in the warm sun of late afternoon, Buster appeared from behind the woodpile proudly carrying a nearly dead vole. He was back in cat heaven.

†

Beverly was nervous to the point of panic as she sat in the conference room waiting for Ayers to show up. It was bad enough being a woman in a profession dominated by males with overactive aggression glands, but the prospect of having to deal with a self-righteous black ops madman was scary as hell. She tried to calm herself through meditation, but it was not working.

The door opened and Agent Phillips walked in, accompanied by a large portly, man with round face, red hair, disturbing beady eyes, and a ruddy complexion – sort of a combination between Tweedle Dum and Hannibal Lecter. When Ayers was introduced, she stood and extended her hand, but Ayers just sat down. Bad sign – he was already asserting his dominance and setting the tone for a confrontational meeting.

Ayers got right to the point. "We want you to stay away from Robert Fenstrom."

"Who is we?" asked Agent Phillips.

"'We' is a special intelligence branch attached to Homeland Security. I assume your boss has already informed you of our status and our need to be primary on this investigation."

"Okay, I'll accept that because I don't have any choice. We'll agree to leave Fenstrom to you, but we intend to continue our investigation into the drug operation that started this whole thing. I want it clearly understood that Fenstrom is known to have killed one man and is suspected in the murders of two others, so he is clearly a dangerous person. If he kills someone else, it will be on your head. Obviously, we aren't the only law enforcement agency interested in him."

"I'll take care of the other agencies," said Ayers. "And we don't intend to let him kill anyone else. By the way, how did you know that Fenstrom was using the name George Miamoto?"

"We got an anonymous tip," Agent Phillips said.

"Where exactly did this tip come from?"

"I got a call in the evening on my home land line," Beverly answered. "The caller ID showed 'out of area.' A man using some sort of voice alteration equipment simply said that Robert Fenstrom was using the name George Miamoto and that he was in California. He then hung up."

"I think that's bullshit," Ayers said.

"Nevertheless, it's true," Beverly said, with all the calmness and sincerity she could muster.

"If I find out that you're lying, you little bitch, I will make your life a living hell."

Agent Phillips stood and said, "This meeting is over. Get out of our office."

"One other thing," Ayers said as he stood to leave. "If your investigation leads to any information relating to Robert Fenstrom's location, I want to hear about it." And he walked out the door.

"Well, that went well," Beverly said after Ayers was far down the hall.

She went back to her office and tried to focus. At this point, she was more angry than intimidated by Ayers. As far as she was concerned, there was no place for people as unpleasant as Mr. Ayers in contemporary human affairs. Looking back on it, Ayers had seemed like a caricature of a cold war tough guy. And what was the deal with no first name? It would have been almost humorous if he had not been such a creep.

Speaking of creepy guys, she opened the spreadsheet that contained her analysis of each of the items relating to Stuart Halburg's affairs, as collected by Mitsy. She had completed going through the box of goodies and had whittled the evidence down to about ten items that seemed particularly damning. Included were a couple of taped conversations, onshore and offshore bank statements, old phone records, and one written note to Mitsy that was essentially a threat of bodily harm if she did not keep her mouth shut and cooperate with his efforts to get custody of Jake and Frank.

Beverly could not believe that he could be so stupid as to put something like that into writing. If it could be confirmed to be Stuart's handwriting, it would represent an important indication of Stuart's true character and a clear indication of a crime. No jury would be able to ignore it.

Beverly's two research analysts had been assigned the task of assembling the background information that would be needed to support each of the evidence items. So far, things were falling into place quite nicely. She started work on a summary letter that she hoped to complete the next day. A meeting was already scheduled with a federal prosecutor in three days, and she wanted to be prepared to present her case for immediate arrest.

Forty-eight

Ironically, the Mole was back where he had started six months earlier. He shuffled down the street in Seattle's Pioneer Square neighborhood dressed in the clothes of a homeless person. But this time he had a definite destination. It was important that he avoid any kind of confrontation – anyone getting a look at the contents of his backpack would either steal it or arrest him. The beat-up pack was full and heavy, containing his basic survival kit – money, ID documentation, clothing changes, satellite phone, and gun. His motorcycle, a few belongings, and extra cash were stashed in yet another outside ministorage facility on the outskirts of the downtown area.

He walked up the front steps of the address Frank had given him. The tiny old frame house had seen better days. It was apparent that the entire block would soon be a candidate for urban renewal. He knocked, and Frank quickly answered. The two almost-brothers embraced and held each other for a long time. It had been three years since they had actually been in the same room together, although there had been many phone conversations. Robert got cleaned up and changed out of his homeless garb. Each grabbed a beer out of the fridge and sat on the ratty couch in the small living room.

"Where's your girlfriend?" Robert asked.

"She's visiting relatives in the Midwest, so we don't have to worry about her for a while. How the hell did you get out of jail?"

"My old boss did not want me to be questioned by the authorities."

"He must have some major juice to be able to do that."

"You could say that. Unfortunately, now he wants me dead because I haven't cooperated."

313

"In other words, not only are international law enforcement agencies looking for you, but also these other guys."

"Yeah."

"So, what are you going to do now?" Frank asked.

"I was sort of hoping that we could do it together, like the old days."

"I'm listening."

"I would like to go back to Alaska and finish our work there, and then I would like to leave the country permanently and stop running."

"Leaving the country sounds good to me – I'm definitely ready to leave here. But since we're both wanted for murder, it seems to me that traveling anywhere by plane and crossing borders is pretty stupid. I would love to get back to Homer, but is it worth it?" asked Frank.

"It's just something I have to do. I will do it whether you come or not."

"Let's take things one at a time. What would we do for money?"

"Money is not a problem."

"All right, where do you plan to escape to, assuming you survive in Alaska?"

"I don't know exactly," Robert replied. "I think Aldo can help us find a safe place."

"Do you know where Aldo is?"

"No. Probably somewhere in the Caribbean."

"Where would we obtain travel documents?"

"I already have a couple sets for myself. We could order documents for you from Aldo's contact in Los Angeles. It usually takes about three days. We would both have to change our appearance, so start growing a beard."

"That brings us to the Alaska part of the plan," Frank said. "What exactly do you hope to accomplish? We're beyond the point of eliminating witnesses."

"I just want to get rid of the three meddling mooseketeers – Charlie Skyler, Kate Perkins, and their hippie friend. I have a feeling you would like to deal with Kate by yourself."

"It seems like you tried that once before. Do you have a better plan this time?"

"Last time I was in a hurry. This time I plan to go slow and take advantage of opportunities as they arise. I want to keep it simple, probably follow people and take care of one at a time."

"What are you going to do about the hippie? His training seems to be as good as yours."

"He may be good at hand-to-hand combat, but he can't fight off a bullet. So, are you going to come with me or not?" Robert asked.

"Let me think about it. Have you talked to Aldo?"

"He has called me a bunch of times, but I haven't returned his calls. I was thinking of calling him tomorrow. How about you?"

"I've talked to him a couple of times. He asked me to keep him up to date on the Homer situation, mostly information relayed from Izzy. Aldo doesn't sound good. I have a feeling he keeps himself pretty drugged up. He's pissed at you and is not going to be happy if you go to Alaska."

"That's too bad," Robert said. "But I have some news for him that should make him happy."

"Does this have to do with money?"

"Yeah. I'm really tired. I've been on the run for three days without sleep."

"Who's chasing you?"

"The DEA and probably others."

"How did they find you?"

"It's a long story."

†

315

Kate and Charlie woke simultaneously as Buster jumped on the bed and then pounced on each lumpy body. Sunlight streamed through the windows of the cabin, illuminating dust motes dancing in the air. The air was cool and had a totally different smell than the air in the harbor – fresh and piney. It was nice, and Kate was glad to be back home in her cabin in the swamp. She and Charlie had agreed to alternate dwellings whenever it was convenient, taking advantage of the best of both worlds. Charlie rolled over and cuddled, caressing the curve of Kate's hip. Buster glared and jumped off the bed.

†

The Super Trooper pulled into the Homer Airport, his old jeep wheezing and coughing. It was his day off, and he was wearing civilian clothes. Julie was due in any minute, and his emotions were totally jumbled. She had completed her three-month stay at the rehab facility in Anchorage, then had received permission from her parole officer to travel to Wisconsin to see her parents. Bob had been confused and hurt that she had not contacted him when she was discharged. He had not seen her since the day he dropped her off at rehab, and had more or less lost hope. He tried to tell himself that he should put the episode behind him, but was not very successful.

Bob was very concerned that she might have relapsed. He had no way of knowing whether she had actually spent the last three months with her parents, so he was hoping for the best, but was prepared for the worst. Julie had called him three days earlier and asked if he would like to see her. Bob was excited that she was coming to Homer, but he had no idea what the future might hold. His experiences as a law enforcement officer with drug addiction did not permit him to be overly optimistic.

Bob watched through the terminal window as Julie exited the plane and walked toward the arrival gate. She looked terrific – less malnourished than when he had last seen her. Her face glowed, and

316

her long hair glistened in the sun. He felt stirrings in his nether regions. When she came through the terminal door, she saw him, ran over, and kissed him passionately. This seemed like a good sign.

They made small talk until her luggage arrived and they were in Bob's car. Then Julie said, "I know I owe you an explanation. When I was discharged from rehab, I was still feeling a little rough. My counselors suggested that one of the things I needed to do to complete my recovery was make peace with my parents. That made a lot of sense to me – I was repressing a lot of guilt at disappointing them, which fed into my addiction. Also, I wanted to make sure that I was in a good place before coming back to Homer. I don't want to create problems for you, and I especially don't want you to be disappointed in me. You're the first person who has cared about me in a very long time. So here I am. I didn't call you earlier because I was afraid that I would lose my resolve to deal with my past. I needed to take things one step at a time. Does any of that make sense to you?"

Bob's eyes were tearing up. He hugged her and said, "Yes."

They drove to his small house on East End Road. He took her bag out of the trunk and carried it into the house. "I'm going to put your stuff in the guest room. I don't want you to feel any obligation. We can take things as slowly as you want."

"Don't be ridiculous." Julie walked into Bob's bedroom. "I appreciate the chivalry, but I'm horny as hell. I haven't had sex in over six months."

"Well, OK then," said Bob.

Forty-nine

"I've been thinking," Frank said. "The safest way to get to Alaska is by private boat. Commercial fishermen run from Seattle to Alaska all the time. They usually take outside waters, because it's faster and they don't have to deal with Canadian customs. Plus, we could take anything with us that we wanted, since there would be no inspections. Fishing season is coming up, so there should be lots of boats going that way. The drawback is that it would take a few days and we would have to find someone willing to take us."

Robert raised an eyebrow. "That sounds like a good idea, but how would we get back?"

"I don't know, maybe find another boat. We're not too far from the docks. We could go prowl around and see if we can find a good candidate. But anyone we ask is going to know that we're trying to avoid other kinds of transport for some sort of illegal reason. We need to find a fisherman who wouldn't turn us in."

"The fishermen's bars might be a good place to start," said Robert. "Watch people, see how they act, identify the ones who are drug users."

"Yeah," said Frank. "We could go and have a few drinks tonight and see what we can find out. My documents should be here tomorrow or the next day then we can think about getting out of here."

Frank went to the store to get beer and groceries, providing an opportunity for Robert to have a private conversation with Aldo. Using the satellite phone, he dialed Aldo's number and was surprised when he picked up right away. The conversation was awkward, to say the least. Robert relayed that he had been hiding out in Malibu until the DEA got wind of his false name. He also told Aldo that he was currently with Frank and that they wanted to permanently leave the country and end up somewhere safe. Aldo said that he would try to come up with some ideas.

Robert told his father that he had accessed the Cayman Island bank account and had withdrawn four million dollars. He gave his father the access code and instructions on using electronic transfer. Aldo was speechless. He had long ago given up hope that Robert retained any shred of humanity, and was touched by the fact that Robert had left most of the money in the account. The timing could not have been better, since Aldo was running low on funds. As Robert predicted, the gesture caused Aldo to forget about his indiscretions. He never even asked about Robert's plans for revenge. Aldo said that he would call back in less than two days with suggestions for escape destinations where he had personal contacts. He sounded pretty clear-headed, so at least he had not been self-medicating immediately prior to the call. Robert was glad that his father seemed OK.

†

The frozen pizza was marginal, but it was fast and easy. Robert and Frank caught a cab to the Ballard Locks area and looked for a tavern that catered to fishermen. They entered a seedy establishment called the Hook, Lime, and Sinker. It was about half full of small groups of grungy guys. They went to the bar and ordered drinks and tried to eavesdrop on several conversations underway. Three men at a table by the window were drinking whiskey and telling fish stories. After a while it became clear that they operated a purse seine boat and were leaving for the Aleutian Islands in a few days to fish for salmon.

Frank knew that purse seiners were usually relatively big boats, which meant that they would likely opt for the open ocean route to reach their destination, rather than the Inside Passage. They would probably have to refuel somewhere in south-central Alaska, which would be perfect. The apparent owner of the boat was a big man with a full beard and shifty eyes. There was an unsavory air about the group that appealed to Frank and Robert.

Leaving Robert at the bar, Frank approached the men and asked if he could buy them a drink. They offered him a seat at the table, and he sat down and joined the conversation. Frank said that he and his buddy were looking for deck hand work for the summer and were looking for a ride to Alaska, preferably to Seward. They would contribute to food and fuel costs. The owner, whose name was Shane, asked why they would choose a two-week boat trip over a four-hour plane flight. Frank looked cagey and just said that they had reasons. Shane then said, "In that case, you should be willing to pay a little extra."

This was exactly what Frank was hoping for. He pretended to think about the idea, then said, "How much extra?"

"How about a thousand dollars apiece, payable in advance?"

"That seems a little steep, but I'll talk to my partner about it. When are you guys leaving?"

"We leave in four days – at five in the morning on Thursday."

Frank got up and talked to Robert at the bar, then went back to Shane's table and told him that they had a deal. They agreed to meet at the boat an hour before departure. If they were not there with the passage money, the boat would leave without them.

†

Beverly was on pins and needles. She had briefed the federal prosecutor attached to their office, Kent Rogers, about the Stuart Halburg case, and he was quite impressed. Beverly was careful to point out that Halburg had powerful local connections and that there were going to be repercussions. The prosecutor hated it when rich people felt they were above the law, and looked forward to locking up Mr. Halburg. He decided to travel personally to Savannah to supervise the arrest operation and subsequent events. The arrest was supposed to take place any minute, and she was waiting to hear how everything had gone.

Meanwhile, Beverly was looking at the email report she had received from the Homer Trooper regarding his questioning of Aldo's brother-in-law, Izzy. Her analysts had tracked the boat name, Esmeralda, using state registration records. It was based in Ketchikan and owned by a corporation named Marge's Seafood, Inc. There was a Ketchikan address for the company, and the principal shareholders were John and Marge Crawford. Tax returns for the company showed a modest profit and appeared to be in order. It occurred to Beverly that Charlie Skyler might have some connections in Ketchikan. She needed to talk to the Homer trio, so she decided to call that evening.

†

Stuart Halburg was sitting on the veranda of his Savannah mansion drinking a bourbon and branch water. His bimbo du jour, Melody, was lying on her stomach at the edge of the pool wearing a thong and a top with no more than three square inches of cloth. Her swimsuit top was currently unfastened in the back, presumably to allow even tanning. But she kept forgetting to retie it, and every time she moved, her boobs achieved total freedom.

It had started to cool off slightly from the oppressive heat of the day, and a balmy breeze rustled through the trees. The humid Georgia summer evening brought back memories of Vietnam. He had come a long way since those horrible times. Quite a contrast between his current opulent surroundings and those days in the jungle where he wore dirty clothes and slept in a tiny tent. He thought of Aldo and wondered how he was doing in his self-imposed exile.

He also thought of John Vander sitting in a Washington jail — that was not supposed to happen. They had been so careful. It was ironic that Vander was the one in jail, since he was the most law-abiding of the A Squad alumnae. Vander was a gentle man and

322

avoided violence unless absolutely necessary. Stuart certainly could not say the same for his son Frank and stepson Robert. Those two were innately violent and antisocial. He was not sure what he would do if he ever ran into Frank again. He was pretty sure that Frank had killed Jake – they had hated each other since childhood. The biggest regret of his life was the way Frank had turned out. Robert, of course, was another story. Robert and Frank had fed off each other, creating a very bad combination. Robert definitely had some misplaced wiring in his brain, which might not have been so bad except that he was also extremely smart. Stuart wished that Aldo had kept the kid with him in Alaska.

Maria, Stuart's Guatemalan "personal assistant," came running out the back door and blurted that men from the drug enforcement agency were at the front door. Stuart immediately picked up his phone and punched his lawyer's number, which he kept in his emergency contacts list. Reaching his lawyer's receptionist, he told her to tell her boss immediately that the DEA was at the door and he needed help.

Hanging up, Stuart went back through the house and greeted the DEA team, who were already running toward him. Federal Prosecutor Kent Rogers introduced himself and informed Halburg that he was under arrest and that the house and grounds would be searched under the authority of a search warrant. Rogers read him his rights. Stuart informed Rogers that his lawyer was on the way to DEA headquarters and that he would not answer any questions until his lawyer was present. Rogers rolled his eyes and hustled Halburg into one of the DEA sedans for the trip downtown. He wanted to get there before the lawyer so he would have some opportunity to put the fear of God into Halburg regarding the overwhelming evidence. Unfortunately, Stuart's lawyer – former Georgia superior court Judge Cletis Fisher – was already there waiting for them.

Kent Rogers escorted them into their nicest interview room, and they all sat down. Attorney Fisher asked what the charges were and Rogers read off the list, "Well, let's see. Drug trafficking, money laundering, tax evasion, fraud, and domestic violence for starters. The investigation is still ongoing."

Cletis tried to play the intimidation card and blustered about the ridiculous charges and lawsuits that would ruin Rogers' career.

Rogers just smiled and said, "We'll see."

Cletis Fisher then said, "Do you have any proof of these so-called crimes?"

"You'll have plenty of time to review all the evidence before the trial," said Rogers. "But for now, just so you know we are serious, we'll give you some indication of what we've got."

The Federal Prosecutor put a small cassette tape into an old tape player and pressed Play. The scratchy disembodied voice of Stuart Halburg was heard to say, "Don't worry about Mitsy. She's been taken care of. Just send me the fuckin' drugs." Stuart's face at first became pale, then rapidly changed to bright red, and the blood vessels in his temples began to throb as he realized where the tape likely originated. Kent Rogers was afraid that his suspect was going to have a stroke and spoil all of his fun.

Judge Fisher asked if he and his client could have a word in private. "Where did that come from?" he asked when the agents had left.

"It had to be Mitsy. I wonder what else she gave them. We need to find her and make sure she doesn't testify."

"If we intimidate her, it will not help your case."

"I wasn't thinking of intimidation."

"I'm not even going to pursue that line of thought," said the Judge.

"In any event, I want her found, and I want to know what she told them."

"OK. OK. I'll see what I can do. Meanwhile, you're probably going to have to spend the night in jail. I'll try to arrange a bail hearing tomorrow so we can get you out. They're going to want you to stay in jail, but I think your reputation in town will overcome that."

†

Beverly's desk phone rang, and caller ID showed that it was Kent Rogers. She excitedly picked up. Rogers told her that Stuart Halburg was now in jail. As expected, he had immediately called his lawyer. Rogers hoped that bail would be refused because of the likelihood of Rogers being a flight risk. Unfortunately, the Savannah office of the DEA was receiving many calls from people insisting that Halburg was a model citizen, and Rogers felt it was inevitable that he would be released on bail. Nevertheless, the arrest had gone smoothly and the evidence package was strong. They were in the process of searching Halburg's large house, thanks to a federal search warrant. There definitely was pressure from local authorities to make the whole thing go away, but such things only made Kent Rogers more determined.

After work, Beverly picked up Chinese food and went to the park. It was another beautiful evening and she enjoyed watching the kids play. The sight of the children stirred some deeply suppressed emotions, and she suddenly became aware that her biological clock was ticking loudly. These thoughts were logically followed by thoughts of JB. She wanted to get back to Homer in the worst way.

Beverly had earlier arranged with Charlie for the four of them to get together for a conference call at six o'clock. She dialed her throw-away phone, and Charlie answered. Charlie, Kate, and JB were gathered around the dinette table on the Shearwater, with the little mobile phone set on speaker in the middle of the table. Beverly brought them up to date on the successful arrest of Stuart Halburg and the unpleasant meeting with Mr. Ayers. She noted that Robert Fenstrom was on the run and could be headed for Alaska.

"But if Ayers is the only one keeping track of Robert's location, then we will have no way of knowing if he is spotted heading in this direction," said Charlie.

"Unfortunately, that's true," said Beverly. "Ayers certainly isn't going to tell us if Fenstrom has been seen or even if he is apprehended."

"Great," said Kate. "Now we have even less information than we did before."

"I will probably be notified if there is a major change in Fenstrom's status," said JB. "But I think it would be a good idea to refresh the memories of our neighborhood watch team."

"Great idea," said Kate. "I can work on that tomorrow."

"Your state trooper questioned Aldo's brother-in-law and got a little more information. Apparently, Izzy told him that they had picked up a drug shipment in the Gulf of Alaska while fishing. They met a boat called the Esmeralda based out of Ketchikan. The boat is registered under the name of a company called Marge's Seafood, which apparently is owned by John and Marge Crawford. I was hoping that Charlie could use his contacts to learn something about the Crawfords."

"I can do that," said Charlie.

"I talked to my brother a couple days ago," said Kate, "and he said that one thing that might help us to tie things together is the apparent use of satellite phones for primary communication among the members of the syndicate. I don't understand how these things work, but I guess the conversations are protected in a number of ways like encryption and scrambling techniques. But Ned thinks he can find a way to get more information."

"That would be great," said Beverly. "As long as any illegal activities don't get traced back to me. There were some satellite phone provider bills in the stuff we got from Stuart Fenstrom's ex-wife. There isn't much on them, but I'll send a copy to you if that will help. Do you guys have any other business to discuss?"

"Yeah," said JB. "When are you coming back up here?"

"I was just thinking about the same thing," replied Beverly. "As soon as I can arrange it. I have a bunch of comp time to use up."

"Would you like us to leave so you two lovebirds can have a private conversation?" Kate asked.

"It's not necessary," said JB. "We're all mature adults."

Beverly laughed. "Some might argue about that."

Fifty

The Mole knew where the bodies were hidden. In fact, he had put some of them there. He was sitting on Frank's ratty couch, deep in thought. Frank had just received a message from Aldo, saying that his father had been arrested and was now out on bail. Aldo told Frank he was pretty sure that Stuart would try to leave the country before going to trial.

Stuart Halburg was no longer of any use to Robert – he had access to all the money he would ever want, and he was pretty sure he could count on Aldo for help if he needed it. All the humiliation of his childhood came back to him, visions of Stuart whacking his bare butt with a belt as Frank and Jake looked on, laughing. He had information that could put Stuart away for life and assure his immediate return to jail, ending any possibility of escape. All he needed to do was provide an anonymous tip to the DEA. Stuart's second wife, Caroline, currently resided under the ground adjacent to the south pasture on the Halburg plantation. One of the Mole's more unpleasant tasks for the syndicate had been to make Caroline disappear without a trace. After killing her, he had manufactured a trail using her credit cards that showed she had moved to California.

He and Frank were scheduled to leave for Alaska the next day, so he had to act fast, but, whatever he did, it had to be kept secret from Frank. Frank would not go along with double-crossing his own father. Picking up his backpack, which he always kept with him, Robert told Frank he was restless and was going for a walk. He walked several blocks to an Internet café and looked up the phone number of the Drug Enforcement Agency in Los Angeles. He then went to a park, sat on a secluded bench, used his satellite phone to call the DEA, and left a detailed message describing the location of Caroline Halburg's body.

Returning to the little house that Frank shared with his girlfriend, the Mole began to pack for the trip to Alaska. He did not have much. Earlier in the week he had purchased a .308 caliber deer rifle with a scope from a newspaper classified add. The owner was an old man who lived only a few blocks away and was more than happy to take a cash payment. An added benefit was that the guy was nearly blind. Robert disassembled the rifle and packed it in the center of his duffle bag surrounded by clothes.

✝

"Did you find the little bitch?" asked Stuart Halburg. It was sweltering hot on the veranda of the restored antebellum plantation house. But there were too many ears inside the house. Judge Fisher sat next to him, and they were both drinking bourbon on the rocks.

"There is no sign of Mitsy anywhere," said the judge. "I've had two detective agencies searching. It's like she dropped off the surface of the earth a couple of weeks ago. Until that time she was home doing normal stuff – then, poof, she disappears."

"Mitsy isn't smart enough to orchestrate a disappearance all on her own. She must have had help. Most likely the DEA are protecting her. Dammit."

Judge Fisher was enormously relieved that he had not been able to find Mitsy. He did not want any harm that might come to her to be on his conscience. He hoped that Stuart would forget his pursuit.

"The way I see it, I'm pretty much screwed," Stuart said. "I can't afford to stick around for the trial. I need to get out of here as soon as possible."

"As your lawyer, I can't recommend or be involved in any attempt to escape."

"Cut the crap, Judge. I'm tired of your sanctimonious cover-your-ass attitude. You're as involved in illegal enterprises as I am. You certainly have no qualms about accepting payments. The only difference is that you can cover up some of it by attorney-client privilege."

"Be that as it may, even if you are found guilty, you probably won't spend all that much time in jail. So you should consider any plans to run very carefully."

"Any time in jail is too much, as far as I am concerned. But if it's any consolation, I'll make sure you aren't implicated in any escape plans. I've got arrangements to make. Keep me informed of any new developments. I think you know your way out."

Stuart sat for a while, then went into the house, entered his walnut-paneled study, and closed and locked the door. He approached the wall-to-ceiling bookshelves, felt for a hidden latch, and pulled open a section of the bookcase. Behind the bookcase was a Civil War era hiding place. The small room was cool and damp, about ten feet by ten feet, with a prominent trap door in the floor opening to a tunnel that had originally been intended as a way to escape from marauding Union troops. Stuart had not been in the tunnel since he was a child, but he knew that it led to the woods south of the house. Against one of the walls was a safe. Stuart opened the safe and pulled out a zipped portfolio. Re-entering his study, he sat at his desk and opened the portfolio, reviewing its contents. The portfolio contained his escape kit, including two sets of state identification documents, two sets of credit cards, two passports, specific disguise features that matched the pictures on the documents, and a money belt with one hundred thousand dollars. He picked one set of documents and memorized the name and personal information associated with it. He locked the bag in his desk drawer. Then, using the Internet, he made plane reservations.

Fifty-one

Kate started giggling and could not stop. Beer was coming out of her nose as she and JB danced wildly in the sand a few feet from the water's edge at the end of the Homer spit. It was 12:15 am and the sun was just starting to go below the horizon. A huge driftwood fire warmed the cool air blowing off the bay. Couples and small groups of people were dancing around the fire to loud Celtic music. The combined effect of the brilliant scarlet sunset, flickering firelight, Celtic beat, and throbbing bodies had all the characteristics of a pagan ritual. Old pilings from a long-abandoned boardwalk emerged from the sand like a coastal Stonehenge, adding to the mystical ambience. The Homer summer solstice celebration was well underway.

Beverly and Charlie sat in comfortable deck chairs at the edge of the madness, both restricted in the range of their mind alteration by the annoying prospect of random drug tests that were a part of their respective professions. Somehow, beer and wine just did not provide the proper degree of inhibition loss. Nevertheless, they were enjoying watching their friends make fools of themselves.

"Wow," said Beverly. "This scene is so weird I feel like I've entered a parallel universe. But I wouldn't have missed it for the world."

"You're fortunate to be able to observe JB in his natural habitat."

"Defining JB's natural habitat seems like it might not be all that easy."

"You're right about that," Charlie said. "He is an enigma. That's what makes him so fascinating."

"Aside from all the black ops mystery, what do you know about JB?"

"I know that he's one of the smartest, most insightful people I've ever met, and I know that he's a loyal friend. That's all I need to know."

"He's not the only one who is a loyal friend."

Kate and JB wandered over during a momentary lapse in the music. Beverly quickly stood up and tackled JB, followed by much rolling around in the sand, JB's wild hair flying above the sand followed by another roll and Beverly's shapely butt. The rolling and giggling gradually decreased, accompanied by an apparent increase in passion.

"Oh, jeez," said Kate. "You guys are embarrassing. There goes my dance partner."

"Not necessarily." Charlie grabbed Kate's hand and pulled her into the swirling mass of humanity that circled the fire.

†

The next morning, a thin stream of smoke rose from the smoldering bonfire, but the beach was deserted except for a dejected eagle picking morsels of food from a long-dead sea creature. Down the way, a few tourists tried their luck at fishing from shore.

It was late Sunday morning, and all were gathered in the Shearwater's galley once again. Hangovers were the rule of the day, and coffee was flowing. Beverly had arrived in Homer on Friday afternoon with the primary purpose of spending a few days with JB. They had avoided the topic of deranged murderers so that they could enjoy the festivities of the solstice weekend; however, now was the time for a situation update.

"So what's new in our disjointed investigation?" asked Beverly.

"To start with, my brother somehow took the satellite phone stuff from Stuart Halburg that you provided and managed to get some information," Kate replied. "Apparently it's possible to view the call traffic, but it's not possible to determine physical locations of the callers or names of persons responsible for the calls. Anyway, by starting with Stuart's number, he was able to reconstruct a web of interacting callers. He thinks there are four persons who have been talking to each other. The interesting thing is that there was very little traffic for about six months, but just lately the traffic has increased dramatically, suggesting that something is going on. The latest flurry of calls corresponded with the time period just after Robert Fenstrom's escape from DEA clutches."

"That's alarming," Beverly said. "The callers could be Stuart, Aldo, Robert, and maybe Frank – they're all on the loose. We should assume that people are moving around. It would be a good idea to be especially vigilant around here. Robert may be tired of lying low and may have decided to return to Homer to take care of unfinished business."

JB chimed in, "One thing in our favor is that it is going to be difficult for Robert to get to Alaska undetected. Not only are national law enforcement officials looking for him, but also his former employers. It's almost certain that airports and border stations have been alerted. So, if you were Robert, how would you get here?"

"I would come by fishing boat," Charlie replied. "A boat that stays in international waters doesn't have to cross any borders or check in at any location. They could bring a bazooka with them and no one would notice. Plus, at this time of year there are a lot of boats traveling from Portland and Seattle to commercial fish in Alaska."

"That makes sense," Kate said. "But the boat would need to drop him off at a port on the road system, otherwise he'd still have to deal with airport security. That means he'd have to go to Valdez, Seward, Homer, Kenai, or Anchorage. Homer is too close to home, and there is no reason for a fishing boat to go to Anchorage, so that leaves Valdez, Kenai, or Seward."

"I agree," Charlie said. "Valdez is too far away and off the path of most fishing destinations, so Kenai and Seward are the likely choices. Boats large enough to take the outside route to Alaska would probably not be involved in Cook Inlet fisheries, so Kenai might be an unlikely choice. Seward, on the other hand, is used as a refueling stop for larger boats on route to Aleutian fisheries. All of this is pretty far-fetched, but I'm betting on Seward as the port of arrival."

"Assuming that your analysis is correct, what do we do about it?" Beverly asked. "I guess we could alert the Seward police to be on the lookout."

"We could also alert the harbormaster and his staff to keep their eyes open for someone getting off a boat with the apparent intent of leaving the harbor – a guy carrying a duffel bag walking off the docks. Also, once there, our guy will need transportation to Homer, so rental car companies are another possible observation point. Unfortunately, Seward is very busy during the summer fishing season. It seems unlikely that suspicious behavior would actually be noticed."

Beverly frowned. "Let's think about that. It may be worth my while to go to Seward tomorrow and talk to some of the authorities."

"On another front," Charlie said, "I looked into the owners of the vessel Esmeralda. They are not well liked in the Ketchikan fishing community, and there are some questions as to how they have managed to maintain such a prosperous lifestyle while most of the other city residents are struggling. But beyond that, I think the next step needs to be taken by the law enforcement community."

"I'll talk to my boss to see whether he wants to dedicate some resources to investigate further, such resources most likely being me."

"What's happening with Stuart Halburg?' asked Kate.

"Well, as we suspected, he managed to get out on bail. He has a high-powered lawyer – a former judge – helping him. But we're treating him as a flight risk and keeping a close watch on his whereabouts. That's all I know. His trial is scheduled for two months from now."

"Can we keep track of the pattern of calls from the satellite phones?" JB asked. "It may give us some more hints what the bad guys are doing."

"I'll talk to Ned and ask him to monitor the calls," Kate said.

JB turned to Beverly. "How about a quickie before lunch?"

JB got up to leave. Beverly was already on her way out the door.

Fifty-two

Stuart Halburg had dismissed his servants, claiming he was short of money for the time being and would not be able to pay them. The big house suddenly seemed very quiet as he packed a large suitcase. The prospect of leaving the family home was not appealing. He blamed Mitsy, as well as other members of the syndicate, for causing the sudden implosion of his comfortable lifestyle. He had been on the verge of becoming a U.S. senator, for Christ sake, and now it was all unraveling.

He heard several cars pull up in front of the house. Peering out a front window, he saw Kent Rogers, along with about ten burly agents, get out and take up posts surrounding the house. For about ten seconds, Stuart considered answering the door, but then he realized that they would not have come in force unless they had some new damning evidence and intended to take him back into custody. His only chance of escape was through the tunnel. He ran to the study, grabbed his escape bag, and entered the safe room, being very careful to close the secret door completely.

He opened the trap door and descended by an ancient wooden ladder into the tunnel, carrying a flashlight that had been left in a strategic spot. A hundred and fifty years of spider webs blocked his way. The tunnel was much smaller than his childhood memory recalled. It was only about four feet high, and his aging body did not do well in a full crouch. He duck walked and crawled as fast as he could, and after about fifteen minutes he reached the end where there was another ladder leading to an overhead hatch. Stuart looked at his knees and realized that they were bloody, plus there was an intense pain in his back from being bent at the waist for so long. Relieved at being able to stand up straight, he climbed the ladder and pushed on the hatch, but it did not budge.

Full panic began to intrude on his original adrenalin-fueled response to the emergency situation. Using the flashlight, he pounded on the edges of the trap door, hoping to loosen it. The light went out. In a last ditch effort, he reared back on the ladder, lowered his head, and threw his shoulders against the hatch. Amazingly, it broke loose and Stuart poked his head into the dappled sunlight of the forest. There was no sign of anyone around, so he crawled out of the hole and lowered the door. Many years of plant roots had grown over the hatch, making it almost invisible.

Now what? He was filthy, with bloody knees and torn pants, he had no other clothes, and he had no transportation. Stealing a neighbor's car was about his only option. He walked toward his nearest neighbor's house. His back hurt like hell, going into spasms with every wrong move. He was coming close to the county road that provided access to his property. He carefully peered through the underbrush at the roadside, and, seeing no one, he started across the road. As he reached the other side, he heard the unmistakable sound of a round being chambered.

"Stop right there!" A federal agent stood up, aiming a large black automatic at him. Stopping seemed like the prudent thing to do.

†

Shortly after Kent Rogers and his crew had arrived, they were followed by a van with two trained cadaver dogs and a flatbed truck hauling a small backhoe. Establishing that the house was empty, they proceeded to follow the instructions for locating the body that had been provided by the anonymous caller. The supposed burial site was toward the back of the plantation gardens, fronting an overgrown area under a large live oak tree. The terrain and landmarks matched the description perfectly. Immediately, the dogs responded to the precise site that the phone message had described. At the same time, Kent's radio blared with the news that Mr. Halburg had been apprehended on the county road. Found on his person was a shoulder bag containing false identification documents, a large sum of money, and a satellite phone.

A broad smile appeared on Kent Roger's face. "I've got you, you son of a bitch."

The backhoe arrived at the site and started digging carefully under the supervision of a forensic specialist. At the first sight of discolored ground, the backhoe was ordered away, and the forensic team began digging with shovels. Bones appeared, and the site was declared a full-fledged crime scene to be treated with appropriate care. After a few minutes, the chief forensic scientist provided Rogers with a preliminary impression – the body was likely that of a young woman. Rogers smiled again. Halburg's political clout was not going to do him any good now.

†

Beverly got the call from Rogers in late afternoon. He congratulated her on a job well done and related the dramatic details of the apprehension and discovery of the body. She had been the one who recognized the importance of the anonymous message and had immediately passed it on to Rogers, who was still in Savannah directing the prosecution of the case against Halburg. He told her that they had been just in time, and that Stuart was about to leave the country. A half hour later, and they might have missed him. But the way things turned out couldn't have been better. Catching him in the process of fleeing guaranteed that there would be no bail this time, further pounding the nails into his coffin.

Beverly wondered how they might be able to use this turn of events to catch the other members of Aldo's clan. She was pretty sure that Stuart Halburg was not going to inform on the other group members, at least not on the original members of Aldo's squad. But it might be possible to use Stuart's satellite phone to get information on the others. She made a mental note to ask her tech guys about it and also to talk to Kate and see whether her brother had any ideas. Beverly was concerned about the Homer trio and hoped that Stuart's second arrest might provide them with an advantage. The anonymous tip had to have come from someone inside the syndicate, and Stuart likely knew who it was. Maybe he would be willing to selectively snitch on other members of the group to avoid the death penalty.

Fifty-three

House-sized swells came from the southwest, one after another in a nauseating slow-motion rhythm. Every twelve seconds the boat fell off the top of the wave into the trough – each drop like a roller coaster – only to be lifted again. The waves, spawned by storms near Hawaii, travelled three thousand miles to the Gulf of Alaska, a journey requiring about two weeks. The large wave fronts passed over schools of salmon pursuing plankton and small fish while being, in turn, pursued by sharks and Orcas. Seabirds sat on the waves, rising and falling, a boring life punctuated by an occasional frenzied binge on a school of bait fish.

"You picked a fuckin' lousy boat," Robert said. "I had more fun crawling through the swamps during Ranger training."

The Mary Ann was the dirtiest boat Robert had ever been on. The smell of old rotting fish, diesel fuel, mildew, and sweaty raingear was constant. The crew quarters in the foc'sle obviously had not been cleaned in years. The boat had spent most of its long life moored at the commercial docks in Seattle and was infested with cockroaches and who knew what else. There were four bunks arranged in two tiers on each side of the central walkway. Robert and Frank had one side, and the two deckhands had the other side, while Shane, the skipper, slept on a bunk in the galley. The shower in the single head was inoperable, and no one seemed interested in fixing it. And, worst of all, the toilet was clogged up most of the time, sloshing as the boat rolled and pitched.

Robert and Frank were lying on top of folds of netting stacked on the back deck. Although it was chilly on the water, the cabin had become too oppressive and they were tired of making small talk with the crew. The fresh sea air felt good and certainly smelled a whole lot

343

better than the inside of the Mary Ann. They were five days into their journey, steaming northward somewhere offshore from the Alaska panhandle. Both of them had spent time on fishing boats, and neither was squeamish or prone to motion sickness, but the Mary Ann took unpleasantness to a whole new level. Frank had butterflies in his gut every time the boat plunged down off the top of a swell, like the feeling he had as a child on his backyard swing, except that there was no end to the motion. He tried not to think about last night's dinner, when the "cook" had fried fish in recycled oil taken from a jar on the top galley shelf. The oil was dark brown and contained chunks of prior dinners, some that may have been decades old.

Robert was beginning to wonder why he was here. He thought of white sand beaches and the beautiful island girl with the smooth brown skin, long black hair, and large eyes that were almost black. One of the peculiar things about Robert's mental condition was his ability to look outside of himself, as if part of him was a psychiatrist trying to analyze the other psychotic part. He knew full well that pursuing vengeance against his foes in Alaska was irrational and maybe even evil, but he also knew that the psychotic side would win – it always did. Put simply, he was turned on by violence.

He knew that the treatment he had received as a child from Stuart Halburg was part of the reason he turned out the way he did. He desperately wanted to find out whether his message to the DEA had been received in time to prevent his "stepfather" from escaping to another country. Unfortunately, his snitching on Stuart could seriously affect his relationship with Frank. Because of their long history and childhood companionship, Robert had no desire to alienate Frank. He had subtly disabled Frank's satellite phone before they left Seattle and had pretended that his own phone was broken.

In general, Frank was a much simpler person than he was. Frank was immature, with modest intelligence and poor impulse control, but at the same time operated with a sort of common sense that served him well most of the time. Robert knew that Frank's thoughts were pretty much centered on demonstrating to Kate Perkins that she was not as great as she thought she was. The way she had treated Frank at FlashFrozen could not be forgiven. That was probably the only reason he had agreed to come along with Robert.

†

JB was actually working on his book. He had reviewed dozens of scholarly and not-so-scholarly articles about popular political movements throughout history and was trying to make sense of present-day political polarization by looking at the past. It was tempting to be cynical and conclude that people are chronically irrational, but he hoped that the truth was more complicated. Otherwise, there would not be much hope for mankind.

As he was pondering these weighty matters, his phone rang. His heart quickened when he saw the caller ID. He was not expecting a call from Beverly until evening, but he was happy to talk to her anytime. Beverly explained to JB about the anonymous tip, finding Caroline's body, and Stuart Halburg's second arrest. They speculated about the source of the tip.

"The tip was phoned in, right?" JB asked. "Were you able to track the incoming phone number?"

"The number was blocked on caller ID, but our tech guys did some analyses and they think it came from some kind of mobile phone, but not a local cell phone. The logical assumption is that it was a satellite phone."

"So, the call probably came from someone on the inside in Aldo's group. Who would want to see Stuart in jail? It seems unlikely that one of the original Vietnam squad members would be involved. All the indications are that they are very loyal to each other. We have to look to the next generation or someone unknown to us."

"I agree. Also, the preciseness of the description of the body's location was so detailed that it seems likely the caller was there at the time of the murder."

"The most likely candidate is probably Robert Fenstrom," said JB. "We know that he was an enforcer for the syndicate. Stuart might have instructed him to kill his wife, or they may have worked together in some way to get the deed done. We don't know what the relationship was like between the young Robert and his pseudo stepfather. Since Stuart had two sons of his own, the dynamics could have been difficult for Robert. I can see Stuart treating Robert badly. Now that the drug business has disintegrated, Robert might have felt that he had nothing to lose by snitching on his stepfather."

"Sounds good to me. If Kate's brother can track the satellite phone call traffic, then he should be able to determine whether one of the phones in his web made a call to the DEA."

"Good point," JB said. "I'll talk to Kate and see whether she can motivate her brother. It might also be useful to get some idea of the call traffic patterns in the last week so that we can get some insight into their recent activities."

Fifty-four

Two days after talking to JB, Beverly was in Ketchikan. She had convinced her boss that she needed to investigate the Ketchikan connection. He had initially been skeptical that another trip to Alaska would accomplish anything. However, while Beverly was running background checks on John and Marge Crawford, co-owners of the Esmeralda, she discovered that Marge's maiden name was Smithson. It was way too big a coincidence that her name would be the same as Carl Smithson, CEO of Offshore Enterprises and one of Aldo's original Vietnam squad members. Further checking confirmed that Marge was, indeed, Carl's sister. Nepotism was obviously a signature characteristic of Aldo's operation.

Beverly's hotel sat on the mountainside above the town, and her room had an expansive view, overlooking the downtown area, the busy shipping channel called Tongass Narrows, and Gravina Island, the site of Ketchikan's airport. She watched the small airport ferry as it crossed the channel every fifteen minutes, carrying travelers back and forth. The infamous "bridge to nowhere" had been intended to link the City of Ketchikan with Gravina Island and provide convenient access to the airport. Loud float planes took off about every two minutes from the Narrows, reminding her of her previous adventures while pursuing John Vander. Somehow the planes managed to dodge all manner of boats as they navigated the crowded waterway, pulling up at the last minute and climbing over approaching cruise liners.

The problem, now that she was here, was what to do in the way of investigation. Simply questioning the Crawfords probably would not get her very far, given past experience with the major players in the operation. She had some leverage in the form of Izzy's informal testimony, but she was not at all sure that Izzy would actually testify at a trial, assuming he survived long enough. Revealing Izzy's cooperation could put him in danger. She decided to hold back on revealing any evidence for now and to approach the situation by first questioning some of the other fishermen and processors in town. The fishing community was small and would probably be anxious to gossip about a competitor, especially since Charlie's inquiries had suggested that the Crawfords were not overly popular.

The first place Beverly went was one of the biggest fish processing plants in town. Using her credentials, she got in to see the owner/manager of the company. He was familiar with Marge's Seafood and not too happy with their independent operation. Apparently they did everything themselves – catching, processing, and marketing – which went against the tradition of Alaskan fishing, where fishermen were often beholden to large processing companies for their livelihood. The processors controlled the price and often were at odds with the fishermen who felt they had no choice but to go along. However, the plant owner had no knowledge of any illegal activity. Beverly went away from the interview with grudging respect for the Crawfords, who seemed to have the courage to buck the system.

Next, she went to lunch with Ralphie, Charlie's old college buddy who had helped out earlier with information on the Rainbow Inn. Ralphie was a friendly guy who seemed to know everything about everybody. Beverly poured on the charm, and Ralphie became putty in her hands. Although he was involved in sport fishing rather than commercial fishing, he knew most of the fishermen and was familiar with the Crawfords. According to Ralphie, they kept to themselves and did not play an active part in Ketchikan civic affairs. The Crawfords lived in a big, modern house on the water near the end of the highway north of town. They had their own dock facilities where they kept their boats along with an ocean side warehouse. Ralphie reckoned that the value of the house, boats, and dock facilities was several million dollars – much more than the average fisherman could afford. He always assumed that they were either independently wealthy or that something else was going on.

As it happened, one of Ralphie's best friends and his wife lived next door to the Crawfords, and he volunteered to introduce Beverly to them. Consequently, an hour later Beverly found herself sitting in a cozy living room with Sam and Marsha Waterston, their black Labrador, Nutjob, and Ralphie, who insisted on escorting Beverly around town. Through the large picture window they could see Tongass Narrows, and, off to the right, the dock and warehouse belonging to the Crawfords. The Esmeralda was tied up at the end of the private dock. Without going into detail, Beverly explained that she was investigating questionable activities associated with Marge's Seafoods.

"It's about time somebody investigated those lowlifes," Marsha said.

"Why do you say that?" Beverly asked.

"Well, first of all, they are very unfriendly. We've lived next to them for five years and never had any interaction with them. We invited them to dinner when we first moved here, and they pretty much told us to shove it. Secondly, there has been a lot of late night traffic to their place, both by boat and car. The noise and activity have been annoying, to say the least. We've suspected for a long time that drugs are a part of the equation."

"Have you ever notified the police?"

"I mentioned the situation to the police chief a couple of years ago, but he didn't do anything," Sam Waterston said.

"Is there any pattern to the comings and goings?" Beverly asked.

"The traffic seems to peak at about 11:30 each night, and Saturdays are always the busiest days," Marsha said.

After driving back to town and leaving Ralphie, Beverly returned to her hotel. He had been disappointed that Beverly was not interested in accompanying him to a local pub, and Beverly felt sort of bad about it, as Ralphie was such a nice, innocent guy. But she was there on a mission. It was obvious that Marge's Seafood was a front for a drug distribution operation, but there was insufficient direct evidence to permit a raid and search of the premises. As long as she was in Ketchikan, she might as well try to get enough information for a search warrant.

She watched lame TV until ten o'clock, then donned her black stakeout clothes and drove her rental car out toward Marge's Seafood. It was not dark. How did Alaskan law enforcement authorities sneak around during the summer when it was not dark enough for optimum concealment? However, it was overcast and starting to rain; with luck, it would be dark enough by the time she got into position to allow her to hide effectively.

When she and Ralphie were there earlier, she had scoped out the terrain and possible avenues of approach. Just beyond the Crawford's property was a state park with a parking area. She left the car there, hiked down to the beach, and proceeded along the water's edge toward the Crawford's dock. Her backpack contained night vision binoculars, a light-sensitive camera, and a small directional sound amplification system. The sound system was connected to a small recorder. She hoped that she could obtain photos and recorded conversation that would prove that drug transactions were occurring. In a holster at the small of her back was her faithful nine millimeter Glock. It was Friday night, and it seemed likely that some deals might go down. It would be her only chance; she had to return to LA the next day.

It was fortuitous that the wooded property next to Marge's Seafoods was densely vegetated and allowed a close approach that overlooked both the dock and the driveway to the house. Additionally, side windows provided some visibility into the house, and an open deck overlooking the waterfront was only seventy-five feet from Beverly's location. The lack of curtains suggested that they were not too concerned about being watched. There was no sign of any outside security or dogs; dogs were always the bane of close surveillance operations.

Beverly found a flat spot behind an elder bush and settled in for a long evening. She had always believed in being comfortable during stakeouts. Her pack also contained a blanket to sit on, a thermos of coffee, and four Twinkies. Normally she ate only healthy stuff, but it was tradition to allow herself the luxury of junk food to alleviate the boredom of endless nights. She was finally settled in by eleven-thirty, and it was getting quite dark.

Shortly after midnight, as Beverly was finishing her second Twinkie, two cars pulled up to the front of the house and disgorged four young men dressed in baggy pants and hooded sweatshirts. The men entered the house without knocking, passed through the main part of the house, and proceeded out to the deck. She could not believe her good luck – she was so close that she could almost hear the conversations without the aid of her directional microphone. While taking multiple photographs, she listened and recorded.

John and Marge Crawford followed the men onto the deck, casually taking seats at an outdoor table while the men stood impatiently nearby. The conversation that followed clearly indicated a drug buy, as the Crawfords asked to see the money and the leader of the men asked to examine the quality of what appeared to be a package of heroin or cocaine. The kicker was when one of the men loudly exclaimed his pleasure regarding the "primo smack."

Beverly elatedly began to pack up her equipment when she saw a brown four-legged blur launch itself from the deck and run toward her. She crammed everything into her pack and backed up toward the beach. It was pointless to run. She pulled her gun and waited for the dog.

Although only a few seconds elapsed, time slowed down, and Beverly's brain assumed a state of amazing clarity. While aiming her pistol she was able to simultaneously catalog various facts – the dog was a scary-looking pit bull mix and was approaching fast; most of the people on the deck had run into the house; Marge Crawford had remained and was aiming a gun toward Beverly's position; intervening trees prevented Marge from getting a clear shot. Beverly squeezed off one shot when the dog was about ten feet away, dropping it in its tracks. She raced down the beach away from the Crawfords and toward the state park parking lot. She heard two shots behind her, but did not turn around to see what was happening.

Beverly realized that the Crawfords were in a perfect position to block her way back into town, so it would not do much good to return to her car. She knew that she was going to have to do what she really did not want to do, which was call local law enforcement.

Her initial good luck was turning into shit. First of all, she had had to shoot a dog – she loved dogs – and, second, she was going to be in a world of trouble for not notifying local authorities about her plans. Having to explain all this stuff to Ketchikan police, not to mention her own boss, was not a happy thought. However, getting shot by drug dealers was even less appealing.

Stepping into the cover of dense second-growth forest, Beverly pulled out her cell phone and dialed 911. At first, the dispatcher did not want to believe that she was really a DEA agent and was really taking fire, but finally her desperation seemed to get through to the obtuse and sleepy 911 operator. The dispatcher informed her that at least two patrol cars were on their way to the state park lot where Beverly would be waiting.

Meanwhile, she needed to stay alive for at least ten minutes until they got here. Beverly sincerely hoped that the Crawfords only had one dog. She moved quietly through the forest until reaching the back edge of the parking lot, then retreated into the underbrush so that she was out of sight but still had a clear view of the lot. Donning night-vision goggles, she watched and waited. Soon, four young men sauntered into the parking lot and approached her rental car. They peered into the car windows in apparent frustration. One of the men pulled an automatic from his belt and fired three shots into the car.

Shit. Something else she'd have to explain. The men did not seem inclined to enter the dark woods in pursuit of a woman with a gun. They stood around for a few minutes trying to figure out what to do, then they ran back down the road. A second later, Beverly heard the sirens and breathed a sigh of relief.

†

Beverly was racking up demerits at a rapid rate. She sat in an uncomfortable metal chair in the interrogation room of the Ketchikan police department. The police chief had been awakened in the middle of the night and asked to come in to the office. Additionally, Beverly's boss, Agent Phillips, had also been awakened and questioned about Beverly's legitimacy. The local cops were not happy with the situation, since it trespassed on their turf and also interrupted their peaceful summer, which was usually dedicated to fishing. And then she learned that the chief was a long-time friend of Marge Crawford – in fact, they had gone to high school together. Beverly did not want to think about the red tape involved with the three bullet holes in her rental car (of course, she had declined the insurance coverage).

Things were not going Beverly's way until she convinced the cops to at least look at the photos and listen to the tape of the drug deal. The evidence was so clear that even the chief had to agree that things were not right. Finally, Beverly was able to tell her whole story about the drug syndicate and the involvement of Marge's Seafoods. The chief's long-term acquaintance with the Crawfords actually became an advantage, since all of Beverly's details jibed with what he knew about them, including the Vietnam experience of Marge's brother.

But what should they do now? The Crawfords obviously knew that they were under suspicion, thanks to Beverly's clumsy surveillance. If an arrest was going to be made, it would have to be as soon as possible, before the Crawfords had a chance to leave town.

On the positive side, Ketchikan was a hard place to leave; there were no roads out of town.

Beverly figured she might as well go for broke. "Look Chief, I know this has all been a hassle for you and I'm sorry for the lack of coordination, but we need to decide how to proceed right away. The Fenstrom syndicate has been involved in at least four murders in recent years, and the Crawfords are definitely a part of the group, even though they may not have been directly involved in the violence. At a minimum, we should keep them under surveillance until we can get arrest warrants. They may try to escape by boat or plane, if they haven't already."

"I agree," the Chief said. "I'll assign some officers to stake out the house and watch the dock. As soon as Judge Sorenson comes in later this morning, I'll ask him for a warrant based on your evidence."

"That would be great." Beverly reached for her pocket, when her cell phone rang. She listened for a few seconds, then became excited. "That was Marsha Waterston, who lives next door to the Crawfords. She says they are loading up the Esmeralda and apparently preparing to leave. She figured there was something going on there tonight because of all the activity and thought I might want to know."

"Crap, what would we do without busybodies?" The Chief groaned. "You've been making all kinds of friends since you've been here. I'll mobilize land and water forces to make an immediate arrest. It may take a little while at this time of night, so we might miss them. I'll also call the Coast Guard. There is a base here in town, and they have a couple of fast boats that could help. It's unlikely that a boat the size of the Esmeralda will get very far."

"Thanks, Chief." Beverly gave him her best alluring smile. The Chief rolled his eyes.

Fifty-five

"I just talked to my brother," Kate said as she stepped aboard the Shearwater. "One of the syndicate satellite phones was definitely used to transmit the tip about Stuart Halburg's ex-wife to the DEA. So, the theory that Robert Fenstrom made the call may be correct. Also, my brother said that there has been no phone traffic from any of the numbers for about three days. I'm not sure what that means."

"It sounds kind of ominous to me," Charlie said. "But I don't know why."

Charlie and JB were lying on lounge chairs on the back deck, each with a bottle of beer. A bowl of potato chips was between them. Kate, having just gotten off work, looked disgusted at the scene of male slothfulness.

"Boy, it's a good thing someone around here works for a living." Kate commandeered the potato chip bowl and started shoving chips into her mouth.

JB's phone rang, and JB checked the caller ID. "It's the beautiful Beverly. I wonder what she has to say." He answered and listened for several minutes, occasionally nodding his head, then uttered some uncharacteristically mushy words of endearment and hung up.

"Our intrepid DEA agent has been busy. Apparently, the Ketchikan connection has been terminated, thanks to her stubborn determination and foolhardiness. The owners of the Esmeralda have been arrested. They were caught by the Coast Guard in the act of trying to escape by boat from Beverly's clutches. It sounds like an interesting story – something about being shot at and having to kill a nasty dog, then being held by the local authorities. In other words, pretty much what you would expect from Beverly."

"There can't be much left of Aldo's distribution system," Kate said. "Almost everybody's in jail except, unfortunately, the most dangerous members of the group. Maybe the reason there haven't been any phone calls is because there is no one left to talk to."

"At least if calls are made, we know that they have to be limited to just three or four people. So who is left? We've got Aldo, Robert, and Frank, and maybe the remaining squad member, Carl Smithson, wherever he may be. We can probably assume that the guys in jail won't be contacting any of the principals," Charlie said.

"The silence is worrisome," JB said. "I have the feeling that Aldo likes to keep track of what is going on. Maybe Robert and Frank have gone silent because they don't want Aldo to know what they are doing. And, if that's the case, it makes you wonder what they might be up to. Coming to Alaska to dispatch us comes to mind."

"I don't like that theory," Kate said.

"Let's talk to the Super Trooper. He will be interested to know that the information he got from Izzy helped to nail the bad guys in Ketchikan, and we can warn him that more bad guys may be on the way to Homer," said Charlie.

†

"Where the fuck is everybody?" mused Aldo. As usual, he was sitting on the veranda of his shack with a cool rum drink in his hand. In his other hand was the satellite phone, which seemed to have become a totally useless hunk of plastic. He might as well use it to club the lizards constantly invading his space. He had called everybody in the network and had received no answers or call backs.

He was feeling totally disoriented. For the last forty years, he had been the ultimate puppet master, orchestrating the activities of a complex organization from his remote Alaska location, but now all the strings were broken and he was unable to find out what was going on.

He even contemplated calling Izzy, but Izzy was normally so clueless that Aldo didn't think it was worth the risk.

As he was trying to think of a way to get information on what was left of his operation, his phone buzzed. He picked it up to find that he was talking to Carl Smithson for the first time since his escape from the north. Carl had slunk away at the first sign of trouble with a substantial portion of the syndicate's assets, and Aldo was not happy with him. However, he listened intently as Carl informed him that his sister and her husband in Ketchikan had been arrested. Additionally, Stuart Halburg's lawyer had tracked Smithson down and told him that Stuart had been arrested for the murder of his ex-wife, thanks to an inside tip from someone in the organization, likely Aldo's son. Aldo was so upset that he forgot to get mad at Smithson. He just thanked him and hung up.

Aldo was severely conflicted regarding his feelings about his son. When Robert's mother had left him and returned to Vietnam, Aldo had tried to raise young Robert, but ultimately it was just too much. The decision to ship Robert off to live with the Halburg family seemed sensible at the time. After all, Aldo was a reclusive heroin addict living in the Alaska wilderness, while Stuart Halburg was a successful businessman living in a comfortable city. But the Vietnam experience had warped Stuart more than Aldo anticipated, and he turned out to be a dismal and cruel stepfather.

On the one hand, Aldo could not blame Robert for wanting to seek revenge, but, on the other hand, Stuart had been Aldo's right-hand man during those awful war days. They had pledged loyalty to each other and he had always demanded loyalty from all members of the organization. The other conflicting element was Robert's recent decision to leave most of the money in the Cayman account for Aldo's use. This was an unexpected act of affection that had completely thrown Aldo off balance. Considering everything, Aldo decided that he could not be too angry at Robert. Stuart Halburg had used up his loyalty quotient by treating Robert badly and by generally putting his own ambition ahead of the needs of the syndicate. He was basically a very unpleasant person who had murdered his ex-wife and bullied many people to achieve his ends.

But what now? The entire network was destroyed, and the drug business was defunct. Robert and his sidekick Frank were still on the loose. Both were dangerous men with poor impulse control – anything could happen. Aldo was worried both for Robert's welfare and the possibility that Robert's activities could somehow lead the authorities to him. He wanted to know what his son was doing, but Robert was not answering his phone.

Fifty-six

It was the height of salmon fishing season, and the Seward harbor was bustling with commercial and sport-fishing craft. The docks were totally full, and boats rafted three deep. After nearly two weeks at sea, the Mary Ann pulled into the harbor and went directly to the fuel dock. Shane intended to head immediately back out to sea after filling the large fuel tanks.

"This is where you get off," said Shane. "I don't know whether to wish you luck or not, but whatever it is you're doing, keep my name out of it."

"Don't worry," Robert said. "No one will know how we got to Alaska. Good fishing."

Robert and Frank stepped onto the floating dock with their duffle bags and walked up the ramp. Shane's crew members looked longingly at the tavern overlooking the harbor. They were tired of canned beans, no alcohol, and lack of female company. The last thing they wanted to do was head back out into the Gulf of Alaska.

Robert and Frank had agreed that they would split up in Seward and each follow their own agenda. Frank had grown a full beard while on the boat, but he was still the more recognizable of the pair because of the extended time spent in Homer. Plus, the Mole always insisted on working alone – he was obsessive about controlling all the variables. In the back of his mind was the possibility that Frank might actually divert attention from him by bumbling his attempts to avenge his rejection by Kate Perkins. It could be perfect cover for his plans.

Robert found the closest grungy hotel and rented a room for one night. He bought a local newspaper and looked in the classified ads for an inexpensive car. He called several of the ads from a pay phone and settled on an old Chevy blazer that sounded like it was in reasonable

359

condition. He arranged for the owner to meet him and, after a short test drive, paid cash for the vehicle. The former owner of the car would mail the title transfer paperwork to the Division of Motor Vehicles using one of the Mole's many identities, assuring that there would be no public record for at least a couple of weeks. It was unlikely that anyone would connect the car to him.

The Mole then decided that he needed a little R&R after the god-awful boat trip, so he took a long shower, changed his clothes, and went out for a good dinner. It was tempting to prowl the bars for a sexual liaison, but he resisted the temptation, deciding that it was too risky. In his hotel room, he took his handgun and rifle out of the duffle bag and spent two hours obsessively cleaning and oiling the precision machines to rid them of rust and residue from exposure to salt air. He slept very well in spite of the apparent rocking of his bed. Two weeks on the boat had thoroughly messed up his equilibrium.

Meanwhile, Frank, taking a more direct approach, went directly to a car rental agency, rented a small sedan, and drove north on the Seward Highway until he came to a fishing lodge, where he rented a room for the night.

†

Beverly tacked a photograph on the cloth-covered partition of her office cubicle. The ink-jet print showed her and JB standing on the deck of Charlie's boat with mountain scenery in the background. Looking at JB's wild face, she had a sudden chill. She knew their relationship made no sense by just about anyone's standards. There were so many things wrong with it that it was totally ridiculous to even consider the long-term prospects. But the fact remained that she could not stop thinking about him. As she pondered the cliché that love was irrational, her phone rang. The caller ID said "Seward Fuel," which sent another chill down her back.

"Hi, is this Beverly at the DEA?"

"It sure is."

"Yeah, this is Johnny at the Seward Harbor fuel dock. You stopped and talked to me a while back."

"I remember. What's up, Johnny?"

"A seiner called the Mary Ann stopped for fuel about an hour ago. Two guys with duffle bags got off and just walked up the ramp and headed toward town. The Mary Ann filled up with fuel and went back out to sea. It looked like there was a captain and two crew members still on board. The two guys roughly matched the descriptions that you gave us. One of them had a full beard, so I can't be sure. The other had a cap and sunglasses, but from what I was able to see his features appeared Asian. Anyway, it's pretty unusual for people to disembark at the fuel dock, so I thought I would call."

"You did right, Johnny. That's excellent information. If these guys turn out to be our bad guys, I'll make sure you get a commendation. Thanks a lot. If you see them again, let me know."

Beverly instructed her assistants to check into hotels and car rentals to get a better description and see if the movements of the mystery pair could be traced any further. Then she talked to her boss and asked his permission to travel to Alaska.

Agent Phillips said, "Again? You're going to go whether I give you permission or not, right?"

"Probably."

"Well then, you better get going. Meanwhile, I'll alert the Alaska law enforcement folks that these guys are likely back in their territory."

"Thanks, Boss." Beverly called and alerted JB and Charlie to the situation, then made plane reservations.

†

The Super Trooper was, once again, trying to clear his desk of endless paperwork when the notice showed up on his computer to be on the lookout for Robert Fenstrom and Frank Halburg, based on a probable sighting in Seward earlier in the day. It was a beautiful summer day in Homer and Bob had planned to go off shift at four o'clock so that he and Julie could go fishing in the bay. His small boat was gassed up and ready to go.

He could see his fishing trip evaporating. If the bad guys went directly from Seward to Homer, they could conceivably be arriving soon. "Damn."

Robert Fenstrom was a truly scary guy who possessed skills that were way beyond anything that Bob had learned at the trooper academy. He was frightened of any kind of a face-off. Since he and Julie had gotten together, he had developed a somewhat different perspective on facing dangerous situations. Julie was doing great, their relationship was prospering, and there appeared to be real prospects for a future together; consequently, he was feeling that he had responsibilities beyond himself. But still, he needed to do his job.

He called Charlie, only to find out that Charlie had already gotten the word – not a big surprise, since Charlie had been one step ahead all through the Fenstrom affair. Next, he got in his cruiser and went to Gertie's Bar. In recent months Gertie had proven to be a good friend, helping to raise money for Julie's rehabilitation and generally being supportive throughout the process. As usual, Gertie was leaning on the bar providing her customers a clear view into her cavernous cleavage and the colorful iguana residing therein.

"Have you no shame?" Bob grinned as he attempted unsuccessfully to avert his eyes.

"Basically, no," Gertie admitted. "What can I do for law enforcement today?"

"You can keep your eyes open for the two guys I told you about a while back. Do you still have their photos?"

"Yeah, they're still right here behind the bar." She pulled out the photos.

"The guy on the left, Frank Halburg, had a full beard when he was possibly seen getting off a boat in Seward, so use your imagination and picture him with a beard."

"So, they were in Seward. When was that?"

"This morning," I figured you know more about the sleazy underbelly of Homer society than anyone, so you may hear something."

"Gosh, thanks. How is Julie doing?"

"She's great. Everything is cool so far."

"That's good, Bob. I'll keep my eyes open."

"Thanks, Gertie."

†

"This has been the longest day ever," Kate thought as the clock on the wall chimed 4:30 and she got up from behind her desk. It was the end of the month, and she was dealing with payroll issues. She said good night to her coworkers and began her short walk back to the Shearwater, stopping at the little fisherman's store for a bag of potato chips. She looked down from the edge of the harbor into the boat basin and noticed that several people were in the cabin of Charlie's boat. When she saw the trooper car parked at the head of the ramp, she got a bad feeling.

Beverly, JB, Charlie, and the Super Trooper were all sitting at the dinette table and looking serious when Kate entered.

"Beverly! Hi. Do I want to know what is going on?" Kate asked. Beverly and Kate hugged.

"Probably not," Charlie said. "There is a good chance that Robert Fenstrom and Frank Halburg were sighted getting off a boat in Seward this morning. We're discussing what to do about it."

"Shit." Kate kicked off her shoes and sat down at the table. "How reliable is the report?"

"I think it's pretty reliable," Beverly told her. "It also fits everything else we know. Charlie says that it would take a seiner type boat about ten days to get from Seattle to Seward, and that matches the phone silence period. They likely left right after Robert tipped us off about the unfortunate demise of Stuart Halburg's late ex-wife."

Someone had to say it. "I assume that everybody thinks the main reason they're here is to get revenge."

"Unfortunately, we can't think of any other reason," JB admitted. "They are taking a significant risk being here, which doesn't say much for their sanity."

Beverly's phone rang. She picked up the call from her home office, listened for a while, then instructed her assistant to inform Agent Phillips of the situation and ask him to put out an APB in south-central Alaska for the rental car. "We've learned that someone matching Robert's description spent the night in a cheap hotel alone. That's all we know about him. Meanwhile, someone matching Frank's description rented a car in Seward and hasn't been seen since. It looks like they've split up. I can't imagine Robert being stupid enough to rent a car, so he must have found another means of transportation." She looked at JB. "What would you do if you were Robert?"

"I would buy a car listed in a classified ad – using a false name, of course. That would leave virtually no trail, since the former owner simply mails a vehicle transfer form to DMV. In fact, that was what we were taught to do in a class I once took. Robert may have taken the same class."

Beverly immediately dialed her data analyst back in Los Angeles and told her to call all the classified car ads listed in Seward periodicals and see if anyone matching Robert's description had recently purchased a car.

Bob appeared to be amazed. "You guys don't mess around," he said. This was the first time Beverly and Bob had met. Beverly was being careful not to appear too aggressive so Bob would not feel that he was being preempted. The fact that Beverly had turned on her special "male manipulation" cuteness also helped. She was not above using her feminine wiles to enhance her relations with male law enforcement officers when necessary. JB surreptitiously glanced at Beverly and rolled his eyes; Beverly smiled back.

"Now that the gang's all here, do we have a plan?" Kate asked.

"The fact that they may have split up and may have separate agendas makes it a little difficult," Charlie said. "Frank seems to have a special dislike for Kate, because of his thwarted advances at FlashFrozen, so he may concentrate on going after her. Robert was humiliated by JB and me, so he may concentrate on coming after us. Frank seems to be acting on impulse, while Robert has been trained to carefully cover his tracks and pursue his prey. We probably need two different strategies."

"My gut tells me that Robert will be more deliberate this time, since he doesn't want to make the same mistakes he did before," Beverly said. "He may play more of a cat and mouse game, waiting for ideal opportunities. So he is likely going to set up some kind of surveillance, get an idea of your habits, maybe follow you guys and wait for the right time to strike. I'm guessing sniper tactics may play a part. One strategy might be for us to surveille the surveillance. Try to identify someone who is in a position to watch what is going on. We know that Robert is a master of disguises, so we need to get into his head and figure out what he may do."

"Since all three of us spend most of our lives at the harbor, he will obviously need to be in a position to see our boats and cars," Kate said. "I know a woman who owns a top floor condo at the end of the spit. If we could get her permission to camp out on the roof, we could look back toward the harbor – it would be a good vantage point."

"That sounds like a great idea," JB said. "The bad guys could be arriving imminently, so we need to get going right away. I can take the first shift if you want. Beverly, do you have any night vision equipment?"

"It just so happens I do."

"I'll call Laura right now." Kate scrolled through her phone directory.

Fifty-seven

Frank Halburg awoke to a beautiful morning with sun streaming through the window and birds singing. The lodge on the Kenai River had the kind of north-woods atmosphere that was common in various parts of the country where city folks came to the "wilderness" to partake of manly sports. He got dressed and walked from his little riverside cabin to the main lodge and its central dining area. The lobby and dining room were predictably decorated with the dusty heads of various dead animals, along with an assortment of antique guns and ancient tools.

He was unbelievably glad to be off of the boat. It had been one of the most unpleasant two weeks of his entire life. It mystified him how Robert had been able to put himself in a sort of trance to help him endure the boredom and constant motion. Robert was not like everybody else, and Frank's relationship with him was complicated – a sort of brotherly love combined with fear and awe. Part of him was relieved that they had agreed to go their separate ways.

He was no longer nauseated and was, in fact, extremely hungry. A perky, but remarkably unattractive, waitress approached his table. She wore a low-cut peasant dress that was mostly unsuccessful in improving her appearance. Frank ordered eggs, bacon, and pancakes and sat back to enjoy the view of the blue-green river. He also asked if they could prepare bag lunches for two people so that he would have enough food for a couple of days if need be. A float plane was anchored to the dock in front of the lodge, and Frank watched a group of city-slickers in brand new fishing vests and expensive high-tech waders load into the plane for transport to some fishy off-road site. He did not really understand why such activities would be fun, but it was entertaining watching the rubes strut their stuff.

367

After a leisurely and very satisfying breakfast, Frank picked up his bag lunches, packed his stuff, got into his tinny, compact rental car, and headed toward the southwestern part of the Kenai Peninsula. His gun was on the seat beside him under a duffle bag. He was still 120 miles from Homer when he left the curvy mountain roads behind and came onto a long, straight stretch where a car could go a hundred miles an hour. Unfortunately, prudence and his current fugitive status required that he maintain a nearly legal speed. He was not particularly concerned about the cops since, as far as he knew, no one knew he was in Alaska. Frank caught a glimpse of a blue and white State Patrol vehicle as he passed an intersection, but did not give it much thought, since his speed was 58 miles per hour. But a few seconds later, a car with lights and siren pulled out behind him.

As often happened in such situations, Frank's instincts took over and he automatically came up with a plan to buy himself enough time to get away. First, he had to get off the main highway to a secluded location. Since traffic was light, it might be possible to do so without anyone else seeing what was going on. A gravel side road appeared on the left, and he made a quick turn onto it, causing the trooper to overshoot the turnoff. Proceeding another thousand feet, he pulled off the road into the trees and immediately stopped, grabbed his gun, and leapt out of the car. After hiding behind a clump of brushy willows, he had to wait only a few seconds for the trooper to screech to a stop even with his car. He did not want the trooper to have time to radio a location, so he stepped out from behind the bush and fired two shots into the side window of the cruiser from about 20 feet away, killing the trooper instantly.

Everything had changed. First, the trooper's pursuit suggested that the authorities were looking for him. How could anyone possibly have known that he was in Alaska? Second, he had just killed a trooper, and a manhunt would begin shortly. He walked out to the road and saw no sign that anyone had witnessed the shooting, so he had at least a little time to get away. He did not know whether the trooper had radioed his license number during the pursuit, but he didn't think there had been time. Regardless, he had to ditch the rental car quickly. He was about fifteen miles from the town of Sterling, where there should be vehicles available to steal. His best bet was to get there as soon as possible. He got in his car and drove. This time, he did not worry about the speed limit.

About ten minutes later, he entered the roadside community of Sterling and turned left on a well-traveled side road. The road led to a subdivision of weekend summer cabins on the Kenai River. It was the middle of the week, and he guessed that some of the cabins would be empty – maybe there were cars that would not be immediately missed. He drove slowly along the river frontage road looking into each of the driveways. Each lot was about two acres in size, and the heavily wooded lots were reasonably secluded from each other.

As he passed one of the drives, he glimpsed a rundown log cabin with an old jeep parked outside. The roadway looked like it had not been used in quite a while, so he pulled in and parked out of sight of the frontage road. Overgrown vegetation in summer proliferation provided a screen from the adjoining lots. The jeep, although old, had plates that were up to date, and it appeared operable. The age of the vehicle made hot wiring a simple process – no annoying safety interlock features – and it started right up. It even had more than half a tank of gas. Frank could not believe his luck. He removed the plates from the rental car and disposed of them in the river, and splashed mud on the car from a convenient puddle in the driveway.

Things were looking up, but he could not decide what his next step should be. Should he simply continue on to Homer and complete his mission? Or should he hide out for a while and wait for things to cool off? Ultimately he decided that there was no advantage to hiding out. Right now, he might still have the advantage of surprise. He might be able to get to Homer before discovery of the trooper's body and before a road block could be set up. He threw his duffle bag in the jeep and began driving.

The Mole rose early, bought pastries at a bakery, and headed north out of Seward (the only way anyone could go) in his excellent newly-acquired Blazer. The weather was beautiful and the scenery was awesome. Shortly after leaving Seward, the Mole stopped at a deserted State Park rest area and applied a simple disguise consisting of goatee, sideburns, darkened facial skin, and a beret. He thought he looked quite jaunty in his new persona, sort of like a Filipino beatnik. He passed the east end of Kenai Lake with its startling, glacially-tinged blue-green water, then headed west on the road toward Homer. The drive was mostly uneventful. The only stressful element occurred after he had been driving for about two hours. Three police cars passed him going the other way with full lights and siren. He thought nothing more about it. Probably an accident.

Passing through the town of Soldotna, Robert stopped at a big box sporting goods store and bought a complete camping outfit, including tent, sleeping bag, mattress, cook stove, utensils, and fishing gear. His intent was to fit in with the group of people known as spit rats that he had noticed during his prior time in Homer. These mostly young, transient folks camped on the beach every summer in an informal community. Some were employed in seafood canneries, and others were just hanging out. Although they annoyed the local authorities, mostly they were ignored.

The Mole arrived in Homer in mid-afternoon. He drove his old Blazer onto the beach and set up camp amongst all the others.

†

The remainder of Frank's drive toward Homer was uneventful. He also passed a procession of rapidly-moving police cars and felt momentary panic until they disappeared from his rear view mirror. So far, so good.

Frank racked his brain for a strategy as he approached Homer. He needed a way to stay completely out of sight and, at the same time, access his quarry. And then it hit him. He would go directly to Kate Perkin's cabin in the swamp. It was a win-win situation. If she was there, he could kill her. If she was not there, he would have a comfortable, secluded place to hide out.

As he approached the outskirts of Homer, Frank turned on Mission Road and drove past the pull-out at the trail head for Kate's cabin – no cars were there. He turned around and went back to the logging road that had previously been used by Brett Fishbein, pulled the jeep off the road, slung his duffle bag over his shoulder, and walked to the cabin. He was somewhat discouraged by the new hasp and lock on the door, but then he discovered that the bear guards had been removed from the windows, and he was able to crawl through.

The cabin was clean and neat and had obviously been used recently. Maybe Kate would be back soon. Frank lay back on Kate's bed, placed his gun at his side, and opened up his first bag lunch. His thoughts went back to the time period when he was employed by FlashFrozen. He thought of the many times that Kate had ignored his attempts to be friendly, walking around him as if he were a pile of dog shit. He grew more and more agitated, only calming down after he had visualized Kate's final moments as he slowly made her realize that she was going to die. He could see the look on her face. Finally, he smiled and prepared to sleep.

And what was the deal with the stupid purple hippo?

Fifty-eight

JB awoke in a state of confusion. The sun was shining in his eyes, his phone was vibrating in his shirt pocket, and, for some reason he was on top of a roof. Fumbling for the phone, he saw it was Beverly, no doubt checking on the progress of his first night at the roof top surveillance post. People were starting to move around in the harbor area. Charter fishing customers were assembling at their appointed craft, ready to embark on a day of halibut fishing. Commercial fishermen were performing any number of endless tasks required to maintain their boats.

"Aha, you were sleeping," Beverly said.

"Yeah, but I did manage to stay awake until well after dawn, which was about 4:30. The Homer spit just isn't all that interesting. I didn't see any obvious suspicious activity, but I'm starting to get a feel for the various patterns of activity and groups of people. The best part is watching the people come out of the Rusty Harpoon when it closes at 2:00. It's amazing more harbor rats don't drown on their way home."

"I'll be up to relieve you in a minute."

JB watched as Beverly walked up the stairs of the ocean-side condo building and entered the third floor apartment. They had worked out a schedule with Kate's friend, Lucy, so that their comings and goings would not interfere with her sleep or other private events. Lucy had already gone to work. Beverly walked up the stairs to the rooftop terrace and observed JB's observation post. Using a combination of air mattresses, sleeping bags, and folding chairs, JB had created a comfortable nest.

"These new generation night-vision goggles are amazing," JB said. "I guess I've been out of the spy business for too long. I could

373

actually identify the faces of folks coming out of the Rusty Harpoon. I could make money by blackmailing selected members of our community for cheating on their spouses."

Beverly grinned. "I don't think that's what we're here for, but I can see how that might add interest to the exercise."

JB summarized his observations from the previous evening and night, pointing out the various centers of activity and making suggestions of areas to watch. He emphasized watching the collection of motor homes and pickup campers parked on the large fill area adjoining the north end of the harbor. Most of those folks were weekend vacationers from Anchorage spending time fishing in the lagoon that had been dredged from the middle of the spit to provide salmon fishing opportunities and attract tourists. An artificial salmon run had been created by stocking young fish in the lagoon while simultaneously releasing a chemical identifier in the water. A couple of years later, the adult salmon returned to the lagoon by following the smell of the chemical signature which they had been tricked into believing was their natal stream. Most of these fish were ultimately caught by the hordes of fishermen that flailed the lagoon with lures cast from all sides.

JB also described the small tent city occupied by the spit rats on the west side of the spit. Many of the occupants were temporary employees of FlashFrozen, processing fish during the peak summer season. They worked twelve-hour days, with shift change at 6:00 am and 6:00 pm. He pointed out that about 30 percent of the tent dwellers were just hanging out – most of them drank and smoked pot at night and slept late. Driftwood bonfires were a nightly occurrence. Unfortunately, part of the tent city was obscured from view by buildings blocking the line of sight. Obviously, there was a lot of activity associated with the harbor itself with its large parking lots and numerous entry points.

JB and Beverly cuddled for few minutes, and then JB left his post and headed for a nap. The whole team had been concerned that, if someone were watching them, they would be seen entering and exiting the apartment building. To counter this possibility, they had agreed to exit out the back door of the building onto the beach and skirt the beach below the elevation of roads and buildings, then enter the harbor on the southernmost ramp. Most of this route would be out of sight of observers from the other direction. It was the best they could do.

Beverly settled in for a long morning – she would be relieved by Charlie at 1:00 pm. She and JB had agreed to get together for extracurricular activities after her shift. Even with deranged murderers on the loose, it was a given that sex would take priority.

†

The Super Trooper was exhausted. He had initially responded with the rest of the law enforcement personnel on the Kenai Peninsula to the shooting death of one of their own. Bob had attended the police academy with the dead trooper, they were good friends, and he was seriously pissed.

Before going silent, the pursuit trooper had radioed the license plate – the rental car presumably rented by Frank Halburg in Seward. In spite of one of the biggest manhunts ever conducted in the area, the shooter and his car had disappeared into thin air. After the initial rush to the crime scene, Bob had returned south and set up a roadblock on the highway just north of Homer. Still no sign of Halburg – no one even coming close to Halburg's description had passed Bob's location. The road block had been pulled in the late evening, allowing Bob to get a few hours' sleep. Back in the office, he was trying to catch up with what was going on.

He was currently on a conference call with Kate and Charlie in the boat and Beverly on the rooftop. JB was sleeping. They had all been kept informed of Frank Halburg's dramatic appearance on the scene and subsequent disappearance. No one was happy.

"He could be watching us right now," Kate said.

"Maybe, but probably not," Charlie commented. "He has too many people looking for him to come out in the daylight. Right now Frank has two prime motivations: first, he has to avoid getting caught, since that would be the end of everything; and second, he wants to get revenge on Kate and me. He is probably crazy enough to continue with the second objective in spite of the risk of getting caught. One possible conclusion from his disappearance is that he was able to get to Homer before the law enforcement community began its manhunt. That seems possible if he was able to steal another vehicle very quickly after shooting the trooper. He had a lead of a couple of hours. So, assuming that he was able to get to Homer, what would a person in his position do? He needs to stay out of sight, but in the back of his mind, he is planning ways to get close to us."

"That's simple," Kate said. "He would go to my cabin. It's secluded and would be a good temporary hideout, plus there would be the potential bonus of being able to whack me in the process."

"That's brilliant, Kate," Beverly said. "But he would have to figure that eventually we would think of that possibility."

"Maybe so," Bob agreed. "But yesterday his primary need was a place to hide out from a massive manhunt. I think it's worth checking out. I'll head out there."

"Do you think it's a good idea to go out there alone?" Beverly asked. "If you can wait a couple hours, I'll go with you."

Bob leapt at her offer. "OK." Normally he would not have hesitated to approach such a situation by himself; usually, he did not have much choice. But the death of his friend and the thought of Julie waiting for him at home made him think twice about his mortality.

†

Some had said that Frank Halburg was not the sharpest knife in the block, but, nevertheless, his survival skills had been honed by years on the wrong side of the law. Waking up in Kate's cabin shortly after sunrise, Frank reflected on his situation. Although the comfortable bed was very seductive, remaining at the cabin was a dumb idea – someone was bound to come and check it very soon. He could lie in the woods and ambush whoever arrived, but what would that accomplish? He needed to move on and actively pursue his mission, as he had been taught in the army. He ate a portion of his second bag lunch, grabbed Kate's shotgun off the pegs at the side of the door, and crawled back out the window. He carefully walked back to his old Jeep and got in.

What now? Should he just drive into town and take his chances, or drive to the outskirts of town and walk to wherever he needed to go? He finally came up with a compromise – he would drive to the closest relatively secluded spot that he could think of where his vehicle could be hidden and walk the rest of the way. He would hide out until nightfall, and then walk along the beach, continuing out along the spit.

As he was sitting in the Jeep contemplating his future, a car key fell out of the sun visor onto his lap. "Shit," he thought. "If I had just looked there to begin with, I wouldn't have had to waste time hot wiring." He stuck the key in the ignition and started the ancient Jeep. He drove to a familiar road west of town and found a good hiding place at the top of the bluff overlooking Kachemak Bay. After dark, he would climb down to the beach, hike to the base of the spit, and continue on out to the harbor. It would be a good six miles, but he didn't have anything else to do.

†

Beverly and Bob pulled the police cruiser into the parking area at the trail to Kate's cabin and walked down the trail. They saw no sign of recent tracks on the trail, but still they proceeded very cautiously, each walking about twenty feet off to the side to avoid an ambush. Guns drawn, they approached the cabin. The lock on the front door was intact and showed no sign of forced entry. Beverly went around the left side of the cabin and Bob around the right. Bob yelled that there was an open window, but no one inside. Beverly, being smaller, crawled through the window and looked around. She saw that the bed was rumpled and there were sandwich wrappers on the floor.

"I have a feeling he's been here," she said. She called Kate and asked about the messed-up bed and trash on the floor and got confirmation that it had not been left that way. Kate asked whether her shotgun was still hanging on the wall.

Bob could hear Kate on the phone from across the room: "That asshole stole my shotgun!" Obviously, somebody had broken in and spent some time there. If it had been Frank Halburg, he was now armed with a shotgun, in addition to the nine millimeter semiautomatic pistol he had used to kill Bob's classmate.

On the way back to town, they stopped at two homes along Mission Road and inquired whether the residents had seen any unfamiliar vehicles in the morning or the previous night. One of the homes was occupied by a grizzled old man who looked like a refugee from the gold rush. He said that he had seen a rickety old Jeep Cherokee with big rust spots heading toward town at about 8:00 that morning. He had not thought much about it, since it was the kind of beat-up car that most people drove in the area.

The Super Trooper wanted to stop at Gertie's Bar before dropping Beverly off at the harbor. As usual, Gertie was leaning on the bar, smoking a cigarette and drinking a Coke. Beverly was totally fascinated by Gertie's tattoos. She could not take her eyes off the iguana scaling the mounds of flesh.

"So, who is this cute young thing?" Gertie asked.

Bob rolled his eyes. "Gertie, meet Beverly. She's a DEA agent."

"Wow, they sure don't make DEA agents like they used to. So, what's up?"

"Our buddy, Frank Halburg, is likely in town. You have probably heard about the trooper who was shot yesterday. Halburg was responsible. He may be driving an old Jeep Cherokee with big rust spots. Maybe you could discreetly inquire if anyone has seen a car like that in an unusual place, but be careful – he is very dangerous."

Gertie raised both eyebrows. "Holy shit. I'll do what I can."

"That tattoo is amazing," Beverly told her.

Gertie beamed. "It brings the bar patrons from far and wide."

"I suspect that the ecosystem that the iguana inhabits may have something to do with it," Beverly said.

"You may be right." Gertie winked at Bob, who blushed furiously.

On the way out, Bob explained that Gertie had been a good friend and had helped collect money for his girlfriend's rehab.

"Yeah, JB told me all about that. That was a very nice thing to do," she said. The Super Trooper got a misty look in his eye and looked away.

Fifty-nine

"Yahhh!" yelled Izzy. He was returning from the store with a bag of groceries, when he walked into his living room and saw the Mole sitting in his easy chair, drinking a beer.

The Mole grinned, enjoying the other man's obvious terror. "Hi, Izzy. How are things going?"

Izzy backed up a couple of steps, clutching his groceries. "Up until now they were going pretty well. What are you doing here?"

"I want to swap cars with you," said the Mole.

Izzy gulped. "What? Why?"

"You don't need to know."

"Where is your car?" Izzy looked toward the window.

"It's parked out back in your shed."

"Is it stolen?"

The Mole snorted. "Actually, no, but I wouldn't drive it unless you want to get shot."

"Great, are you going to bring my car back?" Izzy asked.

"Maybe," said the Mole. "Give me your keys. Any word of this, and both you and your wife are dead."

Izzy seemed eager to hand over the keys, and The Mole walked outside and climbed into Izzy's dirty, nondescript Toyota Corolla. It was the perfect car. During the previous evening, the Mole had joined some of his spit rat colleagues at the nightly bonfire and heard the news about the trooper getting shot on the road between Seward and Homer. He had a strong feeling that the shooter had been Frank.

It was disappointing that they had been there less than a day and already Frank was in serious trouble. On the other hand, it might take some of the heat off him. But he doubted whether Frank would be stupid enough to break the traffic laws, so the only other explanation was that the police had been tipped off and had actively pursued Frank. If that was the case, then they probably knew Robert was in Alaska as well. Frank had probably rented a car, which would have made him immediately vulnerable. Fortunately, the Mole had been smarter and had covered his tracks somewhat. But if the authorities were persistent, they could figure out that he had bought a car and would soon have a description out.

Izzy's car solved that problem. The Mole returned to the spit rat tent community and continued to monitor the movements of Charlie Skyler and JB what's-his-name. Neither of them had left the harbor since he had begun his observations. It was getting really boring.

†

The veranda of the old colonial hotel smelled like cigars, rum, damp wood, salt air, and jasmine. Five old white guys in shorts and sweat-soaked T-shirts sat on oversized mahogany chairs around an oval, felt-topped poker table. It was 11:00 am, and all had rum drinks beside their poker chips. As usual, Aldo had the biggest stack. An officious dark-skinned waiter hovered nearby, more than happy to refill their drinks.

The young Dominican man pretended to be oblivious, but he knew all of these men extremely well, since he had been eavesdropping on their conversations at the poker table for more than a year. In general, it was a pathetic group. They were all alcoholics, they were all hiding from something in their pasts, and they all had enough money to live on indefinitely in the islands. Of all the expatriates, Aldo was the most mysterious and intriguing. The waiter knew that Aldo was a heroin addict, but he also knew that Aldo had more self-discipline than the others. He sensed that Aldo could be very dangerous. He almost always won at poker – he had fleeced the others of thousands of dollars. The waiter was even beginning to learn some of Aldo's tricks. He knew that Aldo did not need to cheat. He just needed to wait until the others became sloppy drunk. The other players were so transparent that he could always tell when they were bluffing. He just let them beat themselves.

†

Even as he raked in another pile of chips, Aldo was feeling restless. He excused himself under protest from the others and went to walk on the beach. He had not heard anything from his homeland in over two weeks and was crazy with worry. Sentiment had never been a big part of his life, especially during the thirty-five years that had elapsed since his wife deserted him. But he could not stop thinking about Robert. Like many aging human beings, he sought immortality through his offspring. He was realistic about Robert's mental problems and poor judgment, and was afraid that this particular route to immortality might not last very long. He wanted to help Robert, but how?

Robert's gesture with regard to the Cayman Island bank account had touched him and reinforced those feelings. He had tested to see whether the money was really available and found that, with electronic transfer, the account was like an ATM machine that contained millions of dollars. The local banks were more than happy to discreetly assist him with his financial affairs. He was set for life from the monetary standpoint, but that was not enough. He needed to know what was happening with his son.

No one was answering calls on the syndicate satellite phone system. He could still contact Stuart Halburg's sleazy lawyer if necessary, but he did not think that would help much. Another alternative would be to call Izzy and see what was going on in Homer. He had toyed with this idea off and on, but had not wanted to take the risk. Now he was rapidly reaching a point of desperation.

After wandering aimlessly for a while, he returned to his cabana and dialed Izzy's number. Izzy answered on the second ring. When

Aldo asked him what was going on in Homer, Izzy reported that the Mole had just been there and had taken his car. He informed Aldo that otherwise Homer had been quiet. He asked Aldo whether he could do anything about getting his car back. Aldo did not say anything – he just hung up. Izzy was still coming to grips with the fact that the creepy person known as the Mole was actually Aldo's son.

"Great," thought Aldo. "Robert is in Homer, probably on the run, and probably about to kill someone." He dialed Robert's satellite phone for the umpteenth time but again got no answer. He was tempted to call law enforcement himself, thinking it might be better for Robert to be captured before he killed again, but he was afraid that Robert would not allow himself to be taken alive. He did not know what to do.

†

Beverly and JB had just finished rocking the boat when she received a call from her assistant in Los Angeles. After numerous tries, the assistant had talked to a man in Seward who had sold a blue and white Chevy Blazer to a man with Asian features. Now they were looking for two vehicles, a rusty Jeep Cherokee and an old Blazer. Beverly relayed the information to the Super Trooper and to Charlie, who was on rooftop duty.

Charlie was starting to get a feel for the pace of life on the spit. He had made notes regarding several people who might be candidates for closer observation. One was a grungy old man who had parked his pickup camper next to the fishing lagoon. He seemed to spend most of his time in a reclining lawn chair with a can of beer in his hand. His vantage point would provide a good view of the harbor and portions of the harbor parking lot. Cars belonging to Charlie, JB, and Kate were parked alongside each other near the harbor ramp and were in plain view. A couple of the spit rats also spent a lot of time sitting around, but the group was young and dynamic, and it was generally difficult to follow the activities of individuals. The distance was too far to get a look at facial features, even with binoculars. Charlie made a mental note to borrow a spotting telescope from a bird-watching friend so he could get a better look at some of the faces.

Sixty

The eagle soared just above the top of the bluff, taking advantage of thermals rising from the sun-heated soil below. The big bird was making its thirty-second trip past Frank's position, crouched under a stunted spruce misshapen from the continual sea breezes buffeting the bluff top. Frank was going crazy. It was taking forever for the sun to go down. It was 10:30, and still it was broad daylight. His plan was to wait until full darkness, then hike out to the end of the spit and hide under the pile-supported FlashFrozen building until the morning shift change.

During his former employment at the seafood plant, he had explored the area and knew that the miscellaneous debris stored under the building would provide a secure hiding place, but, at the same time, provide a line of sight to the trail from the harbor ramp to the FlashFrozen employee entrance. He hoped to ambush Kate as she went to work the next morning. Unfortunately, his plan ended at that point. There were no good options for escape, and he did not really care. One way or another, this would be his final act. He just wanted to make sure that Kate saw him before he shot her so she would know that she was not going to get away with treating him like dirt.

Finally, the eagle retired to his roost tree for the night, and darkness fell. Clouds rolled in from Cook Inlet and intensified the darkness, which Frank figured was in his favor. He slid down the steep bluff on his butt to the beach and started walking. His clothing was all black, and he had smeared dark mud on his face. All he carried was his pistol, two extra magazines, and a water bottle. He had decided that carrying the shotgun was stupid – it was heavy and would be very conspicuous, so he left it in the car. While the beach was mostly flat, the substrate varied from soft sand to mud to round cobbles, all of which were annoying to walk on. It was a long, slow, exhausting hike.

†

JB was bored. It had been a long time since he had been involved in extended surveillance, and he had forgotten how difficult it was to maintain concentration. Nevertheless, he tried to focus on the patterns of activity among the spit residents. Nothing of particular interest had happened since he took over from Charlie at 6:00. The old guy at the fishing lagoon had remained in his lawn chair from 6:00 to midnight and had consumed eight beers during that time. He finally staggered into his camper. JB eliminated him as a suspect, at least until he sobered up. The Rusty Harpoon had emptied out at 2:00 am, with the patrons driving unsteadily toward town, walking to their campers, or going to their boats. It seemed like everyone was accounted for. The tent city inhabited by the spit rats was unusually quiet; a few people sat around fires for a while, then all had gone to bed. So far there were no loose ends or obvious suspicions.

JB picked up Beverly's night vision binoculars and scanned the area. Looking down the length of the spit, he spotted what appeared to be a solitary figure walking up the beach. The dark figure was more than a mile away, and all that he could see was a dark blob silhouetted against the somewhat lighter water in the background. It was nearing 3:00 am, and it seemed a little late for a midnight stroll.

JB continued to watch as the figure walked in a deliberate fashion toward him. A few minutes later, he was able to pick out more detail and noticed that there was no contrast between the person's face and his dark clothing. Either the mystery figure was African American or he had deliberately blackened his face. JB was betting on the latter. The mystery man's attempt to be inconspicuous was backfiring by making him more suspicious.

JB called Beverly's cell phone, hoping that she would not be too sound asleep to hear it. Beverly, who was zonked out in JB's bed in the tiny forward cabin of the Otterly Ridiculous, finally picked up and seemed to be more or less coherent. JB explained the situation, and they agreed to meet at the back door of the condo building. Beverly put on her tight black surveillance outfit, grabbed her gun, and ran down the dock and up the ramp onto street level, trying to stay in the shadows as much as possible.

"Wow, you look totally hot," said JB when they met.

"Thanks, but we have other things to think about right now, you old horny toad. Do you think this night stalker is one of our bad guys?"

"I don't know for sure, but we need to find out. When he reaches the parking lot at the end of the harbor, he is going to have to come up to the level of the road. We need to get somewhere where we can see what he does next. He should be getting pretty close."

"Yeah, let's go under the boardwalk along the harbor. We should be able to watch from there without being seen."

As they carefully crept through the dark corridors between the pilings, JB thought about times gone by when he had been in similar situations. The combination of fear and excitement used to be exhilarating, but now it just seemed stressful. He felt the weight of his sleek little chrome-plated Beretta pistol tucked into the back of his jeans. He had not carried this gun on a "mission" for more than 15 years. Although he had used every conceivable weapon at one time or another, he loved this little gun. It was elegant, graceful, and compact – not like the fat, ugly black plastic things that were currently preferred by law enforcement (not to mention gang bangers and domestic terrorists). The Glocks obviously had much more stopping power than his little .32 caliber Beretta, but he had always thought that finesse and accurate aim were more important than stopping power. Plus people were less likely to get killed with the little gun. And, of course, there was always the fact that Ian Fleming had chosen to arm James Bond with the Beretta .32.

JB and Beverly reached a point at the corner of the harbor where the boardwalk was truncated. They slowly raised their heads above the walkway and peered out. Without the contrast of the ocean in the background, it was very dark and impossible to see much of anything. JB pulled the night vision scope out of his pocket and looked down the length of the spit. He was just in time to see the night stalker climb up onto the parking lot surface and begin to weave his way through the cars.

"I can't tell whether he's headed for the harbor or someplace else," JB said. "We'll have to wait and see. I guess if he heads toward Charlie's boat, we'll have to follow him. That would make us pretty conspicuous, unless we use a different ramp. Should we warn Charlie and Kate?"

"I think we should wait a little while and see what happens. Do you think this guy is Frank or Robert?"

"Robert is too smart and too well trained to walk five miles out in the open to get to his destination, even if it is very dark. I vote for Frank."

"I agree," Beverly said. "If it is Frank, then his primary target is likely to be Kate. Maybe he's going to try and ambush her as she goes to work in the morning. Since he used to work at FlashFrozen, he probably knows the layout pretty well."

The dark figure bypassed the first two harbor access ramps and seemed to be heading straight toward JB and Beverly.

"It looks like your insight may be correct. He's probably going to find a place to hide near the trail to the FlashFrozen employee's entrance until shift change time. We need to take him out before then, while the spit is deserted."

"I agree," said Beverly. They moved back under the boardwalk into the total darkness and watched as the night stalker came closer. At one point, he was only forty feet from their position, then he headed toward the water and went under the FlashFrozen building, which was suspended about seven feet above the beach on ancient wooden piles. Stashed under the building was assorted fishing gear, such as crab traps and buoys. He went out of sight and did not re-emerge.

"He is probably going to hang out there until morning. He would just need to step out from under the building, shoot Kate as she walks by, and then get out of there somehow. If he is obsessed enough to risk coming back to Homer, then I don't think he is particularly concerned about escaping after the dirty deed. You're the law enforcement officer here, Beverly. How do you want to proceed? Do you want to call for backup?"

"The only backup we've got around here is Bob the trooper, and I don't think we have time for him to get here. Do you by any chance have a gun?"

"Why, yes I do, but you're not supposed to know about that."

"Don't be ridiculous, JB. It's going to start getting light real soon. One of us should work around the back of the building, but not a full 180 degrees. As soon as there is enough light to see, we should close in, preferably trying not to shoot each other."

"Sounds good to me. I'm a very sneaky person, so I should probably move around back. You, being the only legal officer of the law, should initiate the arrest. I know you guys are trained differently, but if he starts shooting I would like to keep him alive."

"We'll see," she replied. "I'll begin to approach his position exactly ten minutes from now." They both checked their watches, then JB vanished under the boardwalk toward the back of the FlashFrozen building. Beverly was amazed at how quiet he was, considering his size and ungainly build. A glow of light appeared above the mountains in the eastern sky. It was going to be another beautiful summer day.

The time was up. Beverly dashed from pile to pile under the boardwalk until she reached the open area in front of the building, and then ran across the grassy path to the edge of the processing plant. Looking around a stack of pallets, she wasn't able to see any sign of

Halburg. There was a pile of debris and some fish totes about fifty feet away, near the middle of the building – that had to be where Frank was hiding. Beverly could see light at the other side of the building and no other obvious hiding spots. She did not see JB either, which caused some concern.

She ran from the pallets to a support pile about ten feet under the building and yelled in as authoritative a voice as she could, "Frank Halburg, this is the Drug Enforcement Agency. You're under arrest. Come out with your hands up!"

There was no reply.

†

Frank had given up trying to stay awake and finally succumbed to sleep about a half hour after he had settled in to his hiding place. The next thing he was conscious of was a woman's voice yelling that he was under arrest. What the fuck was going on? How did these people always seem to know where he was? He was lying inside a large fiberglass tote that rested on its side and smelled of rotten fish. It was impossible for him to take any defensive action from his position; he couldn't see anything and couldn't get into a shooting position. Shit!

He scrambled out of the box and peeked around a buoy. He saw Beverly's shoulder sticking out from behind the piling, which was not quite wide enough to hide her. Now he was wide awake and back in survival mode. All he needed was one good shot. The agent's cover was not good enough to completely protect her. Shooting on one side of the pile would force her to overreact and move too far to the other side, and Frank would be waiting with his next shot. He slowly moved his gun into position, his arm resting on a coil of rope. He could still see about an inch of shoulder extended beyond the diameter of the pile on the right side. He aimed carefully and fired, hitting the side of the piling, followed by flying splinters and an immediate curse from the person behind. As part of the agent's body appeared on the left side, he fired again, again peeling splinters off the side of the piling, followed by another curse. Although he had apparently not hit any vital areas, he was emboldened by his strategy and crouched behind the tote, prepared to keep shooting until he was successful.

As he took aim, he heard a pop behind him and felt extreme pain in his right hand. Shit. Another gunshot, and he felt extreme pain in his left ankle. JB stepped out from behind a crate and told him to toss the gun away. Frank tried to grab the gun in his other hand, but noticed that the grip of the plastic pistol was shattered. He looked at it in disgust and threw it onto the ground.

†

Beverly moved out from behind her lousy cover and held her gun steadily on Frank. Blood was streaming down her left arm, and a six-inch splinter of wood could be seen sticking out of her triceps.

Beverly threw her handcuffs to JB, who cuffed Halburg by his left hand to a water pipe. His right hand was pretty messed up. Beverly called an ambulance and the state troopers. JB made Beverly sit down and looked at her arm.

"We should let the docs remove that splinter, but I think you'll be fine. It's a pretty superficial wound."

"Fucking piling wasn't wide enough," said Beverly. "You'd think they would plan for things like this. You could have shot him before he shot me, for Christ sake."

"I don't know. You were doing a pretty good job of keeping him entertained."

Beverly scowled, and JB realized that this was the wrong time to joke. "Seriously, I couldn't see him well enough to shoot until he moved behind the tote. I'm sorry you got hurt."

"How are we going to explain the presence of two tiny bullets in Frank's extremities? Especially since my gun wasn't fired at all."

"I'm just a private citizen helping out an agent in trouble," JB replied. "I can't help it if I'm not a very good shot."

"Right."

The Super Trooper and the ambulance arrived at the same time. Bob made his way through the pilings to the scene of the gun battle.

"Holy shit. Is that who I think it is?" Bob asked.

"Yep." Beverly winced in pain.

"Are you OK?" Bob stared at her shoulder. "That's the biggest splinter I've ever seen."

"I'm fine. Thank you for your concern and your comforting words."

Kate was on her way to work, accompanied by Charlie, who was on his way to the espresso stand. Seeing the activity, they moved with the crowd of onlookers to see what was going on. As they surveyed the scene and put the pieces of information together, they suddenly realized what had just happened. Kate sat down and started crying. Her friends had risked their lives to save hers. Kate looked up, and her eyes met Frank Halburg's. She had never seen such hatred.

Sixty-one

Robert awoke to sirens on the spit road. He emerged from his tent just in time to see an ambulance and a police cruiser pass by the spit rat enclave. Strolling up to the road, he saw the emergency vehicles stop near the FlashFrozen building. All he could see were the EMTs running around to the back of the building. He was intensely curious, but could not risk joining the crowd of onlookers. He waited for some of his fellow rats to come back. Gossip was the grist of the tent city, and people would be more than willing to describe this newest excitement.

Twenty minutes later, the ambulance drove back toward town, followed soon thereafter by the state trooper. A few of the curious spit rats began to drift back to their tents, and small knots of people gathered to discuss the curious events. The Mole casually joined one of the groups and learned that a shootout had occurred under the FlashFrozen building and that a man had been arrested. The arrested man had multiple gunshot wounds, but the wounds did not seem to be life-threatening. The apparent arresting officer was a petite young woman dressed in Ninja-like clothing. She had been wounded in the shoulder, but she was mobile and apparently OK. Another man, a tall, skinny guy, had somehow also been involved, but no one knew exactly what role he had played. The group speculated about which agency the woman belonged to, with most suggesting the FBI was the most likely. The Super Trooper appeared to be friendly with the Ninja lady, so the crowd assumed that they were acquainted.

Robert tried to inquire what the wounded man looked like without sounding too curious. All he could find out was that the man was medium tall and had a full brown beard. The bad guy had apparently smeared something on his face to darken it, suggesting that he had been sneaking around in the dark.

It had to be Frank. They had been in Alaska for less than three days, and already the idiot had killed a state trooper, triggered a statewide manhunt, wounded a federal agent, and gotten himself caught. Worse yet, he was still alive. The tall guy was most likely his nemesis from the failed exploding boat episode. Robert was pretty sure that, given the right circumstances, Frank would talk way too much. However, looking at the big picture, there probably was not much that Frank could say that would make a difference. He actually felt bad for Frank – they had been working and playing together for a long time. But the long run was coming to an end. Nothing mattered any more except finishing his business in Homer. Whatever happened after that was fate.

He needed to make his move quickly, before the law enforcement community had a chance to regroup. A new plan was forming. The federal agent, whoever she was, and Frank would likely both be in the Homer hospital for a while. Consequently, people would be making trips to the hospital to visit the agent or to question Frank. It seemed likely that some of those people might be persons of extreme interest to him.

He trekked to Izzy's old car, which he had parked in a far corner of the harbor parking lot, and drove to the hospital to do a quick reconnaissance. The new hospital was surrounded by forest on three sides. Robert picked out a dense patch of forest that provided a clear view of the hospital entrance. He then explored adjacent neighborhoods to determine how best to access the area without being seen. It seemed like it would be pretty easy. He drove back to his temporary home at spit rat city.

†

The hospital room with its sterile white walls looked quite cheerful as a result of three giant bouquets of flowers. One of the bouquets had been sent by Beverly's boss, Agent Phillips, who, during a long phone call, had congratulated her on her terrific effort to catch the cop killer Frank Halburg. Knowing Beverly, he promised not to ask too many questions about the details of the apprehension. All he cared about was that Halburg was in custody. Charlie, Kate, JB, and Bob were all in the room as Beverly and JB related the events that had taken place in the early morning hours. Kate, Charlie, and Bob professed to be peeved that they had not been called to participate, but, at the same time, they were relieved. JB wanted his name left out of reports relating to Frank's capture, which meant that Beverly would have to maintain that she had shot Frank in the ankle and the hand. In the law enforcement culture, those injuries would be interpreted as really crappy shooting.

"You owe me big time," Beverly warned JB.

The doctors removed the enormous splinter from Beverly's upper arm. The procedure had been painful and her arm was very sore, but the wound was near the surface and was not likely to cause long-term muscle damage. An IV with a continual antibiotic feed dripped into her good arm to battle possible infection from the dirty, creosote-coated hunk of wood. A simultaneous morphine drip contributed to Beverly's very relaxed attitude. Kate, on the other hand, was on the downside of totally freaking out.

"Kate," Beverly reassured her, "I was doing my job. That is what I am trained for, even if I didn't do the greatest job. There is no reason for you to accept any responsibility for what happened. Frank Halburg is a marginal psychopath with a long record of antisocial acts. It's not your fault that I ended up with a small spear in my arm. That fucking post just wasn't wide enough to hide a human body."

Beverly started giggling and could not stop, coming down from the long adrenalin-fueled morning combined with the morphine.

Eventually she pulled herself together. "Sorry, guys. I think I need to get some sleep. Let's meet back here this evening and regroup."

Out in the hall, JB asked the doctor about Frank Halburg's injuries. His wrist was pretty messed up and probably would never be the same. The ankle injury was not too bad. Frank was shackled to his bed on the top floor of the hospital with two private security guards posted outside the door to his room. Bob was making arrangements to transport him to more secure facilities in Anchorage.

†

After Frank's injuries had been x-rayed and bandaged, he was returned to his high-security room. The Super Trooper was waiting for him. He had asked the doctor to go light on the painkillers so Frank would be coherent. Word had gotten around that Frank was the suspected cop killer; consequently, the doctor had no moral qualms about maintaining as high a pain level as they wanted.

"What did you hope to accomplish by hiding under the FlashFrozen Building?" Bob asked.

"My hand hurts like hell. How about asking the doctor to increase the morphine level?"

"If you answer my questions, I'll talk to the doctor. Now back to my question…"

"I'm sure you already know the answer to that. I don't feel any great need to cooperate since I'm already in about as much trouble as a person can get into."

"How did you get to Homer?"

"I drove."

"Where is your vehicle?"

"It's around. Earn your pay and go find it."

"All right, let's try a different tack. We know that you arrived in Seward with Robert Fenstrom. Where is he now?"

"I have no problem answering that question, since I don't know the answer. We split up in Seward, and I haven't seen or heard from him since. But I can guarantee that he's around here somewhere. He is the sneakiest person I've ever known. If he doesn't want to be found, he won't be."

"Why did you split up?"

"We had different reasons for being here, and Robert only works alone. In his mind, he is the only person he trusts."

"Exactly what is Robert's reason for being here?"

"If you don't know, I'm not going to tell you," Frank answered. He tried to move his arm and winced in pain.

"Where is Aldo Fenstrom?"

"I don't know that either. Nobody knows except Aldo."

"Once you get into federal custody, you are going to face some serious questioning. You should start considering the possibility of the death penalty and what you might do to avoid it."

Bob left Frank's hospital room and wandered out to the hospital lobby.

†

After leaving the hospital, Kate had gone to work. Now, she was staring blankly at her computer screen in her small office, trying to process the events of the last few days. She had spent most of a year in fear for her life, and now it appeared to be coming to a climax. While she was frightened of what might happen next, she looked forward to it being over – anything was better than unending suspense. As quitting time approached, she thought about the walk to the harbor, when she would be out in the open for anyone to take a shot at her. But this was the busiest time of day on the spit, and it seemed unlikely that a killer would be that bold or reckless.

A melodic tone coming from her purse broke into her trance and forced her to focus – someone was sending a text message. The message was from her brother and said that one of the satellite phones he had been monitoring had just placed a call to an Isadore Jablonsky in Homer. Wow. So Izzy was involved. She called Beverly and relayed the news.

Beverly, in turn, relayed the information to the Super Trooper, who volunteered to go question Izzy as soon as he was free. Beverly wanted to participate in the questioning, but the doctor said she had to remain in the hospital for another day to monitor for possible infections. Beverly was frustrated. Her intuition told her that the next chapter in the Fenstrom saga was going to happen soon, and she wanted to be there when it did.

†

Kate managed to make it from FlashFrozen to the Shearwater without any unfortunate incidents, such as flying bullets. Charlie had set a huge bowl of potato chips on the dinette table along with an assortment of cheese and crackers. When she arrived, he opened a bottle of white wine.

"How did you know I would be hungry?"

"You're always hungry, and stress makes you hungrier."

"Thanks, Charlie. You always do just the right thing."

"You look pretty depressed. Beverly's going to be fine, and we caught a very bad person today. All in all, it's been a pretty good day."

"I don't think we had much to do with it. JB and Beverly make a pretty good team."

"I agree, but it was your idea to spy from the rooftop. It's been a team effort all the way along."

"I just want it to be over. I'd like to go back to a more or less normal life."

"Let's start right now." Charlie grabbed Kate's hand and led her down into his luxury suite.

"But…the potato chips."

"They'll still be there later."

"They'll still be there later."

Sixty-two

Bright scarlet sky merging into purple and orange and pink extended the full width of the western quadrant – from southwest to northwest. A few bright stars twinkled. The quicksilver ocean glimmered in front of volcanic peaks. Pastel pink painted the southern mountains, gradually turning to slate gray as the sun dipped lower. A crescent moon rose above the peaks to take its place. A solitary ship steamed across the horizon while gulls wheeled overhead. The ever-present eagles observed everything from their lamp post stations.

JB had insisted on assuming rooftop duty in late afternoon. There were several persons of interest that he had noted the previous night, and he wanted to make sure that he followed their activities. By sunset, he was already bored. He had brought a telescope and tripod up to the roof, but none of his suspects had yet come into sight. Soon it would be too dark to make out faces.

One of the persons of interest was a single male inhabiting a small tent in the spit rat enclave. His actions were not overtly suspicious, but it seemed like he spent too much time just hanging around with no particular focus. He looked like he was older than the average spit rat and always wore sunglasses and a stocking cap. His size and build were similar to Robert Fenstrom. JB had watched his quarry spend about an hour talking to other spit rats at the nightly bonfire, and then had gone into his tent. The view through the telescope had not been much help – deep shadows and dimming light again prevented a good look at the man's face, although nothing that he could see eliminated the possibility of Robert Fenstrom.

Surprisingly, at about 11:30, the mystery man left his tent and walked to the far end of the harbor parking lot. From there, he got into an older model compact sedan and drove off toward town. JB

403

noted the interesting and peculiar behavior and wondered what someone would be doing in town at that time of night. He was determined to remain awake so that he could see whether the mystery man returned to his tent. Meanwhile, JB kept himself occupied by watching the comings and goings at the Rusty Harpoon, always an entertaining pastime. He was amused to see yet another local politician stagger out of the bar and head for his car. Fortunately, there was not much traffic.

†

The long hours of daylight were not conducive to covert operations. The Mole had to wait until after midnight before it was dark enough to continue with his plans. He drove to a vacant lot that he had scouted earlier in the day and parked out of sight. Opening the trunk of the old Corolla, he rummaged through the large duffel bag that contained most of his possessions and pulled out a camouflage jumpsuit. The suit had been purchased at a large sportsman's warehouse store in Seattle. This particular camouflage pattern was called "boreal forest" and theoretically would allow him to blend in with the kinds of vegetation found in Alaska.

The Mole thought it was amazing – and somewhat ridiculous – that there were camouflage patterns to match every major ecosystem in the world. He had a hard time imagining a clothing company sending an artist out into the woods to duplicate the texture of the environment. In spite of his skepticism, he had to admit that the suit worked pretty darn well. He hoisted his duffel onto his shoulder and set off into the forest. After a quarter mile, he came to the edge of the clearing that overlooked the hospital and located a suitable spot to hide out. An understory of tall grass and willows with spruce and birch trees on three sides provided good cover but still allowed him to get a clear view of the hospital roadway and the front entrance. He took his time building a nest of sorts that would cover his location after the sun came up in the morning. A young alder provided additional cover as well as a convenient support for his rifle. Even the rifle had a camouflage barrel cozy so that it would not be visible in the daylight.

It had been a while since Robert had used his sniper skills, and he was starting to feel the usual excitement that accompanied the hunt. He had enough food and water to last a couple of days, so he settled in for a long night. Hopefully, the morning would bring visitors to the hospital. It did not matter whether the visitors came to visit the pretty DEA lady or to question his childhood companion, Frank, as long as they came.

Sixty-three

Yesterday had been a terrible day. After dealing with Frank Halburg and the shootout under the FlashFrozen building early in the morning, the Super Trooper had been called to investigate some serious property damage from vandalism. Bob finally finished up the paperwork in late evening, after spending an entire day trying to sort out the vandalism incidents. The perpetrators had been caught – they were all teenagers from prominent Homer families who had gotten drunk and gone on a senseless rampage. The teens themselves were not the problem. They were currently in jail and, after sobering up, were generally ashamed of themselves. Unfortunately, their parents were much less remorseful and were pressuring Bob for special treatment, generally making his life miserable to the point of implying police brutality. Bob hated this part of his job.

But things were looking up as he came into his office the following morning. At least they were looking up until he noticed the sticky note on top of his desk reminding him that he was supposed to be questioning Izzy about phone calls from unknown members of the Fenstrom clan. He did not want to start his day by interviewing Aldo's clueless brother-in-law, but he knew Izzy might have information that could help find Robert Fenstrom.

Pulling up to the front door of Izzy's ramshackle house, Bob noticed that there were no cars in the driveway. As he walked up to the front door, he caught a glimpse of a white vehicle partially visible through the broken door of Izzy's storage shed. He knocked and, to his surprise, Izzy answered.

"Shit, what now?" Izzy asked.

"Just a couple more questions," said Bob. "Can I come in?"

"Sure. Why not."

The TV was on as usual. This time the sportsman's channel was showing a manly hunter crouching over a not-so-healthy-looking moose. They watched as the hunter hung his rifle on the moose's rack, stepped behind the dead animal, and posed for the cameras with his foot on the moose's back and a smug look on his face. Bob turned off the TV.

"We have evidence that a call was made to your number from a satellite phone that we know is used by members of the Fenstrom drug organization. Do you know anything about that?"

"I don't remember anything like that. It was probably a wrong number."

"That's a very lame answer, Izzy. I don't believe you. Who was at the other end of that line? Was it Aldo?" Bob watched Izzy's eyes as he asked about Aldo and saw them get very wide. Izzy was a totally transparent liar. "What did Aldo want?"

"He'll kill me if he knows I talked to you."

"I suspect Aldo isn't anywhere near Homer, so you probably don't have much to worry about from him in the near future. Let me tell you what's at stake here. You probably heard through the Homer grapevine that the guy who shot a state trooper two days ago was caught in Homer yesterday morning. He was known to be travelling with another man, a wanted felon, who's still on the loose. If you keep any information from us about him, you will be guilty of aiding and abetting and you could be responsible for someone else getting killed."

Izzy closed his eyes and shook his head.

"While you are thinking about that, let me ask you another question," Bob added. "Where is your car, and whose car is in the shed? Is the car in the shed a blue and white Blazer, by any chance?"

"Damn, damn, damn!" Izzy shook his head and tears streamed from his eyes. "A man who calls himself the Mole stopped by and forced me to trade cars with him. He threatened to kill me and Astrid if I didn't cooperate. I know he has something to do with Aldo, but I don't know how it all fits together. I think Aldo called me just to find out what was going on. When I told him that the Mole had forced me to trade cars, he got very upset and hung up. I swear that's all I know."

"Describe your car for me," Bob said.

"It's a 1993 light blue, dirty Toyota Corolla."

"Thanks, Izzy. Don't leave town." Bob ran to his cruiser and called Beverly at the hospital on her cell phone. Beverly, in turn, called JB, who was still on the roof and relayed the information to him. JB asked Beverly if she knew where Kate and Charlie were, and Beverly indicated that they were probably on the way to the hospital to pick her up, since she was in the process of being discharged. JB thought for a few seconds, then the pieces clicked into place.

"Shit, Beverly, a suspicious man left the spit rat area late last night and got into what looked like a dirty Corolla. I wondered what the heck he was doing at 3:00 am. He might be planning on ambushing one or all of us as we go in and out of the hospital. I'll call Charlie. You try Kate. Let's try and stop them."

†

Kate and Charlie woke up relatively early. Charlie was due to relieve JB on the rooftop in mid-morning. As they were eating breakfast, they received a call from Beverly at the hospital. Beverly was doing great except for a very sore arm. The doctor had given her a substantial supply of codeine pain killers, and she was looking forward to chilling out on JB's bunk for some well-deserved – and well medicated – R&R. It was not often that DEA agents got to ingest narcotics without getting fired. She was going to be released in about an hour and wondered if they could pick her up. Kate left a message for her boss that she would be late, and she and Charlie left for the hospital in Kate's old Subaru.

The new hospital was located in a previously wooded area and was accessed by a long curving drive on the outskirts of Homer. Kate turned onto the hospital drive, and a few seconds later Charlie's phone rang, then her phone rang. Charlie answered just as they were entering the large hospital grounds, listened for a few seconds, and yelled to Kate to pull over. Kate yanked the wheel to the left and, at the same time, the front passenger window exploded just in front of Charlie's head, spattering fine glass particles in his face. He pushed Kate down.

They both crawled out of the left side driver's door. Another shot went through the top of the door over their heads. They dove into the ditch beside the roadway. The shooting stopped. Charlie had dropped his phone with the still open circuit to JB on the car floor as they exited, and Kate's phone was in her purse in the car. Charlie could hear JB yelling into his phone and saying that he was on the way.

Charlie needed to get his phone, but it would require going back into the line of fire. He was not sure exactly what direction the shots had come from, except that the shooter was to the north of the hospital drive. It seemed like the car would obstruct the killer's line of vision, but he could not be sure. So far everyone in the hospital seemed to be oblivious of what was going on, which was probably just as well. JB would definitely need backup when he arrived.

Before he could think too carefully about it, Charlie crept up the side of the ditch in line with the Subaru's tires hoping that they would block the sniper's view. He eased alongside the back door under the window and peered through the open driver's door into the car. Immediately, another bullet slammed into the car just over his head. Hoping that the rifle was a bolt action, Charlie dove into the car, retrieved his phone, and dove back into the ditch next to Kate, followed by another gunshot, this one going straight through the car and into the woods behind them. JB, still on the line and panicked because of the shots, was very relieved to know that they were OK so far. Charlie filled JB in on what was going on, but JB was still ten minutes away.

Charlie hung up and dialed 911. After some difficulty, he managed to convince the dispatcher that there was a sniper on the hospital grounds, and that she should make sure that the hospital was locked down and to call the troopers immediately. He also asked the dispatcher to have Bob call him so that he could give him details before he drove into danger. Charlie peeked over the edge of the roadway, but was unable to see anything but trees and bushes. It was quiet for a few minutes, interrupted by the ringing of Charlie's phone. The Super Trooper said he was a minute away.

"Whatever you do, don't come down the hospital driveway. Fenstrom will easily pick you off."

"What do you suggest I do?"

"JB should be there in a minute. Wait for him, and then maybe you guys can come up with a plan. Kate and I are pinned down and can't move. Fenstrom is in the woods north of the drive, probably about a hundred yards east of the hospital. I assume he has set up a camouflaged sniper position, and he obviously has a rifle."

"OK, I'll wait for JB."

"But don't wait too long. If Fenstrom actively pursues us, we are totally helpless without any weapons."

†

Robert saw the old Subaru station wagon come around the bend. Through the powerful rifle scope he saw that Charlie Skyler was in the passenger seat and Kate Perkins was driving. He was disappointed that JB was not present as well, but he had to act while he could. He lined up the cross hairs on Charlie's head, carefully synchronized the movement of the barrel with the movement of the car, and pulled the trigger. But the car slowed and swerved to the left just as his brain transmitted the order to his finger, and the bullet hit the front window frame instead of the center of the window. What the fuck? Re-aiming, he fired again, but the targets ducked and the shot went high. By the time he had chambered another round, his targets were out of the car and out of sight in the ditch. Now what?

He saw Charlie approach the car again and fired, but he was sighting through the broken car window and the two shots were off target. He had to assume that one of them had a phone and help would be coming. He could probably survive a standoff for a while and kill lots of people, but then what? He thought about actively pursuing his targets, but that would involve coming out into the open where he would be an easy target. He knew from his reconnaissance the night before that the forest was continuous between his position and the Kachemak Bay bluff, so he would have a good chance of eluding pursuers, especially since he was equipped with camouflage and other supplies that would help keep him going. He decided to wait a while and see if he might still get an opportunity to end the life of at least one of his targets. He could melt into the forest any time things got too hot.

†

JB and the Super Trooper met at the hospital turnoff and tried to develop a plan of attack. JB suggested that he go into the woods and approach Fenstrom's position from the side while Bob made a somewhat more straightforward approach along the edge of the cleared area where he could just keep out of the line of sight from Fenstrom's sniper nest.

"I assume you're armed," said Bob.

"Yeah, more or less," replied JB.

"OK, I don't want to know any more about it," Bob replied.

They drove partway up the hospital road, got out of their vehicles, and proceeded on foot. JB penetrated about 200 feet into the forest and began to move west toward the Mole's position. Bob grabbed his shotgun and moved in parallel along the edge of the roadway clearing. Soon Bob was able to see Kate's Subaru. He texted Charlie's cell phone and notified them of his approach. Charlie peeked over the lip of the ditch and saw Bob waving from the forest edge a few hundred feet away. They discussed whether they should try to get Fenstrom to take another shot so that they could pinpoint his position and also give JB a directional cue.

Charlie found a six foot tree branch in the ditch bottom. He wrapped his jacket around the pole and put his baseball cap on top. Crawling alongside the car, he pushed the pole up and into the open driver's side door, simulating a person trying to retrieve something from the car. A shot immediately rang out, the bullet penetrating what was left of the passenger side window. Charlie pulled the pole back and found a bullet hole through the center of his good cap – a perfect shot.

Kate had been watching to see where the shot came from and was able to narrow down the location to a section of forest about ten feet long with distinctive tall spruce at either end. They relayed the information to Bob. Bob, in turn, texted JB and gave him the update.

The Super Trooper was not a very patient person. He continued to move along the edge of the road clearing until he could see the two trees that Kate described. He wanted to get this over with. The continual suspense accompanying the threat of two psychopaths targeting the citizens of Homer for the past year had taken a toll. Unfortunately, the configuration of the vegetation was such that he would be out in the open for a minute if he continued his current path. The alternative was to go deeper into the woods, but he was afraid that Charlie might mistake him for Fenstrom. He aimed his shotgun and fired two shots at the center of the spot indicated by Kate, then ran across the opening as fast as he could. He heard another shot, and then time slowed down as a bullet hit his shoulder, spinning him around and knocking him onto the ground. It was the worst shock he had ever felt.

Kate and Charlie watched with horror as Bob went down. Then there was silence.

"We need to get some help to him somehow," Charlie said. "If we can get Fenstrom to go on the run, then at least we can get medical attention to Bob. You stay here and call JB to let him know what is going on. Also, call 911 and tell them to be on standby to deal with a bullet wound. I'm going to backtrack and try to reach Bob's position."

"Charlie, that's crazy. Please stay here."

"I can't. I have to try to help."

Charlie crawled along the bottom of the ditch down the roadway until he was no longer in sight of Fenstrom's sniper nest, then crossed the road and climbed up the embankment to the edge of the road clearing limits. From there, he proceeded back toward the hospital along the same route that Bob had taken a few minutes before. He reached the point where Bob was forced into the open and stopped. The Super Trooper was only about ten feet away. Charlie could hear him moaning.

"Bob, it's Charlie. Can you hear me?"

"Yeah."

"What's your status?"

"I'm alive, but I'm bleeding and my shoulder is pretty messed up. It hurts like hell."

"Does Fenstrom have a line of sight to where you are lying?'

"I don't think so. The grass is too high."

"OK, I'm going to crawl over to you. I think there is enough cover to make it."

Charlie lay on the ground and slithered through the grass. He found Bob lying on his back with a substantial pool of blood under his right shoulder. It looked like the bullet had gone all the way through; most of the blood streamed from the exit wound on the back. While lying down, Charlie wriggled out of his jacket and T-shirt, then put the jacket back on. He tore the T-shirt into two pieces. One of the pieces he scrunched up and pressed against the exit wound and the other, larger piece he used to wrap around the shoulder to keep the first piece tightly in place. It looked like the bleeding had stopped, but Bob was in severe pain.

"I need to force Fenstrom to relinquish his position so we can get you some help. What's the capacity of the shotgun magazine?"

"The magazine holds eight and I used two, so there are six left. In a pouch on the left side of my belt is another eight rounds. You're crazy, Charlie. You're going to get shot just like I did."

"Maybe. But I'll try not to." Charlie found the extra ammo, put two shells in the magazine, and put the rest in his pocket. He called JB's phone, informed him of Bob's condition via text, and indicated that he wanted, at a minimum, to chase Fenstrom out of there. They agreed on a somewhat desperate plan.

†

Robert was getting more and more nervous, waiting for something to happen. He felt foolish because he had fallen for Charlie's cap-on-the-stick trick, but he had not been able to see well through the shattered car window until after he had fired, at which time it became obvious that he had not shot at a real human being. They were trying to pinpoint his location. He scanned the open hospital grounds and the edge of the forest, watching for movement. He saw a branch wiggle on his left and moved the rifle into position.

Just then the State Trooper emerged from the trees and ran toward him, firing a shotgun at the same time. Buckshot pellets tore away a shrub to his right, but he was already sighting in that direction and he was able to squeeze a quick shot at the trooper, hitting him in the upper body. The trooper was down, and all was quiet. Unfortunately, tall grass obscured his view and he could no longer see the injured man and, consequently, he had no idea what was going on. It might be time to go.

A few more minutes of quiet were followed by three unexpected pistol shots from behind him in the woods. Just as he turned to look behind him, he glimpsed Charlie running from tree to tree. Three shotgun blasts raked his general location, with some buckshot pellets

415

coming very close. In one motion, he hoisted his pack, grabbed his rifle, and took off into the forest behind the hospital.

†

Charlie caught a brief glimpse of Fenstrom's rear disappearing through the trees and fired another shotgun round, but Fenstrom was already out of effective range. Charlie called JB and told him that Fenstrom was on the move, heading west.

"I'm going to try and track him," JB said.

"That's crazy. Leave it to law enforcement."

"Sorry, but I can't."

Charlie called 911 again and suggested that they come right away to assist the trooper. He stayed with Bob in case Fenstrom decided to come back.

Sixty-four

Rays of sunshine penetrated the forest canopy and illuminated the mossy ground. Dust motes danced in the light between patches of shade. Ground dogwood and star flowers punctuated the greenness with white florets. The total lack of wind seemed to magnify the sounds of small animals going about their business. Chickadees flitted from tree to tree, scratching in the bark, voles rustled through their tunnels in the forest duff, and red squirrels scritched along the trunks of spruce. Occasionally cones dropped from the heights, intentionally detached by the busy squirrels, soon to be added to their caches in the hollows of old gnarly trees. Mosquitos whined and horse flies buzzed and leaves gently rustled. It was a beautiful gentle summer day in the boreal forest.

JB stood behind a large birch and listened. He had located the Mole's sniper nest and tracked him a few hundred feet into the forest. He was well aware that he was embarking on a dangerous path. Within a dense forest, the pursued have a significant advantage over their pursuers, since the pursued can pick their defensive positions and simply wait for the enemy. But the pursuer, by definition, has to keep looking. JB knew that Robert Fenstrom was not going to panic and make pursuit easy. They had both received the same instruction and had been through similar survival training exercises. It was a cat and mouse game, except that this was more like cat and cat. Fenstrom had a rifle, and probably a pistol, so he had a lot more firepower than JB with his little Beretta. But rifles are heavy and awkward, especially in dense woods. JB also knew that Fenstrom had to think ahead if he was going to escape, because the area would soon be crawling with law enforcement from the ground and air, probably including tracking dogs.

The mossy ground allowed persons on foot to travel quietly and did not make for easy tracking. JB summoned back to his mind lessons that he had learned in the swamps of Georgia when he was nineteen years old. He forced himself to enter into a sort of meditative state where he became entirely tuned into the sights, sounds, and smells of his surroundings, while at the same time putting himself into the mindset of his prey. He carefully crept through the trees, following the subtle signs of Fenstrom's ephemeral presence a few minutes earlier. JB could tell that Robert was moving fast because of the length of his strides and the lack of attention to minimizing disturbance. Following his path was actually pretty easy. Maybe too easy. Did Fenstrom sense his presence? As far as he could tell from the signs, Fenstrom was charging forward rapidly and was probably a good distance ahead. But still, JB proceeded with extreme caution, allowing his senses to take in the full scene.

After about twenty minutes, the dense spruce forest made a gradual transition to more open grassland with scattered birch and alder. They had been heading in a southwesterly direction and were approaching the Kachemak Bay bluff, where the strong winds and salt air made growing conditions difficult for trees. As far as JB could tell, he was still on Fenstrom's trail. JB's senses were on full alert as his sixth sense went into overdrive. A glint from a shiny object caused him to instinctively dive behind a tree just as a rifle shot zinged through the air.

That answered the question of whether Fenstrom knew he was being followed. The crucial thing now was to try and predict what Fenstrom would do next. If he were Robert, he would pretend to move away but actually double back. JB decided that he would counter the expected move by moving to the side, where he could surprise Fenstrom and get a clear shot. JB crawled through the tall grass directly toward the bluff and found a clump of alders to provide cover. If Fenstrom behaved as predicted, he would approach the position where he had last seen JB, which would bring him into close enough proximity for a pistol shot. JB dialed Charlie and quietly texted his position.

Another ten minutes went by. Finally, JB caught a glimpse of Robert's head above the grass, but he was farther away than he had hoped. A shot at that distance would severely tax his rusty marksmanship. He liked to be close enough to be able to place his shots, but that was not going to work out. JB rested his wrist in a fork of the alder and aimed carefully, hoping to hit his target somewhere in the upper body.

He fired two shots in quick succession and saw Fenstrom go down into the grass. Unfortunately, that was the extent of his information. He had no idea how badly Fenstrom was hurt, if at all. Robert popped up from the grass twenty feet to the side and began shooting. JB dove to the ground while alder branches were shredded by the high-powered rifle rounds just over his head.

JB decided to stay where he was rather than move out of the line of fire. He found a small opening in the vegetation that allowed him a view of the terrain toward Fenstrom's position. He saw the grass wiggle and decided to take a chance and fired two more shots into the grass where he visualized that Fenstrom's body would be located. This time there was a yell and a curse. That was good. The Mole was getting mad. JB changed magazines so that he would have the full seven shots if he needed them.

"Show yourself, you son of a bitch!" yelled the Mole.

Charlie remained quiet and shifted his position a few feet to the right. The Mole sat up and fired the rifle two more times into JB's hiding place, but this time JB did not duck. While Fenstrom was shooting, JB took careful aim and shot him in the knee. Another curse and a thrown rifle – the magazine was empty. The Mole pulled his Glock from his belt, but this time JB shot him in the hand, causing him to drop the gun.

"Put your hands behind your head and don't move a muscle," JB said as he emerged from behind the alders. Robert Fenstrom did as he was told, and JB retrieved the big black automatic from the ground. "Now lie down and make yourself comfortable."

"How can I be comfortable? You shot me four times. Why didn't you kill me?"

"My killing days are long over," JB said. "I don't want to end up like you."

Another phone call to Charlie described the situation and requested a helicopter with a medic. The chopper, which was already in the air, arrived in a few minutes and was able to land in a clearing not too far from where the Mole was writhing in pain. To JB's surprise, Beverly slowly disembarked and walked over to the scene of mayhem.

"Holy crap, I see you've been busy." Beverly looked at Robert Fenstrom's multiple injuries. "Isn't that kind of a waste of ammo? One well-placed shot probably would have been adequate. Anyway, I thought you might need an actual law enforcement officer to wrap things up."

"Aren't you supposed to be recuperating?"

"Screw you," Beverly replied.

"Now there's an idea," said JB.

Beverly kissed him without ever taking her eyes off of the Mole.

The paramedic knelt beside Robert Fenstrom. "Christ, what happened to this guy?"

†

The medevac helicopter landed on the Homer hospital landing pad, and a gurney pushed by two orderlies rushed out to meet it. Robert Fenstrom was transferred to the gurney, and the orderlies were preparing to push it inside when Fenstrom's head jerked to the side and a red hole appeared in his forehead. The Mole was dead.

Sixty-five

The Super Trooper's small hospital room was filled to capacity. Julie sat on the edge of the bed holding Bob's hand, while Beverly, JB, Kate, and Charlie stood around his bed.

"What's the damage?" Kate asked.

"My shoulder's pretty messed up with shattered bones and stuff, but the orthopedic guy claims that he can fix it up with a couple of operations, starting tomorrow. Anyway, I'm looking forward to some paid time off."

"Me too," Julie said.

"I'm sorry this whole thing turned out to be such a mess," Kate said. "I feel like we're somehow responsible."

"Don't be ridiculous," Bob said. "Thanks mostly to your efforts, several really bad people are out of commission. I shouldn't have gotten in the way of that bullet. By the way, was there any sign of Fenstrom's killer?"

"We searched the area and found a couple possible places where the shot could have originated, but no actual evidence. No one heard a shot or saw anything out of the ordinary."

"The gun was silenced," JB said. "It was a professional hit. We won't ever know who did it."

Charlie nodded in agreement. "Robert Fenstrom's protectors got tired of protecting. He became too big a liability."

"Liability for what?" Beverly asked.

"Whatever he was involved in is probably forever lost in the shadows of unauthorized black operations. I'm guessing that no one is going to pursue his handlers," JB said.

Bob looked at Beverly. "So, after all this, are we any closer to finding out who killed Jake Halburg and Rodolfo?"

"Frank Halburg is being transported this morning to Los Angeles where he will undergo more questioning. I have a feeling he'll be willing to cooperate if it means avoiding the death penalty. Hopefully, that will fill in some gaps."

†

The sun was still high in the sky in the late afternoon, providing luxuriously warm conditions on the deck of the Shearwater. Kate and Charlie had borrowed a lounge chair for Beverly, who was feeling remarkably comfortable and relaxed. Two beers and a pain pill had taken the edge off the throbbing pain she had endured during the dramatic events of the day. JB was lounging on a pile of nets next to Beverly, while Kate and Charlie sat in deck chairs with a large bowl of potato chips and a cooler of beer between them. Buster was zonked out in the sun, fluidly draped over the edge of the cabin top. Kate and JB passed a pipe back and forth. Charlie was dreamily gazing into Kate's incredible green eyes. All were quiet and thoughtful until the reverie was interrupted by the ringing of Beverly's cell phone.

"Hmnn," Beverly answered. "Oh. Hi, sir. Yes, I'm sort of coherent. What's up?" Beverly listened for a while, then thanked her boss and closed the phone.

Kate stared at her. "Well, are you going to make us wait, or are you going to tell us what he said?"

"Apparently the interrogators at headquarters were able to convince Frank Halburg that there was no point in holding back information, given his obvious involvement with the Fenstrom organization. Anyway, he confessed to killing his brother – apparently, the two hated each other, and he had no remorse. But, he claims that he did not kill Rodolfo and neither did Robert Fenstrom. He claimed that Robert had been in the Lower Forty-eight at the time of Rodolfo's death. Our people checked it out and were able to corroborate Robert's location."

422

“So, who did kill Rodolfo?” Kate asked.

423

Sixty-six

Sun shone through the windows of the small cabana and sounds of surf filled the room. Aldo raised his head, looked at the clock, picked up an empty whiskey bottle, and hurled it at the wall. He slumped back down onto his pillow. He was starting to come down from an extended binge of alcohol and heroin. The call had come three days earlier – Robert was dead. Although the news had not been a big surprise, his reaction had come as a surprise. He was devastated, and his first reaction had been to make himself numb. But, now, waking up with a giant hangover, he was angry, frustrated, and restless.

For some time, he had been coming to the conclusion that the life of a beach bum was not nearly as idyllic as some might think – in fact, it sucked. As his mind began to clear, he came to the realization that, if he remained on Dominica, he would be dead in a few years at his current rate of consumption of mind-altering substances. He had been active all his life and could not see himself resigned to a slow death in exile. It would be better to be engaged in life and go out with a splash rather than a whimper.

The details of Robert's death were sketchy, to say the least. Everything Aldo knew, he had learned from Izzy, whose information was based on notoriously inaccurate community gossip. It seemed that there had been some sort of gunfight near the hospital, resulting in Robert being injured. When Robert got to the hospital for treatment, he was dead. Charlie Skyler, Kate Perkins, and JB, the hippie, were somehow involved. Aldo wanted to know the details.

He began to think of alternative ways to get more information. Most of his Homer informants were either dead or in jail. A crazy idea began to form. What if he went directly to the source? What did he have to lose by talking to the people actually involved in Robert's last days? In his prior discussions with Frank and Robert, he had learned that the guy known as JB was a formidable adversary and had a level of knowledge greater than the others. He needed to get JB's phone number. He made another call to Izzy and asked him to get JB's cell phone number by any possible means. He then got cleaned up, injected himself with the minimum maintenance dose of heroin, put on his best shirt, and went into town for his first meal in three days.

When Aldo got back to his cabana, he was feeling much better. He was surprised to find a message from Izzy with JB's number. Izzy had gotten the number from a friend at a marine supply store where everyone in Homer did business. Aldo began to think that he had underestimated Izzy. He picked up the satellite phone, stared at the number for a few minutes, then dialed.

†

JB was sitting at his tiny desk gazing at his manuscript, when his phone rang. The caller ID indicated out of area. JB answered.

"This is Aldo Fenstrom."

"You're kidding."

"Did you kill my son?"

JB sat back, closed his eyes, and took a few seconds to figure out what approach to take to the strange turn of events. He decided that, since Aldo was addressing things head on, he would do the same. "I captured your son because he tried to kill my friends, but I didn't kill him. In fact, I did my best to keep him alive."

"Then who did kill him?"

"He was shot by a sniper as he was being transferred from the ambulance to the hospital."

"Who would do that?" Aldo asked.

"As you probably know, Robert was involved with some people in the clandestine intelligence community. They got tired of trying to keep Robert out of trouble, so they killed him. Robert knew stuff that made him dangerous, and the last thing they wanted was a trial that might expose them."

JB thought it was time to turn the tables on the discussion. "Did you kill Rodolfo from the taco stand?"

The line was silent for a few seconds. "It was sort of an accident."

"How do you accidentally bash someone's head in? Rodolfo was totally innocent of anything having to do with your operation."

"He had something of mine, and I wanted it," Aldo replied.

"Ah, yes. The Cayman bank account."

More silence.

"Look, Aldo. I don't know why you called me. I assume you feel pissed about what happened to Robert. I was not too happy about Robert's death either, especially since I almost got myself killed while trying not to kill him. None of us in Homer was responsible for Robert's death. If you want to be mad at somebody, you should be angry with the sleazy black ops people responsible for turning Robert into a trained assassin."

"Tell me what you know about the people who killed my son."

"I don't know very much, but if I tell you what I do know, will you stay away from Homer?"

"You and your buddies fucked up a network that I spent my whole life building. We had a good thing going. It's hard to just forget about it."

"Think about it, Aldo. You're almost seventy years old, two of the other syndicate founders from your Vietnam squad are in jail, and several people are dead. I assume you have enough money. Maybe it's time to cut your losses."

"All right. Fair enough. I'll leave you guys alone. So, what do you know?"

JB told Aldo about the man named Ayers and provided what little other information he had that might help Aldo track him down. As incredible as the story sounded, Aldo knew that JB was telling the truth. He had no reason to lie, and the facts fit with Aldo's knowledge of Robert's activities and proclivities.

†

JB sat back and thought about his next move. Beverly deserved to know what was going on. He knew that she would have mixed emotions concerning the fact that JB had taken it upon himself to make deals with a fugitive and murderer. And what was worse, he had provided information that could be used by Aldo to track down and do harm to a government official. He wrote an email to Beverly that simply asked her to call him. A few minutes later, Beverly called JB, using her throw-away cell phone. He described the situation, and Beverly was predictably angry. But, after some thought, she agreed that he didn't have much choice. Because of her affection for Kate, Charlie, and JB and her dislike of Ayers, she ultimately decided that JB had acted brilliantly.

JB hung around his boat until FlashFrozen quitting time. When he saw Kate walking down the dock, he casually joined her and Charlie on the deck of the Shearwater. He had a shit-eating grin on his face.

"OK, what's going on?" Kate asked.

"I need a beer first."

Charlie threw a can to him, which he opened accompanied by a beer foam geyser. "I just had the most amazing phone conversation."

"Who with, pray tell?"

"You have to guess."

"Dammit, JB. Just tell us," Kate said with frustration.

"I just talked to Aldo Fenstrom."

"What?"

"He called me and wanted to know the circumstances of Robert's death. I told him the truth."

Charlie grimaced. "Did he believe you?"

"I think so."

"Is he pissed at us?"

"He's not happy with us, but I made a deal with him. I traded the little information I have on Ayers and his crew for a promise not to come back to Alaska."

Kate looked skeptical. "Will he keep the deal?"

"I think so, at least initially. His first priority is to seek revenge for Robert's death. He seemed sincerely angry with the people who had had so much influence over Robert's life. Oh, and he also admitted to killing Rodolfo."

"Do you have any idea where Aldo was calling from?" Charlie asked.

"I heard bird and surf noises that suggest a tropical beach location, but that doesn't narrow it down very much."

"Have you talked to Beverly yet?" Charlie asked. "She might not be too pleased that you are making deals with Aldo."

"Yeah, she seems OK with it. She agreed that I had a one-time opportunity to try and keep you guys safe. Also, I don't think she will care if Aldo causes trouble for Ayers and his merry band of scofflaws. Plus, if Aldo comes back to the U.S., he will be more vulnerable to capture by the DEA, especially if he actively pursues Ayers."

"So where does this leave us?" Kate asked.

"I think JB's quick thinking allows us to put the whole sorry episode behind us," Charlie answered.

"Are we out of potato chips?" Kate asked.

Epilogue

Fourth Page, *Washington Reviewer* (six months later)

Washington, D.C. High-ranking intelligence analyst Clarence Ayers was found dead in his bed in his upper north side apartment on Tuesday. It is suspected that he died of a heart attack. During his long career, Mr. Ayers worked for a variety of government agencies, often serving as a liaison between intelligence gathering groups. He began his career during the early Cold War and continued to be involved in classified intelligence activities until his death. He had a well-deserved reputation for toughness and single-minded approach to whatever tasks he was assigned.